If the
BOOT
FITS

Books by Karen Witemeyer

A Tailor-Made Bride
Head in the Clouds
To Win Her Heart
Short-Straw Bride
Stealing the Preacher
Full Steam Ahead
A Worthy Pursuit
No Other Will Do
Heart on the Line
More Than Meets the Eye
More Than Words Can Say

HANGER'S HORSEMEN

At Love's Command
The Heart's Charge
In Honor's Defense

TEXAS EVER AFTER

Fairest of Heart
If the Boot Fits

NOVELLAS

A Cowboy Unmatched
Love on the Mend: A Full Steam Ahead Novella
The Husband Maneuver: A Worthy Pursuit Novella
from *With This Ring? A Novella Collection of Proposals Gone Awry*
Worth the Wait: A LADIES OF HARPER'S STATION Novella
The Love Knot: A LADIES OF HARPER'S STATION Novella
Gift of the Heart from *The Christmas Heirloom*
More Than a Pretty Face from *Serving Up Love:*
A Four-in-One Harvey House Brides Collection
An Archer Family Christmas from *An Old-Fashioned Texas Christmas*
Inn for a Surprise from *The Kissing Tree:*
Four Novellas Rooted in Timeless Love
A Texas Christmas Carol from *Under the Texas Mistletoe*

TEXAS EVER AFTER

If the
BOOT
FITS

KAREN
WITEMEYER

BETHANYHOUSE
a division of Baker Publishing Group
Minneapolis, Minnesota

© 2024 by Karen M. Witemeyer

Published by Bethany House Publishers
Minneapolis, Minnesota
BethanyHouse.com

Bethany House Publishers is a division of
Baker Publishing Group, Grand Rapids, Michigan

Printed in the United States of America

Library of Congress Cataloging-in-Publication Data
Name: Witemeyer, Karen, author.
Title: If the boot fits / Karen Witemeyer.
Description: Minneapolis, Minnesota : Bethany House, a division of Baker Publishing
    Group, 2024. | Series: Texas ever after
Identifiers: LCCN 2023045271 | ISBN 9780764240423 (paper) | ISBN
    9780764242892 (casebound) | ISBN 9781493445325 (ebook)
Subjects: LCGFT: Christian fiction. | Romance fiction. | Novels.
Classification: LCC PS3623.I864 I36 2024 | DDC 813/.6—dc23/eng/20231003
LC record available at https://lccn.loc.gov/2023045271

Scripture quotations are from the King James Version of the Bible.

This is a work of historical reconstruction; the appearances of certain historical figures are therefore inevitable. All other characters, however, are products of the author's imagination, and any resemblance to actual persons, living or dead, is coincidental.

Published in association with Books & Such Literary Management, BooksAndSuch.com.

Baker Publishing Group publications use paper produced from sustainable forestry practices and postconsumer waste whenever possible.

24 25 26 27 28 29 30   7 6 5 4 3 2 1

To my daughter and fellow fairy-tale fanatic.
Bethany, you are my book buddy, my craft partner,
and the musician who fills my life with beautiful harmonies.
My life is richer because it is shared with you.

It is better to trust in the Lord than
to put confidence in princes.

PSALM 118:9

1

THREE CEDARS RANCH
PALO PINTO COUNTY, TEXAS
SUMMER 1889

She'd only been home from school for two weeks, and already her father was trying to marry her off. Silently fuming, Samantha Dearing yanked open the door to her father's study and stepped inside.

Her mother had raised her to be a lady, insisting she never raise her voice or engage in disagreements in public, so when Samantha discovered the true purpose behind this evening's event, she'd not dumped the punch bowl over her father's head or engaged in a childish tantrum. No, she'd approached the mighty Eli Dearing with a smile, waited patiently for him to conclude his conversation with one of the wealthy bachelors he'd invited to his daughter's ~~auction~~ welcome home party, and sweetly asked for a private word with him.

The silk skirt of her azure ball gown swished loudly as Samantha swept past the sitting area on the left to reach her father's desk on the right. Her impassioned stride stretched the limits of her narrow skirt, and the bustled train felt slightly unbalanced when she swirled around to face the man entering behind her.

A scuffling noise by the bookcases drew an instinctual glance, but when she saw no evidence of vermin ready to dash across her path, she turned her full attention—and ire—on her father.

"I will not be sold to the highest bidder!"

Her father frowned and pulled the door closed behind him. "Keep your voice down."

"Of course." She sketched a most irreverent curtsy. "Whatever the cattle king demands."

His mouth tightened. "I don't know what burr got stuck in that bustle of yours, girl, but I expect to be addressed with respect."

"And I expect to be *treated* with respect."

A fierce light flared in her father's steel blue eyes. The tendons along his throat stood out from his neck as he stepped closer to her. "Did one of the guests do something improper?" The question rumbled from his chest in a dangerous growl.

Samantha blinked, taken aback. Could it be he actually cared more about her well-being than she'd assumed? After being banished to finishing school for the last three years, she'd calculated her rank to be somewhere below the steers and above the chickens.

Her stance softened just a touch. "No, Daddy. No one behaved improperly. But the gentlemen you invited to this little soiree seem to be under the impression that I've returned to Texas to seek a husband. They all appear determined to apply for the position, rattling off their assets as if they were fabrics in a dress shop competing to be made up into my next gown. The expensive imported lace that would raise my social status. The handsome blue silk that would match my eyes. The pragmatic poplin that would work hard while still allowing a splash of elegance."

The fierceness drained from her father's eyes, replaced by a rather hazy fog. "What does dress fabric have to do with anything? Talk plainly, Sam."

"My name's Samantha."

"I know what your name is, girl. I gave it to you."

Was that hurt in his eyes? She didn't think a man as tough as Eli Dearing could be hurt by something as insignificant as a daughter's rebuff. A pang vibrated through her heart at the visible evidence to the contrary, but she stifled the throb before it softened her. He had no right to use the pet name from her childhood. The day he'd stopped taking her up on his horse with him and banished her to the house, he'd made it clear that he had no use for a daughter. Then when Mother finally birthed a son, Samantha had all but ceased to exist in her father's eyes.

Sam was the name of a girl trying to be the son her father wanted. Samantha was the grown woman whose dreams no longer relied on her father's approval.

"You want plain speaking?" Her fingertips tingled with strange energy. She'd never stood up to her father in so bold a manner. Exhilaration warred with terror inside her breast, but if ever a situation called for reckless courage, this was it. "I won't be forced into an unwanted marriage just so you can expand your holdings."

The sudden darkness of her father's scowl nearly had her backing up, but she fisted her hands and held her ground. Daddy might have passed the fifty mark a couple of years ago, but he was still in his prime. Tall. Strong. Frightful when angry. Yet never cruel. Knowing that allowed her to stand firm despite the trembling his glare induced.

"Do you see a shotgun in my hands?" He held out open palms. His sleeves retracted to expose tanned wrists. He might be dressed in a formal evening suit, but he was still a man of the outdoors, honed by hard work. "No one's forcin' anyone to do anything. It's just a party."

She said nothing, simply lifted her chin.

"All right! So I might have made it known among my acquaintances that my daughter was coming home from Boston and that I hoped to see her settled before long. What's the harm in that? It's a father's job to see that his daughter is provided for." He slapped his hands against his thighs and paced away from her, veering toward the large mahogany desk, where he conducted his written business. "You're nineteen years old, Samantha. Most girls with your beauty and advantages are already married and setting up their houses."

He wasn't wrong, but he also wasn't right.

Samantha crossed her arms, her long white gloves pulling tight at the elbows. "Deciding who I'll spend my life with should be *my* choice, not yours."

He leaned against the side of his desk and heaved a sigh. "I never said it weren't your choice. All I'm doin' is wranglin' the bulls into a pen so you can look them over and pick the one that suits you."

As if she wasn't disgusted by the prospect enough already.

"Yes, well, the *bulls* you seem intent on wrangling all bear a remarkable resemblance to one another. All wealthy and highly invested in the cattle market. Makes me think you're less interested in my personal happiness and more interested in what advantage my marriage can bring to your ranching empire."

Her father scowled as he straightened away from the desk. "You think you got everything figured out, don't you? I'm a coldhearted snake who only cares about profit, willing to sell my daughter to the highest bidder."

Well . . . yes. Wasn't he?

He ran his palm over his face, suddenly looking older than she'd ever seen him. Uncertainty nibbled at her conscience.

"I'll admit to knowin' precious little about raisin' a girl. I probably made a mess of things more'n a few times, especially after your mother passed, but never in all my days have I wanted anything but the best for you."

He jabbed a finger toward the door. "That ballroom is filled with cattlemen and investors because those are the men I've had an opportunity to observe over the last two decades. I know which are men of honor and which are thieves. I know who will stand strong in hard times and who will seek the easy path. I know the ones who honor God with their lips and those who honor him with their lives. I culled out the best of the herd and invited them to this here shindig to meet the daughter I value more than all the beeves in Texas, but it seems she's too busy makin' assumptions and casting stones to give any of them a second look."

Samantha staggered backward as his disappointment speared her heart. She'd thought herself calloused, so accustomed to his rejection that nothing he said or did could hurt her. How wrong she'd been. Moisture flooded her eyes, forcing her to blink back the tide.

Had she misjudged his motives? Was he really trying to do right by her?

His high-handed behavior still rankled. He'd never once asked her opinion or preference. Yet she couldn't honestly say his tactics were any different from how the fathers of her Eastern schoolmates secured husbands for their daughters. Arranged marriages happened all the time among the elite. Mergers of families for wealth, connections, or status. Affection was beneficial but not essential. And tales of love seemed only to exist on the scandal pages.

"Daddy, I . . ."

He waited, but she couldn't find the right words. She hadn't meant to hurt him. Heavens, she hadn't even considered she might hold the power to do so. But she wasn't ready to apologize. It hadn't been wrong to stand up for herself. Perhaps she could have chosen a kinder method, spoken with more care, but—

"I've abandoned my guests long enough." Her father left her floundering in indecision and strode to the door. "Don't feel like you have to return to the party. I'll come up with some excuse or another to explain your absence."

Instinctively, she reached out as if to stop him, but he was through the door before she could take a single step. The door clicked closed behind him, setting off a quake that crumbled the walls of the canyon already separating father from daughter, leaving an imposing gulf that might never be spanned.

Asher Ellis peeked under the sofa, praying he'd find no feet in his field of view. Technically, no feet were visible, but only because Miss Dearing's fancy blue dress swept the carpet, hiding everything beneath. Asher bit back a groan. His one chance to find the evidence necessary to reclaim his family's home was obliterated by a petulant princess and her ill-timed tirade.

Please leave. Please leave. Please leave.

The uncooperative woman remained unmoved by his silent pleas. She remained unmoved altogether, stuck in that singular spot as if a pair of needle-wielding mice had scurried beneath her hem and sewn her slippers to the expensive carpet.

Asher's lips twitched at the thought. He'd have to tell Fergus about that one. His little brother was constantly creating stories about mischievous animals, usually when he needed someone to blame his own mischief on, but the kid's imaginative tales delighted their mother, and anything that lightened Mama Bess's load was worth encouraging.

Plus, imagining Miss Snooty squealing and dashing about

the room after discovering said mice was a pleasure too rich to resist. She'd be barefoot, of course, having pulled her feet from the immovable slippers in a panic. Her dress hiked up, her fancified hair askew. She'd scream for Daddy, and of course Daddy and probably half the men in the ballroom would come running, guns drawn.

Asher's amusement died. His little fantasy had taken a dangerous turn. He needed fewer people in the study, not more. And there definitely should not be any weapons involved. Especially since the only creature currently hunkering on all fours in this room was *him*.

A delicate sniff echoed through the still room like a gunshot. Asher flinched and held his breath. Was she going to cry? Crying wasn't good. Crying meant hiding. Which meant not leaving. Crying could also mean collapsing on the very sofa he was sequestered behind. Isn't that why rich people kept fainting couches around? So their women could artfully collapse whenever their emotions became too weighty? This sofa sported arms carved from solid oak, so it didn't exactly fill the bill, but something told him Miss Dearing could make it work. She seemed the determined type.

Another sniff sounded. Followed by a soft rustling of fabric. Was she fetching a handkerchief? Wiping her eyes? Straightening her gown? Impossible to tell when all he could see was the bottom two inches of her skirt.

Just leave, woman. You're not gonna solve any of your problems in here. I, on the other hand, can solve all of my problems if you'll take your disgruntled self elsewhere.

Unbelievably, she complied. Her skirt swayed and swished all the way to the door. The handle rattled. A breath inhaled. Hinges whined. Then Miss Samantha Dearing and her tragic courtship woes slipped out into the hall, leaving Asher blessedly alone.

Finally.

Thank you, God.

Breaking into another man's house might be walking a thin spiritual line, but his cause was just. Eli Dearing had wrongfully evicted Asher's stepmother and brothers from their home. Callously put them out on the street with no way to support themselves. Besides, the Lord had sanctioned the work of spies before. Even helped them escape capture, in the case of the men sent into Jericho. What Asher was doing wasn't much different.

He wasn't here to steal anything or harm anyone. All he sought was proof that Mama Bess had not been late on her payments. With evidence on his side, he could leverage Dearing to get their home back, or at least obtain some kind of restitution to help them get back on their feet. Asher *knew* the rents had been paid. He sent his wages to Mama Bess every month for that express purpose. Had been doing so since his father died six years ago. There was no way she'd been delinquent. Dearing had just kicked them off the land because he'd wanted to, and his wealth and influence kept anyone from questioning his actions.

Not wanting to chance any other unwelcome visitors, Asher locked the door before resuming his search.

The study was large and rather unorganized, making the task more complicated than it should have been. It took ages for Asher to find the ranch ledgers for the last three years on a random shelf near the floor behind Dearing's desk. Deciphering the accounting system required more precious time as he hunted for itemized rent logs as opposed to generalized totals from all land holdings. Not easy since Dearing owned half of Palo Pinto County and over a dozen properties elsewhere.

At last, he found the records he sought. Tenant Elizabeth Ellis. He ran his finger along the column of numbers, his brow furrowing as the numbers failed to line up. This couldn't be right. Had they raised her rent? Surely she would have told him. Wouldn't she?

A rattle of the door handle nearly had Asher jumping out of his skin.

Heart pounding, he shoved the ledger back into its slot on the shelf.

"Samantha? Are you in there? Unlock the door, darlin'."

Eli Dearing. Of course it would have to be the one man in the house who had a key.

"Sam?"

The handle rattled again. Then the door thumped hard against the jamb.

Asher's panicked gaze shot back to the sofa, but hiding wouldn't work this time. Not with a concerned father on the prowl.

The window.

Asher sprinted around to the portal and hefted up the sash. The study sat on the second floor, so the drop would be significant, but he didn't have a choice.

A cool night breeze hit his chest and ruffled the curtains buffeting his sides. The sound of a key slipping into the lock fired like a starting gun in Asher's head. Praying he didn't break an ankle, he ducked through the opening and dropped.

2

Samantha escaped through the French doors in her mother's sitting room into the warm evening air of the garden. The scents of roses and lemony geraniums met her, yet their perfume failed to soothe her disturbed spirit. Pressing her back against the closed door, she exhaled slowly and raised her gaze toward a sky that was just starting to pinken.

Lord, I need some wisdom.

Truths she'd been certain of for years had been shaken, leaving a rubble of questions and confusion.

She closed her eyes, slowed her breathing, and sought the serenity her teachers promised would come to any young lady who deliberately cleared her mind of troublesome thoughts. Only her troublesome thoughts refused to be swept away. She kept seeing the hurt look in her father's eyes. Kept hearing him accuse her of being blinded by her own prejudices.

Could he be right? Was she seeing villainy where none truly existed? *"The daughter I value more than all the beeves in Texas."* Those words floated around her heart seeking entry, dripping into any small crack or crevice they found in her defenses. She wanted to believe he meant them—he'd *sounded*

16

like he meant them—yet they didn't match her experience of being pushed away, brushed off, and ignored. Or had bitterness skewed her memories?

A slight throbbing pulsed behind her eyebrows. Mercy. How was she supposed to find equilibrium when her mind was in such a tangle? Adding to the mess was Mother's voice, urging her back to the ballroom. A hostess never abandoned her guests for more than a handful of minutes, and then only when absolutely necessary—to, say, put out a house fire or take down a rabid coyote in the dining room. No other excuse would be deemed worthy, at least to her mother's way of thinking. Overwrought emotions could be hidden beneath a practiced smile, and shattered perceptions swept under the rug until the guests departed. If Mother were alive, she would have tracked Samantha down by now, given her a brief sympathetic hug, then sent her back inside with explicit instructions to pack away her upset and focus on entertaining the guests with witty conversation and kind consideration.

Despite her mother's spirit whispering in her ear, Samantha remained in the garden. She stepped closer to the rose trellis and rubbed a finger along one of the red petals, drawing comfort from its smoothness, even as she took care to avoid the thorns. Yes, Mother would disapprove of her loitering, but Samantha daren't return without properly armoring her heart.

Unfortunately, the garden was woefully void of shielding material. No hammered metal or hardened leather dangled from the eaves or sprouted along the well-worn trail to the white iron bench. All she had at her disposal was a collection of water lilies floating atop the dark pond that stretched past the trio of cedars that gave the ranch its name. The water garden painted a peaceful picture as dusk descended, but its serenity drifted just out of reach.

Deep down, Samantha knew why. No matter how many

times he'd stomped upon her heart in the past, she *wanted* to believe her father cared. That he thought about her, prayed for her, and maybe even missed her a little when she'd been away at school. In the secret places of her soul, she longed to recapture the childish joy of riding within the shelter of his arms, laughing together over the antics of frenetic prairie dogs and gaping in wonder at hawks soaring on the breeze. What daughter didn't crave the love and attention of her father?

But she didn't trust him. As much as she secretly longed for emotional connection, experience warned that hoping for such from Eli Dearing would only lead to disappointment. Besides, except for the surprisingly earnest conversation they'd had a quarter hour ago, all other evidence pointed to the idea that he was still trying to get rid of her. Instead of relegating her to the house or shipping her off to finishing school, this time he planned to pawn her off on a husband, making her somebody else's problem. Permanently.

"Whatcha doin' out here?"

Samantha whirled, lifting a hand to her chest to press against her suddenly racing heart. "Clinton Abernathy Dearing! You scared me."

Her little brother shrugged. Twelve-year-olds rarely concerned themselves with the palpitations of big sisters. "It's *your* party. Figured you be dancing or flirtin' or doin' whatever grown-up girls do to land themselves a man."

Good heavens. Who'd been filling his head with tales of man-landing women? Maybe Clint should spend less time in the bunkhouse with Duke and more time in the schoolroom with his tutor.

Samantha gave an exaggerated sniff. "I'll have you know that *this* grown-up girl has no intention of *landing herself a man*. If I marry, it will be to someone who loves me for who I am, not for the dowry I bring or the career advancement my father can provide. And if I never find him . . ." She gave a shrug of her own. "Then I'll just have to live with *you* the rest of my life." She ruffled his hair, grinning when he cringed and pulled away.

"Only if you make me oatmeal cookies and blackberry cobbler."

She chuckled. "Deal."

Mother had discouraged her from working in the kitchen when she'd been alive, but after her passing, Samantha had found comfort in baking. Or, more accurately, in Mrs. Stewart. The grandmotherly cook at the Three Cedars wielded her wooden spoon like a weapon against any cowboy who thought to sneak a taste before dinner, but to a grieving young girl, she'd been a haven of sweet treats and warm hugs.

"Duke thought you'd marry a fancy gent from back east." Clint peered up at her, his face meticulously nonchalant, but worry shone in his brown eyes. "Dad was hoping you'd stay closer to home if he introduced you to some rich Texas fellers. Something about new money bein' just as good as old in the West." His brow wrinkled. "That never made no sense to me. Why do Eastern folks like old money better? It's all dirty and crinkled. I'd much rather have shiny pennies in my pockets than grimy ones."

Samantha smiled as she fingered his dark brown hair, straightening the strands she had rumpled earlier. "Shiny pennies are definitely better."

She'd never cared for the snobbish types who considered themselves above others just because their money had been handed down through multiple generations instead of earned through honest labor. In her mind, a man who worked for his money understood its value and was less likely to squander it.

"So you think you might end up liking one of the fellas in there enough to stick around?" Clint jabbed a thumb over his shoulder toward the house. "I don't like it when you're in Boston."

Her heart squeezed. All this time, she had focused on what *she* was missing by being sent to school a thousand miles away. She'd given little thought to how Clint might feel, assuming that a young boy who was the apple of his daddy's eye would want for nothing. He'd be riding the range and learning the ropes of ranching, cutting up with the hands in the bunkhouse, and doing all the things a daughter wouldn't be allowed to do. Until this moment, she hadn't considered that a boy of twelve might actually miss having his sister around.

After they lost Mother, Samantha had filled the maternal role to the best of her ability. While other ten-year-old girls played house with their dolls, Samantha had lived it with three-year-old Clint. They'd grown close during those years, but the older Clint became, the more interest their father showed in him. By the time she left, Clint was spending the majority of his free time outside with the men, his sister forgotten. Or so she'd thought.

Whipping an arm around his shoulders before he could remember that sisterly displays of affection were embarrassing to young men, she squashed him into her side and grunted in exaggerated effort as she hugged him tightly. "I missed you, too, little man. And I'm not in any hurry to return to Boston."

She missed her volunteer work there, though, the calling that had breathed new purpose into her empty life. Yet it seemed the Almighty wanted her here. Why, she wasn't quite sure, but maybe Clint was part of the reason. Despite the physical distance that had separated them these past three years, she loved her little brother ferociously, and if he needed her, she'd give up Boston in a heartbeat. Besides, she'd much rather believe God had brought her back to Texas to help Clint than to yoke her to one of the self-important bulls her father had penned in the ballroom.

Clint started squirming inside her embrace, so she dropped a kiss on the top of his head with an obnoxiously loud smack and let him go.

"Eww." He rubbed a hand over his hair. "No kisses, Sam."

She nudged his shoulder with the side of her arm and winked. "I only slobbered a little. I promise."

His nose scrunched in brotherly disgust. "Maybe you *should* go back to Boston."

Laughter bubbled out of her, easing the tension that had been making her head ache for most of the evening. Heavens, but it felt good to get the weight of her future off her shoulders for a few minutes.

"Nope. I've decided to stay. Just so I can torture you with kisses."

He groaned and rolled his eyes, but there was a twinkle shining in their depths that had been missing earlier.

"You slime me with kisses, and I'll slime you with frogs in your bed!"

"You wouldn't dare!"

He smirked and tipped his head toward the pond. "Plenty of ammunition in there."

She shivered, knowing he'd do it. Might be best to check her sheets tonight to make sure he—

A scraping sound above her cut off the thread of that thought. Was that a window? She lifted her chin to look. None of the guests should be on this side of the house. The ballroom was on the other—Good grief! Was that a—?

"Look out!" Samantha lunged for Clint and shoved him away from the house. Away from the witless man who'd just leapt out of a second-story window. Air whooshed from her lungs as she tumbled atop her brother, his elbow jabbing her midsection.

"Stop! Thief!" Her father's voice boomed above her, startling her almost as badly as the reprobate crashing through her mother's rose trellis.

She struggled to rise, determined to protect Clint from whatever evil threatened, but her twisted ball gown fought her at every turn. Worse, Clint slipped out from under her like a greased eel and charged after the intruder.

"No, Clint! Come back!"

Merciful stars. Had the boy no sense? The man stumble-running toward the pond could have a weapon.

Please, God, don't let him hurt Clint.

Yanking her skirt hard enough to pop seams, Samantha finally freed her legs and scrambled to her feet. She set off after them, calling her brother's name. Forced to slow as her breathing grew labored, she cursed her vanity for insisting on wearing a gown that required tighter corset lacing.

Thankfully, no shots had been fired. Although that might change when Daddy and his men caught up to them. For now, the villain's focus seemed centered on winning a footrace. Which he was doing handily. His long legs had smoothed out their cadence, lengthening his lead. He'd already circled the far end of the pond and would soon disappear into the trees beyond. Probably had a horse stashed nearby to make his escape. A fact Clint must have calculated as well, for he changed direction at the edge of the pond and made for the first cedar tree.

Realizing his intent, Samantha snatched up her skirt and ran for the water. He couldn't. It was too dangerous.

Some of the ranch hands used the pond as a swimming hole. They'd built a platform in the tree and installed a rope swing. A swing a too-clever-for-his-own-good boy might attempt to use as a pendulum to launch himself to the opposite side.

But the rope was old. Weatherworn.

"Stop, Clint! It's not safe!"

He paid her no heed. Using the rungs nailed to the trunk, he scampered up the tree like a squirrel, snatched the rope, and vaulted off the end of the platform.

Wood cracked. Rope fell. Water splashed. And Clint disappeared beneath the murky green surface.

3

Heart pounding, muscles straining, Asher stretched his legs to their limit as he rounded the far side of the pond. He stole a glance over his shoulder to see if that kid was still dogging his trail. No sign of him. Good. He had enough guilt riding his conscience already. Didn't need to add scuffling with a kid half his age to the mix.

His lungs burned as he fought against slowing his pace. If Dearing's men got him in their sights, bullets were sure to fly, and he really preferred his hide without holes. Unable to afford a misstep, Asher locked his gaze on the ground before him as he raced through the underbrush.

Just a little farther. Bruno waited on the other side of those trees, saddled and ready. Asher's cow pony was nimble and as fast as they came. He'd outdistance any pursuit. If Asher could get to him.

Crack!

Asher flinched, and his steps stuttered. A gunshot? He turned just as a loud splash exploded.

"Clint!" The woman's heartrending scream froze Asher in his tracks.

No man with an ounce of character could ignore such a scream. He pivoted toward the pond and took in the scene.

A woman in a blue dress ran toward the water's edge. A broken tree limb floated in the middle of the pond. Someone floundered a few feet from it, slapping ineffectually at the water's surface.

"Help him!"

Not a demand. A plea.

The pampered princess from the study stared at him from across the pond. Dusk and distance hid her features from him, but nothing could hide her fear. Her anguish.

"Please. He can't swim." Tears roughened her voice. She didn't wait for him to respond, though. She waded straight into the pond, dress and all.

It had to be the boy who'd been chasing him. Clint Dearing. Heir to the Three Cedars, the outfit that had cheated Asher's family out of their home.

Clint Dearing. A boy no older than his brothers. Helpless to save himself.

Heart pumping with shifted purpose, Asher sprinted for the pond, tearing off his jacket as he ran. He paused at the shore long enough to yank his boots from his feet, then waded into the murky water. As soon as it reached his waist, he dove into the depths and stroked with all his might.

If this kid drowned because of him . . .

Please, God, help me reach him in time.

Asher lifted his head for a breath and spotted his target. The splashes were smaller. Sparser. Clint was struggling. Asher turned his face back into the water and kicked harder.

Ten yards. Five yards. Two . . . He lifted his head again. Squinted. The boy should be right in front of him. Nothing. He scanned right and left before turning back to the last place he'd seen him.

"Clint!" The woman screamed her brother's name, then surprised Asher by shouting amazingly level-headed instructions as she jabbed a finger at him from where she stood knee-deep in pond muck. "Your eleven o'clock. Dive."

He obeyed, sweeping his arms wide as he descended, praying he'd connect with the boy. Heaven knew he couldn't see anything, though he opened his eyes anyway, just in case he might distinguish a boyish shadow.

His lungs ached for replenishment, but Asher continued his underwater hunt. Two more sweeps, then he'd come up for air. He stretched his arms in a broad stroke. Nothing. He twisted to his left and tried again. His wrist knocked against something hard.

Praise God!

He grabbed for the shadow, fumbled, then finally grasped what felt like a collar. Holding tightly, he kicked for the surface.

When his head broke through, he gasped for breath, then immediately turned to the limp boy beside him. He flipped him onto his back, making sure his mouth and nose cleared the waterline. Then he positioned himself behind Clint's head, grabbed his underarm, and swam for the shore. About halfway there, the kid coughed and flailed, his panic returning with his consciousness.

"I've got you." Asher struggled to keep himself, and the boy, above water. "Stop fighting, or we'll both go under."

Clint tried to turn his head, but water lapped into his face, setting off another bout of coughing. Thankfully, he had enough presence of mind to stop his thrashing.

"Just stare at the sky, kid. I'll get you to shore."

And hopefully still have time to get himself off Three Cedars property before Dearing's men chased him down. Now that he knew the kid would survive, his own troubles resurfaced, urging his fatigued muscles to swim faster.

Testing the pond's depth, Asher stretched a leg downward and knocked into something relatively solid. It took a moment to steady his feet in the mud, but once he was stable, he shoved upward. Dragging the boy from a standing position proved much easier than swimming. Night air chilled his face and chest, while the muted sounds of faraway shouts urged him to hurry.

Once they reached the shallows, Clint batted Asher's arm away and crawled out under his own power. The kid hunkered on the shore on all fours, his head hanging low as he coughed and wheezed.

Asher gave him a couple of firm whacks on the back to help dislodge some of the water he'd taken in, then spared a quick glance toward the house.

The woman in the soggy blue dress was nearly upon them. Skirt hiked to her knees, she scurried around the west end of the pond as fast as her ruined dance slippers would allow. She didn't worry him as much as the three men running from the house with rifles in hand.

He needed to get out of here.

He thumped Clint's back a final time. "You good, kid?"

Still on all fours, the boy looked like a drowned rat and sounded like a creaky door hinge with all that wheezing, but his head bobbed up and down, giving Asher the permission he needed to beat a hasty departure.

"All right. Take care."

He ran over to where he'd left his boots and snatched them up.

"Clint?"

The woman. She was close. No time. Asher tucked the boots under his arm and sped away in his stockings. He bent sideways to grab his coat from the ground as he sprinted past, but a swath of blue flashed in his peripheral vision. He stumbled. His armful shifted. Something fell, but he didn't have time to go back. If Miss Dearing saw his face, his escape wouldn't matter. She'd just identify him later.

Turning his back to her, he tightened his grip on what remained in his arms and raced for Bruno. Thanking God for hard-packed dirt with few rocks and sticks to jab his feet, he fled down the game trail, not slowing his pace until he was in the saddle, bent over Bruno's neck, galloping for home.

Samantha barely spared the thief-turned-hero a glance as he bounded away from the pond. Her brother, sputtering and coughing at the water's edge, demanded her full attention.

Her heart ached at the sight of him on his hands and knees, hair plastered to his head, chest heaving for breath, limbs shivering as the night air chilled his drenched form.

But he was alive.

"I'm here, Clint." Finally. Never had a distance seemed so long.

She threw herself onto her knees in the mud beside him, her own chest heaving from fear and exertion. Wrapping her arms around his shoulders, she helped him straighten.

"Are you all right?"

He managed a nod as another cough wracked his body.

"Thank God." She folded him into her arms and rocked slightly, unsure if she was trying to soothe him with the motion or herself. Then, as if they weren't soaked enough already, a torrent of gratitude and relief poured from her eyes.

She could have lost him. God have mercy. She could have lost her brother. The very idea seared her soul like a branding iron.

Yet now was not the time to fall apart. Clint needed dry clothes and a warming brick. She'd send for Dr. Abbott. Have him listen to Clint's lungs. Prescribe treatment. Her work in

Boston had shown her the destructive power of pneumonia and consumption. Lung fever could take a healthy person and turn him into a withered, empty husk. That would *not* happen to Clint.

"Come on," she said after giving him one more squeeze and brushing his dripping hair out of his face. "Let's get you back to the house, shall we?"

His eyes looked past her. She turned to see what had captured his attention and found a boot lying discarded on the ground a few feet away. A rather distinctive boot. Usually a man's boot was either brown *or* black. This one was both. Brown lower, black upper with some kind of fancy stitching along the top.

"He saved me." Clint's voice emerged raspy and rough, but it was the awe beneath the sound that drew Samantha's attention back to her brother. "Why did he do that?" His brow creased. "I thought robbers were bad. That they stole and cheated and only cared about themselves. But this one saved me."

What could she say? That things were rarely black and white? That sometimes bad people did good things, and good people did bad things? Samantha's mind turned back to her father. Or maybe actions that seemed bad at first glance had more complicated explanations.

"Well, whoever he was," she said as she dried Clint's face with a dry spot on her sleeve, "I thank God for his help. I don't know what I would have done if I'd lost you." Samantha clamped her lips together and willed her tears not to return. Her father was almost upon them, and she wouldn't have him think her a weak, weepy female who was worthless in a crisis.

She pushed to her feet, then offered a hand to Clint. He shivered and wobbled on unsteady legs, but when she offered support by taking his elbow, he brushed away her aid.

"I can manage." He cast a glance at the approaching men.

It seemed she wasn't the only one who felt the need to display strength in front of Eli Dearing. "Go hide the boot."

What?

Clint shot her a glance, his eyes pleading. "He saved my life, Sam. The least we can do is cover his tracks."

Samantha frowned. Being grateful was one thing, but sacrificing one's integrity was quite another.

She wagged a finger at him. "I'll hide the boot, but I'll not have you lying to Father. A man of honor lives uprightly in all circumstances, and you, Clinton Dearing, are a man of honor. Remember that."

He rolled his eyes and gave her a little push. "Just do it, Sam. Hurry."

Obviously, he was feeling more like himself. She supposed she should be thankful for that. Hiding a smile, she darted over to the boot and kicked it beneath a nearby juniper bush. She toed it deep beneath the ground-scraping branches, making sure no part of it was visible before hurrying back to Clint. Her brother had already started walking toward the approaching men, cleverly taking a path that would angle their attention away from where his rescuer had dropped his belongings.

Her father led the charge, a rifle in his hand and outrage on his face. Until he got a good look at Clint. The anger darkening his face immediately melted into concern.

"What happened to you, son?"

Clint hung his head. "I heard your shout and tried to catch the man running away from the house. He was too fast for me, though. I thought I could cut him off by swinging over the pond, but the limb broke, and I fell."

Duke Kendrick, foreman for the Three Cedars, came alongside, looking nearly as shaken as her father. "What were you thinking, boy?" he scolded. "That fella coulda been armed.

You got no business chasing down trespassers on your own like that."

"Especially not swinging over your mother's pond when you can't even swim. Thunderation, Clint. You could've drowned!" Her father pulled the boy into a rough embrace, his face tipping heavenward. Moist eyes gleamed in the fading light.

Seeing the evidence of her father's love for his son made Samantha's chest ache with longing even as it made her feel closer to him than she had in years. Their own relationship might be rocky, but their love for Clint fostered a common ground they would never forfeit.

"What do you mean, the boy don't know how to swim?" Duke's brows arched almost into his hat. "How could you let him get this old without teachin' him, Eli?"

"Can't teach him something I don't know how to do myself."

She couldn't recall ever seeing her father look anything close to sheepish, but that was exactly the expression he wore as he offered his foreman a shrug.

"Well, good night, man. Why didn't ya say somethin'?" Duke patted Clint on the back as he eased out of his father's hug and swung his gaze to the foreman. "You and me are gonna start swimmin' lessons tomorrow."

"Let's make sure he's recovered first, shall we?" Samantha smiled to take some of the sting out of her words. She knew Duke meant well and had Clint's best interests at heart, but her brother had just coughed up half a lake. She had no intention of letting him anywhere near a body of water for at least a week. "For now, let's get him back to the house and send for Dr. Abbott. We don't want to risk a lung fever developing."

"Of course, Miss Dearing." Duke gave her a deferential nod. "I'll ride for the doctor myself."

"What about the thief?" Martin Hanover, one of the top hands at the Three Cedars spoke up for the first time. He was younger than Duke by at least a decade, but the quiet man had a deep reservoir of ranching knowledge and unmatched observation skills. Had a sixth sense about where to find strays when they went missing, too. Which made him a little *too* well-suited for tracking Clint's rescuer. He jabbed a thumb in the direction the mystery man had fled. "Shouldn't someone try to round him up?"

Clint grabbed his father's arm. "He saved my life, Dad. He could have taken advantage of my fall to make his escape, but he didn't. When he saw I was in trouble, he swam out to rescue me. Can't we just let him go?"

Indecision etched Eli Dearing's face. He wasn't exactly known for his leniency, and Samantha could tell his gratitude warred heavily with his demand for recompense.

"Did you recognize him?"

Apparently forgiving and forgetting were not on the menu, even if he was willing to temporarily call off the chase.

Clint shook his head. "No. 'Course I didn't really get a look at him. He dragged me out backward. And when I made it to shore, I was too busy trying not to choke on all the water I swallowed to pay him much mind."

"What about you, Samantha?" Her father's piercing blue eyes turned in her direction for the first time.

She fought the urge to squirm under his attention. "I only saw him from a distance. All I can tell you is that he was tall, lean, and had brownish hair."

Duke took his hat off and slapped it against his leg. "Shoot, that describes half the men in the county."

Samantha dipped her chin. "Sorry. After Clint fell into the pond, all of my attention fixated on him."

"As it should." Her father seemed to come to some kind of conclusion. His gaze took in her ruined gown, stained with water and pond scum, and he tentatively touched her shoulder.

The touch was awkward for both of them, but the approval inherent in the gesture softened a few of the hardened edges around her heart. He turned to his men and did what he did best, issue orders.

"Martin, see what tracks you can pick up before we lose the last of our daylight. Fellow probably had a horse stashed nearby so it's doubtful you'll find him, but maybe he'll have left a clue behind that can help identify him. Duke, fetch Dr. Abbott. I'm going to take my children back to the house and send our guests on their way."

Duke shoved his hat back on his head and nodded. "You got it, Boss."

Martin headed toward the pond, his gaze glued to the ground.

Worried he'd discover the one thing that might successfully identify Clint's rescuer, Samantha called out to him. "I saw him running down the game path toward the trees over there." She pointed in the direction the man had fled.

Martin tipped his hat and started striding in that direction. "Much obliged, ma'am."

She nodded to him and held her breath until he passed the boot-infested juniper bush.

Letting her father steer her back toward the house, she made a mental note of the bush's position. She'd be taking an early morning stroll tomorrow. With a basket. One large enough to hide a man's boot.

If anyone was going to puzzle out the identity of Clint's mystery rescuer, it was going to be her.

4

The cover of Mark Twain's *Roughing It* creaked slightly as Samantha eased it closed. She'd continued reading for several minutes after Clint's breathing had deepened to make sure he slept soundly. Rising from the chair next to her brother's bed, she laid the book on the night table and turned down the lamp.

His hair had nearly dried after the hot bath she'd insisted he take while they'd waited for Dr. Abbott to arrive. Samantha brushed a curling piece off his forehead with a featherlight touch. He needed a haircut. A smile curled her lips. With his features relaxed in sleep, it was easy to see glimpses of the toddler he'd been. Yet manhood would reach him soon.

Grant him wisdom and a healthy dose of common sense as he grows, Lord.

Hopefully, today's misadventure would teach him the value of caution. Heaven knew he could use a tad less impulsivity.

"Sleep well, Clint," she whispered as she bent down and bussed his forehead.

She turned to leave, then pulled up short when she spotted her father's large frame filling the doorway. He was leaning against the jamb, one ankle crossed over the other as if he'd been observing them for quite some time. Not sure how she felt about that, she frowned slightly as she crossed the room. He shifted to give her access to the hall, his expression hard to read.

"How long have you been there?" she whispered when he pivoted to follow her.

A grin creased his weatherworn face. "Since the camel ate Twain's overcoat." His smile widened. "Of all the outlandish yarns in that book, that one's my favorite."

Samantha blinked. He knew Twain's stories? Strange, but she'd never considered that he actually *read* the books on his study shelves. She'd thought them merely a symbol of his wealth. Hadn't Mother emphasized the importance of him presenting himself to business associates as a man of intelligence and learning in order to secure their respect? Samantha remembered being a young girl and helping her mother unpack the books she'd ordered to line the new shelves the carpenter had installed. The books had seemed dreadfully dull at the time, since none of them contained pictures. Literature. History. Scientific texts. Religious tomes. Classical works. All placed at eye level, their spines a dignified display.

The lower shelves had filled more slowly. She'd hadn't given much thought to who had purchased the additional titles. The books had just appeared little by little over the years. As her love of reading had grown, she'd explored them, of course. Finding most of them to be dry volumes discussing animal husbandry, agriculture, and business. An entire shelf had been dedicated to the annual release of the *Farmers' Almanac*. But there'd been novels, too. And children's stories. All with a boyish adventure flavor. She'd seen them as further proof of her father's preference for Clint, but what if he'd procured them simply because they matched his personal reading preferences?

She'd always assumed that when her father retired to his study in the evenings, he was working on payroll and other business matters. That had likely been true, but perhaps when the work was done, he had stretched out on the sofa, picked up a book from one of those lower shelves, and relaxed by getting lost in an entertaining story. The picture that idea painted so unbalanced her perceptions, she had to shake it away with a wag of her head before it dismantled the guard she'd learned to retain in her father's presence.

"Your mother would be proud of you, Samantha." The quiet rumble of her father's voice drew her out of her woolgathering. "Taking care of Clint the way you have." His big hand touched the small of her back as he guided her down the hall away from her brother's room.

"I miss her," Samantha murmured.

Even though she'd lived at the ranch for six years without Victoria Dearing before leaving for school, there was something about coming home from Boston that made the missing more keen. As if the distance had seduced her into believing that *all* her family waited for her in Texas. No matter how sternly her intellect warned her heart not to get lost in irrational wishes, each time she came home and found her mother gone, the resulting ache took weeks to fade.

"I miss her, too." Her father sighed. "You remind me of her, you know."

Samantha halted and swiveled to look at him. "I do?"

A nostalgic smile curved his lips as he nodded. "She was always ready to take charge of any situation involving family." He chuckled softly. "She never tried to insert herself in ranch business, granting me full reign over anything dealing with livestock or property, but when it came to dealing with people, she insisted I yield to her greater understanding. It seems I was wise to heed her counsel, for you've grown into exactly the sort of young lady she hoped you'd become. Confident. Cultured. Resourceful." He shrugged. "'Course I'd like to think you get some of your gumption from me. As much as I loved your mother, I can't imagine her wading hip deep into a pond while wearing a fancy ball gown."

Uneasy with his praise, Samantha dipped her chin. "Yes, well, Mother possessed a level-headedness I never quite mastered. When I saw Clint fall, I waded in without considering my own lack of swimming skill or the fact that the heavy layers of fashionable froth I wore would likely sink me straight to the bottom. Not the most intelligent maneuver."

A large hand curled gently around her shoulder. "Never underestimate the power of heart, Samantha. You feel things strongly and care deeply. It's how God made you." His hand lifted from her shoulder to rub the back of his neck while his gaze slipped away from hers in favor of staring at a spot on the wall. "I'm more of a doer than a feeler. It's why I struggle to understand you sometimes, but that doesn't mean I don't admire your passion."

Tears misted her eyes as his approval soaked into the scars left from past hurts. He *admired* her? Why had he never said so? Why had he let her believe she held no particular value in his eyes?

"I'm more of a doer than a feeler."

Could it be that he truly had no idea how she'd been feeling all these years? She'd not exactly been subtle in depicting her displeasure, especially during those last few years before being sent away to school. Thinking back on her sullen moods and angry tirades made her blush with chagrin. Missing the rift spreading between them would be like missing Palo Duro Canyon on the way to the JA Ranch—impossible. Yet a person couldn't fix something if he didn't understand what had been broken.

Fathers were larger-than-life. Capable of fixing anything. Or so she'd believed as a young girl. If he had the power to fix the problem and chose not to, it must mean he didn't care enough to try. Looking at him now, his uncertainty and nervousness in her presence evident, her childish beliefs fell away. He wasn't larger-than-life. He was just a man. One with weaknesses and flaws. One who probably had no idea how to relate to a daughter who shared virtually nothing in common with him outside of the Dearing name. Yet he'd paid her a rare compliment tonight. Two, in fact. Perhaps the time had come to cease waiting on him to fix what was broken between them and take on some of the responsibility for bridge building herself.

She lightly clasped his arm. "Hearing you say that means a lot to me, Daddy. Thank you."

He started to open his arms, and for one heart-stopping moment, she thought he might hug her. The child inside her longed to be wrapped in those bearlike arms, to be her daddy's little princess again. But the moment passed. His arms returned to his sides. He cleared his throat and stepped back.

She tried not to be hurt. She really did. But something inside her shriveled at his withdrawal.

"The, uh, doctor told me he expected Clint to make a full recovery."

Samantha nodded, accepting the change of subject and the distraction it provided. "He recommended that Clint not exert himself for the next few days in order to give his lungs a chance to recover."

Her father straightened, a glow of pride coloring his face. "If I know my boy, he'll be champing at the bit to get back to ranchin'."

"But you'll insist he rests," she said pointedly. "Won't you?" It really wasn't a question. More of a demand for consent.

Her father arched a brow. "I'll let you and Mrs. Stewart

coddle him tomorrow, but after that, if he shows no signs of lung fever, and if he feels strong enough to get back to work, I ain't gonna force him to stay in the house with the womenfolk."

Her jaw tightened. As if the house were the only space "womenfolk" were allowed to occupy. Her sense of justice bristled. Samantha might not agree with all the rhetoric espoused by Lucy Stone and the Massachusetts Woman Suffrage Association, but she'd attended enough lectures to conclude that it was constrictive assumptions like this that kept men from viewing women as viable candidates for the vote.

That's a fight for another day. You're supposed to be building bridges, remember, not taking an ax to the few support beams still standing.

Some of her displeasure must have shown on her face, though, for her father got that bulldog look of his that typically predicted the arrival of a bout of stubbornness.

"I ain't gonna argue with you on this, Samantha. He's my son, and I'll decide what's best for him." He opened his mouth to say more, then stopped himself. His shoulders slowly lowered, like a pair of barking dogs being ordered to stand down. When he finally spoke, a deliberate calmness colored his tone. "I promise not to run the boy into an early grave. Duke and I'll keep an eye on him. Make sure he doesn't overdo."

"I know you will." And she did. Clint was his whole world. He'd never do anything to jeopardize his son's well-being.

She fiddled with the sleeve on the loose housedress she'd donned after changing out of her sodden ball gown.

"I meant to ask you," she said, taking a page from his book and switching topics to avoid delving too deeply into uncomfortable waters, "did you discover what our uninvited guest took from your study?" *Uninvited guest* sounded so much better than *thief.* The man had saved her brother's life, after all. That should earn him a more favorable descriptor.

Her father shook his head. "I must've chased him out before he could take anything. Far as I can tell nothing's missing."

He *wasn't* a thief. Even better!

As if that bit of knowledge unlocked the door she'd pushed his memory behind, a vision of him rose in her mind's eye—his strong strokes propelling him across the pond, the way he pulled Clint from the water, the aid he'd administered, taking time to ensure her brother's fitness, even though it hampered his escape. She couldn't imagine any of the self-important dandies of her acquaintance back east making such a sacrifice. His actions had been noble, heroic.

"So you won't be reporting him to the sheriff, then?"

He gave her a look that made her feel like a naïve schoolgirl. "He's still a trespasser and a housebreaker, Samantha."

She deflated a bit at the reminder but held firm to the most important truth she knew about the intriguing intruder. "He saved Clint's life."

"Yes, and if he's found, I will ask the judge to be lenient with sentencing because of that, but I can't let a crime go unreported."

If he's found.

Samantha twirled a lock of her hair around her index finger. "Martin didn't uncover any clue to his identity, did he?"

"Nope." Her father peered at her oddly, as if he suspected her growing interest in the stranger who'd invaded their home. "Whoever he was, he's no concern of yours. Understand?"

"Yes, sir." She understood just fine.

Agreeing was an entirely different matter.

5

Asher woke early the next morning to scrub the pond out of his clothes. Mama Bess wouldn't have minded him tossing his laundry in the family pile, but his conscience insisted he clean up his own mess. Plus, he'd prefer not to answer any questions about why he took an evening swim fully clothed.

Water sluiced off his forearms as he lifted them out of the bucket of soapy water he'd propped on a tree stump. The dilapidated lean-to that housed the family cow stood behind him, blocking his activities from anyone who might peer out the kitchen window. Asher examined the front of his best white shirt and frowned. Still dirty. He gave it another swipe of soap and rubbed it against the washboard again.

He wished he hadn't donned his best duds for the party. He thought they'd help him blend in with the rich gents who'd come to woo the cattle king's daughter. He'd even worn his Sunday boots. The ones he saved for special occasions. He loved those boots. Won them in a rodeo contest last year for riding Old Red longer than any other hand at the Bar 7 Ranch. That bronc nearly busted Asher's hip when he finally unseated him, but seeing those fancy boots on his feet had made the platter-sized bruise and five days of limping worth the trouble. A man walked a little taller in boots like those.

Until he lost one. Wearing half the pair didn't exactly elevate a man's standing. Made it rather lopsided, as a matter of fact. His confident swagger would end up resembling the strut of an inebriated rooster. Not exactly a look to draw a lady's favor or a man's respect. Asher plunged the shirt into the depths of the bucket with a little too much vigor. Water sloshed over the brim and onto his denims. Asher grimaced. All his good intentions were going awry lately.

"Whatcha doin' back here?"

Asher jumped, sloshing another wave of water onto his trousers. "Gallopin' goose feathers, Fergus! Don't scare me like that."

His youngest brother snickered as he rounded the lean-to, milk bucket in hand. His blond hair stood on end, and his shirttails dangled untucked. Must've come straight from bed. Fergus resisted rising like a cat resisted swimming. Especially on a Saturday when there was no school to motivate him. Yet even at seven in the morning, he had that ever-present pencil behind his ear. The kid might only be ten, but he knew what he'd been put on the earth to do—write stories. He could entertain himself for hours with his sketchbook and writing tablet and rarely went anywhere without them. Even the milking stall.

Fergus pointed at Asher's trousers, his pudgy cheeks straining to contain his guffaw. "Thought you were too old to wet your pants, Ash."

Asher released the washboard and grabbed hold of the bucket handle. "I'm not too old to wet *your* pants." He pulled the bucket off the stump, grabbed the bottom, and pretended to toss the contents onto his brother.

42

Fergus squealed and dodged backward out of range, though his chuckles proved he trusted his big brother not to carry out the threat.

Asher grinned and set the bucket back on the stump. He shook the water off his hands and wiped them on the backside of his trousers. One of the few places dry enough to do any good.

"What's on the menu this mornin'?"

Asher had been craving Mama Bess's hotcakes ever since he'd returned home three days ago. Butter denting the fluffy middle as it melted, and her blackberry syrup dripping over the sides of the stack to puddle at the edges of the plate. Mmm. No ranch cook could match that sweet perfection. He'd dropped a few hints yesterday after the second morning of oatmeal, and the kiss she'd pressed into his head as he cleaned his bowl had promised good things.

Fergus shrugged. "Not sure. I didn't see the oat bin out, so we might get hotcakes, but she's been real stingy with the eggs ever since we moved. Sells most of them to the dry goods store. Butter too." His slightly somber expression brightened as he met Asher's gaze. "But now that you're home, she's bound to let us have jam and cookies again. It'll be like Christmas!"

Because Christmas was the only time he came home. At least that'd been true for the last five years. He'd tried to find local work after his pa died, but stringing together odd jobs didn't pay enough, and no one wanted to hire a wet-behind-the-ears kid at a man's salary. He'd finally found work as a cowhand, riding drag on a trail drive. He'd eaten more dust than chow on that drive, but it gave him something he'd desperately needed—experience.

After that, he managed to hire on with different brands whenever an outfit needed an extra hand. The work was sporadic and kept him moving from ranch to ranch, until two years ago when he landed a permanent position at the Bar 7 over in Callahan County. His foreman had given him two weeks off with no pay to tend to his family and promised another one if he needed it. Anything longer, though, and he'd likely be out of a job. Which wouldn't help Mama Bess or the boys get back on their feet. Jack had already dropped out of school to work as a stableboy at one of the liveries in town to bring in extra money. A fact Mama Bess had failed to mention in her letters, and one that stuck in Asher's craw worse than a swallowed fish bone.

The boy should be in school, not mucking out rented stalls. He was only twelve. This wasn't his burden to carry. It was Asher's.

Thank God Fergus was still free to be a boy. Taking school away from the youngest of the Ellis clan would be akin to stripping him of his skin. Never had Asher known a boy more fond of books.

And sweets.

Asher grinned, grabbed his brother in a mock headlock, and ruffled his not-yet-combed hair. "Now we know the real reason you like having me home. All those jams and cookies."

Fergus chuckled as he squirmed free. "Well, that and having extra help with the chores." He held out the milk pail. "You know, Mrs. Merriweather mentioned just last night how much she missed seeing you. I'm sure she'd love to have you pay your respects this morning."

Everyone else called the cow Cindy, but Fergus insisted on a more elegant title. He'd written her into his stories a couple of years ago, dubbing her Mrs. Lucinda Merriweather, matron of the barnyard. A woman of high moral standards and proper etiquette, she disapproved of all the trouble Fergus's more mischievous characters got into under her nose. Yet having a heart as big as her udders, she'd saved the little scamps from more than one misadventure.

"I'm afraid you'll have to pass along my regrets," Asher said, backing away from the milk pail palms up. "Let her know I'll stop by to work on her roof later this afternoon, though. Patch up some of those holes for her." The rotted wood on the lean-to surely leaked like a sieve when it rained.

Fergus dipped his chin. "She'll be glad of that. She gets a bit out of sorts when the weather doesn't stay outside like it's supposed to. Everything in its place, you know."

His brother's voice took on the prim tones of a schoolmarm, and Asher fought back a grin. Pressing his lips together, he crossed his arms over his chest and managed a solemn nod of agreement.

Fergus and his milk pail disappeared into the lean-to, and Asher got back to his laundry. Thirty minutes later, his shirt, trousers, underdrawers, and socks hung on the line in an adequate state of cleanliness, and the worst of the wetness had dried from the clothes he wore. He'd just finished putting the washboard and bucket away in the shed when Mama Bess called him to breakfast.

Feeling like the boy he'd been when Mama Bess had first married his pa and wooed her stepson with kindness and sugary treats, Asher hurried for the kitchen door, anxious to see what delights waited for him at the table. One of the hens pecking about the yard tried to waylay him with a flurry of flapping feathers, nearly flying into his belly. Asher dodged the airborne poultry and jogged up the back steps, satisfaction filling him when the step he'd replaced yesterday held his weight.

The ramshackle cottage on the edge of town that Mama Bess and the boys had moved into after being forced from their home needed more repair than Asher had time or know-how to provide. Nevertheless, he intended to improve it as much as possible before he left.

Pulling open the back door, Asher inhaled the aroma of fresh-made biscuits. His mouth watered, and his stomach growled.

"Mmm, that smells good."

Mama Bess looked up from setting a bowl of white gravy on the table. A smile blossomed across her face. "Asher. Come help me with this platter, would you?"

"Of course." He met her by the stove and reached for the large platter heaped with golden brown biscuits, but she placed a hand on his forearm, forestalling his assistance.

"I'm sorry it's not the hotcakes you wanted," she whispered low enough to ensure Jack and Fergus didn't overhear while they set the table. "I don't have the funds right now for extras like sugar. There's no more coffee, either, I'm afraid."

She looked distraught at the idea of disappointing him.

Asher wanted to kick himself. He never should have hinted at wanting hotcakes. He'd been remembering things as they'd been, not thinking about present hardships.

He grinned and planted a kiss on her cheek. "You know I love your biscuits." He lifted the platter over her head, not difficult since her dark brown bun barely reached his chin. "And what goes better with biscuits than milk?"

Asher hadn't had a glass of milk in years. The hands at the Bar 7 would rib him good about drinking a child's beverage, but if it kept the sadness out of Mama Bess's green eyes, he'd drink milk with every meal.

How had things gotten so bad that she couldn't afford basic staples? She must've depleted her entire savings trying to keep the house she'd shared with his father. He didn't have

46

much put by himself, but he'd be sure to stock her pantry before he left.

"Can I use my jam, Mama?" Fergus stood in front of the open cupboard, a half-filled jar of strawberry jam in his hand.

Fergus wasn't overly fond of gravy.

"Yes, love. Just remember, that's the last jar. When it's gone there won't be more until I can put in a new garden."

Fergus cradled the jar as if it were filled with precious gems instead of fruit. "I'll just eat a little. I promise."

"Share with your brother," she admonished gently.

"That's all right." Jack waved a dismissive hand. "I don't need any. I'm in the mood for gravy."

Jack met Asher's eye from across the table, and Asher gave a nod of approval—big brother to big brother. The kid had really grown up while Asher had been away. Taking on a job. Watching over Fergus. When was the last time he'd allowed himself just to be a kid?

"What time do you have to be at the livery today?" Asher asked him as he took a seat at the table.

Jack slid into his chair and placed his napkin in his lap. "Nine. Haggerty likes me to have all the stalls mucked out before noon."

"So if we finish breakfast by eight, you might have time for a quick spot of fishing in Eagle Creek if Bruno and I give you a ride?"

Jack's eyes lit with excitement. "I can be ready in ten minutes!" He grabbed a biscuit off the platter.

"Jonathan Ellis. We say grace before we eat in this family." Mama Bess froze his hand in midair with a look.

Slowly, he placed the biscuit back on the pile. "Yes, ma'am."

She smiled at his compliance, then turned to Asher. "Would you do the honors?"

"Of course." Hoping she could hear the apology in his voice,

Asher extended his hands to Jack and Fergus, who were seated on either side of him. They completed the circle by clasping their mother's hands. Asher's eyes closed as he soaked up the feeling of family.

"Heavenly Father," he prayed, "your mercies are new every morning, and we see that in the bounty spread before us. Thank you for good food to eat and loved ones to share it. Give us strength to tackle the challenges that await us today. May we honor you with the choices we make and the actions we take." Thoughts of last night's disaster pinched his conscience. "Forgive us when we fail you, and grant us courage to make amends. We ask you to meet our needs and help us to meet the needs of others. In the name of Jesus, amen."

"Amen."

As if a racing gun had fired, Jack's hand shot out to claim a pair of biscuits from the platter. In a blink of an eye, he had them ripped open and gravy poured over their fluffy middles. Mama Bess shook her head but gave no reprimand. Deciding he best be ready, too, Asher wasted no time tucking into his own breakfast. Until he noticed how quietly Fergus was sitting.

Asher set down his fork and reached for his milk glass. "You want to come with us, Fergus?"

Fergus wasn't much of an outdoorsman, but Asher hated for him to feel left out.

The boy shook his head as he spread a thin, nearly transparent layer of jam across one biscuit half. "Nah, I got things to do around here."

"All right. But when I get back, remind me to tell you about the mice I met last night who sewed a girl's slippers to the carpet."

Fergus dropped his knife with a clatter as his mouth hung agape.

Asher hid his grin behind a drink of milk.

"Sewing mice?"

"Mm-hmm." Asher swallowed and set his glass down. "I thought you might like to introduce them to your barnyard friends. They're uppity house mice, though, so they might not get along with everyone."

Asher swore he could see the cogs turning in Fergus's mind as his imagination cranked.

Within ten minutes, both boys were finished with their breakfast and excused from the table. Jack to dig out the fishing poles. Fergus to dig out a fresh writing tablet.

Mama Bess reached across the table and grasped Asher's hand. "It's good to have you home. The boys miss you so."

"I miss them, too." He rubbed his thumb over her thumb. "And you."

She flushed with pleasure at his words.

He hated to chase away that smile, but he wasn't sure when he would next have a chance to talk to her alone. "Why didn't you tell me they raised your rent, Mama Bess? I could have sent more money."

She pulled her hand away and crossed her arms over her chest. "No." She shook her head with adamant force. "You give us too much already. You should be saving that money to start a family of your own."

Asher frowned. "You *are* my family. You and Jack and Fergus."

She turned her face toward the stove and nibbled on her lower lip. "It would have beggared you, Ash. I couldn't allow that. Not when I really didn't need all that land. They started charging me the same rates as a tenant who made a profit from farming or ranching. I thought I could bargain with Mr. Dearing, perhaps renegotiate an agreement that permitted me to keep the house and yard while allowing him to reclaim all the acreage we weren't using. His manager refused my petition. He said the land was worth more with the house than without. He also hinted that Mr. Dearing had plans for the property, though he didn't share the details.

"In hindsight, I should have agreed to leave when they first raised the rents, but I was in a state of denial. I couldn't imagine living in a place that held no memories of your father. Jonathan found that job at the livery, and I convinced myself that the additional funds would buy us more time. Even if it didn't cover the bulk of what I owed. When the first eviction notice arrived, I had just put the garden in, and you know how much we depend on that harvest to see us through the winter. I ignored the warning, hoping for a few more months of grace, but . . ." Her brow furrowed as if an idea had interrupted her train of thought. Slowly her head pivoted back toward him, her gaze rife with suspicion. "How did you find out about the rent?"

Asher was saved having to answer when Jack ran into the kitchen, fishing poles in hand. "I found 'em!"

"Great!" Asher grinned at Jack and rose from the table. "Go saddle Bruno for me, would ya? I'll be right there."

Jack dashed off, too excited about the prospect of fishing to read the tension in the room.

Mama Bess stood and took Asher's arm. "Promise me you won't do anything foolish. We're fine where we are. Money is tight, and things are hard, but the Lord will see us through."

His jaw tightened. "What Dearing did to you was wrong. I aim to do what I can to set it right."

Her green eyes bored into his with such intensity, heat singed his chest. "If you pit yourself against Eli Dearing, you'll lose. He's a powerful man with the wealth and connections to ruin your life should he so choose. I won't allow you to throw away your future over a patch of dirt. That's not what your father would have wanted. Please, Asher, leave it be."

Asher bent down and kissed her forehead, hoping to soothe her fears in a way honest words could never do. Because after what he'd done last night, there was a better than average chance that *leaving it be* was no longer an option.

6

Samantha strolled around the churchyard Sunday morning, making a mental catalog of the boots worn by the men milling about after services. She doubted her mystery man would stride through town with one boot that matched the orphaned footwear she'd hidden in her wardrobe and a second boot from a different pair. Nevertheless, curiosity compelled her to look. Well . . . maybe a little more than mere curiosity.

She'd dreamed of him the last two nights. Only, in her dreams, the stranger had rescued *her*, not Clint.

Samantha had always considered herself a sensible woman, not the type to get swept up in unrealistic romantic fantasies. Yet the idea of a handsome man of mystery dedicating himself to her protection proved far too tantalizing to dismiss. And the fact that he was a housebreaker? She'd never admit it aloud, but a tiny rebellious part of her liked the fact that he wasn't afraid to defy her father. Too many men kowtowed to Eli Dearing in an effort to gain his favor and his business. It was refreshing to meet someone unswayed by the cattle king's influence. She might not know why he'd broken into her house, but she knew he wasn't a thief and hadn't intended anyone harm. Surely a man honorable enough to risk his own freedom to rescue a floundering boy had to possess a noble heart. Like Robin Hood. Finding him would give her the opportunity to investigate his character, to determine whether he was the hero her dreams portrayed.

Or a petty thief run off the property before he had the chance to snatch anything of value.

Focusing again on the footwear ambling about the churchyard, Samantha continued cataloging boots. She ruled out the men who had feet either much too large or far too small to fit in the boot she'd found. A handful of others were eliminated due to age and physique. She'd not seen Clint's rescuer up close, but even from a distance it'd been obvious that he had no paunchy middle or gray hair. Still, there were likely scores of men in Palo Pinto County who met her broad specifications. Close to a dozen roamed the grounds of the First Christian Church this very minute. None of whom wore the boot she sought.

She meandered through the parked wagons, trying to catch a glimpse of boot tops hidden inside trouser legs. When a gentleman propped his foot on a wagon wheel or reached for a stirrup while mounting, he might reveal a glimpse of either the front or back shaft. Enough to tell her if the leather on top was the same as the leather covering the foot.

The brown-footed boot snagging her attention at the moment rose off the ground and twisted inward, offering her a few additional inches of leather to view. Brown leather. Not the contrasting black she'd been seeking.

"Did I step in something unsavory?"

Samantha jerked her attention upward, hoping her cheeks weren't as fire red as they felt. "Mr. Rutherford! Forgive me. I was . . . admiring your boots. Which are respectably unblemished, by the way." A nervous giggle slipped from her throat

53

before she could clamp off her windpipe. "Are they custom made?" she rambled. "I'm considering purchasing a pair for my father's birthday." As of two seconds ago. "Do you find them comfortable?"

Close your mouth and stop talking!

Samantha bit her tongue. Good heavens. She could have simply ignored his question and commented on the weather. That's what her etiquette instructor would have advised. *"Never allow a conversation to lead you where you don't want to go. If it veers off course, steer it to safer ground."*

Too late now. The train had already derailed.

The lines smoothed from Mr. Rutherford's brow, however, as if he noticed nothing amiss. "Ah yes, I had these made by a bootmaker in Fort Worth two years ago when I attended the annual meeting of the Northwestern Texas Stock Raisers Association. Such a memorable occasion. Charles Goodnight himself addressed the group." He aimed a pretentious smile her way. "He and I spoke afterward."

What did that have to do with boots? His expectant expression indicated he thought the revelation rather meaningful. Oh dear. Was he trying to impress her by mentioning his brief interaction with Mr. Goodnight? Not the wisest strategy, seeing as how Charles Goodnight had dined at the Three Cedars on more than one occasion. James Loving too. Besides, she cared little about who a man *knew*. Who a man *was* carried much more weight. And none of this had any bearing on the actual conversation at hand. They were discussing the comfort of Mr. Rutherford's boots, after all.

"So would you recommend him?" She batted her lashes. Just once. Not enough to flirt. Just enough to portray innocuous interest in his opinion.

The utterly blank look on Mr. Rutherford's face was really quite comical. "Recommend who? Mr. Goodnight?"

"Your bootmaker." Samantha lifted her brows in a quizzical fashion. "That is what we are discussing, isn't it? Boots?"

"Yes . . . of course." His imaginary plumage retracted and drooped while he stammered. "I'll, uh, look up the name for you when I get home this afternoon."

"That's very kind. Thank you."

Seeing that her praise restored a bit of his composure, Samantha determined to beat a hasty exit before he could shake any new tailfeathers in her direction. "If you'll excuse me, Mr. Rutherford. I must find my brother."

He fingered the brim of his hat. "Of course, Miss Dearing."

She turned to make her escape, but his next words halted her retreat.

"It was good to see young Clint recovered enough to attend services."

Hmm. Perhaps Mr. Rutherford wasn't completely self-absorbed.

"Yes," she said. "He's doing much better, thank the Lord." And already asking to resume ranch work, just as their father had predicted.

"I'm glad he suffered no ill effects from his accident." A sincerity shone in Mr. Rutherford's eyes that gave her pause.

Samantha nodded. "As am I."

Her father hadn't mentioned there being an intruder when he'd dismissed the party guests, only that Clint had suffered an injury. He probably hadn't wanted to chance spooking any of her suitors with the possibility of nefarious shenanigans being afoot. Yet someone was bound to have heard the commotion and pieced things together. Her father hadn't exactly been whispering when he'd accused their uninvited visitor of thievery.

Feeling slightly more charitable toward Mr. Rutherford, Samantha offered a genuine smile as she made her departure.

Maybe her father was right. Maybe she *was* too eager to

find fault in the suitors he'd selected for her. Dorian Rutherford might be a peacock, but it seemed he possessed a measure of compassion beneath all the plumage. If only he and the others would cease trying to impress her and simply get to know her and let her get to know them in return. She wasn't hiring someone to manage her affairs. She sought a relationship—one to last a lifetime. A man's financial pedigree and understanding of the cattle market meant less to her than mutual respect, shared values, and camaraderie. She wanted someone who would make her laugh and hold her when she cried. One who would listen to her opinions and consider them of equal worth to his own. One who enjoyed her company and sought her out instead of relegating her to a role separate from his. One to whom she could pour out her love without fear of rejection.

A sigh slipped from her lips as she wove her way through the dispersing congregants. Did such a man exist? She wanted to believe he did. That God would cross his path with hers when the time was right. But would she recognize him when that day came? Or would she be so jaded by past disappointments and fearful of future hurts that she failed to take the risk required to find love?

"That's a rather dour expression for someone who just spent the last hour worshipping the God of unending grace."

"Aunt Regina!" Samantha pulled up short at the base of the church steps, chagrined to be caught in her own moment of self-absorption. "I'm sorry. I really did attend to Uncle Obadiah's sermon on Ephesians chapter two. I promise. I just . . . have a lot on my mind."

Regina Hopewell wrapped an arm about Samantha's shoulders and squeezed her close. "I'm sure you do. I'm not criticizing, dear heart, just trying to tease a smile onto my favorite niece's face."

It worked, of course. Aunt Regina was rather magical that

way, always lightening the load of the people around her with her encouraging spirit and kind ways.

"I'm your *only* niece," Samantha teased back, her grin widening.

Aunt Regina winked, her eyes dancing with merriment. "That doesn't mean you can't be my favorite." She steered Samantha to the side of the church building, to a place that afforded a bit of privacy. Her expression grew serious. "What is it, dear heart? Are you worried about Clint? He seems much recovered." Her gaze lifted to a place in front of the building.

Samantha turned and spotted a group of boys running and slapping at one another's back in what seemed to be a team version of tag. Clint ran with the rest of them, laughing and not appearing the least bit winded by the activity.

Thank you, Lord.

"Looking at him, one wouldn't know he almost drowned two nights ago." Samantha shook her head, then turned back to face her aunt. "I do worry about him pushing himself too hard, too fast, but Dr. Abbott said his lungs sounded clear when he checked in on him yesterday, and Daddy saw no reason to keep him home from church. On the way here, I made Clint promise to slow down if he felt winded." She shrugged. "I think he agreed just to keep me from harping at him, but I trust him to honor his word."

"So if not Clint," Aunt Regina nudged, "who or what is weighing down your thoughts?"

"Daddy thinks it's time for me to marry."

"You disagree?"

"Yes. Well, at least with the way he's going about it." Samantha blew out a breath. "He thinks it's his job to wrangle a husband for me, but it should be my choice."

"Have you chosen someone?" Aunt Regina's eyes held no judgment, only patience and curiosity.

"Not yet, but that doesn't mean I want him shoving random cowboys down my throat."

Aunt Regina laughed softly. "My, but you do love a dramatic turn of phrase."

Well, yes. But that didn't mean there wasn't a layer of truth beneath it.

"If I know your father," Aunt Regina said with a gentle smile, "those cowboys he's herding your way are anything but random."

"That may be true, but I still don't like the idea of him trying to control my life."

"Oh, honey, it's not your daddy who's been controlling your life."

What?

"Mrs. Hopewell?" Dottie Philpot, leader of the Palo Pinto quilting club and usurper of private conversations, closed in on them, hand waving. "Mrs. Hopewell, I really must speak to you." She spared a brief glance for Samantha. "Pardon me, Miss Dearing, but this is an urgent matter. It has just come to my attention that the Benevolence Committee Picnic is scheduled on the same day as my quilting bee. Something must be changed. Immediately."

"Is that so?" Without agreeing or disagreeing, Aunt Regina slid her arm around Mrs. Philpot's and deftly aimed her away from Samantha. "Why don't we seek out Mrs. Henshaw? I'm sure between the three of us, we can resolve this complication."

As the older woman shuffled past Samantha, buzzing about her quilting bee always being on the third Saturday of the month, Aunt Regina cast a look back to her niece.

"Call on me tomorrow afternoon," she said. "We can talk more then."

Without interruption.

"All right." Samantha's mind whirled as the ladies left her to her own devices.

What could her aunt have possibly meant by that comment about her father not controlling her life? He'd been making decisions on her behalf since childhood. Had she been trying to make some kind of spiritual point about God being the one in control? Possibly, but Samantha didn't think so. Something about the way her aunt said it had felt much more . . . earthly.

She'd call early. Right after lunch. Aunt Regina wouldn't mind. She knew patience wasn't one of Samantha's stronger virtues. Besides, Samantha had another matter to discuss with her aunt. One requiring guidance from a minister's wife more than a family member. It might take two pots of tea to get everything sorted. But if anyone could navigate the muddy waters of suitors, fathers, and a woman's desire for autonomy, it was Aunt Regina. She was the wisest woman Samantha knew.

Aunt Regina and Uncle Obadiah hadn't been blessed with children of their own, which was probably why they'd made such a concerted effort to be involved in the lives of their niece and nephew. After Mama passed, Aunt Regina had stayed at the Three Cedars for two months, taking care of Clint and soothing Samantha's broken heart. It had been a balm Samantha had desperately needed since her father had dealt with his grief by burying himself in work. Feeling abandoned by both parents, Samantha had begged Aunt Regina to take her home with her. Her aunt didn't consider it for even a moment. She'd hugged Samantha tightly, then said words Samantha would never forget, even though she found them hard to believe.

"Your father needs you. And you need him. If I took you away, it would break his heart, and it would harden yours. I don't want that for either of you."

Yet her heart *had* hardened. Even now, it was still a little crusty around the edges. If her father needed her, loved her, why had he never invited her into his life the way he had Clint? Was being a girl such a sin? He hadn't even taught her how to ride. He'd brought in some fancy Easterner to teach her how to ride sidesaddle. Sidesaddle! As if she didn't feel ostracized enough from her peers. She'd given her instructor fits and never finished her lessons, hoping her father would give in and teach her to ride like a normal Texan. She'd even gotten Mrs. Stewart to help her remake one of her skirts into a split style so he couldn't make the modesty argument. Not only had he refused to teach her to ride astride, he'd sold the horse he'd bought for her lessons the next day.

How could Aunt Regina think he hadn't controlled her life? He'd controlled everything.

7

The following day, at precisely one o'clock, Samantha knocked on her aunt's door. Regina Hopewell greeted her with a hug and a cheery smile.

"I thought you might come early." She ushered her niece into the front parlor, where a tea tray stood ready for service atop a small table. "I'm glad you did. It gives us more time to visit."

Samantha smiled as she rounded the settee and took a seat in the adjacent armchair. She'd always liked this parlor suite. Smooth wood, free of the intricate carvings one found on more expensive sets. The dark blue upholstery with the floral needlepoint design was feminine and inviting. A simple style that welcomed a guest into the room, no matter their station in life. Perfect for a minister's home. Yet so different from the richly ornamental furnishings her mother had selected for the Three Cedars. Strange how two sisters could have such disparate tastes.

"I'd intended to call sooner after returning from Boston," Samantha said as she pulled her gloves from her hands, "but when Daddy sprang that ball on me, things got a little hectic."

Aunt Regina's soft laugh tinkled like fairy bells. "I can imagine. Your father's not one to do things halfway."

"That's the truth."

Aunt Regina slid gracefully onto the settee and reached for the white-and-blue porcelain teapot. She filled the first cup, added two teaspoons of sugar, and gave it a thorough stir before handing it to her niece. Samantha's stomach knotted as she reached for the saucer. The sweeter the tea, the more serious the conversation that lay ahead.

"First," her aunt said as she stirred a generous spoonful of sugar into her own tea, "give me an update on Clinton. How is he faring?"

"Dr. Abbott paid a call this morning and pronounced him fit, much to Clint's delight. He spent most of the morning riding fences with Martin. Daddy promised to keep him in the saddle and away from the more strenuous tasks, but I still worry he'll overdo." She lifted her teacup to her lips and took a small sip.

"If he does, you'll be there to scold him and tuck him into bed." Aunt Regina's smile held a hint of longing but no bitterness.

Did her heart ever ache over her barrenness? She always seemed so content and joyful, but she must have mourned the loss of the children she would never hold. When she was younger, perhaps? Had she and Uncle Obadiah prayed for children only to have God refuse their petition? How had they let go of the pain and moved forward free of resentment, serving the Lord without reservation?

Samantha would love to learn their secret. To rid her heart of the resentment she felt toward her father and focus on the ministry the Lord had placed on her heart. They had made some progress over the last few days, but the distance left to travel stretched inordinately long and left her disheartened.

She and Aunt Regina chatted a bit about school and the friends she'd left behind, but instead of easing her tension, the longer they avoided the topic that had brought her here, the more knots formed in her belly. When the conversation turned to fashion and the size of Eastern society bustles, Samantha's tolerance for small talk evaporated.

Setting her cup and saucer down on the side table with an indelicate clatter, she bounced her rear down to the edge of her chair and reached for her aunt's arm. "We can talk about Boston later. I need to understand what you meant by your comment yesterday after church. About Daddy not being the one controlling my life. It makes no sense. He's controlled *everything.*"

Aunt Regina's posture sagged slightly as she set her own teacup down. Her gaze traveled to the ceiling and lingered there. Samantha retracted her hand and tucked it into her lap. Was her aunt praying? Trying to find the right words?

Just spit it out!

Several seconds of torturous silence elapsed before her aunt finally spoke. "Do you remember how angry you were when your father first sent you to Boston?"

Samantha nodded as old hurt sliced into her anew. Never had she felt more unwanted or betrayed. Her father had turned deaf ears to her pleas to stay. He'd even ignored Clint when her brother petitioned on her behalf.

What jabbed the knife even deeper was the fact that Aunt Regina and Uncle Obadiah had moved to Palo Pinto only four months before. The people who had always accepted her, loved her unconditionally, and mentored her through letters and annual visits had finally moved to town. They'd lived two counties away for most of her life, her uncle a circuit-riding preacher serving small congregations within a fifty-mile radius. His ministering to a scattered flock made it difficult for them to get away for family visits, though they were faithful correspondents. When the First Christian Church of Palo Pinto found themselves in need of a full-time preacher, Samantha had begged Uncle Obadiah to apply. He did and won the position easily. She was certain a more dedicated shepherd of souls could not be found in all of Texas.

Samantha still remembered the day they moved to town. She'd squealed and laughed and hugged them twenty times each, so excited that the Lord had answered her prayers. Yet that abundant joy calcified into anger when her father revealed she'd been accepted into a prestigious girls school back east and would start in the fall. He'd stripped her of everything she loved in one fell swoop.

Samantha swallowed. "It took months for me to forgive him for that." Truth to tell, the forgiving was an ongoing process. Whenever she prodded those memories, bitterness threatened to creep back into her heart. It took an act of will, and a healthy dose of God's grace, to refuse it entrance even now.

"I remember. You didn't answer a single letter from him during that time."

It had been petty. The actions of a hurt child. Thankfully, Aunt Regina had shaken her out of her callowness.

Samantha's lips twitched in chagrin at the memory of the letter her aunt had written that November. "I never knew ink could leap from its page to write upon a human heart with such ferocity until I read your letter of admonishment. My knees bore bruises for a week after the hours I spent petitioning the Lord for mercy."

Aunt Regina's small smile didn't remove the shadows from her eyes. "Your silence nearly broke him, Samantha."

"What?" Her heart thudded hard in her breast.

Her aunt nodded. "I'll never forget the day he showed up at my door. He looked like he hadn't slept in three days. I

64

thought he'd taken ill and called for Obadiah, but he insisted on talking to me in private."

Samantha leaned back in her chair, suddenly in need of its support.

"He was convinced that he'd destroyed his relationship with you. That you'd never forgive him or see the good in what he'd been trying to accomplish by sending you away." Aunt Regina smoothed the fabric of her dress across her lap. "He asked me dozens of questions about you. Had you made friends? Did you like your teachers? What was your favorite class? What was the weather like in Boston? He was a starving man begging for crumbs. It made my heart ache."

Moisture rose to Samantha's eyes. The picture Aunt Regina painted was hard to fathom. Her father . . . begging? The cattle king—a man as strong as iron, who had built an empire with his own two hands. A man whose decisions were law, whose heart was impervious to a daughter's wishes.

"There are things you don't know about him, Samantha. Reasons for the choices he's made. I might not agree with all of his decisions, but I can promise you, they were never made from a callous heart. That man loves you more than his own life."

"Then why . . . ?"

Aunt Regina held up a hand. "I can't share secrets that don't belong to me. You need to talk to him. More than that, Samantha, you need to *listen* to him. Listen not with the ears of a child, but with the ears of a woman, one who understands how complicated this world can be."

Complicated enough that a man who broke into her house seemed less a thief and more the heroic savior of overzealous boys. Perhaps there were complications with her father that she'd never considered. But why would he hide them from her?

"After you finally wrote to him," Aunt Regina continued,

"he carried your letter in his billfold for weeks. I lost track of how many times I witnessed him pull it out when someone at church would ask after you. He'd beam with pride as he unfolded your missive and shared a few tidbits about your life in Boston. I wouldn't be surprised to learn he carries it with him still." She reached for the teapot and poured a stream into her cup. "That letter didn't just contain idle tittle-tattle from a girl in boarding school, it contained proof that he hadn't lost you."

Samantha's chest throbbed as she extended her own cup for a refill. "If he was so worried about losing me, why did he constantly push me away?"

Silver clinked against porcelain as her aunt stirred sugar into her tea. "He thought he was doing what was best for you."

Why would he think cutting her off from the people and place she loved would be best?

"I can see you're struggling to accept the idea," her aunt said as she handed Samantha her teacup, "but not everyone sees things from the same perspective. Your mother and I certainly didn't."

"How so?" Samantha's memories of her mother had faded over time. The large portrait hanging in the front parlor kept her physical image alive, but the rest was rather hazy. She remembered admiring her mother's beauty and her ability to handle any household crisis that arose. The cattle king might have mastered the business of ranching, but his queen managed everything else—including him.

"Victoria's aspirations were far grander than mine," Aunt Regina explained. "Even from the time we were children. My favorite toy was a rag doll that I could hold and carry about, while Vicky favored paper dolls that she could dress in elaborate costumes and use to practice proper conversation. I rolled about in the hay with barn kittens, while your mother preferred playing the piano. I read dime novels. She poured over fashion magazines. I loved people and wanted to make friends with everyone. She analyzed people and maximized their potential. If you needed a task accomplished or an event organized, Victoria would work her fingers to the bone to ensure its success. Those who needed cheering up or who wanted someone to share their troubles with gravitated more toward me.

"God created us with very different personalities and interests, which led to us viewing the world through very different lenses. One wasn't better or worse than another. Both had value. And both had pitfalls."

Her aunt dipped her chin, no longer meeting Samantha's gaze. "I gave my heart too easily." Her soft admission bore the heaviness of regret. "To a handsome young man who knew how to spin a sympathetic tale. I was so determined to prove my devotion to him that I nearly sacrificed my devotion to God. Had my conscience not stopped me that night, I don't know where I'd be today." She looked up to the mantel where a small wedding photograph stood in a place of honor. "Likely, I'd not be married to a man who puts the Lord first in everything he does and who loves me with such selfless affection that he'd sooner lay down his life than cause me one moment of physical or spiritual harm."

That was what Samantha craved. A marriage built on love where both parties cared more about the other's well-being than their own.

Had her parents enjoyed such a marriage? She wasn't sure. She couldn't recall a single time her mother's eyes had gone soft and misty like Aunt Regina's just had when speaking about her husband. Respect had abounded between them, but affection had only been expressed behind closed doors.

"Your mother's weakness was that she trusted a little too much in chariots."

Samantha scrunched her forehead. "Chariots?"

Aunt Regina smiled. "Proverbial ones, of course."

"Of course." Samantha waited for the epiphany to descend upon her, but it must have gotten hung up in the rafters because after a long thoughtful moment she still hadn't a clue as to what her aunt referred.

"Psalm 20:7. 'Some trust in chariots, and some in horses: but we will remember the name of the Lord our God.' Your mother valued social status and judged herself on her ability to achieve it. So when it came time to marry, she discouraged any suitors who lacked wealth or significant prospects. Eli Dearing had both. And even more important, he possessed a willingness to be molded into the man of standing she wished him to be."

"She didn't love him?"

Aunt Regina set her tea aside and captured Samantha's hand. "Perhaps not at first, but love grew in her heart. I know it did. And your father . . . well, he fell head over heels for Victoria the first moment he saw her. He held her up on a pedestal so high I sometimes worried what would happen if she slipped off. Not only to him but to her. She placed so much pressure on herself to succeed. Then you came along, and new dreams were born. Your parents were so full of plans for you."

"But I wasn't a boy."

"That didn't matter. You were theirs, and they loved you."

Samantha frowned. "Daddy wasn't disappointed? When I was little, Mama talked a lot about giving me a little brother, about how daughters were the apple of their daddy's eye, but sons were necessary to build a legacy. I didn't know what that meant, exactly, but I knew I wasn't enough."

"You listen to me, Samantha Jane Dearing. You are more than enough. You are exactly who God intended you to be. If your parents had failed to see you as such, it wouldn't have made it any less true. But, dear heart, your parents were not blind. They adored you. They bragged about you all the time. How smart you were, how fearless. And that didn't stop after Clint was born."

Samantha stared at her aunt, her proclamation crossing swords with every long-held insecurity banging around in her head. Hard to tell which side was winning.

She really needed to have a hard, honest conversation with her father. Not so he could give her value or shape her identity—she'd found that in her Lord and in his work—but to gain a better understanding of his thoughts and motives. Perhaps it would heal old wounds and help them find a path to reconciliation.

"I love you, Aunt Reggie." The name she'd called her aunt as a young girl slipped out, but it felt right for the moment.

Moisture glistened in her aunt's eyes as she squeezed Samantha's hand. "I love you, too, Sammy girl." She sniffed a bit, then released her niece's hand, giving her arm a pat before scooting back on the settee and taking a deep breath. "Enough talk of the past. Let's turn to the future. What do you plan to do with yourself now that you've finished school?"

Samantha's pulse fluttered with new excitement. "I'm so glad you asked." She straightened her posture and smoothed the front of her dress. Why was she suddenly nervous? This was Aunt Regina, for pity's sake. Not her former headmistress. "I'd like your help in finding a way to minister to the less fortunate here in Palo Pinto."

Her aunt blinked at her.

Samantha rushed to continue. "I don't simply want to be Eli Dearing's daughter. Privileged and prized for my dowry. I want to make a difference in my community." Her voice rose as passion ignited. "I wrote you about my work in Boston. The soup kitchens and hospitals where I volunteered. The class for illiterate girls I started, teaching them to read and write so they could better themselves."

Leaving her girls behind had been the hardest part about coming home. The five girls she taught worked long hours in factories to help support their families. Yet despite their exhaustion, they came to her class three nights a week and drank up knowledge with a thirst she envied. Thankfully, one of the ladies from church had agreed to take over the lessons, but Samantha still prayed for each of her girls by name every night.

"Please, Aunt Regina, I believe God wants me to serve. I'm just not sure how to do that here."

"God wants all of us to serve, but you must be careful in how you go about it. In a big city like Boston, I imagine you rarely crossed paths with the people you served. Here, however, it will be impossible *not* to cross paths with them."

"Why does that matter? We are called to love our neighbors as ourselves, aren't we?" Samantha hadn't expected resistance. She'd expected support. Eagerness, even. "I thought you'd be glad to have another volunteer to help with your charity work."

"That's just it. People don't like to be thought of as charity work."

Samantha sputtered. "That's not what I meant."

"But I'm afraid that's how you might be perceived. The people around here know you. They know your station. Your wealth. Whether it is your intention or not, they are predisposed to see any help you offer as an act of condescension." Her aunt took a breath, then reached out and patted Samantha's knee. "I'm not trying to discourage you. Truly. I'm proud of you for seeking ways to be involved in the Lord's work. You have a kind heart and a holy passion. But to be effective in this place, you need to serve from a place of humility, otherwise people will likely reject the help you wish to give. They must feel respected, not pitied. Ministry is not about you helping those in need, it's about God helping those in need through you. Do you understand the difference?"

Not really, but she did understand a person's need for respect. To be seen as an equal. That was the basis for the women's suffrage movement, after all.

Samantha took a long breath before she responded. "I understand that I have a lot to learn." She'd be foolish to ignore her aunt's experience, yet she couldn't ignore the Lord's call. "Perhaps we can start small? Maybe there is a child I can help in some way or an elderly widow?"

Aunt Regina smiled. A proud, satisfied sort of smile that sent a wave of warmth radiating through Samantha's chest.

"I'll pray about it tonight and discuss the idea with Obadiah." Her aunt's enthusiasm blossomed as she spoke. Her words picked up speed, and her eyes danced as possibilities stirred to life. "Oh! I'm lunching with the other ministers' wives tomorrow. I'll mention it to them as well. There might be needs within their congregations that would be suited to your situation."

This was the reaction Samantha had hoped for. Energy zinged inside her midsection as she leaned forward in her seat.

"I'll come see you on Wednesday," she said. "And I'll be praying that God leads me to the place where I can do the most good."

8

Asher sat in Clyde Milton's office on Monday afternoon, hat in his lap, heart in his throat. His knees bounced incessantly as he waited for the lawyer to read over the rental agreement Mama Bess had provided. There had to be a clause or stipulation somewhere banning the raising of rent. A new rate should require a new contract, shouldn't it? The tenant had rights, too.

Unfortunately, Asher hadn't recognized anything actionable when he'd scoured the document this morning, but the convoluted lingo had been hard to decipher. That's why he'd decided to pay for an interpreter. Someone he hoped could find him a legal leg to stand on when he faced off with Eli Dearing.

After many scowls, a handful of thoughtful hums, and one rather laborious sigh, Clyde Milton sat back in his desk chair and met Asher's gaze. "I'm sorry, Mr. Ellis. I don't see anything in this contract that prohibits the owner from raising the rent price. In fact, it seems Mr. Dearing could have evicted your mother after your father died. The fact that he allowed her to stay without a credible source of income will likely endear him to the judge. Make him seem long-suffering, especially since he didn't raise the rent for six years."

Asher jumped from his chair and paced in front of Milton's desk. "Can't we argue that the price increase was exorbitant? That it placed undo hardship on my mother?"

Milton stood slowly, his bones creaking slightly as he straightened his middle-aged frame. "I'm afraid your mother's poverty does not have any bearing on the case. The owner can set the rent to any figure he deems appropriate as long as he communicates the change to the tenant in advance. Which he did, judging by this letter." He slid the second paper out from behind the first and pinned it to the desktop with his index finger.

"What about the improvements she made to the land? Shouldn't she be compensated for that in some way?" Asher was grasping at straws, and he knew it, but he couldn't come away from this with *nothing*.

"I'm afraid not. Mr. Dearing owns the land, and therefore any improvements made to it belong to him as well."

Asher's hand fisted around the brim of his hat. "What about the garden? Mama Bess could feed half the town with her harvest. Shoot, she gives away as much as she keeps, so she probably *has* fed half the town over the years. The seeds planted were hers, not Dearing's. The labor was hers, not Dearing's. And since she left, the plot just sits there, rotting. What good does that do anyone?" He flung his arms wide. "The land is his, sure. But the food growing in and above that soil belongs to her. She should be allowed to harvest it."

"I'm sorry, Mr. Ellis. The law cannot compel him to do so. And if your mother"—he raised a pointed brow—"*or anyone else* trespasses on the property to collect items growing there, that person will be subject to criminal charges and a steep fine. If said parties are unable to pay such a fine, jail time could be imposed, or the family might be relocated to the county's poor farm."

The fight drained from Asher's stance. "Please, Clyde. She depends on that garden to feed herself and the boys. Taking that away from her is stealing food from their mouths. There has to be something we can do."

The lawyer moved out from behind his desk, shedding his professional persona in favor of the one the Ellis family saw when they sat across the aisle from him in church. He clapped Asher's shoulder and wagged his head. "I'm sorry, Ash. I wish I could help, but legally there's nothing I can do." He turned back to the desk and collected the papers. "Personally, though, I can bring some supplies by the house after work. I've been on the receiving end of Elizabeth's generous nature. It's only right that I return the favor."

"That's kind of you," Asher said, his mouth tightening, "but unnecessary. I'll see she has the supplies she needs."

Even if it bankrupted him.

Offering a final word of thanks, Asher accepted the lease papers and took his leave. The sun hit his face when he exited the courthouse, the brightness momentarily blinding. He took a moment to reshape the brim he'd mangled during his unproductive meeting with Clyde Milton, then fit the hat back to his head. Nodding to a man in a suit striding purposefully toward the courthouse entrance, Asher stepped away from the doorframe and headed to the street and the hitching post where he'd left his horse.

Bruno lifted his head and snorted, almost as if asking how Asher's meeting had gone.

"Not well, buddy." He patted the paint's black-and-white neck, then tucked Mama Bess's papers into his saddlebag. "Not well at all."

Asher gritted his teeth as he slid his foot into the left stirrup and mounted. Men like Eli Dearing shouldn't be allowed to toy with people's lives whenever the whim struck. They should honor the spirit of agreements made instead of using the letter of the law to circumvent the original intent. What could he possibly need with that one small plot of land that justified turning out a widow and her two children?

Nudging Bruno into a walk, Asher headed away from the square. He scanned the conveyances surrounding him in the street. A ragged buckboard driven by a man in stained overalls rolled down one side while a man in a tall hat and fancy suit pranced down the other on a high-stepping thoroughbred. Kids without shoes dangled bare feet off the tailgate of a farm wagon parked outside the general store, and a lady in a stylish pink dress and fashionable hat drove her pony cart down a cross street as if she were in some sort of parade.

Why did the Lord allow such disparity among his people? Why did some work all their lives and only scratch out a meager living while others worked with similar diligence and received riches upon riches? Where was the justice in that? Even worse were those who gained wealth through illicit means. Eli Dearing might not be conducting illegal business, but neither was he loving his neighbor. It wasn't right. Society should hold him accountable, not turn a blind eye to his callous choices. Yet no one wanted to stand against a man with wealth and power, too afraid of the price they might be called to pay. Then again, Asher was no better. He could have stormed the cattle king's castle and taken the man to task for turning out his stepmother and brothers, but he hadn't. Not because he was afraid of the repercussions for himself, but because he didn't want to bring more trouble to Mama Bess's doorstep.

I'm sorry, Pop. I've tried everything I can think of to fix this, even a few things I'm ashamed of, but there's no putting it right. The house is gone.

75

Nothing to do now but make the new place as habitable as possible before he left. Which was why he reined Bruno to a halt in front of Patterson's Hardware. If he was going to weatherproof Mama Bess's roof, he was going to need some supplies.

A bell rang as he entered the shop. The clerk behind the counter glanced up from the customer he was assisting and smiled.

"Afternoon, sir."

Asher fingered the recently reshaped brim of his hat. "Afternoon."

"Farm implements are along the back wall. Ironware to your right. Carpentry tools in the center. Cutlery and kitchenware to the left."

"Much obliged." Asher strode toward the center aisle in search of nails. He'd probably have to special order the shingles he'd need, but—

A pile of wiggling pink froth stole every thought from his head as he rounded the corner and stepped into the aisle.

It was a woman—obviously—but what she was doing, he had no earthly idea. Hunkered down in front of a display of chisels, she seemed to be trying to peer beneath the shelving to view something in the adjacent aisle. Asher eased backward, took a couple of steps to his left, and peered down the next walkway. A pair of men stood about even with her position, discussing the merits of whitewash versus paint.

Not exactly the type of conversation to entice an eavesdropper.

Inching back to his right, he found the woman where he'd left her, now holding two gloved hands in front of her, as if measuring the length of something, though the spread of her hands failed to match any of the items housed on the nearby shelf.

Deciding it might be best to pretend he didn't see her, Asher turned his gaze away and stepped into the aisle. Unfortunately, his elbow clipped a dangling handsaw and sent it flying off its nail and onto the floor. The woman gasped and lurched to her feet, spinning toward Asher as he gave chase to the runaway saw.

Her cheeks flushed pinker than her dress, and her eyes darted to him, then past him as if checking to see if anyone else had witnessed her odd behavior.

Instinct prompted Asher to look over his shoulder to see if anyone was there. But he didn't. He couldn't seem to look away from her.

Blue. Her eyes. Summer sky blue. Rimmed with thick lashes. And returning their attention to him.

Feeling his own cheeks heat, Asher held up his hands in apology. "Sorry to startle you. I, uh, accidentally knocked it with my arm." He took a few steps forward and bent to retrieve the errant saw.

"That's all right." She offered a shaky smile and ran a hand down the front of her dress.

Asher straightened, the saw clutched awkwardly in front of him. *Say something, you dolt!*

"I'll just, uh, put this back."

Ugh. Something intelligent, Ash.

He sidled down to the front of the aisle, where the other saws hung, keeping her in his peripheral vision. His mind spun but failed to grip anything worth saying out loud.

"Are you . . . interested in carpentry?"

Her downturned gaze jerked up to meet his, a hint of guilt playing about her face. Had she been staring at his feet? Why would a woman wearing a dress that probably cost more than his saddle be interested in a worn-out pair of boots? Wait . . . had that been what she was looking at while she'd been hunched over? The boots worn by the men on the next aisle over?

"Carpentry?" Tiny lines etched her forehead. "Not particularly. Why?"

He grinned, feeling more himself now that he had the upper hand in the conversation. He tipped his head toward the shelf beside her. "You seemed quite enthralled by those chisels. I thought you might be a hobbyist."

"Ah yes. Well. My father has a birthday coming up." She fiddled with a bit of lace at her cuff.

"And he's a carpenter?" He really shouldn't derive so much pleasure from teasing her, but it felt good to let go of his worries for a few minutes and flirt with a pretty girl.

"A rancher, actually, but tools are always handy to have around, wouldn't you agree?"

"I would." He grinned. "A ranch can never have too many chisels."

Her lips twitched, and amusement gleamed in her vibrant eyes, but she managed to keep it contained. Unfortunate, since he found himself intensely curious about what her laugh would sound like once unleashed.

"Everything all right back here?" The clerk who had greeted Asher from behind the front counter hurried into the aisle, his smile strained. "I heard a crash." He scanned the shelves, no doubt looking for evidence of an avalanche.

"Sorry," Asher said. "That was my fault. I clipped a saw with my elbow. The stray's been wrangled and is back with the herd now, though, so no harm done." He nodded to where the saw hung, nice and tidy.

The clerk, however, didn't bother looking at the cutting-edge display. His attention remained riveted elsewhere. Not that Asher blamed him. What fella wanted to look at saws when there was an attractive young woman a few feet away?

"Miss Dearing? Are you sure there's nothing I can assist you with? I'd be happy to lend you my expertise."

Asher's ears rang. Miss Dearing? As in *Samantha* Dearing? The pampered princess he'd nearly flattened when jumping out of her daddy's study window? The one whose little brother almost drowned trying to chase him down?

Had she recognized him? Slowly, he turned his face away, thankful for the distraction of the overzealous clerk. He hadn't recognized her, but then he'd not seen her up close that night. But what if she had seen him? In the study or after he'd leapt from the window.

Breathe, Ash. It had been dark. A boy had been drowning. She'd had other concerns on her mind. Plus, no recognition had registered in her eyes while they'd been talking. He would've seen it with as hard as he'd been staring at those blue beauties.

But what if it wasn't his face that could give him away? His gut tightened as her interest in men's boots suddenly made a dreadful sort of sense. If she'd found the boot he'd dropped . . .

Asher yanked his fingers away from the handsaw he'd been pretending to inspect. He needed to get out of here. Now.

Lengthening his stride, he left the carpentry aisle behind and made a beeline for the door. Shingles and nails would have to wait. He couldn't chance being recognized by the one woman in town who could send him to prison.

9

Samantha bit back a sigh as the intriguing gentleman with the kind eyes and teasing smile disappeared from the aisle. His bootheels echoed against the wooden floorboards, then faded beneath the jangle of a bell. He'd left.

"Miss Dearing?"

"Hmm?" She refocused on the annoyingly helpful clerk. "Oh yes. Mr. Flanders." She manufactured a polite smile for the man with the heavily pomaded hair and lopsided mustache. "Thank you so much for your kind offer." She was pretty sure he'd offered something. Pointing out items in the store perhaps? Whatever it was, she had no desire to take him up on it. "I just stopped in today to do a little light browsing. My father's birthday is coming up, you see."

That excuse had become remarkably handy, even if the occasion was three months away. It might not reflect the real reason she chose to visit the shop, but the statement itself was true.

Mr. Flanders grinned, the gesture tipping his already lopsided mustache into an even steeper asymmetrical position. He held out his arm and stepped toward her. "We have some sturdy work gloves that would make a fine gift for a rancher. Or perhaps a new saddlebag? We have a special collection of hand-tooled leather goods I think you'll like."

He attempted to herd her in that direction, but she side-stepped and dipped her chin in apology.

"Excellent ideas, sir. I will certainly bear them in mind." She squeezed past him, wiggling her fingers in a small wave as she went. "For now, though, I have other business to attend to. If you'll excuse me?"

"Of course." His arms dropped to his side, and his mustache leveled out as his smile dimmed.

She felt a little bad about dashing his hopes, whether they'd been centered on her in a personal manner or strictly attached to her pocketbook. Best not to encourage either. Although . . . she might have to return later and buy one of those chisels. The oddity of the gift would be vastly entertaining. Stepping outside onto the street, she fought a giggle as she pictured her father's face scrunched in confusion when he unwrapped her package.

The real pleasure would come from the memories sure to be prompted whenever she ran across the chisel among the tools in the barn. Memories of a handsome cowboy who teased and flirted with her as if she were any other woman. No exaggerated efforts to impress. No effusive compliments. No recitation of his pedigree. Just friendly conversation. He even had the good manners not to ask about her peeping beneath the store shelves like a child spying through a keyhole.

Warmth spread through her chest as she lifted the hem of her skirt and climbed into the horse cart she used when driving to and from the ranch. He'd dressed like any other cowboy—denim trousers, tan shirt with a bibbed front, dusty brown boots that looked nothing like the one she'd found with the fancy stitching. She'd hadn't gotten more than a glance at his feet, but they seemed to fit within the size parameters she'd set. What if he was the man who rescued Clint? Her heart pounded as she picked up the reins and clicked her tongue to signal the little mare that she was ready to depart.

His physique matched what she remembered of the man fleeing her ball. Tall. Lean with sinewy strength. Of course, that description fit most working cowhands. Still, it didn't rule him out. Her pulse pounded at the possibility that she might have just conversed with the mystery man who'd been invading her dreams of late. A man possessed of rugged good looks and a pleasant manner. One might even consider him charming.

She'd tried to convince herself that her search for her brother's rescuer had been motivated by a desire to express her gratitude, but if she were brutally honest with herself, it probably had more to do with besting her father. Solving the case of the unknown intruder while her father remained in the dark would be incredibly satisfying. She'd control the knowledge and decide how best to use it, not him. If the man she found ended up being more hero than thief, she'd protect his identity out of loyalty to Clint. On the other hand, if she discovered a man of murky character, one in possession of nefarious intentions toward her family, she wouldn't hesitate to have the intruder brought up on charges.

Although, after her encounter in the hardware shop, she had to admit to a third possible motive at play—romantic curiosity. Could the real-life man compare to the dream version she'd built up in her mind? Samantha silently scoffed at the thought, the answer obvious. Of course he couldn't. Her dreams glossed over the trespassing, choosing to focus solely on the courage and compassion on display during the rescue. Only a fool would employ such willful blindness in reality, and Samantha was no fool. She'd not give her heart to a man she didn't trust, and she'd not trust a man who acted without honor.

Reaching Cedar Street, Samantha turned her cart left onto the road that would take her out of town and back toward the ranch.

"Get up, Dolly," she called to the small black mare. She clicked and jiggled the reins until the horse sped to a trot.

Once out of town, her mind wandered back to the man in the hardware shop. He hadn't seemed like the housebreaking type. Not that she was terribly familiar with such characters, but surely a criminal wouldn't have eyes that danced with good humor and kindness. Or a manner that put a young lady at ease after being found in an embarrassing position. Besides, he'd carried himself like a man who understood the value of hard work. His hat alone bore testament to that. Beaten up, sweat stained, the brim misshapen. It matched any of the hats she'd seen her father's men wear. Men who wrangled cattle, strung barbed wire, dug fence-post holes, and hauled hay for a living. Did he do the same?

She wished she'd asked his name. Found out where he was from. Why had he left so abruptly? He hadn't even purchased anything.

Had it been because he'd learned *her* name? The thought demolished her pleasure with the same sudden efficiency as a speeding wagon splashing mud over a new dress.

It might've been a coincidence. He could have remembered an appointment or caught a glimpse of someone he needed to speak to outside. He could have taken ill or . . . or . . . Samantha sighed, unable to come up with any other plausible explanations. Not that the ones she'd manufactured bore much plausibility, either. Her mystery cowboy hadn't seemed the slightest bit peaked, and the front windows weren't even visible from the aisle where they'd been standing.

No, the simplest explanation was likely correct. The cowboy heard Mr. Flanders address her as Miss Dearing and left because of it. But why? Did the difference in their stations intimidate him? Did he bear a grudge against her father that tainted her by association? Had he heard stories about her father wanting to marry her off and feared for his bachelorhood?

Oh for pity's sake. She'd conversed no more than ten minutes with the man. For all she knew, he'd been looking for an excuse to extricate himself from her company all along and had simply grasped the opportunity provided by the clerk's interruption.

Nothing like a dose of humility to flatten a girl's spirits. Oh well. She'd be better served by turning her thoughts to the conversation she needed to have with her father. Another spirit-flattening endeavor, yet one she could no longer shy away from. Not if she wanted to be a woman of maturity instead of a child who buried her head under blankets and plugged her ears whenever difficult topics arose.

As she turned off the main road and passed under the wooden archway that proclaimed her arrival at the Three Cedars Ranch, nerves pricked her belly.

I'm going to need your help, Lord. It's hard to open old wounds and not focus on the pain. Give me eyes to see things from his perspective instead of merely my own. You make all things new, Lord. Soften my heart so I can join your work of reconciliation instead of hindering it.

Aunt Regina had given her much to think about today, and the mirror she'd held up had not displayed a flattering reflection, depicting more petulant child than gracious woman. That wasn't who she wanted to be. No matter the outcome of this conversation, she couldn't allow herself to be mired in old hurts any longer. She needed to forgive her father and move forward.

Despite her determination to conduct herself as a mature, sophisticated woman, Samantha's hand still shook when she raised it to knock on her father's study door that evening after dinner.

"Come in."

Pulse fluttering, she pushed the door open and stepped into the room. Her father glanced up from the papers strewn across his desk. His eyes widened when they settled on her.

"Samantha?" He pushed back his chair and rose to his feet. "What is it?" He rounded the desk. "Has something happened?"

Shame dipped her chin. Of course he assumed something dreadful had occurred. Outside of meals, church, and the occasions when she needed money, she tended to avoid him.

"Nothing's wrong, Daddy." At least nothing of immediate consequence. "I just . . ." She took a breath and lifted her chin, forcing herself to meet his gaze. "I wanted to talk to you about a few things. If that's all right."

He stood frozen at the edge of his desk for a moment. Then he blinked, cleared his throat, and moved forward to meet her. "Of course." He gestured to the seating area across the way. When she moved toward it, he stepped behind her to close the door.

She took a seat on the sofa and waited for him to settle into the armchair on her right.

"Is this about the ball?" He frowned slightly, his voice taking on a defensive edge. "I realize now I should have asked your opinion before sending the invitations, but those men who came would be good providers and—"

Samantha stopped him by placing a hand on his arm. "Daddy, it's not about the ball."

His eyes searched her face. "All right." He gave her hand a pat. "What's on your mind, then?"

She nibbled on her lower lip as she gathered her courage, then pictured the woman she wanted to be. She straightened her posture, settled her hands in her lap, and lifted her chin. "Why did you send me away to school when you knew I didn't want to go?"

Her father rubbed a hand over his face as he exhaled a heavy breath. "I thought we were past this, Samantha." He shook his head and leaned backward in his seat. "Kids don't always know what's best for them. It's not a parent's job to give a child everything she wants. Sometimes we gotta look past what we want and do what's best, even if it's hard."

"No, Daddy, that's not what I mean." She scooted to the edge of her chair, careful to keep all hint of accusation from her voice. "Why did you think sending me to school in Boston was the best thing for me? Why did you think I needed lessons in deportment and the chance to make social connections back east if I was going to return to Texas and become a rancher's wife? Wouldn't learning the cattle industry be more beneficial?"

He quirked a half smile and a nostalgic look passed over his face. "I asked your mother the same question. She would not be dissuaded, though. She insisted on sending you to Boston when you turned sixteen." His smile faded. "Even made me swear to see it done when she realized she . . . would not be around when the time came."

"So finishing school was Mama's idea." Samantha had started to suspect as much after her conversation with Aunt Regina, but seeing her father's nod made her feel as if someone were pushing heavy furniture around in her heart—rearranging what she'd always understood to be true.

He sat up and leaned toward her. "Your mama wanted the

best for you, and she had very specific ideas of what that entailed. Some days I thought her dreams were too lofty, too . . . far-flung. She talked of you becoming the wife of a steel baron or a senator. Of using your position in society to make a difference in the world. Personally, I just wanted you to grow up to marry a local boy and stay close to home." He shrugged.

"If you wanted me to stay, why did you still make me go to Boston? Mama was gone. Her dreams were gone."

Her father pinned her to the back of the sofa with his gaze. "I made your mama a promise as she lay dying, Samantha. I *had* to carry it out. Even if you and I both hated it." He fell silent for a long minute, then finally slouched back in his chair, the action releasing the tension that had held her captive. "Can't say I was disappointed when you showed no interest in any of them Eastern bigwigs and came home anyway."

He grinned, and for the first time in a long time, Samantha found herself grinning back at him, sharing a moment of camaraderie.

"Mama might have raised me to be a socialite," she said, "but I've got too much of your Texas blood in me to be happy in that kind of life."

He chuckled softly. "Yeah. You might've gotten your good looks and your determination to make a difference in the world from her, but you got your grit and orneriness from me. I still remember how you screamed the house down when I told you that you couldn't ride with me anymore. You were about four, I think. Chased me out of the house and into the barn. Stood in front of the stall with your arms above your head, refusing to let me leave without you. 'My turn to ride, Daddy. Up!' I nearly gave in. Probably would have if your mother hadn't caught up to us. She scooped you into her arms and took you to the house. You kicked and screamed the entire way. I felt like the worst parent on the planet. But then, I knew nothing about raising a little girl. I let your mama take the lead with that. She read enough of those etiquette books and magazine articles to be an expert. When she read that it was considered vulgar for a young lady to ride a horse astride, she insisted I cease taking you up on my horse. Wouldn't even let me buy you a pony. She said you'd learn to ride sidesaddle like a proper young lady when you were older. Maybe if she had still been alive when I hired that instructor, you would've actually completed the lessons."

Samantha clutched the sofa arm as she fought to get her bearings in a sea that suddenly seemed to be in an entirely different hemisphere. The stars that had been her navigational guideposts had vanished. New stars glimmered in the darkness, pointing out a path she didn't recognize but somehow knew to be true.

"She told me that girls ran houses, not ranches." The words slipped from Samantha's lips almost without her awareness as she tried to view the past through different eyes. "She said you would have a son one day and would train him to run the ranch, but that wasn't the place for me." Her vision blurred, and she blinked back tears as she found her father's face. "All this time, I thought you didn't want me. That I had no place in your life because I was a girl."

"Oh, darlin', nothin' could be further from the truth." He left his chair, sat next to her on the sofa, and opened his arms. "Come here, sweetheart."

She hesitated a moment, then fell against him. She wrapped her arms around her daddy, buried her face in his shirt, and sobbed out two decades of hurt. And when a warm wetness penetrated her scalp from where her father's cheek pressed against the top of her head, the last bit of crustiness dissolved from the edges of her heart.

10

A sher? Would you come into the house for a moment?"
Mama Bess's call stilled Asher's hammer.
"Be right there!"

He swung the hammer two more times, driving a nail through the siding of the chicken coop. Four more along the edge ought to secure the patch. Holding the gaping board flat against the coop with his hip, he pulled a nail from the wide-mouthed jar by his feet, then pounded one after the other into the board until it hung flat and sturdy.

It had been two days since he'd run into Miss Dearing in Patterson's Hardware, yet he hadn't gone back to order those shingles. Foolish, really. The woman didn't live there. The chances of running into her a second time in the same week were practically zero. Still, he'd been avoiding the place. He'd purchased a couple of pounds of nails from one of the general stores in town, but he'd have to go back to Patterson's tomorrow if he hoped to get the shingles in time for him to complete the repairs before he had to head back to the Bar 7. The coop needed a new roof even worse than the house did, and he wasn't about to leave Mama Bess and the boys with a roof that would let in the wet and cold once the seasons changed.

Asher dropped his hammer into his father's old toolbox, grabbed the jar of nails, and did a quick scan of the work area to make sure he wasn't leaving anything unsafe behind before heading up to the house. Chickens squawked as he crossed the yard, and Mrs. Merriweather raised her bovine head to watch the undignified parade of man and fowl. One would think the feathered ladies would show more appreciation to the man refurbishing their house, but these particular birds preferred lying in wait and ambushing him the moment he entered their territory. Made a man wish there were such a thing as a chicken-herding dog. If he could employ one, maybe he'd be able to walk in a straight line between the shed and the house once in a while.

Thanks to peck-proof work boots, Asher made it through the yard relatively unscathed. He set the toolbox down on the back porch, then took a minute to wash up at the basin Mama Bess left out for that purpose. He banged the heels of his boots against the edge of the porch to knock off the worst of the dirt before walking into the kitchen.

Mama Bess stilled the broom she'd been wielding and greeted him with a smile. "Poured you a glass of water." She nodded toward the table as she propped the broom in the nearest corner.

"Thanks." Asher hung his hat on the wall hook and rubbed the sweat from his brow with his sleeve before reaching for the refreshment.

He'd never understood why children's stories portrayed stepmothers as selfish and evil. Mama Bess was an angel in calico as far as Ash was concerned.

He gulped down half the water before he noticed the tentative look in Mama Bess's eyes, one very similar to the look she'd worn before she'd admitted to not telling him about the increased rent. Asher lowered his glass. "What is it?"

She gestured to the chair nearest him as she slid into one herself. "Nothing to worry about, I assure you."

Ironic how that statement intensified the very thing it had been designed to eradicate.

Asher took a seat, steeling himself for whatever bad news was coming. Mama Bess didn't have many faults, but she did have a frustrating tendency to ignore or postpone unpleasantness until the last possible moment, leaving a man precious little time to prepare for whatever battle loomed.

"Mrs. Stephenson called on me yesterday afternoon."

The preacher's wife? That didn't sound too bad. Although, from what little interaction he'd had with her from his few visits over the years, she struck him as one of those organizing and interfering types. Always with the best of intentions, of course. Yet once she set her mind on a path she believed to be right, turning her from it was like trying to turn a stampede without a horse—impossible to avoid getting run over. A woman as gentle-natured as Mama Bess wouldn't have stood a chance.

Asher set his water glass down and focused on keeping his tone mild. "And . . . ?"

"And she presented me with a wonderful opportunity. One I was happy to accept for Jonathan's sake."

Asher frowned. "This isn't another job, is it? Jack already works more than he should at the livery."

It still stuck in Asher's craw that his little brother had to work to help make ends meet. When Mama Bess had mentioned Jack's job in her letters, she'd made it sound like it was just a few hours a week. A way for him to earn a little spending money. He'd had no idea that Jack's earnings were going toward family necessities.

This rundown place on the edge of town didn't have any of the acreage the farm had, yet it cost nearly as much to rent since it was within the city limits and had access to city water and municipal services like coal delivery. That, combined with greater food costs and no place for the animals to graze, stretched them thin. Asher's wages could keep the roof over their head, but half of what a cowhand earned was paid through room and board. Only a portion came to him as cash. He sent Mama Bess all he could, and it chafed that it wasn't enough.

"No, it's not about a job. It's about his schooling." Mama Bess turned pleading eyes on him as if she expected him not to be in favor of Jack's education. "There's a young lady who recently arrived in town who has some experience with teaching. She's volunteered to help Jonathan get caught up on the work he missed last term after he began working at the livery. She's agreed to come for two hours in the evenings, three days a week. But since it will likely be getting dark by the time she needs to return home, Mrs. Stephenson insisted on the young lady having an escort. I assured her that you would see the teacher home, at least for as long as you are here."

Asher grinned. "Is that all? Of course, I'll see her home. Least I can do." He lifted his glass to his mouth, thanking God all the dread he'd felt had been worry over nothing.

Then Mama Bess's hand pressed into his forearm, and her gaze grew fierce. "You will treat her with respect, Asher Ellis. You will be a gentleman at all times and do nothing to discourage her from returning. She's doing Jonathan a great favor, and we must not jeopardize this opportunity."

Affronted, Asher gulped down the rest of his water in order to keep his tongue from firing off something he'd regret saying. What did she think he was going to do? Assault the young lady on the way home? Did she trust him so little?

Setting the glass back on table, Asher kept his fingers circled around its base and squeezed tightly. "You have my word that I will behave as a gentleman at all times."

She patted his arm, her face lighting with relief. "Excellent. I knew I could count on you. Miss Dearing will be here at six thirty this evening, so we'll move supper up to five thirty."

"Miss *Dearing*?" He nearly choked on the surname.

Mama Bess swirled out of her chair and crossed the kitchen to retrieve the broom as if she hadn't just dug a hole and pushed him in. "Yes, Miss Samantha Dearing. I understand she's a lovely young woman. Cultured. Intelligent." Her frantic sweeping slowed as she finally looked Asher in the eye again. "I'm willing to look past her family connections for Jonathan's sake. I pray you will, too."

Looking past *her* family connections wasn't the problem. It was hiding *his* connection to her family that had him worried.

Samantha reminded herself to breathe as she pulled the mare to a halt in front of the Ellis home. After setting the brake on her gig, she smoothed a hand down her sensible navy bodice to press lightly against her stomach.

You can do this. Just smile and act like a professional.

If only her nerves would settle. She hated feeling unprepared, and even though she'd spent an hour with the local schoolmarm figuring out precisely where Jonathan Ellis's education had ended and what needed to be covered for him not to be held back a grade should he find a way to return next year, butterflies the size of chickens fluttered in her belly.

She knew why, and it had nothing to do with teaching. If she could successfully instruct a room of illiterate working girls, teaching one young man should present no difficulty. No, it was the welcome she might receive that had her on edge.

Mrs. Stephenson, one of Aunt Regina's friends, had recommended this assignment. She'd met with Samantha this morning to go over the specifics, explaining about the widowed Mrs. Ellis and her two boys who had fallen on hard times after her husband passed six years ago. Those hard times had been compounded when they'd been evicted from their home earlier in the year. Evicted by none other than Eli Dearing. The Baptist minister's wife believed Providence to be at work, directing the daughter of the man who had cast out the family to be the one to help them find their footing again.

Learning of her father's involvement had only fueled Samantha's determination to serve this family to the best of her ability. He might have to protect his investments and put business above charity in order to care for his family, men, and stock, but she was under no such constraint. The question was, Would the Ellis family see her as a custodian of blessing or a stark reminder of all they had lost?

Only one way to find out.

Samantha climbed down from her two-wheeled cart, then reached to the floorboard to collect the basket she'd packed for her visit. Schoolbooks, slate, writing tablet, and a little something that hopefully would sweeten her reception.

Someone must've been watching at the window, for the front door opened before she'd made it halfway down the walk. A young boy stood in the doorway, inspecting her from hair to shoes. His eyes lit on the basket with interest, then found their way back to her face.

"Are you Miss Dearing?"

Samantha smiled and nodded. "I am. Are you Jonathan Ellis?"

The boy shook his head. "Nope. Jack's inside. I'm Fergus."

She thought he looked a little small for twelve. He stood several inches shorter than Clint, but he seemed to have taken it upon himself to play the role of guard dog. A role she respected, having played it once or twice herself over the years.

Samantha extended her hand to him. "Nice to meet you, Fergus. Will you be joining us for lessons?"

Fergus gave her hand an arch look before deciding to grasp it. He pumped her arm as if he expected water to sluice from her mouth, then stepped back.

"Mama said the lessons were just for Jack since I'm already ahead in school. But if you got any extra books in your basket, I might take a look. Especially if you got stories."

A boy who liked to read. What a refreshing change. "I'm afraid I didn't bring any storybooks with me this time, but I'll be sure to put a few extras in my basket for my next visit."

His shoulders slumped.

"I might have something else in here you'd like, though." Samantha opened the basket flap and held it toward him in invitation.

Fergus inched closer and peeked inside. His gaze flew to hers. "Is that a cobbler?" His voice echoed with reverence.

"Mm-hmm." Samantha dropped the basket lid back into place as she fought to keep her amusement in check. "Blackberry."

Fergus sprinted back into the house. "Mama! Mama! The teacher's here, and she brought cobbler!"

Samantha loosed a quiet giggle, enjoying the boy's enthusiasm even if it meant she was left standing on the doorstep.

"Fergus Leopold Ellis. Where are your manners?" The hushed reprimand echoed in the evening air a moment before Elizabeth Ellis appeared. She hurried to the front door, an apologetic smile stretching across her face. "I'm so sorry, Miss Dearing. Please, come in."

"Thank you."

The house was small, the walls slightly warped with dingy

paint and peeling paper. The floor slanted to the left, and the boards creaked with every step, yet the rooms were tidy, and the furnishings were free of dust—the mark of a woman who took pride in her home.

"I thought you and Jonathan could work at the kitchen table, if that suits you?" Mrs. Ellis led her into a room that was obviously the heart of the home. Hats hung from hooks, aromas of a meal recently eaten filled the air, and people mingled about.

Four people. Two boys pushing and jostling each other near the table. A mother who scurried over to referee. And a man at the table sipping coffee. A man who rose to his feet when she entered. A man who set her heart to thumping as she took in his familiar sandy hair and brown eyes.

Mrs. Ellis brought her two boys forward, forcing Samantha's gaze away from the man by the table.

"You've met Fergus," she said with a nod toward her youngest. "This is Jonathan."

The older boy didn't seem particularly pleased by the prospect of spending his evenings cooped up with a tutor and a pile of books, but Samantha refused to take it personally. "Pleased to meet you, Jonathan. I'm Miss Dearing."

"Call me Jack."

"All right. I look forward to working with you, Jack."

A movement behind the boys drew her attention back to the table.

Mrs. Ellis turned and waved the man forward. "This is my oldest son, Asher. He rides with the Bar 7 Ranch down in Callahan County." Her voice rang with obvious pride.

"Mr. Ellis."

"Miss Dearing." Gone were the levity and flirtatious manner that had so captivated her in the hardware store. In their place was a guardedness that warned her to keep her distance.

She dipped her chin and dragged her attention away from her mystery man who was no longer a mystery—Asher Ellis.

Offering Elizabeth a smile, she set her basket on the edge of the table. "The rumors are true," she said. "I did bring a cobbler. If you wish, you can dish it up while Jack and I figure out the best place for us to begin."

Samantha pulled out the small baking dish.

"It looks divine," Mrs. Ellis said, taking it from her, "but you didn't need to do this. You're our guest."

"It was no trouble." Samantha waved away the concern. "I enjoy baking." She leaned close to Mrs. Ellis and whispered. "Besides, I figured the boys might like me better if I sweetened them up first."

Mrs. Ellis chuckled. "Wise woman. You're going to have all three of them eating out of your hand."

Samantha's gaze darted to the man standing solemnly by the stove, refilling his coffee. She hoped his mother was right, because at the moment, the oldest Ellis male seemed more interested in bucking her out of his corral.

11

Asher had to give the woman credit. She baked a fine cobbler. He scraped his spoon around the inside of his empty bowl to collect the last little bit of sweet blackberry filling and crust crumbles. Sitting on the rear stoop with the house at his back and one knee bent upward to support the arm that held his bowl, he licked the spoon clean and gazed across the yard.

She knew his name now and where he was staying. Would a lawman bang on his mother's door tonight? The temptation to leave town after he took her home flickered through Asher's mind, but he discarded it. Mama Bess had told Miss Dearing about the Bar 7 when she introduced him. Running would only delay the inevitable. Besides, he couldn't abandon his family. Not when this place needed so much work. He scanned the yard, seeing all that needed to be done. The cowshed really should be rebuilt from scratch if he wanted to ensure it didn't collapse on Mrs. Merriweather the first time a blue norther blustered in. The chicken coop still needed a new roof. The rickety fence was riddled with half-rotted boards. And then there was the house. He'd barely scratched the surface there.

Asher dropped the spoon back into the bowl with a clink.

Maybe he could talk his way out of jail time. He hadn't actually taken anything from the Three Cedars, after all. Not to mention that the house had been open to guests for the party, so he really hadn't broken in, either. He couldn't quite rationalize away the trespassing charge, but maybe dragging Clint Dearing out of the pond would generate enough good will to wipe out that particular stain. Doubtful, but possible.

Feathery clouds lining the horizon began turning pink at the edges, cuing him to cease his cowardly hiding and face his responsibilities. He'd avoided the kitchen as long as possible, finishing up the siding on the chicken coop before sneaking in to snag some cobbler while Jack had Miss Dearing distracted, but the time had come to face his nemesis.

Biting back a groan, Asher pushed to his feet and walked into the kitchen. He kept his eyes averted from the tutoring session happening at the table and slid his empty bowl into the basin of dishwater Mama Bess had left in the sink.

"I don't see why I have to learn this stuff," Jack grumbled. "I know my numbers good enough to get by. I'm never gonna use . . . What did you call it?"

"Algebra."

Even without looking at her, Asher could hear the smile in her voice. The woman had a way with kids, it seemed. Patient. Good-humored. Skilled in the art of bribery. Probably came with having a younger brother.

"Yeah, well, I'm never gonna use algebra in real life, so why don't we just skip this part?"

"You might be surprised how handy algebra can be," she countered.

Asher dallied, interested to see how she handled the situation. Jack was a good kid, but he could be ornery when he set his mind to it. Unable to think of another way to busy himself in the kitchen, Asher dunked his hands into the dishwater, dug around for the washrag, and set about cleaning his bowl in the slowest manner possible.

"Let's say your boss at the livery asked you to take two horses to the farrier to get new horseshoes," Miss Dearing proposed. "He gives you three dollars. You get to the farrier, and his sign says that he charges sixty cents per shoe. Do you have enough money?"

Asher peeked over his shoulder to find Jack's face scrunched as his fingers ticked off imaginary cost.

Miss Dearing placed a hand over Jack's. "No counting."

Jack groaned. "This is stupid. The farrier can just send Mr. Cooper a bill."

"Here." She scooted the slate in front of her and picked up a spare slate pencil. "Let me show you how easy it can be to figure. We'll use an x to represent how many horseshoes we can get for three dollars. How much do they cost again?"

"Sixty cents." Jack's tone echoed with impatience, but Asher detected a touch of interest as well.

The slate pencil scraped against the small board. "All right. So point six times x equals three dollars. Our first step is what?"

"Get x by itself."

"Good!" she praised. "So we divide each side by point six . . . move the decimal . . . how many times does six go into thirty?"

"Five?"

"Correct. So you can pay for five horseshoes. Is that enough for two horses?"

"Not if all four shoes need replacin' on each horse."

"Precisely. Now, if Mr. Cooper gives you five dollars instead of three for the same job and says you can spend the change on penny candy at the general store, how many pieces of candy will you be able to buy?"

"Sixty times eight is four eighty." Jack stared at the ceiling as the wheel in his brain turned. "Take that from five hundred ... Twenty! Twenty pieces of penny candy. That would last Fergus and me for at least a week. Well, only if I hide it and give my brother one piece a day. He'd eat it all at once if I let him."

Asher grinned as he pulled his now-spotless bowl and spoon out of the water and rubbed them dry with a towel.

Miss Dearing clapped her hands and exclaimed over Jack's success. The woman might not know much about how farriers worked, but she understood algebra and little boys. Did that understanding stretch to men as well? A beautiful nemesis with political connections was bad enough. Add clever to the mix, and his odds of escaping unscathed shrank dramatically.

Turning to face the pair at the table, Asher cleared his throat and waited for faces to lift and eyes to shift in his direction. "Sun's settin'. Time to wrap things up."

His voice emerged gruffer than he'd intended, but he hadn't been prepared for the impact of those smiling blue eyes. How could he have forgotten the way they sparkled? They shone even brighter now with the added glow of pride over her student's accomplishment.

"Thank you, Mr. Ellis." A touch of pink colored her cheeks, making her even prettier. Which was completely unfair. Enemies were supposed to be foul, disagreeable people who turned a man's gut sour when forced to interact. Samantha Dearing had an odd effect on his gut, all right, but *sour* was not the word he'd use to describe it.

Best he minimized his exposure before he actually started liking the woman who held the power to destroy his life. "I'll saddle my horse and meet you out front."

She nodded. "I'll be ready." She turned her attention back to Jack and began listing off assignments for him to work on before their next tutoring session.

Asher tromped out the back door, irritated at his reaction. He should *not* be attracted to the daughter of the man who tossed his mother and brothers out on their ears. As he fetched his saddle and tack from the cowshed, he tried to recall the pampered princess who'd been throwing a tantrum when he'd first encountered her. Spoiled. Demanding. Threatening his personal safety. But even that didn't help. She'd been arguing with Eli Dearing, which brought the whole enemy-of-my-enemy-is-my-friend thing into play. And then there was the fact that she was fighting against being married off to one of her daddy's rich cattlemen friends, which he actually found rather commendable. And blaming her for threatening his personal safety was hypocritical at best, since *he'd* been the one committing a crime at the time, not her.

He heaved the saddle off his shoulder and onto the fence railing with a grunt that had more to do with frustration than effort. Bruno trotted over and nudged Asher's shoulder with his nose. Asher patted the paint's neck.

"I might need you to buck some sense into me tonight if I start going soft in the head over that woman in there." He spread the saddle blanket over Bruno's back, then reached for the saddle. "She's too pretty for my own good. Not to mention smart. And kind." He reached under Bruno for the cinch. "But she's a Dearing. Educated. Refined. Rich." Any one of which was enough to place her well out of his reach. All four should send him scurrying in the opposite direction.

So why was his heart picking up speed at the prospect of seeing her home?

Because I've got rocks for brains.

Rocks or not, he'd promised Mama Bess to see the woman home, so that's what he'd do. Asher finished cinching the saddle, then fit the bit to Bruno's mouth and fastened the bridle straps.

Just keep your eyes on the road. Not the most sophisticated strategy, he acknowledged as he led Bruno around to the front of the house, but it had potential. Gave him an excuse to avoid conversation. Easier to ignore her if he couldn't see her. Or hear her. Maybe he'd run through a mental list of all the supplies he needed to purchase. That should keep his mind engaged in a productive direction. *Nails, shingles, lumber, paint, fen—*

"I'm ready."

The supply list evaporated the instant she came into view. He'd obviously overestimated the effectiveness of his diversion tactic. An entire lumberyard couldn't distract a man from that cheerful smile. Especially when it came packaged in such a comely face. If she'd had the decency to wear one of her fancy dresses, like that pink fashion-plate outfit she'd had on in the hardware store, it would have been easier to recognize the difference between their stations, but her dark blue dress looked so . . . *normal.* It made it hard to remember she was Eli Dearing's daughter.

Knowing Mama Bess was likely watching from the front window, Asher left Bruno to introduce himself to the little mare pulling the cart and came forward to assist Miss Dearing with her basket. Good manners were good manners, after all, and he preferred avoiding motherly scoldings whenever possible. Even if he did have to hold his breath to keep from inhaling the smell of blackberry cobbler that lingered in the basket linens. Far too dangerous to associate the woman with words like *delicious* and *sweet.*

He slid the basket onto the floor of the small cart, then offered a hand to assist Miss Dearing into the gig. He felt her gaze on him as she fit her hand to his, but he kept his eyes trained on the ground.

"Thank you." Her soft words floated over him, the tinge of disappointment in them jabbing his conscience.

He glanced up, but she'd already turned her attention to settling herself in the seat and collecting the driving lines. He figured saying anything at this point would have a greater chance of going wrong than right, so he clamped his jaw shut, strode over to Bruno, and mounted.

Asher kept Bruno even with the black mare he'd heard Miss Dearing call Dolly. Made it easier to avoid conversation that way. Not that Miss Dearing had made any efforts in that direction, a fact he should be thankful for, yet oddly . . . wasn't.

The vibrant pinks and oranges slashing across the sky began to fade as they left Palo Pinto behind and entered open country. He expected Miss Dearing to urge her mare into a trot, but she seemed in no hurry. At this rate, it would be near to full dark by the time they reached the Three Cedars. He'd ridden through the dark before and wasn't concerned for himself, but he didn't need an overprotective father sending out a search party to hunt down his little princess and blame Asher for her tardiness.

Reining Bruno in, he slowed to a near crawl until her cart drew alongside him. "We should probably pick up the pace a bit," he suggested.

She swiveled her neck to face him, and the earnestness radiating from her blue eyes caught him off guard. "I want to apologize first."

Apologize? For what? He was the one acting surly.

Before he could question her, words starting spilling out of her like milk from an overturned bucket.

"I'm so sorry about what happened to your family. Mrs. Stephenson didn't share any details, but she did mention that your mother lived on property owned by my father and that he recently evicted her. I don't know his reasons, but I do know how hard it is to be evicted from a home you love and be forced to start anew elsewhere."

How that statement could be true, he couldn't imagine, yet the sincerity in her gaze had him believing her.

"You must be so angry at my family. I don't blame you. It's clear you don't approve of me tutoring Jack, but I promise I'm just here to help."

"Whoa, now. I never said anything about not approving."

"You didn't have to. That day we met in Patterson's Hardware, I saw the change that came over you after you realized who I was. And tonight, you've done everything you can to avoid me."

Just lay him across the road and let Dolly trample him with the cart. "I didn't mean to—"

"I understand. Really, I do. But I'm hoping you might be willing to look past my family connections. I think I can help Jack. I want to try, at least." Her words slowed to a trickle. "You and I will likely be seeing a lot of each other over the next several weeks, and I hope we can . . . Well, if not be friends . . . perhaps we can at least be amiable with each other . . . for Jack's sake."

"For Jack's sake."

What if he wanted to be amiable with her for his own sake?

She smiled as if accepting his mindless parroting of her words as agreement. "Thank you, Mr. Ellis. I promise to treat your family with the utmost respect." Her eyes visibly brightened. "Now, let's get this distasteful duty of yours discharged without further delay, shall we?"

She snapped the driving lines and clicked her tongue. "Get up, Dolly."

Before Asher could argue with her faulty assumption that he found escorting her distasteful, she pulled away from him at a fast clip.

He hung back a moment, still trying to process all of what she'd just said. Yet as he watched her go, it dawned on him that while she had painted him as a grumbly, grudge-holding grump, she *hadn't* described him as a trespassing thief. Maybe she didn't recognize him after all. Maybe he *could* have a friendly relationship with her without worrying about the sheriff knocking on Mama Bess's door.

The weight on his heart had just started to lighten when the cart in front of him hit a deep rut, and a sharp crack rent the air. A piercing squeal followed, hardening his core in an instant.

The right wheel of the cart broke from the carriage and rolled off the side of the road. The cart crashed sideways, its axle dragging through the dirt as the spooked mare bolted.

"Hold on!" Asher kicked Bruno's side and set out in pursuit.

It was a miracle she hadn't been thrown. Somehow, she'd had the presence of mind to grab hold of the carriage frame, but if she lost her grip or the cart hit another rough patch, she'd be bucked out at a speed that could prove deadly.

12

Samantha clung to the shelfed edge of the cart that extended over the left wheel, desperate to keep from being thrown from the conveyance. Drawing her knees to her chest to prevent her dangling feet from dragging on the road, she squeezed her eyes shut and prayed for Dolly to stop.

Every bump in the road magnified a hundred times as the quaking of the carriage coursed through Samantha's limbs, threatening to shake her loose. She clamped her rattling teeth together and strained to maintain her grip.

The wheel hit something in the road, hurtling the cart into the air. Samantha felt her body lift away from the bench. She clenched already tight fingers even harder against the far too flimsy armrest. Her stomach lurched. Her legs flung outward. Visions of Clint and her father flashed through her mind. She didn't want to leave them.

The cart crashed back down to earth, and the impact broke the grip of her right hand. A scream tore from her throat as she skated down the slanted bench toward the road. Her left arm twisted awkwardly as her body slid, those fingers her only remaining tether. Eyes flying open, Samantha scrabbled for something else to grasp.

A voice ordered her to hold on. Deep. Commanding. Close. *Asher.*

He leaned low in the saddle, drawing alongside. His eyes met hers for a fraction of an instant as he raced past, but determination and conviction radiated from him to her in such an overpowering wave that pain and panic receded.

The dash rail! An image of the thin brass rail atop the front of the driver's box, where Clint liked to prop his boots when they rode together, crystalized in Samantha's mind. Grunting against the wrenching ache in her left shoulder, she twisted and flung herself to the right. Another small bump in the road aided her momentum. Her hand banged against the dash. She grabbled for purchase, but the jostling of the broken cart made it nearly impossible to lock onto her target.

Her left arm weakened. Her right floundered. As did her hope.

Samantha set her jaw as words she once thought of as harsh echoed through her mind in her father's firm voice. *"When life's hard, you gotta be harder. Dearings don't quit."* So she tried again. And again. Until her fingers finally closed around the rail.

Belly flat against the driver's bench, face mashed between her left arm and the unforgiving wooden shelf that was keeping her alive, she closed her eyes and focused on nothing more than holding on as her heart prayed a single word. *Please.*

Every rattle loosened her grip a little more.

Please.

Her handhold became a fingerhold.

Please.

Then a man's shout echoed above pounding hooves. "Whoa, Dolly! Whoa!"

Her heart leapt, and her fingertips tightened. Asher had

made it. He'd reached the mare's head. He'd get Dolly to stop. He *would*. Samantha just had to hold on a few more seconds.

Dearings don't quit. Dearings don't quit.

She chanted the words to herself over and over as the cart slowed. Tears rolled down her cheeks as she let herself believe that she wasn't going to die.

When the vehicle dragged to a stop, she continued to cling to its frame, her arms and legs shaking. She knew she should let go. Crawl away from the cart. Put space between herself and the danger in case Dolly took off again. But she couldn't move. She could only cling.

"Miss Dearing? Are you all right?"

She tried to answer, but her vocal cords seemed as incapable of movement as the rest of her. The tiniest mewl was all she managed to push past her lips.

Boots thudded against earth. "Samantha?"

Large hands cupped her shoulders, their warmth seeping into her frozen bones and starting a thaw.

"You can let go now."

Could she? She wasn't so sure.

"Here." One of his hands left her shoulder and covered her fingers above her head. "I'll help." He started prying her fingertips away from the shelf.

She panicked and tightened her grip. "I'll f-fall."

"No, you won't. I've got you."

He stepped closer, his chest resting lightly against her back. Then he looped an arm beneath her right elbow and locked his grip on her shoulder. He secured his hold on her and pulled her firmly against his chest.

This time, when he attempted to peel her fingers off the ledge, she offered no resistance. In fact, once he had the left hand free, her right hand fell away from the dash rail all on its own. He took her weight upon himself and eased them both away from the cart. She turned toward his chest, seeking his warmth as she shivered in the aftermath of her brush with death. He slipped an arm beneath her legs and carried her to the edge of the road. Slowly, he lowered her legs to the ground, holding her steady until both of them were sure her knees wouldn't fold the instant he let go.

"You're shaking," he murmured, his lips close to her ear.

It wasn't a question, so she didn't feel compelled to answer. A good thing, since her mind seemed rather numb and blank at the moment.

"Here," he said. "Lean on me." He cupped the back of her head and gently pressed her cheek against his chest as he shifted his feet into a wider stance.

Not able to think of any reason not to comply, Samantha rested against him, thankful for his sturdy support. He took her weight as if it were nothing, then ran his hands up and down her arms. The friction soothed and warmed, even though her cold came from inside. His heart thumped a hypnotic rhythm beneath her ear, soothing her agitation.

Eventually, the rubbing stopped, though, and reality returned.

"Are you hurt?" Mr. Ellis set her away from him slightly, careful to keep a hold on one of her arms just in case she wobbled.

Taking a mental inventory, Samantha found nothing more serious than a sore left shoulder. "Just some bumps and bruises, I think."

"Thank God."

Yes, thank you, Lord.

"You gave me quite a scare." He pulled his hat off and rubbed his sleeve across his brow. The hat quivered as he fit it back to his head, and for the first time, she realized she wasn't the only one shaken by what had transpired.

Her lips twitched in an almost smile. "I gave myself a pretty good scare, too."

A grin stretched wide and full across his face. "I imagine so."

Heavens, but the man was handsome when he smiled. Well, he was handsome all the time, but that smile threatened to put the wobble back in her knees after they'd finally firmed up.

Pulling her gaze from his face, she steered it over to the shambles that used to be her horse cart. "How could this happen? Wheels don't just fall off their moorings."

"They can if they lose the nuts that hold them in place."

She glanced back and caught his frown. "Surely that's rare, though. Right? I've heard of broken axles and busted wheels, but never something like this."

Mr. Ellis scratched at a spot on his jaw. "Saw it once at the Bar 7. Some of the hands were moving a hay wagon backward across the field, and a nut dropped into the grass. No one noticed until the wheel fell off. Thankfully, the wagon nuts on the other three wheels had been tightened better. Never seen it happen on a buggy rolling forward, though." He met her gaze. "Wheel nuts are reverse-threaded, so they tighten when the wheels roll forward and loosen when they roll backward. Yours must've been either off altogether or too loose to catch the threads. The wheel must not have been able to maintain its position on the axle once you increased your pace."

"But Daddy always has one of the hands check the rig for me when they hitch up Dolly. Wouldn't he have noticed?"

She took a few steps toward the gig, thinking back to earlier in the day when she'd left the ranch. The cart had been ready and waiting for her when she left the house. She hadn't seen any of the hands around, but then, she'd been distracted with thoughts of the lessons she wanted to teach.

"If the nut had been completely missing, a competent fella would've noticed, but if it was just loose . . ." He shrugged. "It coulda been missed."

Samantha's head started to ache. "This still doesn't make sense. I drove to town without incident. If the wheel rolling forward is designed to tighten the nut, wouldn't it have been tighter on the return trip?"

————

Asher blew out a breath. "I wish I had answers for you, but I don't." And that bothered him. An accident like this shouldn't have happened. "Have your father check the cart over real good when he retrieves it. His men need to know what to look for to make sure nothing like this happens again."

The very thought chilled his blood. If she'd been alone . . . Thank God Mrs. Stephenson had insisted he provide an escort. For as long as he lived, he'd never forget the abject terror in Samantha's eyes as she clung to the edge of the speeding cart. Had she not had the presence of mind to grab the nearest handhold, she would have been thrown. A fall at that speed would have left her seriously injured if not dead.

"Might be good to have a wainwright take a look." Asher cleared his throat when what he really needed to do was clear his mind of the horrible image plaguing him of Samantha Dearing lying broken on the side of the road. "An expert might be able to determine what went wrong."

Although his gut told him this was more than a mechanical malfunction. Either gross negligence or out-and-out sabotage. He couldn't imagine anyone wanting to hurt Miss Dearing, though, so it must have been negligence. But even if no malice had been intended, such carelessness had to be addressed to ensure it didn't happen again.

"I'd offer to search for the wheel and nut on my way back to town, but it'll likely be full dark by then. Better to have someone from the Three Cedars hunt for it in the morning."

Peering at the sky, she rubbed her arms as if his mention of the lateness of the hour had induced a sudden chill. The desire to hold her as he had when he'd pulled her from the cart hit him with surprising intensity. With no immediate threat around to excuse such familiarity, however, Asher settled for shrugging out of his coat and wrapping it around her shoulders.

She glanced over her shoulder and offered him a small smile. "Thank you."

All at once her eyes widened, and she turned to face him fully. She grabbed his hand between both of hers and squeezed tightly, her unexpected touch setting his pulse to pumping.

"*Thank you.*" She shook her head slightly. "I can't believe I let myself get distracted by wheel nuts and reverse threads when I hadn't even thanked you properly." Her blue eyes melded with his, and something in his chest tightened. "You saved my life, Mr. Ellis. Thank you."

Feeling his neck heat, Asher ducked his head, but he couldn't resist the pull of her eyes for more than a heartbeat. His gaze found hers again, and he spoke the only words he could find. "I'm just glad I was here."

"Me too." A touch of pink dusted her cheeks, bringing much-needed color back to her face.

Standing in the middle of a deserted road with a fading sunset painting the sky and a beautiful woman looking at him with adoration in her eyes put far too many ideas in a man's head. None of which he had any business acting upon. So before he could do something foolish, he tugged his hand away from her hold and strode for the horses.

"I'll get Dolly unhitched so you can ride the rest of the way." That'd be good. Her on her horse. Him on his. Plenty of distance between.

"I don't ride."

He'd just reached for the first strap when her words froze his hands in midair. Surely he'd misheard. "What?"

She stood a few feet away from him, her arms wrapped around her middle. "I don't ride."

Asher straightened away from Dolly. "You were raised on the largest ranch in the county, and you don't know how to ride a horse?"

"Ironic, isn't it?" She smiled, but something in her eyes hinted at a past hurt. "My parents didn't think it ladylike for me to ride astride, and I refused to use a sidesaddle. No compromise could be found, so I turned my attention to carts and buggies and left the riding to my brother."

"I could teach you." Asher clamped his mouth shut as soon as the offer formed on his tongue, but the words must have slid sideways past his teeth, for his ears heard them echo in the air.

Galloping geese. What was he doing? He needed to spend less time with this woman, not more. But when her eyes lit with hope, he knew he was done for.

"Really?"

Now you did it. "Sure. You can come early to a few of Jack's lessons, and I can put you up on Bruno. Lead you around town a bit."

"No, we can't do it in town. Too many witnesses. If I'm going to make a fool of myself, I'd prefer to do it in private." She nibbled her bottom lip, making him wonder if eliminating witnesses had more to do with keeping her father from finding out than hiding her lack of skill.

"I don't know if that's such a good—"

"The old mill!" Her eyes lit. "It's been abandoned for at least a decade. There's a large field and water for the horses. We could meet there at four in the afternoon. Ride for an hour and still get home for supper. What do you think?"

He thought he was in a whole heap of trouble.

13

Samantha did her best to set her hair and clothing to rights while Asher unhitched Dolly from the cart. He took time with the little mare, stroking her neck and praising her courage and fortitude. He had a knack for consoling unsettled females, it seemed. The edges of Samantha's mouth turned upward slightly around the collection of hairpins wedged between her lips.

Asher Ellis. She'd been drawn to him the moment they crossed paths in Patterson's Hardware shop. His charm. His rugged features. The gentlemanly way he pretended he hadn't noticed her spying on other men's feet. Seeing him at the Ellis home tonight had delighted her. Until she realized he likely despised her because of what had transpired between their parents. She'd planned to clear the air between them, then put him out of her mind to better concentrate on tutoring his younger brother. Then he went and saved her life and obliterated all her good intentions. Putting him out of her mind was no longer an option. The moment he'd lifted her in his arms and carried her away from the crippled buggy, he'd carved a permanent place for himself in her memory. And when he'd offered to teach her to ride? Well, that had etched his name into her heart.

Don't get ahead of yourself, Samantha. He's not staying. He'll head back to Callahan County the moment he finishes helping his mother.

Although . . . Callahan County wasn't so terribly far away. Just a few hours by train.

"Oh for pity's sake," she muttered under her breath as she twisted her hair into a long rope. "Have you completely lost your wits?"

Apparently she had, for when Asher turned and started walking both horses over to where she stood, Samantha failed to recall a single reason why she shouldn't allow her pulse to leap about like a sugar-fed rabbit at the sight of him.

Square jaw shaved clean. Tanned face and hands. Wide shoulders. Lean hips. A sauntering stride that instilled confidence without the need for arrogance. Soft brown eyes full of concern and chivalry. Courageous. Capable. Kind. *This* was the type of man she'd been waiting to meet. One who valued family and was willing to help a woman accomplish her goals instead of placing her in a box of his own making.

"You all right?" His brows arched, and he slowed his approach. "Don't worry. I'm not gonna put you up on Dolly. You can ride with me on Bruno. I'll lead the mare behind us."

Good heavens. He must think her a complete ninny. Arms frozen above her head, hairpins dangling from her mouth as if she'd forgotten what she'd been doing. All right, she *had* forgotten what she'd been doing, but not because of the horses. She'd been too busy cataloging the finer points of her companion to do more than register the animals' existence. Not that she'd admit that truth to anyone save herself.

Giving her head a little shake, she ignored the rising heat in her cheeks and finished winding her hair into a simple bun. Extricating one pin at a time from between her lips, she secured the knot in place.

Samantha offered a smile as she reached for the hat she'd set upon the ground near her feet. "I'm fine," she assured him. "Just got swept up in my own thoughts for a moment."

She straightened and set the small beribboned toque on her head, feeling around with her fingers to position it just above her bun. Finding what she hoped was a central location, she held it in place with her left hand while extracting and repositioning the hatpin with her right.

"Does it look straight?" She lowered her hands to her sides and waited for a response.

Mr. Ellis blinked at her as if he couldn't believe he'd been asked to comment upon her personal appearance. "Uh . . . yes?"

Nothing like an uncertain answer to invigorate feminine confidence. Oh well. It would have to do.

"Daddy will be less likely to overreact if I don't look like I went through a harrowing experience when we show up at the ranch."

"But you did go through a harrowing experience."

She waved off his concern as she swept past him to coo over Dolly. "The cart lost a wheel, but you intercepted Dolly before any serious damage could be done."

The hand she lifted to pet the mare's neck trembled, belying her casual tone. She'd likely have nightmares about clinging to that narrow wooden shelf. And that horrifying moment when she'd nearly been catapulted to her death? A shudder coursed through her, threatening to weaken her resolve.

The danger had passed, she reminded herself as her fingers tangled in Dolly's mane. God had seen her through. God and Asher Ellis. No good would come from getting worked up by a list of things that could have happened. What *could* have happened didn't. She was safe. That's what mattered, and that's what she'd focus on when she saw her father. They were just beginning to mend things between them. She didn't want to jeopardize their truce by antagonizing him. If he decided to play the role of overprotective patriarch, he might try to ban her from future tutoring. She'd be unable to comply with such a prohibition, of course. Jonathan Ellis needed her, and she'd not allow a little mishap to keep her from fulfilling her calling. No, it was best for everyone if she took steps to reduce the likelihood of a flare-up of overprotective tendencies.

"Hey." The gentleness in Asher's voice seeped into her and smoothed the raw edges of her nerves. Then his hand settled against her back, and her racing thoughts stilled.

Samantha twisted to face him, and his eyes nearly melted her where she stood. They brimmed with kindness, patience, and more sympathy than she likely deserved.

"It's up to you how many details you want to share with your father, but remember, pretending something didn't happened isn't the same as dealing with it. You have someone who already knows all the details, so don't hesitate to come find me if you need to talk, all right?"

Samantha's eyes stung with new tears as she pressed her lips together and nodded.

"Good. Now, let's get you home before we lose all our daylight."

Despite the fact that darkness stalked them, Asher slowed Bruno to a walk when the Three Cedars ranch house came into view. He was reluctant for this particular ride to end. Having Samantha's arms twined loosely around his waist and her body pressed close against his back tempted him to find a longer route to the Three Cedars. She'd been stiff at first, her inexperience evident. But after he'd encouraged her to relax and hold on to him for balance, she started to absorb the horse's movements instead of fighting them. Her tension seemed to be returning, however. The closer they came to the house, the stiffer she became.

He couldn't blame her. He'd gone a little stiff himself. Seeing the house again had tied his stomach in knots. His forehead throbbed as if the truth of the crime he'd committed when last here was trying to climb through his skin to declare his guilt in scarlet letters upon his forehead. He tugged his hat brim a little closer to his eyes.

The outline of a man separated itself from the shadows of the porch. Fellow was a little on the short side, but when he cupped his hands to his mouth, his voice boomed across the yard. "She's home!"

Clinton Dearing jogged forward, his gaze locked on his sister. "You had us worried, Sam."

Miss Dearing shifted behind Asher. "Help me down," she whispered, her tone urgent.

Asher reined Bruno to a stop and offered his arm to her. "Grab hold, then lean to your left and slide off," he murmured. "I'll steady you."

It wasn't the most graceful dismount he'd ever witnessed, but she made it to the ground in one piece and even managed to fluff out her skirt before her brother squashed it flat when he wrapped his sister in an embrace.

"You shouldn't scare me like that," he scolded, emotion causing the words to tremble slightly.

She rested her cheek atop his head as she rubbed his back. "I'm sorry. But I'm fine. I promise." She lifted her head and looked him in the face. "I had a little trouble with the cart, but Mr. Ellis saw me safely home."

Asher fought from rolling his eyes as he dismounted to stand beside the queen of understatement.

Clint thrust his hand toward him the moment his feet hit the dirt. "Thanks for taking care of my sister, Mr. Ellis."

Asher shook the boy's hand, doing his best to hide all recognition from his face and act as if they were strangers meeting for the first time. "Glad I was there." Not so glad he was *here*, facing another Dearing with the power to send him to prison. Hopefully, the distortive shadows of twilight would protect Asher's anonymity.

Clint's face scrunched slightly as he withdrew his hand. "Your voice sounds familiar. Have we met?"

Asher's gut turned to stone. A lie jumped to his tongue, but he bit it back, searching for something honest to say that didn't incriminate him.

"Mr. Ellis is the older brother of the boy I'm tutoring in town," Miss Dearing explained, covering his awkward hesitation.

Seemed tonight was a night of rescues for both of them.

"Samantha?" Eli Dearing emerged from the barn, his anxious gaze seeking his daughter. When he found her, he strode across the yard with quick, long strides. "Thank the Lord above. You're all right." His hand settled on her shoulder, but he held her at arm's length while he scanned her for any sign of injury. "Duke and I were about to ride out to search for you. What happened?"

"I had some trouble with one of the buggy wheels," she said, completely glossing over the entire nearly-falling-to-her-death part of the story. "Thankfully, Mr. Ellis had agreed to escort me home and was on hand to offer assistance."

Dearing turned his attention upon Asher for the first time. He scanned him from head to toe, then thrust out his hand. "I'm obliged to you, Ellis."

Asher forced his hand into Dearing's, somewhat surprised that flames didn't ignite to scorch his palm. Shaking the hand of one's enemy shouldn't feel this . . . normal. Yet in this moment,

Dearing wasn't the callous landlord who'd evicted Mama Bess. He was a father concerned about the safety of his daughter. A concern Asher shared.

Clenching his jaw, Asher gripped Dearing's hand firm and strong. He jerked a quick nod of acknowledgment, then released his grip and turned his attention to the horses.

"Here, I'll take Dolly for you." A middle-aged man in a blue shirt and tan hat stepped around Clint and held out a hand to Asher.

Presuming this was the Duke who'd been preparing to ride with Dearing to fetch Samantha, Asher handed over the lead line. "I didn't notice any injuries," he murmured, "but you might want to give her a thorough inspection when you brush her down. She had a rough time of it."

The dark-haired man nodded. "I'll take good care of her."

As the foreman led Dolly back toward the barn, he called out to Dearing over his shoulder. "I'll take Martin with me to collect the cart first thing in the morning, Boss. See what kind of repairs it might need."

And likely see the drag marks from the axle scraping the road for close to a quarter of a mile. Samantha might prefer downplaying the danger she'd been in, but any man with half a brain would be able to piece together what had happened when he saw the cart.

"Thanks, Duke." Dearing waved a hand at the fellow, but his focus remained firmly attached to his daughter.

Clint grabbed his sister's hand and started dragging her toward the house. "I wanna hear everything that happened. How did the wheel get busted? How far from town were you? Did you fall out of the cart?"

Samantha laughed as she traipsed after him. "Goodness. One question at a time." She paused long enough to glance back at Asher and lift a hand in farewell.

Asher grinned and saluted her with a tug on his hat brim. If Clint was anywhere near as persistent at pestering as Fergus and Jack, she'd have a hard time keeping the details hidden. Little brothers made cunning interrogators.

"I'd invite you up to the house for coffee, Ellis, but it's getting darker by the minute, and I know you need to get back."

"Yes, sir." Asher fit his left foot to the stirrup and swung onto Bruno's back.

Dearing's gaze trailed after his children as they wound their way toward the house. "I lost their mother when Clint was just a babe, then came close to losing Clint last week. Now a scare with Samantha. Makes a man want to tighten his hold and never let his family out of his sight."

How well Asher understood wanting to protect loved ones from hurt and harm. "I guess it's good that the Lord never sleeps."

Dearing peered up at Asher, then gave a nod. "That it is, boy. That it is."

Asher dipped his chin, then reined Bruno around and nudged him into a trot. As he left the Three Cedars behind, an uncomfortable realization unfurled inside him.

Vilifying a man when one knew little about him beyond the wrong that had been committed was easy. Justifying the characterization when one found himself sharing a piece of common ground with the fellow proved much more difficult.

14

The next day and a half sped by in a blur as Samantha prepared not only for her next tutoring session but for her first riding lesson. The anticipation had climbed to such dizzying levels, her fingers tingled as she examined the lines of her new split skirt in the full-length mirror. She'd hidden behind the locked door of her bedroom all day yesterday, making over the most serviceable skirt she owned—a chocolate-brown gored skirt with button front. Its lack of trim and excessive pleating in the back made it the most suitable piece for the purpose. She'd crafted a panel out of the buttoned section to conceal the pantaloon seams she'd sewn beneath. When the time came to ride, she could unbutton the panel to hip level and gain the mobility needed to straddle a horse.

Twisting to the side, she eyed the skirt from the back, then walked three paces away from the mirror. Hmm. The pantaloon legs flared wide, hiding most of the separation, but it might be best not to wear this in town. She'd hate for some bored biddy to crank up the rumor mill over the Dearing girl's scandalous skirt. Daddy would not be pleased. By either her attire or the fact that she was defying him by learning how to ride astride. It was possible he'd respect her choice to take lessons now that she was a grown woman and no longer a child under his jurisdiction, but she didn't yet possess enough confidence in him to take that chance. She'd stuff the skirt into her satchel and change at the old mill. No one need be any the wiser. Well, except Asher. But he didn't seem the type to scandalize easily.

First, though, she required a sturdy pair of boots. Neither her heeled white-kid half boots or her stylish satin slippers would serve her well when it came to tromping through fields and sticking in stirrups. Her sensible Oxfords might fare slightly better, but they were cut too low on the ankle. Men always wore boots that covered their calves when they rode. She'd do the same.

Duke had made good on his promise to fetch her cart yesterday morning. Thankfully, the damage to the vehicle hadn't been too severe. He and Martin tracked down the missing wheel and managed to get it back on the buggy long enough to pull the cart into town. Best of all, he'd not made a big to-do over the drag-mark evidence of her adventure left behind in the road. Maybe he hadn't noticed, or maybe he didn't see the point in getting her father all worked up about something that had done no lasting harm. Either way, she appreciated his discretion. As a result, Daddy hadn't tried to stop her tutoring sessions. He'd even given her permission to use the ranch's buckboard for running to and from town while the axle on her cart was being repaired. Unfortunately, using the buckboard meant leaving sweet Dolly behind. Her father's team of Morgans intimidated her just a smidgeon, but draft horses would be better suited to carrying her out to the old mill, so she'd not complain.

Samantha stepped out of her handcrafted riding skirt and replaced it with a petticoat, small bustle, and one of her favorite fan-style skirts. The vertical stripes of garnet and cream matched the ivory blouse she'd already donned. Plus, the stripes made her look slightly taller, which boosted her confidence. She dug through her wardrobe until she found the solid garnet vest that matched the skirt. She slipped her arms through the holes and fastened the shiny gold buttons at the front, then nodded with satisfaction. Stylish and professional. Perfect for a shopping excursion followed by a tutoring session later that evening. No one would suspect her secret riding rendezvous in between.

Her hands shook slightly as she fit a red-trimmed straw bonnet to her head, trailing the thin ribbon behind her ears before tying it under her chin. She'd waited years for this chance. Yet it wasn't just the riding that had her stomach fluttering.

Heroic rescuers with dashing aplomb and considerate ways made for exceptionally romantic daydreams, and Asher had figured prominently in hers the last two days, successfully supplanting the faceless mystery man she'd encountered the night of the ball. Sewing might busy the hands, but it left the mind free to wander. And hers had wandered back to Mr. Ellis, time and time again. Recollecting strong arms that carried her from danger, a firm chest that offered shelter and support, tender words, gentle touches. Goodness! If she wasn't careful, she was going to get lost in the weeds of her imaginings and squander half the day.

Samantha shoved thoughts of Asher into a box at the back of her mind and got down to business. She rolled up her riding skirt and hid it inside the satchel with her teaching materials, then made her way to the barn, where Martin had the buckboard and team waiting for her.

An unexpected shiver coursed through her as she approached the wagon. Her steps slowed as trepidation pushed aside all the lovely excitement that had been propelling her through the day.

"Need a hand up, Miss Dearing?" Martin set aside the rope he'd been coiling around his elbow and hurried over to assist.

Samantha swallowed. The team of Morgans loomed so much taller than sweet little Dolly. Broader shoulders. Stronger backs and legs. Two horses would certainly create twice as much speed as one should they spook.

You're the one spooking. Do you want your riding lesson or not?

The pair of bays appeared docile—bored even—as they waited to do their duty. Samantha set her shoulders. She could do this.

Forcing a smile to her lips, she turned to Martin. "Yes, thank you."

She handed him her satchel, which he tossed beneath the driver's seat. Then he pivoted back to offer her a hand. She hesitated.

"You checked all the wheel nuts, right? They're all present and tightened appropriately?"

"Yes, ma'am. Everything is in good working order." Sympathy shone in his eyes, ruffling her pride.

"Well then," she said, injecting a note of cheerfulness into her voice she didn't yet feel, "I'm sure everything is fine."

Though she did eye the hub on the wheel in front of her, ensuring the presence of a nut before she set her hand in his. He steadied her with a grip to her elbow as she climbed the wheel spokes and made her way into the driver's box.

"Thank you for your assistance, Martin," she said as she unwound the driving lines from the rein hitch on her left.

Reaching to her right, she released the brake, then clicked to the team, encouraging them with a light flick of the reins. Surely the Lord hadn't preserved her life only to take it from her two days later. He was watching over her. She could trust him.

The horses moved. The wagon jolted. Samantha's heart lodged in her throat. She grabbed the edge of the seat with her left hand.

A Bible verse jumped to mind from one of the psalms she'd memorized as a child. The final promise of Psalm 121. *"The* L ORD *shall preserve thy going out and thy coming in from this time forth, and even forevermore."*

She mouthed the promise as the buckboard pulled away from the barn. And again when they reached the drive.

Yes, Lord. Preserve my going out and my coming in.

She repeated the verse over and over in her mind until her heart started to believe. By the time she reached the road, her pulse had calmed, and she urged the Morgans into a trot.

God be praised, the wheels stayed on! Samantha's exuberance returned in full force, and an unfettered laugh burst from her throat as the wagon's increased pace drew passing air across her cheeks.

Heart lightened and spirits high, Samantha smiled all the way to town. The sun seemed brighter, the passersby friendlier, and even the practical black boots she'd purchased seemed more charming than ugly. They weren't quite as tall as a man's boot, but they would lace up a few inches past her ankles and offer plenty of protection. She plucked a pair in her size from the shelf the dry goods clerk had directed her to when she'd asked for the sturdiest shoes in the store. He'd touted them as double soled, which apparently meant they were twice as durable as the average ladies' shoe. Samantha attempted to bend the shoe in her hand, but the leather was so stiff it barely budged. Good heavens. How did people walk in these things? They had to be dreadfully uncomfortable. She supposed they'd soften with use, but in the meantime, perhaps it would be wise to purchase an extra pair of stockings to protect her feet from blisters. She selected a pair made of thick black wool and headed to the front counter.

"Shall I charge these to your father's account, Miss Dearing?"

Samantha shook her head. "No, I'll be paying for these myself." She extracted her coin purse and counted out one dollar and fifty-five cents.

"Very well, miss. Shall I wrap your purchases for you?"

Distracted by a young woman pacing outside the store window with a toddler perched on one hip, Samantha didn't answer at first.

Was that . . . ?

"Miss?"

The woman outside turned, giving Samantha a full view of her face. It was! Ida Mae Forrester. She hadn't seen Ida Mae in ages. They'd exchanged letters for several months after Samantha first moved to Boston for school, but their correspondence dwindled over time. After a year, Ida Mae ceased writing altogether. When the few sporadic letters Samantha sent continued to go unanswered, she stopped writing as well. But it seemed God was giving them a chance to reconnect, one Samantha didn't intend to waste.

"Never mind the wrapping." She scooped the items off the counter and into the crook of her arm. "I'll just take them like this." She hurried to the door, calling out a thank-you over her shoulder as she exited.

Pivoting to the left, she expected to see Ida Mae still pacing the edge of the boardwalk, but her friend had disappeared. Samantha scanned the street and spotted Ida Mae marching with purpose toward Patterson's Hardware, where a cowboy was loading coils of fencing wire into a green farm wagon that displayed a CCC insignia on the side. The brand of the Three Cedars. One of her father's wagons.

Samantha started across the street. She didn't recognize the cowboy loading the supplies, but her father employed dozens of hands, many of whom she'd never met. Only a handful were allowed up at the house, trusted men like Duke Kendrick and Martin Hanover who had been with her father for years. This fellow looked young, probably around the same age as Asher, though he had a shorter, stockier build.

A pair of ladies passed by the wagon, wiggling their fingers in a flirtatious wave. The cowboy stopped his work to tip his hat and flash a cocky grin at the girls, his well-chiseled features the type many would consider handsome. The way his gaze followed the women after they passed seemed rather roguish, though, and left Samantha less than impressed.

She'd navigated halfway across the street when Ida Mae reached the cowboy and started having words with him. Heated, animated words. The man's demeanor changed in an instant. his swagger disappeared, replaced by a cascade of irritated frustration. He took Ida Mae's free arm and steered her into the narrow alleyway between Patterson's and the drugstore next door.

Alarmed, Samantha picked up her pace. Surely he wouldn't hurt Ida Mae or the baby. Yet something was wrong, and Samantha refused to be one of those weak women who buried their heads in the sand, pretending not to see trouble in the hopes of keeping themselves from being tainted by it. She'd not barge in on a private conversation, but neither would she leave her friend to face trouble alone.

"You gotta do right by me, Leroy."

Ida Mae's raised voice ricocheted off the alley walls, slamming into Samantha's chest and bringing her feet to a halt. She spun around to face the street, keeping her back to the alley in the hopes of shielding Ida Mae from anyone milling about the nearby shops.

"Keep your voice down, woman."

"I'm done bein' hushed up," Ida Mae declared. "By you, by my folks. Jimmy needs a daddy, and I need a husband."

"Well, don't look at me. I ain't applyin' for the job."

"There's no *applyin'* to it. Jimmy's your boy, and you know it."

Samantha's chest squeezed, and tears moistened her eyes. *Oh, Ida Mae. No.*

"I know no such thing."

How could the man sound so smug? So uncaring?

Ida Mae gasped. "I've never been with any man but you."

"So you say. Just because I was your first don't mean I was your only. You coulda rolled around in the hay with half the cowboys in the county since we were together."

The crack of a slap echoed through the alley.

"You ruined me, Leroy." Tears clogged Ida Mae's voice, twisting Samantha's heart. "Don't ruin your son, too. Take responsibility. Do what's right."

"You ruined yourself, Ida Mae. The boy's your mess to clean up, not mine."

Bootheels thumped against packed dirt as a woman's quiet sobs mixed with a baby's plaintive cry.

Indignation roared to life in Samantha's breast. Such injustice could not stand. Why should a woman alone bear the consequences of a sin in which the man was an equal participant? Likely even the instigator. The world might excuse and minimize this man's shame, but she would not.

15

Whirling around, Samantha blocked the alley's exit and glared at the cowboy striding out of the shadows, apparently unconcerned about the devastation left in his wake.

She said nothing aloud yet communicated her disapproval and disdain in the sharp slant of her brows and the rigidity of her stance. Leroy stumbled slightly when he saw her. His eyes widened with recognition, and his self-assurance withered.

He jerked his hat from his head and held it against his chest as if to shield himself from the invisible daggers she threw.

"M-Miss Dearing." He nodded deferentially, but when she made no reply, he sidled around her and made his escape.

Oh, how she wanted to whack him with her new double-soled, extra-sturdy leather shoes as he slid past. A dent in his skull would serve him right, the cad. She restrained the impulse—barely. Justice would have to wait.

Turning her attention to more important matters, Samantha hurried into the alley and wrapped her arm around her whimpering friend.

"Shh," she soothed. "He's not worth it."

Ida Mae spun away from Samantha's offer of comfort, shaking her head as she pressed her back against the alley wall. "You d-don't understand." She clutched her son close to her chest. "In three months, Jimmy will t-turn two." She sniffed and wiped the back of one hand under her dripping nose. "When that happens, my pa is kickin' us out of the house."

"What?" How could a parent do that to his own child? His grandchild? Samantha and her father had had their disagreements over the years, but she knew without a doubt that her daddy would never banish her from his home. No matter what she'd done.

"He wanted to kick me out when he first learned I was carryin'. Said I'd shamed him and tainted the family honor. Mama convinced him to let me stay through my confinement and until the baby was weaned. We both prayed he'd soften. That he'd fall in love with Jimmy the way we had." She loosened her hold on her son and smoothed his blond hair with her hand, smiling at him through her tears. "He really is the sweetest boy. And smart. He's already talking. Aren't you, little man?"

Jimmy's pudgy hand patted Ida Mae's cheek. "Mama. Uv Mama."

"And Mama loves *you*." She kissed his head and hugged him tightly again, her smile fading as soon as her face shifted out of Jimmy's line of sight. "Getting Leroy to marry me is the only way to provide for my boy. Heaven knows that philandering louse would make a horrible husband, but I'd put up with his womanizing ways if it meant restoring my respectability and giving Jimmy a name."

Outrage hummed through Samantha's blood. "Jimmy already has a name. *Yours*. Seeing the way Leroy turned out, it might be better for Jimmy not to have that particular role model as his father."

Ida Mae stiffened, and her voice grew caustic. "Unlike you,

I don't have the luxury of turning down a houseful of wealthy suitors because they don't meet my far-too-particular preferences. I have to think of my son instead of myself."

Samantha fell back a step, tiny needles jabbing her heart. Is that truly what Ida Mae thought of her? A self-absorbed, pretentious rich girl who considered no suitor good enough? Heavens. If Ida Mae thought such a thing of her, chances were good that many others did, too. A sick feeling settled into the pit of her stomach. Were they right?

"I've looked for employment," Ida Mae continued, "but no respectable place in town will hire a woman with a tarnished reputation. And even if someone looked past the stain on my character, I have no one to tend Jimmy while I work. Pa says he's done providin' for us, and while Mama will do whatever she can to help, she won't defy him outright."

A weight pressed against Samantha's chest as she realized for the first time how small and petty her problems really were. So she'd never been taught to ride a horse. What did that matter compared to the plight of a young woman being thrown out onto the street with no way to support herself and her child? She'd thought herself so noble and enlightened for valuing relationship over riches in a marriage partner. How utterly frivolous such "nobility" must seem to someone scraping the bottom of the matrimonial barrel in a desperate bid to reclaim respectability.

Tears stung Samantha's eyes. "Ida Mae, I'm so sorry."

"Yeah? Well, so am I. But sorrow won't feed my baby." The defiance drained from Ida Mae's gaze, leaving only haggard despair. "Oh, Sam, I don't know what I'm going to do. It'll rip my heart out to give him up, but I might not have a choice." She bit her lip and pressed her cheek against Jimmy's head, her eyes closing in defeat.

Every feminine instinct Samantha possessed roared to life

in opposition to that outcome. Tears evaporated beneath the flaring heat of ignited passion. "That's not going to happen." She clasped her friend's arm. "We have three months to figure this out. And with God's help, we *will* find a solution."

Ida Mae shook her head. "God quit helpin' me the minute I let Leroy sweet-talk me into his bed."

"It might feel that way, but it's not true. He worked through your mother to keep a roof over your head for the last two years, and he gave you a healthy, intelligent boy with a loving disposition."

Ida Mae wagged her head. "He abandoned me. Left me alone. Just like Leroy. Like my father."

Samantha tightened her grip on her friend's arm and waited for her eyes to lift. "You're not alone, Ida Mae. You've got Jimmy. Your mother. And now you've got me, too. And you *know* how I am when I get a bee in my bonnet."

A hint of a smile touched Ida Mae's mouth. "You're a force to be reckoned with."

"Better believe it." Samantha grinned, then nodded her head toward the street. "Why don't you let me give you a ride home? We can start scheming on the way."

"You sure you want to be seen associating with me? People are bound to talk."

Samantha waved off the concern. "Let them. I have more important things to focus on." She stepped around Ida Mae to make a silly face at Jimmy. Her heart flipped when he grinned at her and waved his fist in excitement. "Like getting to know this adorable little man."

He made some nonsensical happy noise that delighted Samantha more than the most well-penned prose.

"You and I are going to be great friends, Jimmy." She voiced the vow aloud and echoed it in her heart.

This boy would *not* go hungry, and he would *not* be separated from his mother. God had crossed her path with Ida Mae today on purpose. To reveal a need. To invigorate hope in one and instill humility in the other. And to lay a calling on Samantha's soul that could not be denied. God had already planned an escape from the trap holding Ida Mae captive. They just had to find it.

"I'm headed out for an hour or so." Asher passed through the kitchen, where Mama Bess sat at the table snapping beans into an oversized bowl. He moved behind her and gave her shoulders a quick rub. "Gonna take Bruno out for a ride. I'll be back before supper."

She reached up and caught his hand, the small touch carrying the warmth of a full hug. She set the beans aside and shifted in her seat to meet his gaze. "I'm glad you're getting out, Ash. You've been working so hard. It's good for you to take some time for yourself. Besides . . ." She grinned and a touch of mischief sparked in her eyes. "I could use a break from all that hammering."

He'd spent the last two days reinforcing the milking shed by shoring up the support pillars and patching up the siding.

"If you think the noise has been bad the last couple days, just wait until I get started on the roof." He rolled his eyes toward the ceiling and chuckled when Mama Bess groaned.

"I might need to pay some social calls when those shingles you ordered come in."

Asher laid a hand on her shoulder. "I hope you do." He gave her shoulders another quick massage. "You've endured a lot of upheaval the last couple of months. Being forced to move, scrambling to make ends meet, worrying over the boys. That's a heavy load for these slender shoulders to carry."

"God has been faithful." She sagged a bit beneath his hands.

"I might wish for the security of a full larder, but I'm learning to trust him for our daily bread." She crooked her head toward him, her eyes alight with the cheerful enthusiasm that never failed to inspire him to give his best to any task that lay before him. "And since you're around to watch Fergus for me, I just might start paying those calls tomorrow."

He chuckled. "Good. Fergus and I will get along just fine. I might even convince him to set aside his stories long enough to learn a few things about carpentry."

"Just be patient when his attention wanders. You might be able to get him to set down his pencil in favor of a hammer for a few hours, but that won't stop the stories from spinning through his mind."

"I know, Mama." Asher gave her shoulders a final squeeze, then headed for the back door.

Fergus's stories were a part of who he was, and Asher never wanted him to lose that piece of himself. Yet at the same time, a man had to understand how to navigate the real world, and Asher wouldn't be much of a big brother if he didn't prepare Fergus for that side of life.

It saddened him slightly to think about all the things he wouldn't be around to teach Fergus. Jack, too, for that matter. His middle brother considered himself the man of the house and postured accordingly, but underneath that confident veneer lived a scared twelve-year old kid forced to grow up too fast. Asher knew exactly how that felt, and he'd tried for years to spare his brothers from that kind of pressure. But thanks to Eli Dearing and his rent increases, that layer of protection had disintegrated.

The anger that usually accompanied thoughts of his step-mother's former landlord didn't burn his gut with the same ferocity as it had a week ago. More like banked coals than roaring flames. Mama Bess's acceptance of her new circumstances no doubt played a role in that change. His lack of legal recourse combined with the sweat he'd already poured into making the new house livable had forced Asher to come to terms with the reality of the situation. He couldn't change what had happened. Couldn't restore what had been lost. All he could do was help his family move forward.

He urged Bruno into a canter as he left Palo Pinto behind and followed a path winding north along Eagle Creek. The ruins of the old mill came into view, and his pulse picked up its pace.

He spotted a buckboard near the abandoned building but didn't see Samantha. He slowed Bruno to a walk and scanned the area.

"Miss Dearing? You here?"

She stepped out from behind the stone mill, her smile beaming as she waved and watched him approach. Man, but the woman was beautiful. She wore the drabbest colors he'd ever seen her in, a plain brown skirt with an ivory blouse, yet that smile of hers sparkled like the sun. She ran over to greet him, giving him a front-row seat for the blue of her eyes. The woman could be covered in coal dust, but with those eyes and that smile, she'd still be the most vibrant woman he'd ever seen.

"Mr. Ellis, you came!"

"Did you doubt I would?" Tearing his attention away from her eyes, he concentrated on dismounting, a maneuver that wouldn't normally require thought, but in his current state of distraction, there were no guarantees he'd not end up with a boot stuck in a stirrup. He'd rather not hop around like a one-legged rabbit while she watched.

"Not really. You strike me as being a man of your word. But it dawned on me this afternoon that riding lessons are rather . . . frivolous compared to the important work you're doing for your mother." She picked at the decorative buttons running down the front of her skirt. "I would understand if you felt like your time could be put to better use elsewhere."

She glanced up at him, and all contending ideas for how he should use his time immediately bowed out of the running. Nothing could compete with being in her company.

He pivoted to face her fully. "Do you want to learn to ride, Miss Dearing?"

She nodded, her eyes alight. "Very much."

He grinned. "Then let's get to it."

That beaming smile returned accompanied by a giddy excitement that had her bouncing on her toes. "Thank you!"

Keeping his pulse in check was going to be tricky during these lessons if she kept looking at him like that.

Thankfully, she broke eye contact and glanced downward, giving him a chance to recover. Until he realized what she was doing. His pulse jumped to full-throttle panic.

She was unbuttoning her skirt.

16

"Whoa! What are you doing?"

"Well, that's a silly question." Bent at the waist, skirt placket in hand, Samantha craned her neck in order to peer up at Asher from the corner of one eye. "I'm preparing to ride."

Asher's face had gone quite red. He held up his hands and backed up a step as if he expected her to pull a derringer from her garters at any moment.

"I don't know what you thought we'd be doing, but this ain't no Lady Godiva school of riding."

What on earth was he talking about? What did Lady Godiva have to do with—

A gasp seized her lungs. Good heavens! He didn't think she was actually *disrobing*, did he? Samantha released her skirt as if it had caught fire, though all the heat traveled directly to her cheeks.

"I'm not . . ." Her voice squeaked, so she cleared her throat and tried again. "I'm wearing a split skirt. Rather like extra-wide pantaloons. The buttons hold the placket in place to give it the appearance of a regular skirt. Unfastening them allows

140

me greater range of movement with increased coverage of . . . ankles . . . and so forth." Mercy. Could this conversation get any more awkward? She lifted her chin, determined to brazen it out. "I promise all clothing will remain fully in place."

"That's, uh, good to know." Asher took up a sudden interest in his horse's saddle, pivoting away from her in order to fiddle with whatever straps happened to be within reach. "I'll just, uh, shorten these stirrups a bit while you . . . finish your, er, preparations."

A giggle slipped free before Samantha could catch it. She tried to close her lips to prevent more escapees, but that only caused them to erupt from her nose in an embarrassing snort, which ironically generated more amusement. She clapped a hand over her mouth, the sheer ridiculousness of the situation making it almost impossible to stem the flow. Striving for the dignity her mother had always exuded, Samantha bit the inside of her cheek and ordered herself to cease acting like a child. She'd nearly bullied her mirth into submission when a deep rumble vibrated the air. Her eyes flew to Asher's back. Another rumble. Correction—that was definitely a chuckle. Which, of course, unlocked the door on her poorly imprisoned hilarity. It erupted all at once in a completely unladylike guffaw.

Dignity didn't stand a chance.

Asher joined in the laughter, turning to face her, hunching slightly as he wrapped an arm around his midsection. She swore she could feel his laughter vibrate inside her own chest. The sound was so contagious and inviting that she withdrew her hand and allowed her amusement to run free. She laughed until her ribs ached and tears formed in her eyes. Wiping at the moisture, she struggled to catch her breath and calm her racing heart, but then she met his dancing gaze, and the laughter started all over again.

They must've spent five minutes in that uproarious state

before wearing themselves out. Samantha had given up on standing early on and had collapsed onto the grassy field.

"Come on," Asher said, offering her a hand up along with a smile so handsome it almost hurt to look at him. Being the brave woman she was, she suffered through the discomfort.

She slipped her hand into his and let him pull her to her feet. Her legs still wobbled a bit, but she managed to hold herself upright. Their eyes met and awareness swept across her skin and seeped into her bloodstream. Slowly, her smile relaxed as something other than humor played havoc with her breathing.

The moment stretched. He didn't release her hand. She didn't tug it free. Why would she when it felt so lovely inside his?

Heavens, but he had nice eyes. A dark, rich brown. Like expensive French coffee. The kind you sipped slowly in order to make it last. But nothing lasted forever.

Asher's smile quirked up on one side as he finally let her hand slip from his hold. He turned to pat Bruno's neck, then circled around to the horse's other side. "I'll get this stirrup set, then we'll be ready to start."

"All right." Samantha nodded, doing her best to hide her disappointment. She swiveled to present him her back as she finished unbuttoning the placket on her skirt. Her lips twitched as she worked the buttons through their holes, memories of the laughter they'd shared too fresh to abolish completely.

She straightened and turned to find him watching her. He averted his gaze quickly, but not fast enough to keep a little thrill from dancing around in her belly at the notion that he might find her attractive.

Clearing his throat, he moved to the front of the horse and hooked a lead line to the bridle beneath Bruno's jaw. "First thing for you to do is to introduce yourself to the horse."

Samantha shot Asher a teasing grin. "Should I curtsy?"

He grinned back, warming her blood as he shared her jest. "There's no rule against it, but I haven't taught Bruno how to bow, so maybe we should skip that part, so we don't embarrass him."

"Good thinking." Samantha smiled up at her teacher. "What do you suggest, then?"

Asher nodded toward Bruno. "Offer him your hand as if you're at a fancy ball and expecting some fine gentleman to kiss your knuckles."

Heat rushed to Samantha's cheeks. Did he have to mention kissing? Good heavens. Now all she could think about was presenting Asher her hand. Would he take it? Touch her knuckles with his lips? Would it make her toes tingle? How could it not? Her toes were practically tingling now and all he'd done was mention the word. In the context of his horse, even.

Praying Asher couldn't read her thoughts, Samantha extended her arm toward Bruno's head, her fingers draping downward in a relaxed pose.

"Pleased to meet you, Sir Bruno. I'm Miss Dearing, but you may call me Samantha."

The black-and-white paint's head bobbed a couple of times before he stretched out his neck and touched his nose to the back of her fingers. The simple gesture lit her up from the inside.

"Good," Asher praised. "Now move closer and pat his neck. Talk to him, too. It's good for him to get to know your voice as well as your scent."

Samantha obeyed. She patted Bruno's neck and ran her fingers through his mane. "What a fine fellow you are," she murmured. "So gallant, coming to a lady's rescue the way you did the other night. I hope you'll be equally gallant today and help me look like I have at least a little skill in the saddle."

"Bruno's used to making people look good," Asher said with

a self-deprecating grin as he moved to Samantha's side. "He covers up my mistakes all the time."

She dipped her chin, suddenly shy to have him so close. "You don't seem the type to make many mistakes."

An odd look crossed his face. "I've made my share. A few of them were real humdingers, too. I would've been in a heap of trouble if Bruno hadn't been around to save my bacon."

The way he looked at her . . . so probing. As if seeking absolution for something. But what? He'd never wronged her. He'd saved her life, for pity's sake.

"Well, I for one am glad that Bruno kept you out of trouble. We all need a trusted friend we can count on to get us back on track when we veer off course." Like Aunt Regina was for her. Like she hoped to be for Ida Mae.

A deeper thought stirred, and Samantha's hand fell away from the horse as she gave the notion her full attention. "My aunt stayed with Clint and me after my mother passed. He was three at the time and seemed to ask a thousand questions a day, most of them starting with *why*." She smiled at the memory. "Whenever I complained about his pestering, Aunt Regina would tell me how blessed Clint and I were to have each other. She'd quote a verse from Ecclesiastes. I don't remember it word for word, but it went something like 'Two are better than one, for if one falls, the other can help him up, but woe to the one who is alone when he falls, for he has no one to help him up.'"

A stillness came over the man at her side. He stopped fiddling with the rope, and his posture tensed slightly. Samantha bit her lip. She'd gotten too personal. They'd been talking about a horse, not actual friendship. And what prompted her to start spouting Bible verses? She hadn't thought about that particular passage in years. Why now? She was just here to learn how to ride, not to delve into the depths of human relationships. She ought to apologize. Make some silly quip and get their conversation back on level ground. But before she could think of the right words to smooth things over, Asher broke the silence.

"I lost both my parents. My father most recently. Six years ago."

Samantha touched his arm. "I'm sorry."

"I was eighteen. Old enough to work to provide for Mama Bess and the boys, but too young to have the experience needed to make more than a piddlin' wage for the first several years. I felt the woe that verse was talkin' about. Being alone with no one to help me up. Still do sometimes."

Asher was the one providing for his mother? Samantha had never had to worry about money, so she'd paid little attention to what things cost or how people made their living. She'd assumed Asher was a cowboy like most of the hands at the Three Cedars, earning a wage for himself, perhaps putting some funds aside to start a ranch of his own someday. But he wasn't working for himself. He was supporting his family. And had been for years. Since he was eighteen. She was only a year older than that now. What would she do if her daddy and his money disappeared? How would she provide for Clint and herself?

"It must be hard," she said. "Bearing the weight of that responsibility."

"Sometimes." He shrugged. "But family is worth the sacrifice." He leaned an arm on the saddle and gazed across the open field. "I just wish I could do more for them. It grates my hide that Jack had to take a job at the livery and that Mama Bess lost her garden."

"Her garden?"

A smile spread across his face. "The finest in Palo Pinto County. I used to hate it when she would make me weed when

I was a kid, unless the strawberries were ripe. Then I'd eat while I worked. Mama Bess would pretend to scold and fuss about me not leaving enough berries for her to put up jam, but she kept sending me to that section of the garden to work, so I think it actually made her happy to see me enjoying the fruits of her labor." He shook his head. "Mama Bess has a gift for growing things. Squash, tomatoes, cucumbers, beans, carrots, potatoes, corn, beets, watermelon, chickpeas, greens. There's nothing she can't grow. Early spring through late autumn, she was in that garden, planting, nurturing, and harvesting. She'd can enough of the surplus to keep us in food all winter long. Any excess above that was shared with neighbors and friends. Nothing went to waste." His smile dimmed. "Losing the house she'd shared with my father was hard, but losing her garden ... I think that tore out a little piece of her soul."

He made no mention of the role her father played in those circumstances, but Samantha felt the weight of guilt settle over her at his words anyway. The urge to cast her father as the villain rose within her, but she wouldn't give the accusation voice. She'd blamed her father for far too many things over the years that weren't actually his fault. He was her father, and she owed him her loyalty and respect. She'd not speak ill of him in front of others. But she *would* speak to him in private. Tonight.

Asher straightened away from the horse and offered her a smile that didn't quite reach his eyes. "Boy, that turned melancholy all of a sudden, didn't it? Sorry about that. You're here to ride, not to get mired in my family troubles." He opened his stance and waved her close to the horse. "Come take the reins, and we'll get you in the saddle."

"Asher."

His eyes met hers.

"The riding can wait."

His brows arched in question.

"Friends share thoughts and worries with each other. It's how we lighten the burden and find the strength to keep moving forward when situations try to beat us down. You and I haven't known each other long, but I hope you consider me a friend . . . as I do you." Although *friend* seemed a rather mild word to describe the connection she felt with this man. "I might not be able to help you repair a roof or reconstruct a chicken coop, but I can listen and pray on your behalf. It might not be much, but—"

"It's a lot. Thank you." He gently clasped her arm. The touch lasted only a moment, but it carried a wealth of emotion that stirred an answering response within Samantha's breast.

This time when he grinned, his eyes danced, causing a strange flopping sensation in her belly. "Now, about those lessons."

She smiled and moved close, both to him and the horse. His arm brushed against hers as he handed her the reins, and tingles erupted in her midsection.

Focus, Samantha. You don't want him thinking you're an empty-headed ninny.

"Keep the reins short and grab a fistful of mane with your left hand. Good. Now I'm going to give you a leg up. When you're ready, bend your left leg at the knee, bringing your shin parallel to the ground. I'll grip your knee and ankle, and on the count of three, you'll jump, and I'll boost at the same time. Got it?"

Samantha nodded. "I think so."

"When I lift, reach for the saddle horn with your right hand and swing your right leg over Bruno's back." He offered a smile of encouragement. "Ready to give it a try?"

"Ready." She turned and targeted her gaze on the saddle horn as she lifted her left foot from the ground.

Feeling Asher's hands grip her leg proved extremely distracting, but the minute he started counting, her attention sharpened.

"One. Two. Three!"

She jumped off her right leg at the same time he lifted her left. She felt as light as dandelion fluff as she flew upward. Remembering her job, she grabbed the saddle horn and found her balance as she straddled the horse. Excitement zinged through her along with a generous helping of nerves.

"Now fit your toes into the stirrups and loosen the reins slightly."

She had to peek over the side to find the stirrups, but she managed to get both feet in place.

"I'll be leading him," Asher said, "so you won't have to worry about directing him, but I want you to get a feel for holding the reins. Let go of the horn and find a comfortable seat."

She really didn't want to let go of the horn. That handle seemed the most stable piece of the entire operation, but she didn't want Asher to think her afraid, so she released her hold and shifted slightly until she found a position that felt relatively natural.

"Good. Now, when we start walking, I want you to continue sitting straight but don't be stiff. Feel his rhythm and let your body sway along like you would if he were your dancing partner. Don't fight him. Move as one."

"I'll try."

He grinned. "You'll do great."

And she did. Until Bruno grew bored and kicked their slow waltz into a bouncy polka.

17

With the sun warming his shoulders and back, Asher slipped into a bit of a lull as he rotated at the focus point of the riding circle while Bruno plodded around the circumference. The rope tugged gently against his hand as he pivoted, his gaze riveted on the woman in the saddle as his mind replayed their conversation.

"I hope you consider me a friend. . . . I can listen and pray on your behalf."

How had he ever mistaken Samantha Dearing for a self-absorbed princess? She might be the daughter of the wealthiest cattleman in the county, but she cared about people. Not only cared but looked for ways to help. Like with his brother. And now with him.

She'd offered to pray for him. When was the last time a woman other than Mama Bess had made such an offer? He couldn't recall a single instance. Of course, he'd been so busy working over the last six years, he hadn't had many opportunities to converse with women. Still . . . the experience seemed rather extraordinary. *She* seemed rather extraordinary.

"Whoa, Bruno. Whoooooa!" Her squeal sharpened Asher's focus in an instant.

Bruno had transitioned into a trot. The paint had been trained to respond to changes in his rider's seat, so it was likely that Samantha had bumped him with her heel or shifted in the saddle enough to make the horse believe it was time to pick up the pace.

"Tilt your hips forward," he called as he jogged toward her, reeling in the lead line as he went. "Keep your heels down and your shoulders over your hips."

"It's too b-bouncy." She clung to the saddle horn but started listing to the left.

Asher dropped the lead and sprinted forward. "Ho, Bruno. Ho!" His voice rang with an authority the paint recognized.

Bruno stopped, but Samantha kept sliding.

He reached her side right as she fell from the saddle. Her face smooshed against his chest when he wrapped his arms around her waist, and her left foot tangled in the stirrup, leaving her suspended like a human bridge between horse and man. After a bit of wiggling and twisting, she managed to free her foot and slide the rest of the way off the horse and into Asher's arms. A situation he enjoyed more than he probably should.

Once her feet found the ground, however, Samantha straightened and created some distance between them.

"I'm sorry." She reached up to straighten the bonnet that had gone askew after crashing into his chest during her less-than-elegant dismount. "I panicked. I didn't expect Bruno to start running."

Asher willed away the grin that clamored for release. "That was a trot, not a run, but it *is* one of the trickier gaits for new riders to master. You'll like the canter. It's faster, but much smoother."

She gave him a dubious look. "I don't think I'm ready for faster."

The grin he'd been fighting found its way onto his face. "Not yet, but you will be. You've got a great teacher, after all."

Her eyes danced. The fear from a moment ago faded behind a tide of rising sass. "Oh, I do, do I?" She placed a hand on her hip and raised a brow as she looked him over. "Well, my instructor *did* manage to save me from taking a nasty tumble, so I suppose he deserves credit for the rescue. Probably shouldn't tell him how much I appreciated his gallantry, though. I'd hate for his head to swell. Just imagine if his hat no longer fit. He'd be a bareheaded cowboy in Texas. The laughingstock of cattlemen statewide. We must guard him against such shame."

Asher chuckled as he folded an arm over his chest in a show of solidarity. "I'll take your secret to my grave, milady."

She nodded with a regal air. "Your nobility is commendable, sir. Now, help me back onto this steed before I talk myself out of trying again."

Asher helped her mount, yet her playful words stung his conscience. He'd been far from noble or trustworthy when he'd broken into her home last week. What would she say if she learned the truth? Would the admiration warming her gaze chill into a frosty disdain? The thought speared him in the chest. In the short time he'd known her, he'd come to crave her good opinion. Yet how could he be the noble gentleman she thought him to be if he hid the truth from her?

Asher collected the lead line and moved back to the center of their imaginary circle. Maybe it was a good thing he was leaving in a couple of weeks, because if he stayed, and he and Samantha continued to see each other, he'd eventually have to confess all. And that confession would either solidify their trust or utterly destroy it.

151

Later that evening, Samantha hummed softly to herself as she unpacked items from an old trunk in the attic at the Three Cedars. Each tiny shirt, sleeping gown, and pair of booties stirred an odd mix of nostalgia and new longings. The nostalgia she'd been prepared for. The longings? Those had taken her by surprise. Finding a silver rattle, she lifted it out of the trunk and gave it a shake. The bells at the top jingled, eliciting a smile.

What would it be like to hold a baby of her own? After being forced into a mothering role at an early age to care for her brother, her dreams had centered less on home and hearth and more on independence and freedom from familial responsibilities. Yet her father's eagerness to see her married, combined with her encounter with Ida Mae, had caused something inside her to shift.

All right. The shift wasn't only because of Daddy and Ida Mae. Asher Ellis carried most of the blame. After spending an hour with him for her riding lesson, then having him escort her home after she'd tutored Jack, he occupied most of her thoughts. When he'd offered to drive the buckboard home for her, she'd tossed all her independent ideals out the window and accepted his offer. Mostly because the memories of what had happened on her last drive home still plagued her with lingering anxiety, but she'd be lying if she failed to acknowledge that she'd *wanted* him to sit next to her on that bench. So she might admire him up close. Perhaps even brush up against him should they hit a jostle-inducing rut. Having him near would allow them to converse or even just to sit in companionable silence as they watched the sunset.

Was it any wonder that when domestic ideas invaded her mind, he was the husband she envisioned at her side? His hand gently caressing her back as he peered into the crook of her arm to smile at the imaginary child she held—a child possessing Asher's sandy brown hair and her blue eyes.

"Whatcha doin' up here?"

Samantha startled so badly the rattle slipped from her hand and clattered onto the hardwood floor. "Clint! Must you always sneak up on me?" She pressed a hand to her chest in an effort to calm her pounding heart as she craned her neck around to scowl at her snickering brother.

"What? I'm just walking. It's not my fault you were too busy woolgathering to hear me coming." She might have believed him had his eyes not been glowing with triumph as he held up his hands in manufactured innocence.

Biting back a sigh, Samantha retrieved the rattle and added it to her *keep* pile, then turned back to the trunk. "I'm going through your old baby clothes."

"Why?"

"I ran across a friend in town today. She has a little boy, and I thought I would let her borrow some things."

Her brother knelt beside her in front of the trunk, then leaned over the edge to look inside. "Hey! I remember this blanket." He pulled out the stained and misshapen knitted baby blanket he'd slept with until about four years ago.

After their mother died, Clint had often lain awake crying until Aunt Regina got the idea to dab a little of Mother's perfume on his blanket and place it in bed with him. The scent had soothed him and allowed the entire household to sleep. After Aunt Regina left, Samantha had continued the practice, applying dots of perfume every few weeks until the vial on her mother's dressing table was empty. By then, Clint had grown accustomed to sleeping with the small blanket tucked beside him and refused to go to bed without it. At least until Daddy and Duke started training him to run the ranch, and he decided he was too manly to sleep with a baby blanket.

Clint rubbed the sky blue knit against his chin, an expression of fond remembrance passing over his face that tugged on Samantha's heartstrings. It didn't last long, however. He seemed to recall the threat baby blankets posed to his masculinity and tossed it aside, nearly toppling her *share* pile.

"Careful." She lifted the blanket off the wobbling stack of toddler-sized clothing. "I can't have you messing up my system."

Clint eyed the piles stacked in a semicircle around her knees. "What system?"

"I'm stacking them by age-appropriateness." She pointed to a pile on her right. "These are for infants and are too small for Ida Mae's baby." Shifting to the left, she pointed to a stack by her knee. "These are clothes that would likely fit Jimmy now and over the next year or two." She shifted her hand to lie atop a pile by her hip. "This pile contains larger items that we can pass along in a few years. And this small pile," she said as she touched the few items between her knees and the trunk, "is things too sentimental to part with." The rattle, a wooden horse on wheels her father had made, Clint's first pair of tiny cowboy boots.

Her brother eyed the piles a little more seriously, then took the baby blanket from her hand and dropped it into the pile with the rattle and boots. Samantha bit back a smile. He might do his best to act like one of the men, but his heart still retained a boyish tenderness.

Samantha reached inside the trunk for the next item. "Was there a reason you came to find me?"

"Oh yeah." Clint sat back on his heels. "Daddy sent me to fetch you. He's done with the payroll accounting and ready to meet with you."

Samantha dropped the set of short trousers she'd just collected and pushed to her feet, her belly tightening. She and her father had been getting along better the last few days. He'd been particularly solicitous after her accident, checking in on her before going to bed and staying close to the house the following day just in case she needed anything. She would hate to reinstall the cold formality between them, but the conversation she was fixing to have with him could do just that. Yet it had to be done. Injustice must be brought to light. If she pretended not to see it because confronting it complicated her life, she'd have no one to blame but herself when it struck again. Perhaps closer to home.

"I'll have to finish this later, then." She bent to retrieve the lamp she'd placed on a nearby table and headed for the stairs at the end of the long narrow room. "Come on. It's too dark to be up here without a light."

Clint had just straddled a rocking horse he'd last ridden around age six and was poised to fold his lanky adolescent frame onto the unsuspecting equine when she made that comment. He moaned quietly to register his protest of her bringing an end to his fun, then traipsed after her.

They separated on the second-floor landing, Clint continuing downstairs, likely to the kitchen to pilfer a snack, while Samantha made her way down the hall to her father's office. She set her lamp on the hall table, then smoothed her skirt, brushing off the thin coating of attic dust that had collected around her knees. Once she felt sufficiently tidied, she inhaled a steadying breath and knocked.

"Enter."

Her father stood behind his desk, an open book in his hands. When he saw her, he smiled and slid the book back into its place on the shelf. He gestured for her to join him on the furniture across from his desk. "Did everything go well with the Ellis boy tonight?"

She smiled. "Yes, Jack is quite bright. I imagine he'll be

caught up to the other children his age by the end of the summer."

"Good, good. And your journey home was uneventful, I trust?" He waited for her to settle on the sofa before lowering himself into the chair to her right.

The ride home hadn't *felt* uneventful with Asher at her side, but she kept that little detail to herself. "All four wheels performed their duty admirably. Not a single mishap to report."

"Excellent. I'd prefer neither of my children have any more mishaps. I think I've added a hundred gray hairs to my head over the last week." He ran his hand through the dark blond hair that had begun to thin and fade with age. "So you said at dinner you had a couple of things you wanted to talk to me about. What's on your mind?"

Deciding it might be wise to ease into their discussion, Samantha opted for the easier of the two topics. "Why did you evict the Ellis family from their home?"

Her father expelled a sigh and ran a hand over his jaw. "I felt bad about that. Elizabeth bein' a widow and all. I went as long as I could without raising her rent, but after I lost so many Shorthorns to Texas fever a year ago, I had no choice. I raised rents across all my properties to cover my losses. I was glad her eldest boy was able to help her find a new place in town. She really didn't need all that acreage anyway. It's gone unused since her husband died."

Keeping her voice as bland as possible, Samantha picked at a spot on the upholstery of the sofa's arm. "Have you rented the property to anyone else yet?"

"No." His face reddened slightly. "I'd thought to gift it to you as a wedding present." He held up a hand as if to ward off a coming attack. "I know that's not really in the works anymore, but it's some of the best land I own. Fertile soil. Plentiful water.

Smooth terrain. It'd make a great starter ranch or even a farm, should your, uh, husband be . . . agriculturally inclined."

"And if he's not?" she couldn't help but ask. "What if he prefers town life? What if he were a . . ." She tried to think of an example her father would take exception to. "A store clerk?"

Her father stiffened. "A *clerk*? Tell me you haven't fallen for that weaselly Flanders fellow down at Patterson's." He looked so utterly horrified by the prospect that Samantha had to stifle a giggle.

"No. I have no interest in Mr. Flanders. I was just curious about what would happen to the land."

"Thank goodness." He slumped back in his chair. "Don't scare me like that, girl."

She bit back a smile. "The land, Daddy?"

"Oh yes. The land. Well, if you up and married a town fella, I guess you could use the land as an investment or sell it. 'Course, now that I know you're not in a hurry to settle down, I should probably put a notice in the paper about the place being available again."

"Could you wait a few months?" Samantha leaned forward in her seat. "Mrs. Ellis left behind a garden. One she depended on to keep her family fed through the winter. I was hoping you would allow her to salvage what was left of the plot. I could oversee things as your representative. Maybe she could even teach me a few things about planting and harvesting. It would be a good skill to have should I ever marry a man who is . . . agriculturally inclined."

He rubbed his chin. "The house is already closed up."

That wasn't a no.

"We wouldn't need the house, Daddy. Just access to the garden. Please. It would really help Mrs. Ellis, and you know what the Good Book says about taking care of orphans and widows."

"I'm aware." His dry tone made it clear he didn't appreciate her biblical manipulation. Nevertheless, he nodded his head. "I suppose it won't hurt anything if you agree to supervise. But come September, I'm opening it up to renters." He gave her a sly side glance. "Unless you happen to be engaged by then."

Now who was doing the manipulating?

Not that it mattered. He'd granted access to Mama Bess's garden. Her first mission had been accomplished.

She leaned back in her seat. "I guess we'll have to see what September brings."

"That we will." He grinned and patted her knee. "Now, what is the second thing you needed to talk about?" He stretched his legs out in front of him and visibly relaxed as if the worst were over.

Unfortunately, the worst was yet to come.

18

Filling her mind with images of Ida Mae and sweet little Jimmy, Samantha gripped the sofa arm and braced herself for rough seas. "I think you need to fire one of your cowhands."

Her father stiffened, and his expression darkened. "Did someone get out of line with you?"

She shook her head. "Not with me, but I discovered today that Leroy Thompson fathered a child with one of my friends, and he refuses to take responsibility and marry her."

Daddy sighed and pulled his knees up in order to brace his forearms on the shelf they formed. "You know I don't hold with immorality, but it's not my job to police the men when they're off duty. I work them hard, so I don't begrudge them the chance to let off steam during their personal time. Some drink, some gamble, some . . . seek female companionship. As long as their work doesn't suffer from their choices, I got no reason to interfere." He leaned back and scratched at a spot behind his ear. "Shoot, if I only employed straightlaced fellas, I'd be out of business by the end of the year from a lack of manpower. Leroy Thompson is a good hand. I ain't gonna fire him just because some young woman claims he's the father of her babe."

"Claims?" Samantha bristled. "Do you think Ida Mae would lie about something like that?"

His hand slapped against his leg, and he expelled an exasperated breath. "I don't know, Samantha. I'm not familiar with Ida Mae's habits, nor am I privy to the workings of her mind. And neither are you. You haven't seen her more than a handful of times over the last three years. She might not be the same person you remember."

Samantha stiffened her spine. "She's definitely *not* the same person I remember. She's a mother now. Her reputation has been slaughtered, her father plans to kick her and the baby out of his house in three months, and the man who sired her son not only refuses to marry her, but he won't even provide for the boy's basic needs."

"How is that my problem?"

Unable to sit still a moment longer, Samantha lunged off the sofa and paced to the edge of the rug. She spun around with enough zeal to bell out her skirt as she pointed a finger at her father when he rose from his chair. "It's *your* problem because as long as the older and wiser men of our society turn a blind eye to the bad behavior of their young protégés, nothing will change. Someone has to take a stand and demand integrity."

She curled her hand into a fist and pounded it against the flat of her hand. "Why is it that when a man and woman have relations outside of marriage, the woman is a harlot, but the man is simply 'sowing his wild oats'? Why is the woman's reputation destroyed while the man escapes unscathed? Why is raising the child born from this union solely the responsibility of the woman when the man is equally responsible for the child's existence?"

"Cool your kettle," her father snapped. A muscle in his jaw twitched.

"'Cool my kettle'?" That's all the response he could manage? Samantha stalked forward. "What if it had been me, Daddy? What if Leroy Thompson had gotten *me* with child? Would he still be working for you?"

"He'd not be workin' for anyone 'cause he'd not be breathing."

The grumbled response injected her with hope, even though she knew he'd never actually harm another person.

She halted in front of her father and looked up at him, silently pleading with him to understand the severity of the issue. "Because what he did was dishonorable."

Hard blue eyes stared down at her. "No, because what he did hurt my little girl."

Samantha laid a hand on her daddy's chest. "Ida Mae is someone's little girl, too. It shouldn't matter if she is personally connected to you or not. The crime is the same. If you would punish Mr. Thompson for hurting me, then you should punish him for hurting Ida Mae."

"I'm not Ida Mae's father, Sam. It's not my place to get involved."

Samantha's hand fell away from his chest as her hope deflated. "I wish you *were* her father," she said softly. "Then she'd have a safe place to raise her child instead of being kicked out the house with no way to support herself."

Her father groaned and strode over to his desk. Bracing both hands on the mahogany surface, he leaned into the wood and shook his head. "You're putting me in a tough spot. I can't fire a man simply based on a woman's accusation. If I confront him about it, he'll deny that the child is his, and there's no way for me to prove him a liar."

Samantha balled her hands into fists. If only Leroy had admitted his guilt when Ida Mae confronted him. Then Samantha could've corroborated her friend's side of the story. But the shifty skunk was too slippery for that. "I overheard him admit to . . . having relations with Ida Mae." Speaking about it brought heat to her cheeks. "But he insisted he wasn't Jimmy's father. His tone was so smug, though, I know he was lying."

Her father pushed away from the table and pivoted to sit on its edge. "Women's intuition ain't proof, Samantha. And even if he did admit to fathering the kid, I still wouldn't have cause to fire him. Leroy's actions weren't moral, but they weren't criminal, either. And while I agree that it's unfair for Ida Mae to bear the consequences alone for a sin they both participated in, the truth is that she chose to give herself to a man not her husband."

"Someone's got to change things, Daddy." Passion flared in Samantha's breast. She flung her arms wide as she begged him to be part of the change. "Men have been covering for the sins of their brothers since Bible times. Look at the woman they dragged to Jesus. Scripture says she was caught in the very act of adultery. The very act. That means the man had to have been there. Yet they didn't drag *him* to Jesus for punishment, only her. These were religious men. Pharisees. Men leading the church of that time. Men who knew adultery was just as sinful for men as for women. Yet they ignored the man's sin and publicly disgraced the woman. They picked up stones to take her life. They would have killed her and thought themselves justified, their self-righteous fervor blinding them to their hypocrisy. Thank God that Jesus stopped them." Her arms flopped back to her sides as she moved toward the desk. "If society is going to punish the woman, it should punish the man, too."

"I'm not society, Samantha. I'm just one person."

"But you're a person in a position to take action. Someone who can demonstrate that integrity matters."

How could she convince him? How could she make him see how important this was?

Then she saw it. The photo frame standing on the desk next to his hip. It faced away from her, but she knew the image by heart.

"What about Clint?" she blurted. "Do you want him influenced by men who think nothing of seducing women and leaving illegitimate children in their wake?"

Her father jerked to his feet. "Enough of your speeches. You see everything in black and white, right and wrong. But things are rarely that simple. You're fighting for your friend, and I appreciate that, but there are layers to this that are more complicated. I might have the power to fire an employee on a whim, but doing so would undermine the trust I've fostered with all my other hands. If a man does his work well, his job should be protected unless there is proof that he broke faith with his employer. I need concrete evidence of wrongdoing before I can take action against him."

"But—"

"There has to be a check in place, Samantha. I've seen the way Leroy flirts with the ladies, so I'm disposed to believe Ida Mae's story, especially with you vouching for her, but what's to keep someone who bears a grudge against one of my men from concocting some outlandish lie to sabotage his employment? What if someone accused you of stealing things from the houses where you tutored students? Wouldn't you want the parents you worked for to seek proof before taking action against you? Our justice system is predicated on the idea that we must presume innocence and only find a person guilty when evidence proves him to be so."

Some of the wind fell out of Samantha's sails. She didn't have any proof. Only Ida Mae's word, which would be cancelled by Leroy's lies. It was just so unfair!

"What about the love shack?"

The sound of Clint's voice spun Samantha toward the hall. Her brother pushed open the door that had only been halfway closed and took a step into the room.

Good heavens! Had he overheard their conversation? Fire blazed in Samantha's cheeks. She should have ensured the door was closed. He was far too young to be exposed to such talk. Mercy. Mother would be horrified. Not only had her daughter initiated a conversation that was completely improper for any unmarried young woman, but she'd exposed her innocent baby brother to it as well.

"Clint!" She scurried forward and tried to shoo him from the room. "You shouldn't be here."

He sidestepped and skewered her with a dark frown. "It's Three Cedars business. I have every right to be here. How else am I supposed to learn to be a good manager?"

"But you're too young to understand—"

He pulled himself up to his full height and looked her straight in the eye. "I help breed cattle, Sam. I know where babies come from. And I think Ida Mae's baby came from the love shack."

"What on earth is a love shack?" She looked to her father, but his expression mimicked her confusion.

"I have no idea." He turned to his son. "Clint?"

"A couple months ago, I heard Leroy bragging to some of the other hands about some old line shack he found a few years back. Said someone had fixed it up as a twisting place."

Samantha shared a look with her father. A *trysting* place, perhaps?

"Instead of having a narrow cot inside like the other shacks, it had an actual bed, one big enough for two people." Clint's face reddened. "Leroy said he'd been takin' girls out there for years. I bet Ida Mae was one of them."

Her father scowled. "I lay in supplies once a month at every line shack we have, and I know for a fact that none of them sport a bed like that."

"This ain't a regular Three Cedars cabin. It's over by Dry Creek Gulch. We haven't run cattle over there for as long as I can remember."

"Not since the creek dried up back in '74. Before you were born. That area ain't good for nothing 'cept cactus farmin' these days. You say there's a cabin there?"

Clint nodded. "I've seen it."

"Why didn't you say something to me, boy?"

Clint shrugged. "I assumed you already knew. You know everything about the Three Cedars."

Her father crossed his arms over his chest and frowned. "Apparently not." He raised a brow at Clint. "What else can you tell me about it?"

"Only that Leroy calls it the love shack and that sometimes when he goes to town, he'll pay a girl from the saloon to meet him there."

Samantha's knees wobbled. "Good heavens, Clinton. You are far too young to be discussing saloons and the . . . the . . . women who work in them."

Her brother rolled his eyes at her, but it was their father who surprised her most. He circled around behind his desk, opened the side drawer, and took out the gun belt he always wore when working on the ranch. "Fetch Martin," he told Clint as he strapped on his gun. "Ask him to saddle a pair of horses and prep two lanterns."

Clint nodded and dashed from the room.

"I don't understand." Samantha frowned. "Where could you possibly need to go this time of night?"

Her father grinned, his smile rather wolfish. "Leroy went to town today to pick up an order of barbed wire for me."

"I know. I saw him. . . . You don't think . . . ?"

"Men who run town errands are assigned night duty with the herd. Leroy volunteered for the north pasture. If he's out with the stock like he's supposed to be, I'll make up some excuse as to why I'm checking on him. But if he's at this cabin with a woman . . ."

"You'll have a legitimate excuse to fire him."

Her father nodded. "A good reason to take a ride in the dark, don't you think?"

Samantha blinked a sheen of fast-developing moisture from her eyes. "Thank you, Daddy."

He touched her arm, then strode for the doorway. He stopped on the threshold, though, and turned back. "You know, I've been thinking about hiring someone to help Mrs. Stewart with the cooking and cleaning. She's not as young as she used to be. Talk to her in the morning. If she's amenable to the idea, you can offer Ida Mae the position. Ten dollars a month, plus room and board."

Too stunned to speak, Samantha barely managed a nod before her father left.

How she'd misjudged this man. All the resentment she'd carried around during her teen years had hardened her heart and obscured her vision, but now she could finally see clearly.

Eli Dearing wasn't a cold cattle king who cared only for his ranch. He was a man of justice who harbored a tender and kind heart. A man any girl would be blessed to call Daddy.

19

◦⟋∽⟋◦

Asher stepped out of the telegraph office the following afternoon, his heart heavy. The foreman from the Bar 7 had replied to the wire Asher had sent that morning with the expected answer. Mr. Tremaine, owner of the Bar 7, had approved an additional week of leave, but he made it clear that Asher's position at the ranch would be filled at the end of that time if he did not return. Whoever they'd hired to fill his vacancy on a temporary basis would become a permanent hand by the end of the month. The terms were fair. Generous even. Yet the deadline failed to inspire any urgency.

The last eleven days had been filled with hard work, but they'd also been filled with family—a blessing he hadn't enjoyed to this extent in years. He loved spending quiet evenings with Mama Bess, listening to Fergus's imaginative stories, and stealing time away with Jack at the fishing hole. He'd missed nearly half of his brothers' lives, more than half in Fergus's case, and a craving was building inside him. A craving to be a regular part of their lives. To be not just their provider but their brother. One who actually spent time with them and

167

had a relationship built on more than letters and a few days at Christmas.

Asher turned down the boardwalk and nodded to a couple he recognized from church who were strolling toward him. Mr. Johnson smiled and dipped his chin as he covered his wife's hand where it lay in the crook of his arm. A touch of pink colored Mrs. Johnson's cheeks at her husband's show of affection. Asher grinned and scooted closer to the buildings to give them room to pass. The Johnsons had to be in their forties, maybe even fifties, yet they acted like a newly courting couple. What must it be like to share that kind of closeness with someone for so many years?

An image of Samantha Dearing popped into his mind unbidden, but he didn't shoo it away. Spending a lifetime with a woman possessing her unique combination of sweetness and spunk would be a pleasure indeed. The chances of him being the man she hitched her wagon to were slimmer than a paper's edge, but the idea of another fella doing so stirred up a strong case of indigestion.

She was the daughter of the cattle king, for pity's sake. Even if, by some miracle, she did develop feelings for him, her father would never approve a match between them. Why would he when he could fill an entire ballroom with more suitable candidates? Men of wealth and prestige. Men who owned land and fine houses. Men free to make his daughter their first priority without the constraints of providing for a stepmother and brothers.

Yet none of those men had been by her side when she'd needed rescuing from a runaway cart. And none of those men were teaching her how to ride or sitting beside her in a wagon seat while the sun set over the Texas landscape.

Of course, none of those men had trespassed on her father's property, either. Or riffled through his study. Eli Dearing had more than Asher's meager bank account to support a rejection of his suit. And what about Samantha? Would her admiration turn to disdain when she learned the truth?

Stepping off the boardwalk, Asher clenched his jaw and turned down a side street. He'd learned long ago not to dream too big. The bigger the dream, the bigger the disappointment when it failed. A man needed realistic goals and hard work to find success. Dreaming was best left to boys like Fergus who had the imagination and cleverness to see those dreams to fruition. Asher had been built for work, not for scaling castles built on air.

He aimed his feet toward the livery where Jack worked, intending to check in on his brother before he returned home. As he walked, his surroundings grew rougher. No boardwalks to keep a lady's skirts out of the dirt here. No picture windows filled with goods to entice shoppers inside. A blacksmith's hammer echoed from somewhere behind him. The smell of leather wafted through the window of a saddlery shop to his right. The occasional raucous shout came from the saloon up the street, blending with the quiet nickers of the livery nags. This street was a man's domain.

So why in the world was Samantha Dearing standing in the middle of it? Asher's boots locked in place as he blinked at the vision before him. Her fashion plate of a dress, the color of a cloudless sky, stood out from the drab browns and grays like a cornflower in a gravel pit. Beautiful. Delicate. And completely out of place.

She lifted a hand and waved, but not at him. The distance kept him from seeing her expression, but he swore he could feel her smile all the way down the block. Something ugly twisted in his gut until a boy jogged over to the corral fence and climbed onto the bottom rung. Jack.

Get your head on straight, Ash. She doesn't belong to you.

Oddly enough, that truth had virtually no effect on the possessiveness spiking through his chest as he watched her approach his brother. It actually made it worse as instinct warred with logic. Not only was she beautiful, intelligent, and as feisty as an unbroke filly, but somehow she just . . . fit . . . with his family, despite the differences in their background. Fergus had declared his fealty to her last night when she'd brought him an illustrated edition of *Gulliver's Travels* from her home library. He and the book had been inseparable all day today. And Jack, as much as he might grumble about forfeiting his evening leisure for lessons, obviously didn't object to the tutor herself. If he leaned any farther over that fence rail, he'd end up with a permanent crease in his middle.

Asher chuckled softly as he started toward the livery. It seemed Miss Dearing had charmed *all* the Ellis men.

"Well, if it ain't Miss High and Mighty." The overloud, slurred voice came from a man staggering out of the saloon. A nearly empty whiskey bottle in his hand, he raised an unsteady arm to point an accusing finger at Samantha. "I knowed it wuz you. Interferin' in my business. You got no right!"

Asher frowned and lengthened his stride.

Jack moved to straddle the top rung of the fence and scowled at the obnoxious fellow. "Leave the lady alone, mister. Get on home, and sleep it off."

"Ain't got no home, no job neither, thanks to this meddlin' cow. Ran right to Daddy, didn't you? Ya little tattler." The line he walked might be crooked, but it was taking him directly to Samantha. Asher kicked into a jog. "Someone ought to teach you to stay out of other folks' business."

Instead of retreating like a sensible woman, Samantha squared off with the fellow, her voice vibrating with indignation. "What was it you said to Ida Mae? Oh yes. 'You ruined yourself.'" She jutted her chin. "Doesn't feel good to be on the receiving end of censure, does it? Your own choices and bad acts have brought about your demise, Mr. Thompson. Nothing else. You are finally reaping what you have sown."

"Shut up, you slanderin' hussy!" He lunged forward and grabbed hold of her wrist. "You're gonna pay for what you done to me."

Samantha tried to pull free of his grasp, but he held firm. "Let me go!" she cried.

Asher heard the tremor of fear beneath the anger in her voice, and flames flared inside him as if someone had just thrown kerosene on his campfire.

Jack hopped off the fence, ready to do battle, but Asher caught his attention and waved him off as he slowed his approach and planted himself at Samantha's side.

"Release her." Asher's low voice resonated with authority.

The drunken cowboy's eyes widened for a second before they narrowed into stubborn slits. "Step aside, stranger. This ain't none of your concern."

"Any lady being threatened is my concern. Now release her."

Red-rimmed eyes stared Asher down as Thompson's bravado battled with whatever common sense hadn't yet pickled inside his brain.

Asher didn't like to fight, but he could hold his own when the occasion called for it, and if this lout of a cowboy didn't let go of Samantha's arm in three seconds, Asher was going to answer that call by breaking Thompson's nose.

"One . . . two . . ."

"Fine!" Thompson threw Samantha's arm away from him with such force, she stumbled back a step.

Asher took the opportunity to angle himself in front of her, but he didn't turn to check on her. His focus remained locked on the threat as he thrust his face an inch from Thompson's. The sour smell of whiskey turned his stomach, but he steeled himself against the fumes. "Touch her again—ever—and I'll break that hand so badly you'll never rope another steer. Got it?"

Thompson's Adam's apple bobbed, but the defiant light in his eyes didn't dim. He backed up a step, though, and lifted the bottle to his mouth. He took a long swig, then offered a parting jab. "You ain't always going to be around, cowboy." He shifted his gaze to Samantha as he staggered away. "Watch your back, missy. What goes around, comes around."

Asher kept his eye on Thompson until the man made it back to the saloon and gathered his horse. Took him three tries to get his foot in the stirrup, but he eventually found his way into the saddle and set off down the road.

The instant Thompson turned the corner and disappeared behind one of the buildings, Asher pivoted to face Samantha. "Are you all right?" He didn't like the way she was rubbing her wrist. "He hurt you, didn't he?"

She shook her head, not meeting his gaze. "It's just a little sore. I'll be fine." She lifted her head and scowled in the direction Thompson had left. "I hope he keeps riding and never comes back."

"Men say thickheaded things when they're drunk." The threats Thompson made rang loud in his ears. How much louder must they be ringing in hers? "Whiskey loosens their tongue and props them up with false courage. When he sobers up, he'll regret his words against you."

"If he even remembers them," Jack muttered as he joined their little circle.

"Oh, I'm not worried about myself," Samantha protested. "It's Ida Mae I'm concerned about. If Leroy blames me for losing his job, he might blame her even more. And she doesn't have two strong Ellis men to protect her like I do." She grinned brightly at Jack, then aimed a slightly more serious look of gratitude in Asher's direction.

His chest ached with the urge to pledge to protect her always. But he kept his jaw locked down until the words dissolved on his tongue. He was in no position to make her any promises. Not now. Maybe not ever.

"Who's Ida Mae?" Jack asked.

"A friend of mine who was treated poorly by that man." Her face scrunched in distaste. It didn't take much imagination on Asher's part to surmise what that poor treatment entailed. "But if everything goes according to plan, she won't have to worry about him anymore." Her eyes brightened. "Daddy gave me permission to hire her on at the Three Cedars as a housemaid and assistant cook. She and Jimmy will be safe from Leroy there."

"You should still let your father know about the threats." Asher collected her hand and smoothed the pad of his thumb over the red marks on her wrist. The idea of her being in any kind of danger rattled him more than he wanted to admit. "I doubt anything will come of it," he said as he gently released her hand, "but it's always better to be prepared than taken by surprise."

Her eyes met his, and his gut tightened.

"I will." Her soft voice roughened slightly, and the sound set his blood to pumping as if he were sprinting down a hill instead of standing perfectly still in the middle of the street.

"I, uh, better get back to the livery." Jack retreated. The teasing look in his eyes as he glanced from Asher to Samantha made Asher want to throw his brother in the nearest trough, but thankfully, Samantha didn't seem to comprehend the implication.

"Wait!" She grabbed Jack's hand and drew him back. "Before you go, I've got news." She glanced back at Asher, her eyes dancing with the kind of joyous secrets that usually only came on Christmas morning. "I've secured permission for us to work your mother's garden!"

"What?" Asher's world tilted slightly off-balance.

Samantha practically bounced where she stood. "Isn't it wonderful? No one has rented the property yet, so Daddy didn't see a reason to deny the request. I have to be there to represent the Three Cedars to keep anyone from claiming theft, and the house will remain locked, but that shouldn't cause any difficulty. I just came from visiting with your mother. She thinks that working a couple mornings a week would be sufficient to get the garden back into shape. I know the two of you won't be able to help because of your other responsibilities, but I'll lend a hand, and if Ida Mae takes the job I offer, she can help, too. Fergus can keep an eye on Jimmy while we ladies work. My knowledge of gardening is woefully inadequate, but your mother assures me it's easy to learn. I'm rather looking forward to it, if you can believe it."

Believe it? He could barely comprehend it.

Asher traded a look with Jack, both of them unable to do more than stand there and blink. One didn't often witness miracles packaged in fancy blue dresses.

20

Samantha drove the half mile out to Ida Mae's home, trying to convince her pulse to return to normal after her encounter with Asher. One would expect her run-in with Leroy to have the more unsettling effect, but memories of Asher's staunch defense and tender care had her pulse skipping more beats than a one-handed drummer.

He'd insisted on walking her back to his mother's place to collect her wagon. He didn't have much to say during their stroll, but that didn't dim the pleasure she took in his company. Asher was the kind of man to warm a lady's heart just by standing at her side. No poetic words or sophisticated airs required. His eyes said everything her heart longed to hear. They glowed with respect, with protective concern, and with a heated interest that would have had her scrambling for her hand fan had she been in a ballroom instead of on a dusty Texas street.

For the first time since her father broached the subject of marriage, the idea didn't completely leave her cold. Not if Asher Ellis presented himself as a matrimonial candidate.

Easy, girl. You just met the man.

Yet she felt like she'd known him so much longer. Like a sauce that had reduced down to a thick syrup, they might not have a large volume of shared experiences, but those they did have had been concentrated for maximum potency. She'd been courted by enough men to know that what she felt for Asher was special. Worth investigating at the very least. Maybe even worth nurturing, to see how deep the roots might grow.

Hard to nurture a relationship with a man living three counties away, though. She had no connections in Callahan County, no relative or friend there to provide an excuse for her to visit. And from what she'd gathered from talking with his mother, Asher didn't come home to Palo Pinto very often. The next couple of weeks might be all the time she had with him.

Unless he left the Bar 7 and came to work for her father.

Her thoughts skidded to a halt. The Three Cedars *did* have a newly vacated position. Would Asher be interested in a change of scenery? Her heartbeat kicked into a trot at the notion of having him nearby on a more permanent basis. Until she recalled her father's strict policy against any of his hired men fraternizing with his daughter. Ugh. Which was worse—not seeing Asher for months at a time, or seeing him but not being allowed to pursue a relationship with him? Samantha frowned, uninspired by either option.

Reining the team of Morgans to the right, she drove the buckboard down the rutted path that led to the Forrester homestead and forced thoughts of Asher from her mind. Ida Mae hadn't been overly pleased with Samantha's interference in her business yesterday. She'd likely resent her interference today as well. Nevertheless, Samantha intended to stick her nose right back into her friend's private affairs no matter how uncomfortable it proved to either of them. The stakes were too high to let comfort dictate her level of involvement.

The creaking wagon wood and jangling harness must have

announced her arrival, for the front door opened. Matilda Forrester stepped onto the porch, lifting a hand to her forehead to shade her eyes.

"Bless my buttons! Is that Samantha Dearing come to call?" A grin spread across her face like an unfurling welcome flag. She reached behind her back to untie her apron, then draped it over the railing as she hurried down the steps. "Heavens to Betsy, girl. I haven't seen you for ages. What a fine Boston lady you've turned into."

Samantha chuckled as she reined in the team and set the brake. "Don't let the dress fool you. I'm the same headstrong scamp I've always been." She winked at her friend's mother. "No Boston polish can change that."

"No, I don't suppose it could."

Samantha climbed down from the wagon and clasped the woman's hands. "It's good to see you again, Mrs. Forrester."

Matilda's smile slowly faded. "Ida Mae mentioned that she saw you in town yesterday. It's good of you to come by the house. Friends have been in short supply the last couple years."

"I hope I can change that." Samantha pivoted and gestured to the back of the wagon with a sweep of her arm. "I have a box of some of Clint's old baby clothes. I thought Jimmy might be able to use them."

"Well, that sure is kind of you." Mrs. Forrester followed Samantha to the back of the wagon. "Take 'em on up to the house. Ida Mae's hangin' the wash out back. I'll go spell her and give the two of you a chance to talk."

Samantha lifted the large bandbox over the side of the wagon and carried it through the front door. Recalling the location of the parlor from when she'd visited years ago, she found her way into the cozy little den at the front of the house and set the box on the side table next to the settee. The room looked much as she remembered it. Seating for four near the hearth, a floral-patterned rug, a pair of mismatched lamps, a knitting basket next to the chair on the left. Mrs. Forrester always had some kind of project in the works. Afghan, scarf, sweater. The woman never sat idle in the evenings. One of her knitted throws was draped over the back of the settee, its colorful rows of alternating blues, greens, and browns bringing a cheerful richness to a room that had started to fade with age.

The sound of a door closing somewhere at the back of the house tightened the knots in Samantha's stomach as she pivoted to face the doorway. Every footstep that echoed against a floorboard caused her heart to pound a little harder in her chest.

Ida Mae swept into the parlor, her mouth turned down in irritation. "What are you doing here, Samantha? I don't have time for social calls."

Jimmy sat on her hip, his eyes wide, his middle two fingers stuck in his mouth. Ida Mae brushed the hair out of his eyes, then used the edge of her apron to wipe his nose when she noticed it running. She took care to ensure her son looked presentable but made no effort to remove her smudged, damp apron or tuck away the strands of dark chestnut hair the afternoon wind had tugged free of her braid. Her defiant gaze dared Samantha to comment on her appearance.

She wouldn't, of course. Ida Mae had dealt with enough criticism from townsfolk and even her own father. Besides, her appearance showed her to be exactly who she was—a hardworking mother doing everything she could to provide for her son. There was an honor to be found there that no fashion plate could replicate.

Samantha dug out a smile from her emergency supply of pleasant-expressions-for-any-social-occasion and slapped it on her face. "I went through some of Clint's old baby clothes last night and set aside some things I thought Jimmy might be able to use." She gestured to the bandbox on the side table. "There are some larger sizes in there as well." Samantha took a chance by stepping closer to Ida Ma and rubbing Jimmy's back. "I remember how fast little boys grow out of everything.

"Isn't that right, little man?" Samantha diverted her attention to the friendly face *not* glaring at her. "All you do is grow . . . grow . . . grow." The pitch of her voice rose as she walked her fingers up his arm, and she bopped the tip of his nose with her fingertip. He grinned, and drool stretched from his fingers as he pulled them out of his mouth.

He twisted to face her. "'Gin!"

Happy to oblige, Samantha walked her fingers down his arm, this time veering toward his chubby belly. "I know how to slow your growing. Tummy tickles!" Her fingers wiggled against his belly, and baby giggles filled the room with sweet music.

Samantha glanced up at her friend to find the defiance had disappeared from her gaze, replaced by motherly indulgence. "May I hold him?"

Ida Mae nibbled her lip. "He might fuss. Jimmy's not used to being held by anyone other than me or his granny."

"I'm not afraid of a little temper. Besides"—she turned her attention back to the toddler waving a slobbery hand through the air—"Jimmy and I are going to be great friends, aren't we?" Samantha held her hands out, and Jimmy leaned toward her, his trust absolute.

Ida Mae loosened her hold, and Samantha fit her hands to Jimmy's stocky torso. Memories washed over her in a powerful wave. Memories of Mother showing Samantha how to hold her baby brother. Of climbing into Clint's bed after Mother passed, trying to comfort them both and feeling the weight of responsibility slide onto her ten-year-old shoulders. He was hers now, to protect and nurture, to love, and to guide.

Sure, there'd been moments when she'd resented having such responsibility thrust upon her, but she never resented him. He held too much of her heart.

How much stronger must the bond be between actual mother and son?

Samantha played with Jimmy for several minutes, tickling, swinging, and bouncing until he squirmed and demanded to be let down. She lowered him to the rug, and he immediately scampered over to Ida Mae and hid behind her skirt. Once there, he consented to a few rounds of peekaboo before abandoning Samantha altogether.

All in all, a favorable first encounter. One of many to come, she hoped.

Ida Mae lifted out a tiny suit of short pants and matching jacket from the floral-patterned bandbox and turned to Samantha. "These clothes are too fine for the likes of us."

"Nonsense. They're just clothes. Meant to get dirty like any other."

"I don't think I can accept them. Jimmy's bound to tear them up or stain them beyond repair."

Samantha stepped closer and placed a hand on her friend's arm. "I don't care what happens to the clothes, Ida Mae. I care about what happens to your son. These garments have plenty of wear left in them. Take them. Please."

Ida Mae's eyes glistened, but she nodded as she folded the suit back up and returned it to the box. "Thank you." Her voice wavered slightly.

"I have something else to offer you. Something that wouldn't fit into the bandbox."

Ida Mae's face swiveled toward Samantha. Her brows lifted.

"A job. At the Three Cedars. Helping Mrs. Stewart with the cooking and keeping house. Jimmy can come, too. There's a spare room off the kitchen. It's small, but it stays nice and warm in the winter. Daddy would pay you ten dollars a month on top of room and board. Mrs. Stewart loves children, and I just know she'll dote on Jimmy. You can start as soon as you like. Monday, even."

Ida Mae started shaking her head, and Samantha scrambled to adjust her argument.

"Or you can wait. You still have a few months to enjoy being at home with your mother. The job will be there whenever you—"

"I can't." A tear trailed down Ida Mae's cheek as her head wagged. "Heaven knows I want to. A job and a roof over our heads? Mama and I have been praying for the Lord to open a door somewhere. But not at the Three Cedars. Not with Leroy there. Smirking at me every day. Tellin' tales about me in the bunkhouse. I don't want my son growing up to think his mama's a . . . a loose woman."

Samantha bit back a groan at her own thoughtlessness. How could she have forgotten the most important point?

"Leroy Thompson no longer works at the Three Cedars."

Ida Mae's head came up with a sharp jerk. "What?"

"My father fired him last night after finding him . . . engaged in unsanctioned behavior on Three Cedars property."

Ida Mae's expression hardened. "Engaged with a woman, you mean."

Samantha nodded.

"Where were they?"

Heat climbed up Samantha's cheeks. "In a small cabin over by Dry Creek Gulch."

A bitter laugh echoed loudly in the quiet room. "The love shack? Oh, that's rich. He bragged all the time about how secret that place was, how not even Eli Dearing knew it existed." She raised a brow. "How'd your father find him?"

"Let's just say his bragging came back to haunt him."

Ida Mae didn't need to know about Clint. Goodness, Samantha was still scandalized over her little brother knowing about the goings on in that cabin. Best not to give Ida Mae any other potential reasons to balk at accepting the position.

Satisfaction over Leroy's downfall hardened Ida Mae's face for a moment, but in a blink her expression softened, and Samantha saw the friend of her childhood reflected in the woman before her. "You did this, didn't you?"

Embarrassed, Samantha shrugged. "I might have planted the bug in Daddy's ear that Leroy's character did not reflect well on the Three Cedars brand."

A twinkle danced in Ida Mae's moisture-filled eyes. "Planted a bug, huh? If I know you, that bug was the size of an elephant."

"Ida Mae Forrester! Are you implying I lack the feminine grace of nuanced conversation?"

Ida Mae chuckled. "Nuance has never been your gift, Sam. But defending those who are fortunate enough to call you friend?" Her face sobered. "That's where you excel." She clasped Samantha's hand and squeezed it tightly. "I'll never be able to thank you enough for what you've done for me and Jimmy."

Now Samantha was the one with damp eyes. She blinked as she squeezed her friend's hand in return. "My father is the one who deserves your thanks. The job offer was his idea."

"I'll be sure to thank him on Monday when I show up for work."

Samantha left the Forresters' house feeling lighter than she had in ages. She hummed a jaunty tune as she drove the wagon home, her mind busy making plans for sprucing up the room off the kitchen before the new occupants arrived. Distracted as she was, she didn't hear the hooves of the galloping horse behind her until the rider was practically upon her. She tightened her grip on the reins, determined to keep the Morgans to a walk. One runaway carriage in her lifetime was plenty.

The reckless cowboy seemed to slow just a bit as he drew abreast of her. Samantha glanced to her left. He looked like a bandit—black bandanna tied around his face, black hat pulled low over his eyes. He raised his arm. Samantha gasped and turned her face away. But it must not have been a gun in his hand, for a burlap sack dropped onto her feet an instant before the horse and mysterious rider sped away.

Heart about to beat out of her chest, Samantha reined in the Morgans as she examined the sack at her feet.

Something inside it moved.

Yelping, Samantha shifted in her seat, ready to kick whatever it was out of the wagon and into the road.

Then she heard the rattle, and every muscle in her body froze.

21

The burlap undulated with the snake's movements. The top of the sack gaped open. Any moment now, the rattler would find his way out. Should she stay still and pray it mistook her for a rock and slither away? Would it be better to kick the sack out of the wagon and hope it didn't land close to the horses? Or maybe she should try to ease her feet out from under the sack, climb over the seat into the wagon bed, and escape out the back.

Indecision tormented her. Too many things could go wrong no matter what she chose. All she knew for sure was that her shoes and skirts offered more protection than her thin sleeves, so she released the reins and drew her arms up toward her head. She'd just about decided to try to ease her feet out from under the sack when the head of the snake emerged dangerously close to her ankle.

The brownish-gray triangular head loomed large in her vision. Nearly the size of her fist, it pushed the burlap aside and led the way for the rest of its oversized body to wriggle free.

Samantha prayed the creature would simply dismount the

wagon and escape onto the prairie, but instead of taking the straight path to freedom, it curled around behind her heel.

What if it climbed up her skirts? The terrifying thought nearly unseated her.

Don't move. Don't move. Don't move.

The meditation didn't steady her pulse. Her heart pounded harder and harder until she found it difficult to breathe. Foot after foot of scaly diamondback serpent slithered from the sack and disappeared beneath her skirt. The vile thing had to be at least five feet long. She could feel it moving. Over her shoes. Around her ankle. Rustling the fabric of her petticoats.

Something brushed against her calf, above the top of her left shoe.

Samantha whimpered, then pressed her lips together and squeezed her eyes closed.

Take it away, God, please. I can't bear it.

Terror built inside her, urging her to flee. But she held firm, heeding the tiny scrap of logic that remained in her possession. Stillness gave her the best chance to survive. Do nothing to make the snake feel threatened.

But what if the creature tangled in her skirts and couldn't find its way out? What if it was drawn to her warmth and decided to curl up and take a nap?

One of the Morgans tossed its head and stomped a hoof. Samantha's eyes flew open.

Merciful heavens. What if the horses jostled the wagon?

Tears filled her eyes. Her chest throbbed. Her soul cried for rescue.

Panic wound its tentacles around her mind, cutting off her access to rational thought. The weight of it threatened to pull her under. She needed to get away. Now!

She clutched the seat back and prepared to jump up onto the bench. But a movement caught her eye. The snake's head emerged from beneath her skirt on the far side of her right foot. Samantha held her breath but not her prayers as a few ounces of sanity returned. The rattler was leaving. Its long body still slithered between her calf and ankle, but its head dipped over the far side of the wagon and disappeared.

Yes. Oh, please. Go!

The body followed. All five feet of scaly horror along with its rattled tip. Inch by excruciating inch it stretched over the wagon side until finally sliding completely from view.

The instant it vanished, Samantha kicked the empty burlap sack off her feet, her movements jerky and clumsy as desperation fogged her brain. A ravaged mewl vibrated her throat as her feet thrashed until the unholy sack fluttered to the ground. Arms shaking, she snatched the reins and slapped the lines across the Morgans' backs.

"Yah!"

She raced for home as if the snake were giving chase. Tears streamed down her face, and her knees knocked together. A chill settled over her body, exacerbating her tremors and deepening the sense of isolation that gripped her heart.

One of her father's hands must've spotted her wild approach, for two gunshots rang out in quick succession, the signal that trouble was upon them. From the corner of her eye, she spotted Daddy on his big bay gelding riding in at a gallop from the front pasture. Never had she wanted him more.

She reined in her team and scrambled out of the wagon the instant the horses stopped. Picking up her skirt, she ran across the field, straight for her daddy, sobbing as she ran.

A few yards from her, Eli Dearing leapt from his saddle and ran to her. "Sam! What hap—?"

She threw herself against his chest, cutting off his question and forcing him to stagger backward in order to catch his balance. But none of that mattered. All that mattered was her daddy was here, and she didn't have to be afraid anymore.

As if her body had taken in a poison that had to be expelled, she latched on to her father's waist and bawled it all out. His arms came around her. Strong. Warm. Supporting her as she trembled. The anchor in her storm.

She heard the arrival of other horses, heard men asking questions about an attack. Samantha kept her face buried in her father's chest, hiding and wishing everyone away.

Daddy's deep voice vibrated his chest beneath her ear as he spoke, instructing Martin to see to the wagon and warning the others to stay vigilant as they returned to their duties. Saddle leather creaked. Hooves thumped. Murmurs of assent echoed. Then all fell quiet, the hiccups of her subsiding sobs and her father's steady heartbeat the only sounds remaining.

He asked no questions. Didn't even urge her to hush. He just held her until her supply of tears ran dry.

The hand rubbing circles on her back slowed. "You ain't hurt anywhere, are you?"

She shook her head as she sniffed and finally found the strength to stand on her own. Straightening, she rubbed the wetness from her cheeks with the backs of her hands.

"Here." A white handkerchief appeared, and she accepted it with gratitude.

After wiping her eyes dry and blowing her nose several times, she crumpled the wadded linen into her fist and squeezed it tightly.

She inhaled a shaky breath, then stiffened her spine as she lifted her chin to meet her father's concerned gaze. "Someone tried to kill me, Daddy."

His eyes widened in shock before a storm cloud darkened his features. "Tell me exactly what happened."

She did, though she didn't really have any helpful details to share. She hadn't recognized the man. Nor the horse. Nothing about either stood out in her memory besides the fact that the cowboy had been dressed almost fully in black. His horse had been brown with a black tail and mane. Other than that, all she recalled was the snake.

"I was so scared, Daddy." Tears threatened to return, but she forced them back.

Until her stone-faced father grabbed her and nearly hugged the breath right out of her body. "I could have lost you, girl." His voice cracked, and Samantha's heart throbbed as the truth of his love seeped into all her cracks and crevices.

He held her away from him, his eyes scouring her as if searching for bite marks that could have been.

"I'm all right, Daddy." The words felt good to say. So good, in fact, she said them again. "I'm all right."

She *was* all right. She wouldn't be surprised to wake up tomorrow morning and find her hair had turned gray overnight from the fright she'd endured, but thanks to God's provision, that's all it had been—a fright. She'd suffered no physical harm.

"Who would do such a thing?" Her father scowled as he released his hold on her and balled his hands into fists. "I might credit a prank of some kind if there'd been a garter or bull snake in the sack, but a rattler? That's too malicious to be a prank. And too targeted to be random. But why would any man want to hurt you? You're not a threat to anyone."

Memories of angry accusations and a vow for retribution set Samantha's legs to trembling anew.

"Leroy Thompson might disagree."

A muscle ticked in her father's jaw. "You think Leroy did this?"

Samantha shrugged. "I ran into him in town earlier today. He was drunk and none too pleased about my interference in his affairs. Blamed me for losing his job. Threatened to make me pay." Her stomach knotted at the memory until a better recollection surfaced and smoothed out the wrinkles. "Asher Ellis happened across us and took up for me. Leroy backed down after that and slunk away. The man was so drunk it took him three tries to mount his horse."

That particular detail brought a frown to her face.

"Maybe it *wasn't* Leroy." Samantha fiddled with the wadded handkerchief in her hand. "He looked about ready to pass out last I saw him. He'd be in no condition to make such a ride barely an hour later."

Her father crossed his arms over his broad chest. "He coulda hired someone to do it. If he knew you were in town, he could have set someone to watch you, then strike when you were halfway between town and home, where you'd be least likely to find help."

A new chill passed over Samantha's skin at the calculated nature of such a plan. How cold-blooded would someone have to be to plot to take another's life? Did Leroy truly hate her that much?

"Or what about that fella that trespassed the night of the ball?" His frown deepened. "We got no way of knowing what that scoundrel was truly after. I figured he was after money or legal papers of some sort since we found him in my study, but maybe when he didn't find what he was looking for, he decided to go after you."

Samantha hadn't thought of her bootless cowboy in days. Now that she'd met Asher, her obsession with the faceless man seemed a bit naïve, but she still couldn't imagine that the man who'd saved her brother's life would deliberately try to take hers.

"What would he gain from killing me? If he wanted money, kidnapping and demanding a ransom would be a more logical choice. Besides, the man from the ball saved Clint's life. He had a conscience. A code. It doesn't make sense that he would turn so vengeful as to commit murder."

"A lot of things in this world don't make sense. Especially killin'. The truth is, we got no idea who that intruder was or what he'd come here to do. That means he's a suspect. One I plan to report to the sheriff."

Samantha wanted to argue but couldn't think of a logical rationale to present. As her father had said before, a woman's intuition wasn't proof.

"I ought to pack you up and send you back to Boston," her father grumbled. "Ain't no rattlesnakes there."

There was no Asher Ellis there, either. No big-hearted daddy who let his grown daughter cry all over him when she was scared. No baby brother to watch grow into manhood. No Ida Mae, Jimmy, or Jack. No Fergus with his imaginative stories or Mama Bess with her garden.

"Texas is my home, Daddy." Her words might have been soft, but they carried weight from the certainty of her decision. "Snakes and all."

The edge of her father's mouth turned up at one corner. "Figured you'd say that." He raised a brow. "Don't reckon you'd agree to me locking you in your room until the sheriff runs down the varmint who tried to hurt you, either?"

She grinned as she wagged her head slowly from side to side. "Nope."

"Didn't think so." He uncrossed his arms and scratched a spot on the side of his neck. "What about staying with your Aunt Regina for a spell? It'd keep you off that stretch of road where you seem particularly prone to mishap of late."

The idea had merit. She'd be closer to Asher and the rest of the Ellises. She could walk wherever she needed to go, a rather attractive prospect after the two vehicle mishaps she'd experienced. But no. She needed to be at the Three Cedars.

"I'm staying here, Daddy. Ida Mae plans to start work on Monday, and I want to be here to help her get settled."

That muscle in his jaw ticked again. "You're a stubborn little thing. You know that?"

Samantha smiled. "I get it from my father."

Eli chuckled as he wrapped an arm around his daughter's shoulders and started steering her toward the house. "Don't be so sure. Your mama could be mighty headstrong when she set her mind to something."

So Samantha was coming to discover.

They walked several steps in silence, Samantha enjoying the shelter of his arm. Up ahead, she spied Clint in the doorway of the barn. Martin stood beside him, pointing in their direction. Her time alone with her father would be ending soon.

She slowed her step and turned to the man she was finally starting to understand. "Thank you," she said. "For being my daddy, even after all the grief I caused you over the years."

A sheen came into his eyes, but he blinked it away as he hugged her shoulders. "Only natural for a spirited filly to kick and buck a bit as she's learnin' her way. Don't make me love her any less. In fact, it makes me right proud to see that fire in her eyes. Means she's strong. Won't let the world beat her down."

Samantha dipped her chin. "I didn't feel strong in the wagon. I felt helpless and terrified."

"Look at me, girl."

She raised her gaze.

"Feeling fear don't make you weak. It makes you human. Bein' strong means you don't let fear dictate your actions. You kept your head out there. Sure, you were scared. I woulda been, too. But you lassoed that fright and kept it tied down until it was safe to let it go. I'm proud of how you handled yourself."

The last of the chill left her bones as his words wrapped around her heart.

"But that don't mean I ain't gonna take a few extra precautions moving forward." His stern look warned her not to argue. "You aren't to go to town without an escort. That Ellis fellow can see you home, but one of my men will ride with you into town from here on out until we catch the scoundrel who attacked you."

Samantha certainly wasn't eager to make that trip to town again by herself, but she couldn't help worrying about what having an escort might mean for her riding lessons. She had less than two weeks to determine if Asher Ellis might be the man for her. She couldn't forfeit her time with him, but neither could she make herself a target for Leroy or whoever wanted her dead.

She might have to solicit some help. And the young man heading her way might be just the ally she needed.

22

Are you humming?"

Asher squinted through the suds on his face to find Fergus squatting near his knee and peering up at him as if he'd never seen a man wash up on the back porch before. The tuneful vibrations resonating in Asher's throat cut off abruptly.

"Mama says if a fella is humming, it's likely he's got a gal on his mind. You got a gal on your mind, Ash?"

Why the good Lord thought giving little brothers an extra helping of curiosity was a good idea, Asher would never understand. Didn't big brothers have enough to do with protecting and providing to deserve a break when it came to provoking personal questions?

Fergus tugged on Asher's trouser leg. "Do ya? Have a gal on your mind?"

Instead of answering, Asher scooped a handful of water from the basin and tossed it at Fergus's head.

His little brother squealed and scampered backward, but the dousing proved an insufficient deterrent.

"You do!" Fergus shook water from his head like a dog, then

slapped his hands to his knees and continued his interrogation. "Who is she? Do I know her?"

Asher bit back a groan and squeezed his eyes closed as he cupped both hands in the water and rinsed his face before he ended up half-blind from soap sting.

"Are you on your way to see her? Is that why you quit workin' on the roof an hour before supper?"

Asher lathered a cloth and rubbed it over his chest, belly, and arms before giving his armpits a good scrub. "I've got an appointment, that's all."

"With a *girl*?"

Water hadn't slowed the questions. Maybe a soggy cloth filled with sweat stink would do the trick. Asher launched the rag at Fergus's head, but the kid managed to dodge, leaving the wet cloth to splat on the porch floor.

"I'm meeting a friend, if you must know." Asher reached for the towel he'd draped over the side railing and ran it over his face.

"A *girl* friend?"

Asher sighed into the towel before dragging it down his torso. "You know, if your story writing career doesn't work out, you should look into lawyering."

Triumph gleamed in Fergus's eyes. "I knew it! You *are* going to see a girl."

"It's not what you think," Asher insisted as he hung up the towel and reached for the clean shirt hanging on a peg by the back door. "I'm just giving a friend some riding lessons."

At least that's what he kept telling himself.

"I don't remember you cleaning up special to give me riding lessons last Christmas." Fergus crossed his arms and raised his brows in an admirable imitation of one of Jack's smug expressions.

"That's because it was winter, and I hadn't been baking on

a roof for half the day." Asher pulled on his shirt and shoved his arms through the sleeves, trying not to look at the half-full water basin. The longer Fergus tormented him, the harder it was to remember why he shouldn't dump the remaining contents over his brother's head.

"Is it Darla Washington? I saw her talking to you after church yesterday. Or maybe Felicia Hanson? The way she kept stumbling whenever you were nearby seemed mighty suspicious. The third time she tried, you weren't looking, and old Mr. Drummond had to steady her. She recovered twice as quick when he was the one touching her arm."

Asher had felt a twinge of guilt when he'd pretended not to see Miss Hanson's third stumble yesterday, but his sympathy had run short after her second attempt to secure his assistance. Her obvious ploy left him feeling a bit insulted that she thought so little of his intelligence. Miss Washington exhibited no false artifice, but she also exhibited no restraint in her conversation. The woman could drown a man in the sheer volume of words that poured out of her mouth. If Mama Bess hadn't taken pity on him and called him away, he might still be treading water in that churchyard.

"Is it Miss Dearing?"

The suspenders he'd been stretching up to his right shoulder slipped out of Asher's grasp and snapped against his hip. He winced.

"Aha!" Fergus crowed in triumph as he danced a celebratory jig featuring high knees and wiggling arms. "I guessed it!"

Clenching his jaw, Asher fit his suspenders over his shoulders with mechanical deliberateness. "You can throw out as many female names as you want, Ferg. I ain't gonna tell you anything."

Fergus ceased his dance, but the annoying twinkle in his eyes proved he saw more than Asher would have liked.

"For what it's worth," Fergus said, his boyish face seeming to mature before Asher's eyes, "I like Miss Dearing. And not just because she brings me books and makes yummy cobbler. She's nice to Mama." His gaze shifted to the door that led to the kitchen. "And Mama needs some niceness these days.

"When Miss Dearing came by on Saturday to tell us about the garden, she sat with me while we waited on Mama to finish up her bread kneading. I showed her my stories, and she gave me a new idea for how to add those sewing mice you told me about to my barnyard. She said they could make Mrs. Merriweather a fancy hat in exchange for letting them take shelter in the barn. Once Mrs. Merriweather approves of them, the hens and pigs will follow her lead. But first, she thinks I need a story to explain how the sewing mice come to be here. I had been planning to have a cat chase them out of their old home, but she had an even better idea about an owl who snatches them up and carries them off for his supper. One of the mice jabs him with her needle. The owl screeches and drops them into our trough. Now they have to decide if they want to make a new home in our barnyard or have an adventure trying to find their way back home."

Asher chuckled and ruffled his little brother's hair. Good thing Fergus was easily distracted by story ideas. "Sounds like you'll be busy writing for a few days. You'll have to let me know how it turns out."

Fergus blinked a bit, then focused his gaze once again on Asher. "She's real good at coming up with ideas, Ash. She might even be able to come up with one that lets you stay home for good."

The pang he'd been trying to ignore for the last couple of days intensified a hundredfold. Asher tugged Fergus into a rough embrace and rested his chin on his little brother's head. "I wish livin' life was as easy as writing stories, Ferg. 'Cause there's nothing I'd like more than to be around while you and Jack grow up. To help out Mama Bess and be the family our pa wanted us to be."

Fergus tipped his head back to peer into Asher's face. "We got lots of ranches around here. Maybe you could get a job at one of them, now that you aren't so green."

Asher's chest throbbed with longing. If only it were that easy. "The Bar 7's been good to me. I can't just leave them in a lurch." Although, if they already had a man lined up to fill his position, how much of a lurch would it really be? "I tell you what. While I'm here, I'll ask around. See if there are any openings for positions that can match my current pay. If I find something, I'll give serious consideration to staying. All right?"

The smile on his little brother's face made mincemeat of his heart. "Thanks, Ash!"

"Sure." Asher ruffled the kid's hair a final time.

Fergus pushed Asher's hand away from his head, but his smile lost none of its shine.

Brothers might be a nuisance, but they were a nuisance he wouldn't mind having around a little more often. As Asher rode out to the old mill, family nostalgia kept him distracted until he spotted a fella in cowboy gear keeping Samantha company by her wagon.

Asher frowned. He'd thought she'd wanted these lessons kept private. Why had she invited another man along? And why did Asher have the urge to punch the interloper in the nose?

His jealousy waned when he came close enough to recognize Clinton Dearing, but his gut remained tight. He might not have to worry about any courtship competition from that quarter, but the kid still posed a threat. One he needed to neutralize one of these days if he decided to stick around and make a serious bid for Samantha's hand. He would have to confess his actions on the night of the ball, but not until he had Mama

197

Bess set up. If Eli Dearing chose to make an example of him and have him taken before a judge for trespassing, whatever fine resulted could leave him without the funds necessary to complete the repairs. And if he couldn't afford the resulting fine? Well, he'd want to have the repairs finished before they confiscated his horse and saddle and sent him to a poor farm to work off the remainder of his debt.

Samantha's welcoming smile banished his punitory musings and replaced them with much more pleasant ideas. When she hurried forward to meet him, he immediately dismounted, wishing he could take her hand or set his hand at her back. He did neither of those things, of course, just smiled at her in return.

"Mr. Ellis is here now, Clint," she called over her shoulder. "You can meet up with Martin now and head back to the ranch."

"Not before I have a word." The kid might only be twelve, the same age as Jack, but he carried himself with all the protectiveness of a man fully grown, one determined to watch out for his sister.

Asher could respect that. He'd likely feel the same if he had a sister. He braced his legs apart, ready to accept whatever lecture Clint felt like giving about preserving Samantha's reputation.

"She's not to go anywhere alone."

Whatever Asher had been expecting him to say, *that* definitely wasn't it.

"When she's in town," Clint continued, "we need someone watching over her. She'll be eating dinner at Aunt Regina's house instead of driving home between your riding lessons and her tutoring sessions with Jack. Are you available to keep an eye on her, or do Martin and I need to hang out in town until she's ready to head home tonight?"

"For heaven's sake, Clint, you make me sound like a trouble-some toddler who can't be trusted not to get into mischief the moment your back is turned." Samantha shot Asher an apologetic look before resuming her sisterly admonishment. "Father only wanted me escorted when I traveled between town and the ranch. I'll be perfectly fine in Palo Pinto with all the people about. You don't need to task Mr. Ellis with guard duty. He has enough to do already."

Asher glanced from one to the other before his gaze settled on Samantha. His throat tightened a bit as he squeezed out words he didn't want to believe could be true. "Are you in danger?"

"There was an . . . incident on Saturday when I was driving home."

"It was more than an *incident*." Sarcasm dripped from Clint's voice as he glared at his sister. "It was an attack." He turned to Asher, his face set in uncompromising lines. "Some coward in a mask rode up beside her wagon and threw a sack of rattlers at her feet before galloping away."

"There was only one rattlesnake," Samantha corrected, but her fingers trembled as she raised them to fiddle with the button at the neck of her blouse. "But he was exceptionally large."

Land sakes! She could have been killed. Icy dread hardened his gut, then crept through each limb, leaving an unsettling coldness in its wake. He'd known this woman such a short time, yet imagining his world without her vibrant spirit sparkling in it left a bleak hole in the middle of his chest.

Asher believed in loving his neighbor and turning the other cheek, but at the moment, all he wanted to do was hunt down the man who'd attempted to murder Samantha Dearing and beat him to a bloody pulp.

The vision of a man laying hands on her outside the saloon crystalized in Asher's memory and turned his gut to stone. "Was it Thompson?"

"I don't know." Samantha's calm tone softened the violent edges of his rage. "Nothing about the man who attacked me seemed familiar, but I only got a brief look at him. He wore a bandanna over his face, so I can't even give you an accurate description. Leroy is the only person I can think of who might wish me harm, but he was so drunk on Saturday I don't how he could have pulled it off."

Her gaze finally met his, and Asher's breath left his lungs. The incident had shaken her. Badly. Not just the attack itself, he was sure, but the idea that someone actually wanted her dead. He couldn't imagine what that did to a person. Yet here she stood, out in the open, brave enough to continue living despite all that had happened.

He wanted to pull her into his arms, to comfort both her and himself, but Clint's presence kept his arms hanging dutifully at his sides.

"Daddy reported Leroy to the sheriff this morning," Clint said, "along with the fella who broke into our house on the night of the ball. My money's on Thompson, but until he's caught and confesses, we're taking no chances."

Asher's chest went cold. They suspected the trespasser? He'd never hurt Samantha. Ever. But, of course, they didn't know he and the trespasser were one and the same. And if they thought that intruder capable of murder, confessing could mean a lot more than a fine. It could mean a noose.

But saving his own hide wasn't as important as ensuring Samantha's safety. He might have it on good authority that the trespasser wasn't trying to harm Samantha, but *someone* obviously wished her ill, and Asher wasn't about to leave her exposed to danger if it was in his power to reduce the threat.

He pivoted to face Clint and thrust out his hand. "I'll watch over her. You have my word."

Clint shook on the agreement, then strode to his horse and mounted. "Take care of my sister, Ellis. She means an awful lot to me."

"I will." Asher tugged on his hat brim as the young man rode past.

She means an awful lot to me, too.

23

Asher had proved an effective guard. Maybe too effective. Samantha sighed as she packed a basket filled with ham sandwiches, a cheese wedge, a tin of crackers, hard-boiled eggs, and at least two dozen cookies. A watermelon would be joining the party as well, but it was too heavy to pack in the basket, so it would travel in a separate crate.

The idea of having Asher watch over her had seemed wonderfully romantic yesterday, but the reality failed to live up to her fairy-tale expectations. His vigilance during her riding lesson had left no room for laughter or tender glances. When he wasn't instructing, he was watching—but not her. At least not in the way she wanted him to be watching.

They'd enjoyed a nice moment of connection when she'd taken Bruno's reins on her own for the first time. He'd cheered her progress, and his pride in her achievement softened her heart to the consistency of pudding. And that smile. Intimate warmth had radiated from his eyes as he let his guard down, and in that moment, she'd forgotten about the dark cloud looming over her. Until his smile flattened back into a militant line, and his attention skipped over her to analyze the terrain behind.

On the way home after her tutoring session with Jack, there'd been no soft moments of closeness as the sun set. Asher's gaze constantly scoured the landscape for threats, and his battle-ready mentality had him so stiff, he'd felt as cuddly as a rock when she'd scooted close enough to brush her leg up against his.

Don't be ungrateful. He's trying to protect you. If he didn't care, he wouldn't take his duty so seriously.

Still, a woman with such a short time to determine a man's potential for becoming her forever love match couldn't help wishing the man in question would attend a little more to *her* than the surroundings.

"The lemonade's ready." Ida Mae pulled a long-handled spoon out of the half-full milk can they would use to tote the beverage out to the garden site. She curled her fingers around the handles on either side and braced her legs as she prepared to lift the heavy container out of the sink.

"Let me get that for you." Her father's top ranch hand, his cheeks an intriguing shade of pink, rushed through the open back door to assist.

Martin had been filling the wagon with garden tools a few minutes ago and must have come to the kitchen to see if they were ready to load the food.

"I can manage," Ida Mae insisted, raising the can several inches to prove her point. "I'm stronger than I look."

"I got no doubt about that," Martin said as he reached for the handles himself, "but why tucker yourself out when you can tucker me out instead?"

He grinned, and Samantha swore she saw Ida Mae's lips twitch in response. Until his hands brushed hers. She jerked backward, and the milk can banged down into the sink as she tucked her hands inside her apron.

Samantha pressed her lips together and pointedly turned her attention to the lunch basket. She'd never in her life seen Martin flirt with a girl. He was the quiet type who kept to himself, even at church and town socials. He had to be about ten years older than Ida Mae, but he'd obviously taken a shine to her. Even knowing about Jimmy and, likely, her history with Leroy.

Martin was a hard worker, dependable, and as honorable as the day was long. He'd be good for Ida Mae. If she would allow herself to trust a man again.

Lord, you know what is best. I want so much for Ida Mae to be happy and for Jimmy to have a father who loves him. I don't know if your plans for them include Martin or not, but I ask you to work things together for their good.

And for mine, too.

Why was it easier to trust God to work things together for the good of others than for herself? She believed the Lord was at work in her life, but there was so much uncertainty swirling around her, she felt like she was stumbling around in the dark. How much easier it would be if God would light a lamp and show her the full plan so she could step forward in confidence, knowing she was going the right way.

As she shuffled things around in the picnic basket to give Ida Mae and Martin the illusion of privacy, an unexpected bit of insight materialized in her mind. There must be dozens of ways to pack this basket. Sandwiches could be placed on the top right. Or they could switch places with the boiled eggs. The boiled eggs could be divided up, some on the right and some on the left. The crackers could be taken out of their tin. The cheese could be sliced or left in a large wedge. As the one packing the food, she had the choice of how to place everything. There wasn't only one right way to do it. All the food would still end up at the picnic. Some methods might lead to the food being smashed or spilled, so wisdom certainly played a role in minimizing difficulty, but as long as she followed the prescribed menu and didn't trade out the eggs for rocks or the cheese for a cake of soap, the picnic would still be a success.

Could the same be true of life in general? That the Almighty provided godly parameters for his people but gave them the freedom to choose the details of the paths they walked? She could return to Boston and serve the Lord, or she could serve him here in Texas. She could walk in faith as the wife of a rancher, the wife of a banker, or a single woman who never became a wife at all. Her duty was to seek God first and walk in righteousness, but within those parameters, she could make a hundred different choices that would shape the details of her life in a thousand different ways.

Yet not all of those ways were equally good. Dropping a twenty-pound watermelon on top of her sandwiches would lead to considerable bruising, and taking the crackers out of their tin would end in a crumbly mess.

How I need you, Lord. Your wisdom. Your discernment as I seek the best path for my future. Guide me through the tangle of possibilities I face. Show me what is best, and give me the courage to trust your leading above my own desires and limited understanding.

"Samantha? Did you hear me?"

"Sorry. What?" Samantha lifted her head and pivoted to face Ida Mae, who was giving her a curious look.

She must have been ensconced in her thoughts longer than she realized, for both Martin and the lemonade had disappeared from the kitchen.

"Do you need anything else before I fetch Jimmy? Mrs. Stewart took him to watch the horses while we packed."

Samantha shook her head. "No, I'm done with the basket.

I'll take it out to the wagon, then check on Clint. I'll be ready to leave in five minutes."

"Jimmy and I will wait for you in the wagon."

An idea sparked as Ida Mae turned to leave.

"Why don't you and Jimmy ride in the front?" Samantha called after her. "I'll ride in the back and make sure the lemonade doesn't spill."

Martin had been assigned escort duty for their excursion today and would be driving the wagon. Samantha had no doubt which lady he'd prefer to join him on the driver's bench.

"I don't think—"

"It'll be safer for Jimmy," Samantha argued. "Keep him away from the trowels and hoes and such. Plus, he likes the horses."

Ida Mae dropped her protest, but she shot Samantha a look that clearly said she was aware of her friend's meddling and did not approve.

Samantha bit back a smile as she hooked her arm through the basket handle and lifted it off the table. She followed Ida Mae out of the house and into the yard, where the wagon waited. Ida Mae veered right, keeping her eyes glued to the paddock fence where Mrs. Stewart stood behind Jimmy, holding him safely in place as he sat on the top rail, jabbering happily and clapping chubby hands together in delight.

Martin followed Ida Mae's progress with his eyes, barely sparing Samantha a glance when she swung the picnic basket over the side of the wagon and settled it in the bed.

"We'll be ready to go in a couple minutes, Martin. I just want to check on Clint first."

The man tore his gaze away from Ida Mae long enough to nod. "The team and I are ready whenever you need us."

"Thank you. And thank you for being willing to ride as escort for us today. I know cattlemen typically disdain farmwork, so I appreciate your sacrifice."

"Ain't no hardship, Miss Dearing. The way I see it, it's more like a paid holiday. Can't remember the last time I went on a picnic."

Samantha smiled. "Well, I hope you're able to enjoy yourself."

"Be hard not to." His gaze slipped back over to the corral, and Samantha took that as her cue to leave.

Clint had started his swimming lessons with Duke that week. They spent an hour in the pond each morning before resuming their usual duties. Clint hadn't gotten up the nerve to get out of the shallows yet—likely, the memories of his near drowning were still too fresh—but he'd mastered floating yesterday and hoped to add some leg action today. As Samantha circled the side of the house, the sound of splashing brought a grin to her face. Her brother was definitely moving something.

When she reached the pond, she found Duke standing in chest-deep water, his dark hair slicked back from his face, his arms extended in front of him, his hands clasped around Clint's wrists.

"Don't bend your arms. Keep 'em long. That's it. Blow the water outta your nose, then turn your head to take a breath. Good." He walked the length of the pond backward, leading Clint along. "Easy with them kicks, boy. This ain't a race. You wanna be relaxed in the water. Controlled. You don't wanna wear yourself out before you get where you're tryin' to go."

"How's he doing?" Samantha called.

Duke twisted to meet her gaze, then grinned, his pride in Clint's growing proficiency obvious. "Look fer yourself. We'll have him dog-paddlin' on his own by the end of the week."

Clint's head popped out of the water. "Is that Samantha?" His eyes remained closed as he groped for Duke's shoulder. He pulled the older man's shirt down so that it gaped enough at the neck to expose a patch of skin several shades lighter than the tan of his face, neck, and forearms. Duke was quick to straighten his shirt and keep himself decently covered in the presence of a lady. At least as decent as one could be in such a soggy state. Clint, on the other hand, gave his state of undress absolutely no consideration as he raised a bare arm out of the water to wave at his sister.

"Did you see me, Sam? Duke says I'm pickin' it up really fast." His smile was so wide it made her heart ache with gladness. All hints of the overprotective brother worried for her safety had disappeared, replaced by a boy excited by his accomplishments. Exactly how it should be.

"You're doing great! Maybe one day you'll be good enough to teach me."

He stood a little taller in the water, his shoulders just far enough above the surface for her to make out the small crescent-shaped birthmark directly beneath his collarbone. It had been bright red when he'd been born but had faded to a dull brick color over time. Mother hadn't liked the blemish and had asked Mrs. Stewart to handle bathing and dressing the baby. Samantha would help sometimes, and one day she'd asked Mrs. Stewart about the mark. The housekeeper had said it was where the angels had kissed him. Samantha had been rather jealous after that, especially when a search in her own bath had turned up no angel-kissed places on her skin. Eventually, of course, she'd learned that it was simply a birthmark. Nothing inherently ugly or blessed about it. It was just a part of her brother, like his big heart and long feet.

"Where're you off to today?" Duke asked, his expression reverting back to the formal lines typical of her interactions with him. He'd always treated Clint with warmth and familiarity while treating her with cool aloofness. She supposed that was natural since he spent his days mentoring her brother in the skills of ranching while she remained uninvolved on the sidelines.

"We're heading to the old Ellis place," Samantha replied with a matching level of polite detachment. "Daddy gave me permission to help Mrs. Ellis try to revitalize the garden there."

Her brother's smile flattened a bit. "Martin's going with you, right?"

"Yes, as is Ida Mae and half the Ellis family. I'll be fine. We're taking lunch with us, so you can expect me back early afternoon." She made a shooing motion with her hand. "Go back to your lessons."

Clint's eyes didn't leave hers, and an odd sense of foreboding wiggled down her spine. "Stay safe, sis."

"You too. Don't go drinking half the pond again, all right?" She teased him, hoping to dissipate the uneasiness that had snuck up on her, but it lingered all the way to the Ellis farm.

24

Elizabeth Ellis's gentle grace had never been more evident than while she walked the rows of her garden. Samantha marveled at her optimism in the face of such bleakness. Knee-high weeds, shriveled vegetables crawling with insects, dead vines covered in yellowed leaves. Samantha had been utterly depressed at the scene. Yet Asher's stepmother's eyes twinkled with delight over each discovery she unearthed.

Clad in a wide-brimmed straw hat, work apron, and garden gloves, Mrs. Ellis looked completely at home in the half-acre plot while Samantha felt as if she were visiting a foreign land. She recognized the dried-out corn stalks at the back of the plot, but the rest of the plants blended together in a leafy mess her untrained eyes were unable to sort. Afraid she'd uproot plants instead of weeds, Samantha volunteered for water duty, filling the large watering can Mrs. Ellis had brought and traipsing back and forth from the garden to the pump. Martin manned the hoe and shoveled out the worst of the bug-eaten produce while Elizabeth and Ida Mae hand-pulled the smaller weeds among the plants and harvested whatever edible vegetables they could find.

The sun shone brightly, quickly warming the cool morning

air into something more oppressive. Samantha's steps began to drag. She swore the watering can weighed twice as much on her sixth trip as it had on her first. Pausing in the shade of the house, she set the can down and stretched out the kink that had developed in her neck. Her arms ached, her back throbbed, and her glistening shine of feminine perspiration had transitioned into the unattractive dripping of sweat twenty minutes ago. She couldn't say she enjoyed the work, yet it filled her with a singular satisfaction that made her discomfort worthwhile. And every time Asher's mother exclaimed over finding a slightly stunted cucumber or still-tender pea pod, Samantha's arms ached a little less.

Retrieving a handkerchief from her apron pocket, Samantha dipped the cotton square into the watering can and squeezed out the excess water. She ran the cloth over her face and neck, biting back an audible sigh as the dampness cooled her skin. Her gaze traveled to the blanket near the front of the house, where Fergus entertained Jimmy with a pair of sticks representing characters in a very animated story.

"Miss Dearing! Come see." Mrs. Ellis waved her over to a patch covered with dying vines, her face alight with excitement.

Thinking she must have found some hint of life in the plant cemetery surrounding her, Samantha bent to collect the watering can, ready to do what she could to aid the resurrection process, but Mrs. Ellis shook her head.

"Leave the water, but grab one of the gunnysacks." She pointed to a spot near the porch where they'd stacked a pair of bushel baskets topped with a few sacks.

Samantha retrieved a sack and hurried to deliver it.

Mrs. Ellis ignored the sack and reached for Samantha's hand instead. "Look, Miss Dearing. So much bounty." Emotion choked her voice.

"Please, you must call me Samantha."

Mrs. Ellis smiled at her through misty eyes and squeezed her hand. "I'd like that. And you must call me Bess."

Samantha nodded, feeling slightly misty herself. She'd seen the love and warmth that flowed through the Ellis family, had admired their closeness and their willingness to sacrifice for one another. This woman was the family's heart, the source and perpetuator of that envious warmth. To have her respect as Jack's teacher was a blessing, but to be offered her friendship—it touched a place inside Samantha that longed for the nurturing affection she'd never received from her own mother.

"Look." Bess gestured to the yellow vines crawling over the ground in front of them. "They're perfect!"

Samantha gazed at the plot, failing to see anything close to perfection. "They're dead, aren't they?"

Bess smiled and reached for one of the vines in front of her. "Only on the surface. Watch."

She pulled on the vine, and as it released its loose hold on the earth, up came the roots and a pair of red potatoes. A gentle tug was all it took to separate tuber from plant.

"There's another one!" Samantha pointed to a potato visible in mound of dirt left behind.

Bess laughed. "Oh yes, I imagine there's at least two or three more under the soil here. After we pull up the vines, we'll take a fork to the ground and see how many we can uncover. I bet we can fill at least two of these large sacks. Maybe more." She nodded to a vine in front of Samantha. "Give it a try."

Catching the excitement, Samantha bent at the waist and tugged on the plant closest to her. When the roots released their grip, Samantha nearly toppled backward, but she was too delighted by the potatoes dangling from her plant to care. She shared a grin with Bess.

"You made this possible, Samantha," Bess said. "A full harvest of potatoes. Once they've dried and cured, they will last us through the winter. And we're finding other produce as well." Her gaze scanned the rest of the half-acre plot. "Summer squash, beans, cabbage, tomatoes, beets. The corn is dried out, but it can be used to feed our animals or even ground down for grits. The pumpkin seeds I planted in May have put out vines, too. They'll need some nurturing, but I think we can revitalize them enough to have pumpkin pie at Thanksgiving." She grinned. "It's Fergus's favorite." She spread her arms wide. "There's so much here. Yes, there's rot, weeds, and plants too withered from neglect to produce, but beneath the bad is a wealth of good if one is willing to look for it."

Bess peered at her in a way that added extra weight to her words, as if she were talking about more than just her garden.

"I'm willing." The simple words reverberated through Samantha's chest like a sacred vow.

Bess grinned, a twinkle entering her eyes. "I thought you might be."

An image of Asher rose to Samantha's mind, and when Bess winked at her as if she'd just borne witness to said image, heat flamed Samantha's cheeks.

Bess patted her shoulder and nodded toward the plants, graciously giving Samantha something to focus on besides her embarrassment. "Pull up all the vines and set aside the potatoes as you go. When you finish, I'll show you how to use the digging fork to unearth the rest. Then we'll brush off the worst of the dirt and pile them in the gunnysacks. Too much sun turns them green, so we'll want to have them stored before we stop for lunch."

Samantha accepted her assignment and dug potatoes for the next hour. It took some practice to get comfortable with the fork, but by the time she finished the last row, she'd found a rhythm. And a pair of blisters.

When it came time to round up the potatoes into their

gunnysack pen, Fergus offered to help, holding the mouth of the sack open while Samantha emptied her apron load. A few strays escaped each time, but Fergus and Jimmy took charge of those. Until Ida Mae called her son to the pump to wash up for lunch.

"Jimmy, come see Mama."

The toddler squatted down in the potato patch, a mulish look on his face. "No. Help Gus Gus."

Fergus rubbed the boy's back. "You were a good helper, Jimmy, but you better obey your mama. We can do more together later."

"No! Help Gus Gus now."

Fergus glanced at Samantha, his eyes pleading for ideas. She held up a potato and tipped her head toward Ida Mae.

Fergus nodded. He pulled a potato from the open sack and held it out to Jimmy. "Here. Can you help me take this to your mama? Help Fergus?"

Jimmy took the potato and threw it on the ground. "No!"

Fergus looked to Samantha for more inspiration, but all she could do was shrug. Toddlers were rarely logical creatures. Especially when nap time loomed.

Thankfully, Martin jogged into the fray and scooped Jimmy off the ground. "I got you, little man." Holding him securely under his arms, he let the boy's legs dangle as he swung him around. Much zig-zagging commenced along with train sounds and an occasional spin. When the two finally made it to the pump, Jimmy was giggling.

Martin lowered the boy to the ground, but Jimmy immediately held his arms up. "'Gin!"

After a quick glance to Ida Mae for permission, Martin snatched the boy up and did another lap around the yard.

"I think this is the last of them," Samantha said, turning out her apron and letting the potatoes roll down into the sack.

Pressing a hand to her back, she stretched muscles unused to all the bending required for garden work. Jimmy wasn't the only one in need of a nap. A warm bath and lie down sounded heavenly right about now.

"Go on and wash up," she told Fergus. "I'll take the sack over to the porch."

This one was only half-filled, so she should be able to manage it on her own. Martin had toted the others for her, but he was busy toting something else at the moment.

Fergus jogged over to Bess, who quickly wrapped an arm around his shoulders and steered him toward the others.

Mothers and their boys. Samantha smiled at the scene before she turned her back and trudged in the opposite direction. Would she experience that bond one day? Would Asher share it with her—swinging their child up onto his shoulders and galloping around like a horse as childish giggles rained down from on high? He'd make a great father. She saw it in the way he treated his brothers. Patient, fun-loving, supportive. How easy to imagine him in that role. Easy to imagine him in the role of husband, too. The pulse-fluttering thought distracted her so completely, she caught her toe on a tree root and pitched forward.

At the same moment, a distant crack sounded, followed by an explosion of glass over her back as a bullet shattered the house window directly behind her.

Samantha fell to the ground, a scream tearing from her throat.

"Everyone behind the house!"

She heard Martin's shout, but she couldn't move. She needed to stay small. Hidden.

Another gun sounded. Closer. Martin. Returning fire. She squeezed her eyes shut, flinching each time a shot echoed.

Then all at once, arms encircled her. A soft voice urged her to get up.

215

"I've got you, Samantha. Come on. You can make it."

Bess.

Asher's mother had come for her.

In that moment, Samantha forgot about herself. About the man out there somewhere trying to shoot her. She thought only of getting Bess out of the line of fire. She knew the devastation of losing a mother. She couldn't be the cause of Fergus and Jack losing theirs. And Asher—it would crush him.

Forcing her limbs to unbend, Samantha pushed upward. Bess shielded her as the two of them crouched and ran, kicking their way through spilled potatoes until they reached the porch. Fergus waved at them from the far corner of the house, calling for them to hurry.

They huddled behind the house for what felt like an eternity, Jimmy's cries the only sound in the eerily silent air.

Finally, Martin rounded the building, his gaze colliding with Samantha's. "Are you hurt?"

"No."

If she hadn't stumbled at just that moment . . . A shiver coursed over her skin. Bess must have felt her tremble, for her arms tightened around her and her hands rubbed away the chill before it could settle in Samantha's bones.

"Thank God."

Yes, thank you, Lord. I would be dead if it weren't for you.

"I'm going to load up the Ellises' wagon and bring it around here," Martin said. "All of you are to stay behind the house until I return. All right?"

Everyone nodded agreement.

He turned to leave, but Ida Mae touched his arm and brought him to a halt. "Be careful," she murmured.

He dipped his chin. "I will."

The man must have sprouted wings on his boots, for he had the wagon loaded in less than ten minutes. All the harvested food had been collected along with the gardening tools and picnic supplies.

"Climb into the back," he ordered as he reined in the team and set the brake. "I want all of you to lay down flat in the wagon bed."

"Do you think the others are in danger, too?" Samantha asked.

"Don't know, but I ain't takin' any chances."

Bess lifted Fergus into the back of the wagon, then looked to Martin. "Where will you take us?"

"To town. My orders were to take Miss Dearing to her aunt's house if any trouble arose."

But when they arrived, Aunt Regina wasn't home.

"Drive to my house," Bess insisted. "Samantha will be safe with us until you can notify her father."

Martin agreed and set the team in motion, taking Samantha to the one person she most wanted to see.

Asher.

25

❧

Balanced on the roof, Asher pounded a shingle in place, then reached for another from the crate to his right. A movement from the street caught his eye, and he swiveled to get a better look. Then straightened.

That looked like the wagon Jack had borrowed from the livery this morning for the gardening trip. Only Mama Bess wasn't driving it. A man held the reins.

Asher's gut tightened, as did his grip on the hammer. Wanting a closer look, he crept toward the edge of the roof, staying low to avoid drawing any attention.

The driver set the brake, then swiveled on the bench, scanning the street and the few houses scattered nearby.

"All clear," the man called.

Something in the back of the wagon shifted. A blanket slid aside, and heads popped up. Fergus clambered out of the wagon. Mama Bess had an arm wrapped around someone, but her body blocked the second woman's face. All he could make out was her blond hair, but that was all he needed. *Samantha.*

No longer caring about stealth, Asher abandoned his hammer and skidded down the roofline toward the back of the house. He ignored the ladder, opting for the faster descent of dropping over the side and onto the porch railing.

"Ash!" Fergus abandoned whatever he'd been trying to take out of the back of the wagon and ran to his brother. "Someone tried to shoot Miss Dearing!"

Time suspended, much like he imagined it would when a bull gored a man in the chest and tossed him into the air. Asher felt as if he were suspended above the earth, his heart throbbing in agony, his mind a hazy blur.

Thankfully, his feet seemed to know what to do and sprinted toward the wagon.

"Samantha?"

Please, God, let her be all right.

"She's all right, son." Mama Bess's words filtered through the fog of his panic but didn't dispel the cloud.

Only when he got a full view of her, did the clouds start to lift. She raised her face and met his gaze. Her beautiful blue eyes shimmered with unshed tears, and the ache in his heart intensified. She was frightened. He reached for her, wanting to touch her, comfort her, and reassure himself that she was alive and unharmed. She came to him without hesitation. He fit his hands to her waist, lowered her from the wagon bed, then clutched her to his chest and held her for a single precious moment before letting her go.

"Are you hurt?"

Dirt smudged her chin, strands of disheveled hair hung in disarray around her face, and her clothes were covered in garden grime, but he didn't see any blood. Still, he needed confirmation. Needed her answer.

Samantha shook her head. "No."

Thank you, God!

A gentle hand touched his arm. "Better get her inside, Ash, just to be safe."

He turned to face his mother, only then taking in the rest of the wagon's passengers. A young woman cradling a toddler watched the goings on with wide eyes.

"Fergus and I will help Martin unload the wagon," Mama Bess said. "You tend to Samantha."

The driver, Martin, came alongside and hefted a bushel basket filled with vegetables over the side of the wagon. "After I see Miss Forrester to her mother's place, I'll return the rig to the livery, rent a horse for myself, and head back to the Three Cedars to let Mr. Dearing know what happened."

"What *did* happen?"

Martin's jaw clenched. "Long range shot from a protected position. Thought I caught a glimpse of a horse and rider through the trees. Took a shot, but I doubt I hit him. He disappeared over the ridge, too far away for me to identify."

Samantha leaned back into Asher and pressed her face against his chest. The details of what happened ceased to matter.

Asher scooped her up in his arms and carried her away from the wagon and the memories of what transpired. Taking her into the house, he kicked the door closed with his foot, then moved to the kitchen table, thinking to set her down and put on the kettle for some tea. But when he lowered her feet to the floor, her arms tightened around his neck.

"Can you just hold me for a minute?"

Warmth seeped through Asher's body as he wrapped his arms around her back and held her close. "As long as you want," he whispered close to her ear before pressing a kiss to her temple.

His drive to do something, to fix something, faded as he stroked her back, her arms, her hair. She felt so good against him. Like she belonged there. A craving stirred to life in his soul—the urge to hold on forever and never let her go.

He loved her. He no longer doubted that truth. He had plenty of doubts about what that might mean or how things might play out in the future, but in this moment, he didn't care about those things. All he cared about was her.

The back door opened, disrupting the peace they'd found alone together. Samantha lifted her head and stepped away from him, but he kept a hand at the small of her back, unwilling to sever their connection entirely. Martin had deposited all the baskets and bags on the back porch and was striding back to the wagon. Fergus crossed the yard, a precarious armful of hoes, forks, and shovels clanking together as he moved. Mama Bess came inside and laid her big straw hat on the table, then turned her attention to Samantha.

"Why don't you go back to my room, honey? There's water you can use to freshen up and a bed if you feel like lying down."

"I'm fine, really." Samantha pasted a smile on her face, but it failed to light her eyes. "I want to help. Just show me what to do."

Mama Bess took Samantha's hand. "If you want to keep busy, I'll let you wash those potatoes you dug so Fergus can lay them out to cure under the porch. But first, take a minute to be still. Wash up. Clear the ugliness out of your mind with some prayer. My Bible's on the bedside table. Help yourself. I find Philippians 4 particularly uplifting when it comes to clearing out dark cobwebs and letting the light back in." Mama Bess smiled, then nodded to Asher, a clear signal that he was to escort Samantha to her room. "Take your time," she urged as Asher started steering Samantha out of the kitchen. "Those taters aren't going anywhere."

In a small house, it didn't take long to move from one room to the next, so his time with Samantha ended far sooner than he would have liked. But he knew it wouldn't be proper for him to follow her into the bedroom.

Reaching around her, he opened his mother's door, but when Samantha didn't immediately cross the threshold, he focused his attention on her face, and offered a smile as he tucked a wayward strand of hair behind her ear.

"Mama Bess is usually right about things," he said, remembering all the times he didn't heed her advice as a youngster and later rued his choice. "Take some time to recover from the shock of everything that's happened. You've been through a lot lately, and it's only natural to be a little rattled. You don't have to pretend to be fine. I know how strong you are, how brave. I admire you more than any woman I've ever met."

She dipped her chin. "I feel neither strong nor brave," she murmured. "I feel . . . shattered." She lifted her face, and her eyes melded with his. "If you hadn't held me, I think I would have completely fallen apart."

Asher swallowed, his throat thick with emotion. "Then I'm glad I was here."

"Me too." She reached out a hand and laid it upon his chest, directly over his heart. That muscle leapt at her touch, beating with new vigor. "You make me feel safe, Asher. I . . ."

His ears strained to hear the words perched on her tongue, sensing their importance, but she never gave them voice. Her lashes lowered over those magnificent eyes, and he felt her distancing herself. Slowly, her hand fell away from his chest.

"I promise to take my time," she said, lifting her lashes and meeting his gaze again. "But I won't want to be alone for long."

He settled his hands on her shoulders and gave them a gentle rub. "I'll be in the kitchen whenever you're ready to emerge. I'll stay by your side until your father comes to fetch you."

A tiny smile tugged her lips upward. "I'd like that."

Asher released her shoulders and cupped both sides of her face. He drew her toward him and touched his lips to her forehead, lingering over a kiss that should be chaste, but aroused all kinds of longings within him. Then he stepped back and watched while she disappeared into the room and closed the door.

———

Samantha leaned against the door at her back, closed her eyes, and relived the memory of Asher's lips pressed to her forehead and his hands gently cupping her face. Such a perfect moment. So tender. So affectionate and sweet. It almost blocked out the memory of the gunshot and glass shattering. Almost, but not quite.

Merciful heavens. What if something had happened to Fergus or Jimmy? For most of the morning, they'd been playing in the very spot where someone had taken a shot at her. If one of those precious children had been hurt because of her . . .

Her hands trembled. She balled them into fists and stepped away from the door.

Had her brash words to Leroy Thompson outside the livery that day evoked enough hatred to drive him to try to end her life? She'd always been impetuous, even as a girl. Speaking before thinking, jumping to conclusions, not considering possible consequences before taking actions. Her mother had tried to curb the tendency in her, but no matter how many times Samantha counted to ten, when her passions ran high, she threw caution to the wind. Now, it seemed, that wind was throwing things back at her—all of them deadly.

Stop thinking about it. You're safe. No one was harmed. Falling apart will only compound your troubles.

Taking herself in hand, she crossed to the washstand in the

far corner of the room, passing a pile of gear stashed along the wall. A shirt she recognized hung on a peg above the pile of what looked to be comprised of saddlebags, rope, and a satchel of some sort. A pair of trousers lay folded on top of the pile, trousers much too long in the leg to belong to Jack or Fergus. Asher must store his things in here. Samantha reached a hand out to run her fingers along the edge of the tan shirt, then saw the filth on her hand and drew back. He'd not thank her for soiling a clean shirt with her dirty fingers.

Determined to put herself to rights and erase the evidence of what had transpired, she peeled off her dirt-stained apron and washed the grime from her face and neck. Finding Bess's hairbrush on the stand, she pulled the pins from her hair and stroked the brush through the long strands until they shone like spun gold. Next, she twisted her hair into a rope and wound it into a simple bun at her nape, fastened it in place with the pins, then examined herself in the mirror. The disheveled, lost little girl had been replaced by a proper lady. Perhaps one with a shaken confidence and a few extra worry lines along her brow, but a lady nonetheless. And when she lifted her chin and glared defiantly into the glass, she almost believed her mettle had been restored.

Yet instead of pasting on a smile and sweeping out the door, ready to pretend all was well as her mother would have done, Samantha followed the tugging of her heart and reached for the book sitting on the bedside table. Lowering herself onto the edge of the mattress, she clasped the cracked leather cover that had been worn from many readings and drew it into her lap.

Bess had recommended Philippians 4, a passage Samantha knew well. The promise of a peace that passed all understanding was a blessing indeed. And the wisdom of guarding one's thoughts by not dwelling on fear or anger or despair, but on that which is pure, lovely, and praiseworthy, could not be denied. The reminder was timely and appropriate; however, her soul craved a more tangible reassurance. A promise to cling to in adversity.

She fanned the pages with her thumb until a clump fell together, opening to reveal a lace bookmark. Opening the Bible fully across her lap, she smoothed the pages, her eyes snagging on the number about halfway down the left page. *Psalm 118.* The words had been written centuries past, yet the spirit within her resonated as if the Lord were speaking them anew, specifically to her.

> *O give thanks unto the* Lord*; for he is good: because his mercy endureth for ever . . .*
> *I called upon the* Lord *in distress: the* Lord *answered me, and set me in a large place. The* Lord *is on my side; I will not fear: what can man do unto me?*

She stopped and read verse six again, then closed her eyes and let the promise anoint her soul. The Lord was on her side. She need not be afraid. For what attack could man launch that God could not defend? He'd saved her from a runaway wagon, from a viper, and now from a gunshot. Why was she cowering in fear when his protection surrounded her?

> *It is better to trust in the* Lord *than to put confidence in man. It is better to trust in the* Lord *than to put confidence in princes.*

Asher. The cowboy prince she longed to claim for her own. Capable and strong. Tender and caring. He'd already saved her life once. He made her feel safe. Yet as much as she trusted him, or her father for that matter, neither man could be everywhere nor guard against every eventuality. Only God could do that.

> *Thou hast thrust sore at me that I might fall: but the L*ORD
> *helped me. The L*ORD *is my strength and song, and is become*
> *my salvation. . . . The right hand of the L*ORD *is exalted: the*
> *right hand of the L*ORD *doeth valiantly. I shall not die, but*
> *live, and declare the works of the L*ORD.

Her heart throbbed, and in that sacred moment, she knew in the depths of her spirit that the Lord had indeed spoken to her.

"'I shall not die,'" she whispered, "'but live, and declare the works of the Lord.'"

Thank you, Father. It is you who has saved me. You who are at work. Bringing calm from calamity and peace from persecution. You brought Asher to me and restored what had been broken with my father. You reunited me with Ida Mae and blessed me with godly women like Aunt Regina and Bess Ellis to advise and prepare me for the hardships in my path. You are at work. I may not be able to see clearly, but I trust your vision, your plan. Help me to leave my fear behind and walk in gratitude.

She sat on the edge of the bed for a long minute, drinking in the Lord's assurance and leaning on his promise. She grew so relaxed that the Bible nearly slipped off her lap. Catching it at the last minute, she slapped her hand across the open pages and accidentally dislodged the pretty bookmark. The scrap of lace floated to the floor and under the edge of the bed.

Setting the Bible aside, Samantha crouched on the floor and peered beneath the bed. She spotted the tatted bookmark and reached for it, almost missing the item that propped it up from behind. A man's boot. Singular. The only one under the bed. After collecting the bookmark in her palm, she hooked a finger over the edge of the boot and dragged it out into the light.

Her heart knew what she would see before her eyes drank in the sight. Brown leather foot, black leather upper, decorative stitching along the top. A perfect match to the boot hiding in her wardrobe.

26

Asher cast a sideways glance at Samantha as he handed her another wet potato to pat dry. Something had changed. When she'd first emerged from the bedroom a couple of hours ago, he'd noticed a difference in the way she looked at him, not quite meeting his gaze. He'd thought it was shyness or perhaps embarrassment over the intimacies they'd shared in the hallway, but then she'd started digging for information during lunch. As they'd passed around the sandwiches, cheese, and watermelon that were supposed to have served as picnic fodder at the homestead, Samantha had delicately maneuvered the conversation around to him.

At first, he'd been flattered that she wanted to learn more about his life. His job at the Bar 7, things he liked to do in his spare time. She'd wheedled Mama Bess into telling her about his father and how hard it had been for them after he passed. Samantha shared some of her own struggles after she'd lost her mother. How she'd been thrust into a parental role for Clint, and how much she'd hated being separated from her family when her father sent her to school in Boston. Her eyes had met his after this revelation, and he'd felt an invisible thread tying them together. She understood the pressure he felt to provide for his brothers, to help Mama Bess raise them to be honorable men. She could relate to the regret he felt over being separated from them.

But then she'd started quizzing Fergus about whether or not he knew how to swim. A rather abrupt change of subject. Instead of giving a simple "yep" as Jack would have had he been there, Fergus launched into one story after another, recounting not only his own sporadic experience, but diving into Asher's as well. Samantha had seemed particularly interested in the tale of Asher's heroics when he'd swum halfway across the Brazos to retrieve the fishing boat Jack had failed to secure properly on shore.

He'd assumed she was just trying to distract herself from what had happened at the homestead, but something about her manner shifted after that conversation. She'd grown quiet. Introspective. Yet he didn't sense any particular unease. Her withdrawal seemed more contemplative than anxious.

Asher shifted in his chair and pulled the last two potatoes from the scrub bucket near his feet. He placed them on the folded towel positioned between him and Samantha on the kitchen table, then dried his hands on his trouser legs and leaned close to the woman working at his side.

"Are you all right?" He kept his voice low so Mama Bess wouldn't overhear from where she stood at the stove stirring a pot of pickle brine to preserve the cucumbers she'd brought back from the garden.

Samantha blinked as if the sound of his voice had disoriented her for a moment, then offered him a smile and a nod. "Yes, I was just thinking about my father and how he might react." She dropped the potato she'd been drying into the crate on the floor and reached for another. "I'm afraid he'll be angry."

What father wouldn't be angry at the thought of someone

trying to harm his child? Shoot, every time Asher thought about the coward who'd hidden behind a tree, aimed his rifle at Samantha, and pulled the trigger, he wanted to tear into the man with his bare hands. Which was why he'd been doing his best not to think about it.

"He likely *will* be angry," Asher said, "but only because he loves you and doesn't want to see you hurt."

"I know." Her hands stilled. "But one can't find happiness without risking hurt."

Now it was Asher's turn to blink. Happiness? He had the strangest feeling the two halves of this conversations weren't adding up to a whole.

"As important as happiness is, surely safety is more so," he said, watching her face for any clue that might offer insight to the workings of her mind. "This is your life we're talking about, Samantha. You can't take that lightly."

"I don't. I know what's at stake." She twisted to face him more fully, passion glowing in her eyes. "I'm not some fluttery debutante who faints whenever something disagreeable arises. I face challenges like my father, head on. But it's my life, not his. If I'm willing to overlook a small misdeed, he should be, too."

"A small misdeed?" Asher couldn't believe what he was hearing. "Samantha, he tried to kill you. There's nothing small about that. I've already decided that I'm not leaving Palo Pinto until I'm sure whoever is responsible is behind bars."

The fiery intensity in her gaze warned of an argument, but somewhere in the middle of his speech, confusion wrinkled her brow.

"You . . . you'd risk your position at the Bar 7 for me?"

He laid a hand over her arm. "I'd risk my *life* for you."

She peered at him, and for the first time since this odd conversation started, he felt they were truly on the same page. "I pray it doesn't come to that," she whispered.

230

He stroked her sleeve, his chest tight. "If it does, I'm ready."

A shy smile transformed her face and set his heart to hammering like a frenzied woodpecker in his chest. "You're a good man, Asher Ellis."

"Not really." Shame had him ducking his head. He stared at his hand where it lay atop her arm, wishing he was the man she believed him to be. "I've made plenty of mistakes and poor choices." One that might land him in his own jail cell someday. "But I fight for those I care about." He raised his chin and met her gaze. "And you are quickly climbing to the top of that list."

"Asher, I—"

A loud pounding on the front door cut off whatever she'd been about to say.

"That's probably your father," Asher said as he pushed up from the table. "I'll go let him in."

Mama Bess glanced at him over her shoulder. "Seat him in the parlor. I'll bring a pitcher of fresh water and some glasses after I shoo Fergus outside."

Asher nodded. Fergus didn't need to hear the discussion that was about to take place, one that would likely contain more questions than answers at this point. Asher could fill him in on the key points after Dearing left.

Samantha rose and slipped her hand through the crook of Asher's arm. "I'll come with you."

Asher made no argument, though he did wonder how long her hand would linger on his arm once her father entered the house.

Not long, as it turned out. But not because she released her hold. No, it was her bear of a father who swallowed her up in a hug so big it not only pulled her hand from Asher's arm but lifted her feet from the floor.

"Thank God you're all right." Eli Dearing set his daughter down, his expression a mix of guilt, torture, and relief. "When

Martin told me what happened . . . gracious, girl. I think I aged ten years in the last hour."

Samantha gazed up at her father, her eyes moist. "I'm fine, Daddy. Martin did an excellent job of keeping us all safe after the . . . after the shooting."

Asher's hand found its way to her back, lending her what support he could. Her eyes found his, and her lips tipped up a bit at the corners in gratitude. It took several seconds for Asher to look away from her, but when he did, it ran straight into the pointed stare of her father. Asher fought the urge to flinch and instead held Dearing's gaze, letting his intentions be seen. One of Dearing's brows raised a smidge, but the cattleman turned his attention back to his daughter without further challenge.

"Clint wanted to come," Dearing said, "but I made him stay at the ranch. After what Martin learned from the sheriff, I didn't want to take the chance of him being targeted as well."

That statement sharpened Asher's attention. "What did the sheriff have to say?"

Dearing blew out a breath, then reached up to take his hat off. "Leroy Thompson ain't our man."

A dozen questions jumped to attention in Asher's mind, but it was the slight stiffening of Samantha's posture beside him that took precedence.

"Come in and have a seat." Asher motioned her father toward the small sitting area behind him. "We can talk in here."

Dearing nodded and strode into the parlor while Asher closed the front door. Mama Bess bustled in with a water pitcher, glasses, and a plate of cookies that had been left over from the picnic supplies. Samantha jumped in to help serve, pouring the water while Mama Bess took Eli's coat and hat and offered him the place of honor in the armed chair nearest the hearth. She settled on the tufted stool usually reserved for

Fergus and insisted that Asher and Samantha share the settee. Asher was more than happy to comply.

"Tell us about the sheriff, Daddy." Samantha leaned forward in her seat. Her eyes were locked on her father, but her leg pressed against Asher's as if seeking solace to help her bear the bad news to come.

He longed to place his hand on her back, to rub and soothe and support, but under the watchful eye of her father, he figured subtlety would be the wiser option and contented himself with shifting his weight slightly to bring himself a little closer to her side.

"Martin stopped by the sheriff's office to report the shooting and to . . . express our displeasure over the lack of resolution in this case. Sheriff Jeter said he questioned the barkeep at the saloon who confirmed that Leroy had been in a foul mood and drunker than a skunk when he left the day he accosted you in the street, but he hadn't been back since. Jeter notified other law enforcement in the area, giving them Leroy's name and description. Got a wire this morning from the sheriff over in Parker County. Seems Leroy made it as far as Millsap. The local marshal brought him in for questioning yesterday, then locked him up when Leroy took a swing at him. Apparently, he accused the marshal of being on my payroll and enforcing a bunch of trumped-up charges. Anyway, what matters is that he couldn't have been the one behind the rifle today. Not if he's been locked up in Millsap for the last twenty-four hours."

Samantha edged a little closer to Asher as she leaned against the settee's back. "Do you still think he might have hired someone?"

Her father shook his head. "According to the marshal in Millsap, he pawned his cigarette case to cover his bar tab. He's too short on funds to hire anyone."

"If Leroy's not behind the attacks, then who is?"

Dearing grimaced. "Well, we never figured out who broke in the night of the ball. Right now, he's the only real suspect I got."

Asher's throat began to close up.

"We discussed this, Daddy." Samantha leaned forward, her gaze darting back to Asher before settling on her father. "We don't know why the trespasser was there, but we do know that he wasn't a killer. He risked capture in order to save Clint's life. That's not the kind of man who would try to kill a woman."

Asher cleared his throat and braced himself to clear the air. Listening to her defend his crimes rubbed his conscience raw. They needed to know the truth. Especially Samantha. She deserved—

"I'm not as sure of that as you are." Dearing jabbed a pointed stare at his daughter. "But when I stopped by Jeter's office on my way here, I also gave him the names of men who might wish me or my family harm. Men resentful of being left out of business deals and those I had to evict from properties." His gaze narrowed as he aimed it at Asher. "Seems to me someone who grew up at that homestead would know the terrain real well. Where to hide. How best to escape."

Mama Bess gasped. "My son would never!"

"Daddy, you're wrong!"

Dearing flung out an arm in Asher's direction. "Who else knew where you'd be this morning? Maybe he's been cozying up to you in order to seek some kind of twisted revenge against me. He could have even orchestrated that wheel mishap with your cart to weasel his way into your good graces."

"That's outrageous!" Mama Bess jumped to her feet and planted her hands on her hips. "My Ash would never harm Samantha, or anyone. If you had half a brain beneath that thick skull of yours, you'd see how much he cares for her."

"Easy, Mama." How he loved her for believing in him so

completely, but he knew his time of reckoning had come. "Mr. Dearing has reason not to trust me."

He pushed to his feet, surprised when Samantha grabbed his hand and tried to tug him back down.

"Asher, don't." Her eyes pled with him, as if she knew what he was about to confess. But how could she?

"I'm sorry, Samantha. I should have been honest with you from the beginning." He tugged his hand free and turned to face Eli Dearing. The man rose from his chair, hands balled into fists, face as hard as granite. "I *did* resent you when I heard what you'd done to my family. In fact, when I first returned to town, I was determined to prove you a heartless scoundrel who cheated good women out of their homes. I was the one who broke into your house the night of the ball. I riffled through the documents in your study, sure I'd find evidence of fraud or unethical behavior that I could use as leverage to get you to restore our land."

"You thought to blackmail me?" Dearing growled through gritted teeth.

"I suppose I did, though at the time I considered it more an act of justice." Asher shook his head. "I let my anger cloud my judgment, and I've come to regret my actions. I found no proof of wrongdoing. Only raised rents that my mother had failed to mention in her letters." How he wanted to look at Samantha and judge her reaction. He prayed she was only disappointed and not completely repulsed. But the man he'd wronged deserved his full attention, so he kept his eyes on Eli Dearing and forced himself to voice the rest.

"After that night, I made peace with our new circumstances and vowed to do all I could to see Mama Bess and the boys well situated before returning to my job at the Bar 7. I've come to respect you, sir, for the care you show your daughter. If you wish to take me before the judge, I'll go peaceably, but

I pray you'll wait until after we find the man responsible for the attacks on Samantha. She means a great deal to me, and I want to help keep her safe."

"You think I'm gonna trust you, after this?" Dearing's raised voice reverberated through the room like a Texas thunderstorm. His face contorted with all the menacing darkness of a funnel cloud, and his pale eyes shot lightning shards at Asher's chest. "You're a criminal! I don't want my daughter anywhere near you."

Samantha rose from the settee and came to stand by Asher's side. "Well, your daughter intends to keep him close at hand, so you're going to have to adjust your wishes."

Dearing raised a brow and fired a few lightning bolts at his daughter. Not that she seemed to notice. Samantha held her ground and even slid her hand around Asher's, offering him an anchor in the storm.

"Asher would never hurt me, Daddy." Her steady voice soothed Asher's bruised heart as nothing else could. She spoke with absolute certainty, as if the confession he'd just made had bounced off her without leaving a single dent. "I trust him," she said, "and so do you. You assigned him to watch over me in town, remember? If he had wanted me dead, he could have killed me any of the evenings that he escorted me home. Goodness, he could have simply let the runaway cart do the job for him. But he didn't. He saved my life, just as he saved Clint's the night of the ball."

She turned her gaze on Asher, and he had to lock his knees to keep them from buckling. Those glorious blue eyes glimmered with faith and confidence. In him. A man could face anything when his woman believed in him.

"He made a mistake. One he's admitted. It takes courage and strength of character to admit to wrongdoing, but that's what a man of integrity does. That is who Asher is—a man of integrity." She smiled at Asher and gave his hand a reassuring squeeze. Never had his heart felt so full. Then she turned back to her father. "You asked who else knew where I would be this morning. I can think of any number of people, all of whom work at the Three Cedars."

"You think one of my men would harm you?"

"Leroy Thompson was one of your men."

Having no answer to that, Dearing strode away from the group to stare into the empty hearth. His heavy fist banged softly against the mantel. "If it's one of my men and I missed the signs . . ."

Samantha moved to her father's side and placed a hand on his back. "Then you'd be human. Just like the rest of us."

The granite crumbled from Dearing's face, leaving him looking haggard and desperate. "I lost your mother. I can't lose you, too."

She smiled. "You won't. I have the two best men in the county looking after me."

He wrapped an arm around her and pulled her into a side hug. "I love you, girl."

"I love you, too, Daddy."

Dearing cleared his throat, then turned his attention back to the group. His gaze found Asher. "We'll talk later about that trespassing incident," he said.

Asher gave a sharp nod, thankful for the reprieve.

"For now, I'm going to take Samantha to her aunt's house, where she is to stay until this matter is resolved." He gave her a stern look, successfully stalling the protest she had started to make. "Mrs. Stewart packed you a bag. I already dropped it off at the house. Tracked Obadiah down at the church and filled him in on what's been happening. He assured me there would be a room waiting for you when you arrived. I'll go back to the ranch and have Duke round up the men so I can question them. We'll get down to the bottom of this, one way or the other."

Asher rubbed at his jaw, a thought eating away at his gut. "You might focus your attention on those who had access to Samantha's cart on the day of her accident."

Dearing raised a brow. "Why's that?"

"I don't think it *was* an accident." The logic untwisted, leaving a straight path in Asher's mind. "If Leroy's not the perpetrator, then it stands to reason, the accident with the loose wheel was the true attacker's first attempt. If someone had access to the cart ahead of time, he could have sabotaged the wheel nut. Blaming her death on a tragic accident would help remove suspicion."

Dearing's jaw tightened. "And when that didn't work, he changed tactics to something more direct."

Which meant Samantha wouldn't be safe until the fiend was caught. But how could they catch the villain without using Samantha as bait?

27

Asher sat in a rocking chair on Obadiah Hopewell's front porch, three days later, waiting for Jack to finish his lesson with Samantha. He'd been making excuses to stop by the preacher's house every day since Samantha took up residence. If anyone commented about the regularity of his visits, he was quick to explain how he wanted to offer her a distraction from both the danger she faced and the boredom she was forced to contend with while being cooped up in her aunt and uncle's house. All of that was true, yet those explanations failed to take into account his deepest motivation.

He simply wanted to be with her. To see her smile and hear her laugh. To touch her hand and watch her eyes soften when she looked at him.

She believed in him. Not only in his ability to keep her safe but in his character. Despite his criminal actions against her father. He didn't deserve her faith, yet he craved it with a hunger so strong he knew he'd spend the rest of his life trying to be worthy of her good opinion.

To that end, he kept an eye on every man who walked past the parsonage that evening. Oh, he waved and nodded to those who passed by, but his outer politeness hid an inner vigilance. Was that man in the suit taking stock of the upstairs windows or just appreciating the first tinge of pink as sunset neared? Or what about the cowboy whose hat was pulled down so low Asher couldn't see his eyes? Was his hat simply a size too big, or was he trying to hide his identity?

Then there was the large man on horseback moseying toward the house as if it were his destination. Asher's stomach clenched as recognition dawned. This man posed no threat to Samantha. The threat to Asher, however, was a different story.

Asher pushed to his feet and leaned against the porch post. "Evenin', Mr. Dearing."

"Ellis." Eli Dearing dismounted and secured his horse. "Figured I might find you here. When Clint and I stopped by yesterday, Samantha mentioned you've been bringing Jack by for his lessons."

"Yep." Asher eyed him warily as he approached the steps. "Jack will likely be done in about twenty minutes or so."

Dearing clapped a hand on Asher's shoulder, his grip firm. "Good. That gives us time to sit for a bit. Have a nice chat before Regina invites us in for pie."

Asher swallowed. "Yes, sir."

Nothing like a conversation concerning criminal misconduct to put a man in the mood for dessert. Asher stepped aside and gestured for Dearing to select his chair of choice. Dearing claimed the larger rocker, leaving Asher to squeeze his frame into a chair built for the more petite member of the Hopewell family.

Dearing pushed his hat back on his head, then pierced Asher with a stare hot enough to fire a blacksmith's forge. "I'm a man who believes in justice, Ellis. I don't take kindly to folks who break the law. Who got no respect for a man's property nor his privacy. If you and me were the only two stuck in this mire, I'd haul you over to the sheriff right now and turn you in for tresspassin'. You broke the law. Ain't no prettying that up with heartwarming stories about tryin' to provide for your mother and brothers."

Asher's gut turned rock-hard from dread, but he forced himself to hold Dearing's gaze. "You're right. There's no excuse to justify what I did. I regret my actions, sir, and I'll honor whatever decision you make regarding the consequences."

He'd been praying for mercy, but he'd accept justice. It was only right.

Dearing's rocker creaked as the big man leaned back in his chair. "I'm glad we see eye to eye on the matter. And that you take responsibility for your actions. I respect that." One brow lifted. "If you had tried to weasel out of your culpability, this conversation would have taken an unpleasant turn."

Not knowing what to say to that, Asher opted for silence, barely resisting the urge to wipe at the sweat gathering along his hatband.

Samantha's father crossed his arms over his chest and glared at Asher through narrowed eyes. "What are your intentions toward my daughter?"

Asher's mind went horrifyingly blank. He'd been expecting a verdict regarding his crime, not a courtship interrogation. Thankfully, he had only to picture Samantha in his mind for all his intentions to come flooding back into his brain.

He cleared his throat. "My intentions toward Samantha are to keep her safe from whoever is stalking her. We haven't had the chance to discuss much beyond that point, and I'm not so foolish as to think she won't have an opinion on the matter."

Asher wasn't certain, but he thought he caught a mouth twitch that might constitute a smidgeon of a smile before Eli Dearing's lips pressed back into a hard line.

"What I *can* tell you is that I care about Samantha very

much. She's a rare woman. One who is passionate about making the world a better place, not just for herself but for everyone around her. She's smart, kind, and one of the bravest people I've ever met. Her faith in me is humbling and yet invigorating. She makes me want to be a better man."

"Yeah, she has that effect on people."

"I know that I don't have much to offer when it comes to worldly possessions," Asher admitted as he scooted to the edge of his chair, "but if at some future date, she is willing to consider my suit, I can offer loyalty, hard work, and absolute devotion."

Dearing grunted. Not the most encouraging response.

"For now, though, why don't we focus on keeping her safe? We can figure the rest out later."

That eyebrow raised again.

Asher straightened. "Unless, of course, you've decided we need to pay a call on the sheriff."

He held his breath, silently renewing his prayers for mercy.

Dearing unfolded his arms and slapped his palms against his thighs. "I'm not going to haul you off to the sheriff's office, son. Samantha would flay my hide with that sharp tongue of hers, and I ain't fully healed from the last tongue lashing she gave me." He chuckled softly, then thumped Asher on the back, his gaze turning serious. "Truth be told, I feel better knowing you're watching out for her here in town when I can't. You're no good to me behind bars."

"I'll do everything in my power to keep her safe. You have my word."

Dearing groaned softly as he pushed to his feet. Asher rose alongside.

"My daughter believes in you, Ellis. There ain't no higher recommendation than that in my book." He held out his hand.

Asher stared at the peace offering for a brief moment, then clasped the hand of the man he'd once considered an enemy, and who might soon be family.

"For Samantha," Asher vowed.

Dearing tightened his grip. "For Samantha."

28

Ten days had passed at Aunt Regina and Uncle Obadiah's house, and Samantha feared she'd not last much
longer. She looked up from her book to stare at the instrument of her torture—the mantel clock in her aunt's parlor.
The insufferable thing purposely moved as slowly as possible
whenever it caught her alone. Which was far too often. Her
aunt still paid calls on the ladies of the church each afternoon,
while Uncle Obadiah closed himself off in his study to write his
sermons and pray for his flock. Samantha knew she shouldn't
begrudge them their freedom or interfere with their duties, but
each day that passed without her father or the sheriff finding
her attacker fed her restlessness.

Everyone was doing their best to keep her entertained and
busy. Her father and Clint came to supper every few days.
Asher brought Jack for his lessons and stayed for dessert and
coffee after the lessons concluded. Bess even stopped by one
afternoon for tea. Samantha truly had nothing to complain
about. Especially since Asher and her father had mended
fences. Neither man had shared any details of the conversation that had taken place a week ago on Aunt Regina's porch,

but Jack had spotted them shaking hands when he went to invite his brother in for pie, so Samantha had taken that as a sign that her prayers for forgiveness and understanding between them had been answered. Something she'd thanked God for all week. After all the years of estrangement between her and her father, she couldn't bear to have a new rift created between them.

Turning back to her book, she forced her eyes to roam over the words, but concentration proved difficult. Like a little brother bent on pestering, the mantel clock prodded her every second, it's annoying ticktock growing excruciatingly loud. She couldn't focus. Each tick seemed to reverberate like a gong in her head. Controlling her. Confining her.

In a desperate bid to escape the torturous clock, Samantha snapped her book closed, set it aside, and fled to the window. How she missed her afternoon riding lessons with Asher. The wind blowing her hair, the thrill of accomplishment each time she improved, the time alone with the man she had come to love.

The time had expired for Asher to return to the Bar 7. Yet he remained in Palo Pinto, just as he'd promised. The last time they'd talked, he'd told her not to worry about it. He'd find work at another ranch. He'd written to his foreman and explained the situation, and his former boss had mailed back a letter of recommendation that should help him secure a position. As much as she loved that Asher was still here, she hated that she was the reason for his dismissal. She pleaded with the Lord to provide a position for him, one that would allow him not only to provide for his mother and brothers but perhaps to have enough left over that he might afford to take a wife as well.

Letting the curtain fall back into place with a sigh, Samantha made a circle around the sitting room. Aunt Regina would likely end up with a permanent rut worn into the wooden floorboards with how many circles Samantha made on a daily basis, but moving eased the restlessness. At least a little. She'd only been allowed to leave the house once over the last ten days, and that had been for church. Her father had flanked her on one side, Asher on the other, with Clint leading the way and Martin bringing up the rear. Duke had never been much of a churchgoing man, but even he showed up last Sunday to assist with guard duty. Sensing a soul in need of salvation, Uncle Obadiah had insisted that both Duke and Martin join the family for Sunday dinner. She'd never seen a man shovel in his dessert as fast as Duke had that day in his eagerness to escape her uncle's targeted attention. He'd made his excuses and left the house while everyone lingered over coffee and cobbler.

The sound of a key jiggling in the front door lock brought Samantha's circling to a halt. Stepping around the end table with the hand-painted floral lamp, Samantha strode straight for the entry way, eager to greet her aunt.

"I'm home," Aunt Regina called as she pushed the door inward. She drew up short when she spotted Samantha a few feet away, poised like a half-grown pup, delighted by the return of her mistress and ready to pounce.

A sympathetic smile stretched across her aunt's face as she turned to close and lock the front door. "I see boredom's been winning the war this afternoon."

"I know hiding is necessary for my safety, but your lovely home is starting to feel a bit like a prison."

Samantha stepped forward to collect the basket her aunt always carried when paying calls on the sick. It had gone out filled with bread, honey, and her aunt's special blend of herbal tea that was sure to soothe even the sorest of throats. Samantha set the now empty vessel on the front table, where it would be filled with books, yarn, and needles on the morrow for when Aunt Regina paid calls on two of the widowed ladies from her husband's flock. She read to one and knitted with the other, having gone through a dozen novels and at least twenty scarves so far this year.

Aunt Regina laid a hand on Samantha's shoulder. "I've often thought waiting is one of the hardest things the Lord asks us to do. It strains our patience, faith, and self-control. Yet he promises good to those who wait on him." She smiled as she untied her bonnet strings. "Hang in there a little longer, sweetheart. The end is near."

Samantha blew out a breath. "I wish it would hurry."

"I know it doesn't make it any easier, but the Lord's timing is always best. You must trust in that. In *him*." Aunt Regina hung her bonnet on the hall tree, then hooked her arm through Samantha's elbow and drew her toward the stairs with a wink. "Come with me. I've been saving something, and I think today might be just the time to give it to you."

A touch of giddiness awoke in Samantha's tedium-numbed chest. "What is it?"

Aunt Regina chuckled. "You'll have to wait and see."

Samantha groaned in dramatic fashion before dissolving into giggles.

The two ascended the stairs arm in arm, then Aunt Regina steered them toward her bedroom. Once inside, she dropped Samantha's arm and crossed to the cedar chest standing at the end of the bed. She set aside the dresser scarf that had been draped over the top and opened the lid. Samantha peered over her aunt's shoulder to find a collection of keepsakes inside. A handful of photographs in frames, a scrap of lace peeking out from a brown paper wrapping that hinted at a wedding dress, and a beautiful quilt in shades of blue calico. Aunt Regina slid her hand beneath the quilt and withdrew a slender book. She lowered the lid on the chest, then turned around and sat on it. She scooted over and patted the place beside her. Samantha joined her on the makeshift bench.

"I found this among your mother's things after she passed." Aunt Regina stroked the cover. When she pivoted to face Samantha, her expression turned serious, almost . . . troubled. "Your mother's diary."

Samantha inhaled a shaky breath, all playfulness forgotten.

Her aunt gripped both sides of the book as if afraid it would leap off her lap. "I debated whether or not I should give this to you. They are your mother's private thoughts. Not intended to be seen by others. They might be a tad . . . unvarnished."

"You haven't read it?"

Aunt Regina shook her head. "Victoria was always so fastidious about the way she presented herself to others. Everything had to be pristine. Wrinkles pressed, hair done, smile in place. She would want to be remembered as the charming hostess, dutiful wife, and devoted mother she strove to be, so I choose to honor her by thinking of her as such. But a woman so concerned with perfection has no one with whom to share her vulnerabilities and weaknesses. Such a woman might only feel safe exposing such flaws in private. Perhaps in a journal. Hopefully, also in prayer."

Aunt Regina moved the book to Samantha's lap yet kept a hand pressed to the cover. "I know you have many questions about your mother, and this book might provide some of the answers you seek. But it might also reveal a side of her that you never saw. One riddled with imperfections." She glanced up from the book and met Samantha's gaze. "Some of the things you read might hurt, Sam. You need to be prepared for that. But never doubt that your mother loved you. All of you. You. Your father. Clint. The three of you were her world. So I ask that if you read this, you do so with a spirit of grace."

Slowly, Aunt Regina's hand lifted from the cover of the book. Samantha's belly swirled with an unsettling mixture of fear and anticipation. She remembered her mother through a child's eyes. What would it be like to get to know her woman-to-woman? What would she think of the lady Samantha had grown into? Would she be disappointed that her daughter hadn't married a wealthy son of Boston, or would she see worth in the path Samantha had chosen for herself? Her fingers trembled as she traced the embossed lettering that spelled out *Journal* on the red leather cover.

"Thank you for this." Clutching the book in one hand, Samantha twisted and wrapped her arms around her aunt in a warm embrace.

Aunt Regina held her tightly for a long minute. "I love you, darling girl." When her aunt finally relaxed her hold, Samantha was surprised to find moisture glistening in the older woman's eyes. "I wish I could wave a magic wand and make all your troubles disappear."

"You've taken me in, plied me with sweets, and given me access to your library. My troubles might not have disappeared, but you've done a great job of hiding them. I'm so grateful for everything you and Uncle Obadiah have done for me."

Her aunt smiled and patted Samantha's knee. "Well, that's what family is for." She tapped the spine of the journal as she rose to her feet. "I'm sure this will keep you occupied for some time, but try to pace yourself. No need to read it all in one day."

Yet once Samantha started, she found it impossible to put the book down. Back in the parlor, she curled up in her uncle's favorite wingback chair and turned page after page.

Samantha's absorption made her impervious to the torture of the mantel clock's sluggish ticking. Time churned by utterly unnoticed.

Chronicles of everyday household business were mixed with more personal reflections, but a handful of entries jumped off the page to grab Samantha's heart in a viselike grip.

September 2, 1868

My bleeding started this morning. Another month with no baby. Why has God cursed me? For four years, Eli and I have tried to no avail. He says he is not angry or disappointed in me, but I cannot believe him. I have one job, to give him sons, and I have failed. When we were to marry, he promised to give me the security and standing I craved along with his heart, his protection, and his undying loyalty. I vowed to be his partner in all things, to love him, respect him, and stand by his side. To give him sons, so that the Dearing legacy we were building could be passed on to future generations.

Every month that passes with no child eats away at my soul. Eli's hard work is bringing his plans to fruition. He bought a spread of land that will make an excellent ranch. He's building me the house of my dreams, and what am I building for him? Nothing! I am barren, just like my oh-so-pious sister. Regina warned me that her inability to conceive might affect me as well, but I refused to believe it. God would not be so cruel. He might have wanted her to be childless so she would have more time to do his work, but what would be gained by my infertility? Nothing! Am I to be a millstone around Eli's neck, dragging his legacy into an early grave? Please, God, have mercy. For Eli's sake, if not for mine. Give us a child.

March 9, 1869

We moved into the house today. It's magnificent! A house to rival that of any cattleman in the state. It will take a few years to fully furnish it, but my mind spins with the possibilities. A large dining room for hosting dinners, a ballroom for entertaining prestigious guests. Might the governor grace my home someday? I can see him here now. Kissing my hand, complimenting me on my fine home, praising Eli for all he's achieved. I think Eli worries over my bouts with low spirits. I try to hide my growing melancholia from him, but he sees past my false cheer. I think that's why he let me name the ranch. I tried to refuse the honor—the responsibility—but he insisted. So I chose to name our new home the Three Cedars. It pays tribute to the cluster of stately trees that shade our home, but to me they symbolize my greatest wish, that our family of two will soon expand to three. It will happen. It has to happen. I cannot fail him.

October 12, 1869

I am with child! My prayers have finally been answered. Dr. Abbott confirmed the pregnancy today. Our son will be born late next spring. Eli is so excited he can scarcely sit still. He's been strutting around the ranch like a rooster all afternoon. Duke threatened to throw him in the pond the men have been excavating for my water garden if he doesn't quit crowing. All I can do is laugh. My joy is too large to contain.

February 23, 1870

Eli has settled on a name. Samuel. I can think of nothing better. How well I relate to Hannah and her struggle with infertility. When her time finally came to bear her son, she called him Samuel because she had asked him of the Lord.

Just as I have done. And just as the biblical Eli mentored Samuel to become the greatest judge in Israel's history, my own Eli will guide our son to greatness. I have no doubt. God has turned my mourning into dancing, and all is well.

May 11, 1870

The Lord has failed me! I've birthed a girl. Is there no justice in this world? Am I to be a constant disappointment to my husband? A failure in his eyes? Have I endured the disgrace of years of barrenness only to increase my disgrace by bearing a child of no value?

May 15, 1870

Perhaps all is not lost. Eli dotes on the child. He insists on calling her Samantha. I suggested we save the name Samuel for the son we are sure to have in the future. We could call this child something like Catherine, Amelia, or Helena. A regal name befitting her father's status. But Eli will not be swayed. He declares that our little Sam is utterly perfect just as she is. He might simply be trying to make me feel better about my failure to produce a proper heir, but I see love glowing in his eyes every time he holds her. Maybe this is not such a catastrophe after all.

May 11, 1873

Samantha turned three today. Such a little lady! Eli brags that she has my looks and predicts he'll need to keep his shotgun loaded for when the suitors flock to his door. She really is a charming child. I quite adore her. She picked a flower—a weed, really—and brought it to me the other day, and I found myself compelled to press it between the pages of my Bible to preserve the memory. She has quite changed me. I long to see her smiles and ache when she brings me tears. I no longer dream for myself but for her. With the right guidance, she'll excel in society. I'll have to curb her tendency for stubbornness and high spirits, but with her beauty and winsome ways, there will be nothing she can't achieve.

August 17, 1873

I bumped into Mrs. Philpot at the mercantile. She asked when Eli and I would be having another child. I feel the darkness descending again. . . .

29

Samantha had to wash her face before being presentable
enough to attend dinner with her aunt and uncle. Even
with Aunt Regina's warnings, it had hurt to read of her
mother's disappointment at her birth and see how long it took
for her to set aside her despair and learn to love the daughter
she'd been given.

It wasn't only for herself that Samantha had cried, however.
Her heart had ached for her mother. For all the pressure she
put on herself to achieve something outside of her control.
The bitterness and melancholy she carried, the constant fear
of not being able to fulfill her duty to her husband, and the
legacy she wanted so badly to achieve. It made the happy
memories she had of her mother infinitely more precious
knowing the weight she had carried through much of Samantha's early years.

Yes, her mother had been strict in her rules and her gov-
ernance of Samantha's behavior, but she'd also been eager to
praise her daughter's successes. There'd been hugs and kisses
and outings to the river, where they'd sit under a tree and her
mother would read to her until she fell asleep, her head in

her mother's lap. Daddy loved to make his girls laugh with rowdy parlor games that Mother never would have permitted if guests had been present. But in those private family moments, she had let her guard down, and the sweet tones of her laughter filled the room.

"Are you all right?" Aunt Regina touched a hand to Samantha's arm as she gathered the dirty dishes from the table.

Samantha shrugged as she stacked the plates and carried them to the sink. "You were right about it being difficult to peek into the raw places of a person's private thoughts, but even though it hurts to read some of the things she wrote, I feel closer to her for having done so."

"I'm glad, but maybe you should set the book aside for the rest of the evening. I'm sure your uncle would love to challenge you to a game of backgammon."

Samantha considered her aunt's advice, but her mother's journal beckoned, and she had no desire to resist the call.

"I appreciate your concern, but I want to continue with the journal. I don't know if it is the tug of curiosity or something more, but I feel as if I'm *supposed* to keep reading."

Aunt Regina looked as if she wanted to argue, but then something in her demeanor changed, and she smiled. "Well, you are a woman grown and capable of making your own choices. Besides, if it *is* something more than mere curiosity driving you back to that book, I don't want to be guilty of quenching the Spirit. Just remember that I'm here if you need to talk about anything, all right?"

Samantha nodded, then on impulse reached out and embraced her aunt around the basket of leftover rolls she held. "Thank you."

Her aunt chuckled softly. "Go on, now. Get back to your book. I'll see to the dishes."

Samantha pressed a kiss to her aunt's cheek, then hurried

back to the parlor, moving to the settee so her uncle could read the paper in his favorite chair.

The room gradually darkened as the sun set. At some point, her aunt and uncle bid her good-night, but Samantha barely noticed, caught up in the surprising turn her mother's life had taken. One Samantha never would have believed if the recounting had come from any source other than Victoria Dearing herself.

June 20, 1875

Five years. I had prepared myself for a long battle in the Desert of Barrenness, but I refuse to continue wandering aimlessly with nothing to show for my patience. It took five years for Eli and I to conceive Samantha, and it has been five years since her arrival. Yet my womb remains empty. I am weary of praying and receiving no answer. God knows the desire of my heart, yet he withholds his blessing. Eli tells me the child we have is enough, that he is content. Well, I am not. I vowed to give him a son, and I won't rest until I have done so.

July 8, 1875

My sister thinks to comfort me with Bible stories. Does she expect me to wait twenty-five years for a son like Sarah? At least Sarah had a promise to give her hope in the waiting. What do I have? Nothing but silence.

July 12, 1875

Sarah's story lingers in my mind. I've gone back and read it three times since my sister's letter arrived. An idea is forming. One that fills me both with dread and hope. Sarah, too, grew tired of waiting. She concocted a plan to take matters into her own hands. To craft her own destiny. She instructed her handmaid Hagar to lie with her husband. To bear the child she could not. The Lord did not curse Hagar for lying with her mistress's husband. In fact, he took pity on her and her son, making Ishmael into a great nation.

What if . . . ? Dare I even contemplate such action? But I must. Waiting and hoping have achieved nothing. I must be bold, brave, daring if I am to seize control of my destiny. Yet I cannot proceed as Sarah did. For one, Eli would never welcome another woman to his bed. He is far too honorable. And second, it is my responsibility to bear him a son. It would bring more shame upon me if another woman rounded with Eli's child. No, the only way for this to work will be for me to bear the child. I must simply increase my chances of doing so. I must seek a lover. One who can be trusted to keep silent. One who expects no emotional attachment, for despite the rashness of this plan, my love and loyalty belong solely to my husband.

I am the wife of a cattleman. I hear talk among the men about the potency of different bulls. Some sire thirty calves in a breeding season, some only ten or fifteen. And some fail to get a calf on any cow. If bulls can be infertile, it doesn't stretch the imagination to believe the same can be said of men. Doctors might insist that barrenness only afflicts women, but doctors are men with egos that do not wish to believe the fault might lie with them. Cattlemen are much more pragmatic. If a bull fails to service the heifers of the herd, the animal is put out to pasture and a new one brought in. I must do the same.

July 25, 1875

I have done it! My hand shakes as I write these words, for my heart still pounds in my chest. After weighing my options for two weeks, I made my selection and propositioned the man today. I will not write his name, for that will make it feel too much like a liaison. This is a business transaction. Nothing more. There is no romance. No illicit love affair. I seek only his seed. I offered to pay him, but he refused. I believe he has long admired me, and while I worry he might become attached, I know he will keep our secret. For if he doesn't, Eli will send him packing without pay or reference.

He told me of a line shack out by a creek that dried up last summer. He says they moved all the stock to land with better water. No one has reason to ride over there. Not even Eli. My partner has promised to fix it up, make it fit for a lady. Once he has it ready, this bold plan of mine will begin.

August 4, 1875

Today is the day! Eli will be gone for a week on a cattle-buying expedition. I kissed him good-bye this morning, hiding my guilt behind my wishes for safe travels and an eagerness for his return. I keep telling myself that I am doing this for him, but my conscience doesn't seem to recognize the nobility of my quest.

I soaked in the tub for an hour, but I still feel soiled. I scrubbed and scrubbed, but I can't erase the feel of another man's hands on my skin. A man not my husband. What have I done? I have betrayed my Eli! May God forgive me.

I am done with weeping. I cannot undo what has been done. I must move forward. Make the sacrifice worth something. I will meet him again on the morrow. The sooner I conceive, the sooner I can extricate myself from this physical infidelity.

August 10, 1875

    Eli returns home today, and I fear he will read the truth on my face. I'll shower him with affection and welcome him eagerly to my bed. With any luck, he'll never suspect.

March 2, 1876

    Seven months and still no baby. Maybe the problem is with me after all. If I've forsaken my marriage vows for no reason, I'll never forgive myself. My lover has urged me to try a little longer. To give him a year. If I don't conceive by summer, we'll put an end to our encounters.

June 12, 1876

    I am two weeks late for my woman's time. Please let this be what I've been working for.

July 24, 1876

    I'm sick every morning, and I've never been happier. I am with child! I have ended my affair, and my heart is lighter. I will never betray the man I love again. If I bear a girl, I will make peace with my failure. But I feel in my heart that this is a boy. I have risked everything, and I will finally have my reward.

October 7, 1876

    I can feel the baby move inside me. He is more active than Samantha. I'm sure that is a good sign. Eli is delighted. He kisses my round belly every night and talks to the baby as if he can hear him. He loves this child so much already that I'm starting to believe it might be his after all. I want to believe it is his. To erase all memory of what I have done and simply celebrate our family.

February 26, 1877

  Clinton Abernathy Dearing is born. Son of Eli Dearing and heir to the Three Cedars legacy. He is all I could have hoped for. Healthy. Beautiful. Strong. Whatever stain marks my soul, I cannot regret this beautiful life that we've been given.

February 27, 1877

  No! My innocent babe bears the mark of my sin. A crescent-shaped birthmark beneath his collarbone. The cowhand I gave myself to has the same mark. I wanted so badly to pretend that my deeds were nothing but a bad dream, that they hadn't really taken place. But every time I gaze on Clinton's unclothed chest, I am faced with the evidence of my betrayal. Will Eli decipher the truth? Will he reject his son? Will he reject me?

August 14, 1877

  Clinton is nearly six months old, and Eli has never once questioned why the boy's coloring is not as fair as Samantha's or why his features carry different lines. A few months ago, Eli decided that Clint had his chin, and I concurred with great enthusiasm. I pray the boy picks up Eli's mannerisms and speech patterns to further disguise the truth, but I worry for the day Clint reaches his teen years. What if his resemblance to his true father becomes too obvious to overlook?

March 2, 1878

  Clint said his first word today—dada. I thought Eli would burst from the pride puffing through him. Clint IS Eli's son in all the ways that matter. He is such a cheerful boy, always smiling and trailing after his sister. I can't imagine our family without him.

  Yet guilt eats at my conscience. I try to push it aside, tell-

ing myself that the end result justifies whatever tactics were necessary to produce it, but I know that is a lie. I rejected God's plan in favor of my own. There will be a reckoning. I just pray Clint will not be the one to pay the price for my sin.

June 20, 1880

The parson preached on Psalm 51 today, and I can't get the words out of my head. A plea for forgiveness from a man who committed adultery. A man who recognized his folly and wanted desperately to be forgiven by his God. A man whom the Lord looked on with mercy when he presented not a sacrifice but a broken and contrite heart.

Tonight, I fall on my knees, my remorse too great to stand. I pray the prayer of David and beg for the Lord's mercy. That he will blot out my transgressions and cleanse me from my sin. My wrongs are ever before me. In the face of my beautiful son. In the face of the man who fathered him.

"Create in me a clean heart, O God; and renew a right spirit within me. Cast me not away from thy presence; and take not thy holy spirit from me. Restore unto me the joy of thy salvation; and uphold me with thy free spirit. . . . Wash me, and I shall be whiter than snow."

October 20, 1880

The doctor has no explanation for the sickness that plagues me. I can barely rise from my bed. I have no appetite, and what little food I eat runs through me. My head pounds, and I find it difficult to concentrate. Perhaps this is the Lord's judgment.

October 25, 1880

I am getting worse. Eli spends hours at my side. My sweet Samantha comes and reads to me from her storybook. Clint *naps by my side. If it is my time, I will go peacefully and full of gratitude for these precious moments.*

October 28, 1880

He came to my room today while Eli was out with the herd and Mrs. Stewart had the children. I thought sentiment had brought him, but there was no softness in his eyes when he sat at my bedside. They glowed with ambition and purpose. He bid me farewell and vowed to watch over our son after I was gone.

His visit has left me unsettled. He and Eli both will be looking out for Clint's future, but what about Samantha? Regina will offer womanly guidance, I'm sure, but I want so much more for my daughter than my sister can provide. I must make Eli vow to send Samantha back east, to one of the schools I selected for her years ago. Only then will she reach her full potential. If Eli promises, he'll not go back on his word. He's too honorable. He won't want to send her away, but I'll make him see that it is for the best.

My darling Samantha will achieve all I ever dreamed for her and more.

Samantha turned the page, but there were no more entries. And why should there be? Her mother had died two days later. So weakened, she'd barely been able to squeeze her daughter's hand as they said their final good-byes. Eyes burning, Samantha reached for the lamp on the side table, turned down the wick, and blew out the flame.

Darkness surrounded her, a darkness that seemed appropriate after all she had just read. She reached for one of her aunt's knitted throws draped over the back of the settee and cuddled beneath it.

How could Mother have betrayed her husband? The man

who trusted her, adored her, and loved her with his entire being? Why was producing a son so vital that she couldn't feel whole without it? Why hadn't a daughter been enough?

And what of Clint? He was truly the innocent one in all of this. Samantha could never tell him what she'd learned. Her father, either. It would devastate them. She'd have to carry the secret herself. The legacy of a mother who'd craved earthly success more than her own integrity.

At least she'd made her peace with God before she passed.

Thank you for your abundant mercy and forgiveness, Lord. Give me that same spirit. Help me not to grow embittered toward my mother but to remember her through the lens of grace like Aunt Regina mentioned. None of us are perfect. We all fall short of your glory. Me included. Forgive my pride, my past hardness of heart toward my father, and the anger I feel toward my mother. Create in me a clean heart, too. That I might be an instrument of your grace.

The late hour tugged Samantha toward sleep. A part of her wished she'd never opened that journal. Yet as her mind relaxed, a hazy train of thought began to wind through her brain. The man who fathered Clint might still work at the ranch. Should she try to uncover his identity?

A crash from upstairs brought her eyes open. She listened for her aunt and uncle but heard nothing. Deciding it must not be cause for alarm, she allowed sleep to lure her back into unconsciousness.

Until the acrid smell of smoke penetrated her haze of sleep and jolted her upright.

Fire!

30

Samantha jumped up from the sofa and ran for the stairs, tripping over the shoes she'd removed earlier and nearly colliding with a side table in the process. Relying on habit to guide her through the dark house, she stumbled out of the parlor and raced down the hall to the stairs. A haunting glow writhed along the walls of the second floor, like a menacing demon stalking its prey.

God, help us!

"Aunt Regina! Uncle Obadiah!" Her voice quivered from the sobs welling inside her, but she shoved the weakness aside and sprinted up the stairs. "Aunt Regina! Uncle Obadiah! Wake up!"

By the time she reached the landing, smoke burned her eyes, pouring from the west side of the house. Her room. Had she left a candle lit? Forgotten to trim the lamp? But she hadn't been in her room since before dinner, and it had still been light.

Then she recalled the crash she'd heard. How long ago? Five minutes? Ten? Thirty? She had no idea how long she'd dozed.

Drawn toward the undulating light and crackling sounds, she inched to her left. Her door stood open. Smoke crawled along the ceiling as it escaped the room. A wave of heat hit her in the face as she rounded the open door and peered into her room. Flames engulfed her bed. Something that looked like a bottle lay in the center of the mattress. Broken glass shimmered in the windowpane. If she hadn't fallen asleep downstairs . . .

Flames licked up the wall behind the headboard. Wallpaper shriveled and charred. The fire wasn't out of control yet. She might be able to . . .

Smoke stung her eyes. A cough rattled her chest. She backed away from the bonfire that was her bedroom. She needed to wake her aunt and uncle first. If she tried to fight the blaze and something happened to her, they would perish, too. And all because they'd tried to protect her. She couldn't let that happen.

Reaching inside the room just enough to grab the door, she slammed it closed, then ran down the hall and barged into her aunt and uncle's room. "Aunt Regina!"

Why weren't they waking up?

Smoke clouded the room and clogged her throat. Coughs wracked her as she rushed to her aunt's side of the bed and grabbed her shoulder. "Aunt Regina, wake up!" Samantha shook her hard enough to skew her sleeping cap.

Finally, her aunt's eyes opened, though they took a minute to focus. "Samantha?" She pushed up on one arm. "What's wrong?"

"There's a fire in my room. We have to wake Uncle and get out of the house."

Aunt Regina bolted upward and grabbed for Samantha's hand. "Are you hurt?"

Samantha shook her head. "No, I was downstairs when I smelled the smoke."

"Thank God." Her aunt tossed the covers from her legs,

then turned to her husband. "Obadiah, wake up! The house is on fire!"

After a snuffle and groan, her uncle managed to wake. It took him longer to shake off the lethargy that had beset them, but after a push from his wife, he spilled out of bed and fumbled for his glasses.

"We might be able to save the house," Samantha said. "The fire's not too big yet. I'll start filling buckets at the kitchen pump."

"You'll do no such thing." Aunt Regina grabbed her arm and pierced her with a stern look. "You are to leave the house this instant. Rouse the neighbors. They'll help with the fire. You aren't to go anywhere near it."

"But what about you? I can't leave the house until I know you and Uncle Obadiah are safe."

God have mercy. If anything happened to either of them, she'd never forgive herself for bringing tragedy to their doorstep.

Aunt Regina climbed out of bed and reached for her wrapper. "We'll be right behind you." She shooed Samantha toward the bedroom door. "Now go! The best thing you can do for us is to get help."

"But—"

"No sassin' me, young lady." Aunt Regina scowled and jabbed a finger toward the hall. "Go!"

Never in all of Samantha's nineteen years had Aunt Regina ever spoken to her in such a sharp tone. It brought tears to her eyes and an ache to her chest, yet it also brought speed to her feet. A sob choked out of her as she ran for the stairs. Not because her aunt had yelled at her, but because leaving family behind ripped a hole in her heart. She'd run to the neighbors as fast as she could, then she'd come back and make sure her aunt and uncle got out.

266

Please, God, get them out.

Using the banister as a guide, Samantha sped down the hall and onto the stairs. Her stockinged feet slipped on the wooden steps, urging a modicum of caution and bringing the state of her feet to the front of her mind.

Shoes. She'd be faster with shoes.

Ducking into the parlor, she peered into the darkness in search of a pair of shadowy lumps. Her toes registered the softness of the rug a heartbeat before she kicked one of her shoes. She hunkered over and felt around for her other one, thankful that her confinement had led to her wearing house slippers instead of shoes with endless buttons and laces. She sat on the edge of the settee and slid them on. When she bent forward, something pointed jabbed the underside of her thigh. The journal. Not wanting to lose the last connection she had to her mother, she snatched the small book off the settee and shoved it into her skirt pocket before running for the front door.

She unlatched the lock, then grabbed the handle. The knob turned, but the door wouldn't open. Samantha used both hands and yanked with all her might. The door rattled on its hinges but refused to swing inward.

What was happening?

"Come on!" She tried again, jerking the handle every which way to no avail.

Giving up, she abandoned the front door and ran for the kitchen. She banged a hip against a kitchen chair and sent it crashing to the ground. Ignoring both the chair and the pain it inflicted, she pushed past the table and latched on to the handle of the back door. She yanked it toward her. It refused to come.

"No!" She shook the door with all her might, trying to free it from whatever moored it in place. Her own body shook with sobs of desperation as the horrifying truth slashed across her panicked mind.

They'd been locked inside.

Something dropped onto Asher's forehead, waking him from a dream about Samantha. Usually he enjoyed such dreams. In sleep, there were no obstacles to prevent the woman he loved from becoming his wife. No financial barriers, no powerful father with disapproval in his eyes, no murderous threats hanging over her head. Just him and Samantha together beneath a sunny sky, her hand in his, her gaze filled with love, her chin tipped up for his kiss. But tonight's dream had been darker, tying his gut in knots and leaving him on edge. Made him glad something had woken him.

Lying on his back on the bedroll he'd spread on the floor of his brothers' room, he blinked into the dark and reached up to his forehead to figure out what had hit him. The back of a limp hand, apparently. Asher rolled his eyes. Jack. That boy's gangly limbs were always flinging around while he slept. It seemed Asher's forehead had gotten in the way when Jack had flopped onto his stomach. Asher lifted the sleep-slackened appendage away from his face, then sat up. He thought about scooting his bedroll closer to Fergus's bed and going back to sleep, but the disturbing dream he'd awoken from left him restless. Maybe stretching his legs would help clear his head.

Asher rose and stepped into the pair of pants he'd left draped over a chair last night, leaving the connected suspenders to drape over his hips. He shoved his feet into his boots, rubbed a hand over his face to clear away the last vestiges of sleep, then tiptoed out of the room. Thinking to visit the outhouse, he opened the back door and stepped onto the porch. A breeze hit him in the face. One that carried a distinctive odor.

Smoke.

Asher's chest instantly tightened. Fire was dangerous enough during the day, but at night? It could cut a swath through a town before anyone knew what had happened. Heart pounding, he pulled his suspenders up over his undershirt and started jogging north, the direction from which the wind was blowing, thankfully away from the courthouse square and the more densely populated areas of town.

The moon afforded enough light for him to pick out the shadowy outlines of buildings as he trotted past, searching out an orange glow that would pinpoint a source. A dog barked, nudging Asher into a lope. He turned west, then north again, not consciously aware of where he was heading until he reached First Christian Church. His gaze immediately locked on to the two-story house about a block farther down the street. A house he'd visited nearly every day during the last ten days.

An angry orange glow flickered from a window on the second story. The bedrooms. Samantha!

Asher took off at a dead run. A groggy neighbor stumbled onto his porch, where his dog barked and turned at the sound of Asher's pounding footsteps.

"What's going on?" he called.

Asher slowed for only a moment. "Fire at the preacher's house. Ring the bells. Fetch the fire wagon."

Without waiting to see the man's reaction, Asher renewed his sprint, not stopping until he collided with the front door. "Samantha!"

He grabbed the knob and turned it, but it wouldn't allow him entrance. He pounded both fists against the door and shouted at the top of his lungs. "Samantha!"

Please, God.

The wood quivered from the force of his pounding, but it

continued to block his path. He swiveled to set his shoulder to the wood, but something metal glimmered in the moonlight. He pulled back and reached for the object. Long. Flat. He squinted into the darkness, not believing what he was seeing. Someone had screwed a steel plate onto the door, bolting it to the doorframe.

He scratched at the restraint, trying to get a grip, desperate to tear it off.

Growling in frustration when his fingers failed to find purchase, he pounded the door with the pad of his fist.

"Samantha!" The anguished cry ripped through his soul.

He had to find another way in. The back door. No, a window. Whoever the fiend was who trapped them inside would have cut off the rear escape, too.

Asher set his palm to the banister and was about to leap down to the ground in order to access the parlor window when something thumped against the front door, vibrating the wood.

"Help!"

The voice was muffled and raspy, but it was hers.

He ran to the door and pressed his mouth to the crack between it and the jamb. "Samantha? It's Asher. I'm here!"

"Thank God. Can you"—a series of coughs cut off her voice—"open the door?"

He banged his head against the wood wishing for a crowbar or an ax. "No, it's bolted to the frame. You need to open a window. I'll help you climb out."

"I tried," she said. "Someone—" More coughing. Deep and hoarse. God help him. He needed to get her out of there! "None of the shutters will open."

"I'll take a look." *Please let it be a problem I can solve.* "Go to the parlor. First window."

Asher leapt over the railing and ran to the first window. The smoke billowing through the seams of the shutters burned

KAREN WITEMEYER

his eyes, making it hard to see. Groping for the shutters, his
fingers ran over something that felt like leather. Squinting into
the smoke, he discovered a leather strap wrapped around the
closed shutters, right below the hinges, banding them in place.
Looked like cut harness line. Something that would seal the
shutters without alerting those inside, like nailing a board
across them would. Thankfully, a leather band was easier to
remove than a nailed board. Asher jabbed his fingers between
the leather and wood near the crease where the shutters met
and worked the strap downward with a series of sharp tugs.
Finally the leather band fell away, and he yanked the shutters
open hard enough to crash them against the wall.

Smoke poured from the window, forcing him to turn his
head. He coughed and squinted through the smoke. "Samantha?"

Her face appeared in the window, streaked with soot and
tears. "Uncle's collapsed. He's too heavy. I can't . . . I can't drag
him over here."

"Samantha Jane, you climb out of that window this instant.
I'll take care of Obadiah."

Asher recognized the weak, smoke-roughened voice of
Regina Hopewell, but he knew Samantha would never leave
her aunt and uncle behind. He lowered the arms he'd lifted
to help her out of the window and instead shooed her aside.

"I'm coming in."

She stepped back as he pulled himself up and over the sill.
"He's over here."

Her hand touched his arm, and all he wanted to do was tug
her to him and hold on tight. Instead, he followed her to the
fallen form of Parson Hopewell. His wife knelt on the rug at
his side. Nudging past her, Asher moved to the man's head,
flipped him onto his back, then slid his hands under the parson's arms and dragged him toward the window.

Church bells pealed outside. Good. Help was coming. But so was the fire. A chunk of plaster fell from the ceiling and smashed into the settee. Samantha squealed, then grabbed her aunt's hand and hurried her toward the window. Asher glanced at the ceiling and scowled when flames licked through the hole.

They didn't have much time before the entire ceiling came down on their heads.

"Climb out." Asher met Samantha's eye and jerked his chin toward the window. "I'll need you to help me with your uncle."

She nodded and ducked through the opening. The minute she disappeared over the sill, his chest lightened. He turned back to her aunt.

"Now you, ma'am." He released his hold on the parson to offer Mrs. Hopewell a hand. She didn't look too steady. "I'll help you."

She clasped his arm, obviously reluctant to leave her husband. Finally, she moved to the window and sat on the sill. Her eyes found Asher's. "God bless you."

Not knowing what to say to that, he dipped his chin and protected her head with his hand as she bent through the opening. Samantha took her arm from the other side and steadied her descent.

Asher met Samantha's gaze. "Get her away from the smoke."

She nodded and led her aunt away from the house. Asher turned back to the parson. Thanking God Obadiah Hopewell was a slender man, Asher grabbed fistfuls of nightshirt, hefted him onto the windowsill, then pushed him through the opening. Mumbling an apology, Asher climbed out after him, taking care not to step on the poor man's head. Once out, he grabbed the man under his arms and hauled him toward the street. Samantha appeared at his side, ready to assist.

As soon as they cleared the smoke, Asher laid the parson

down beside his wife so she could tend him, then turned to the woman he'd nearly lost.

Not caring who might see, he clasped Samantha to his chest and held on tight. Tears stung his eyes.

She fell against him, her arms wrapping around his back, as all the terror she'd experienced poured out of her in ragged sobs. "Thank God you came."

Asher turned bleary eyes toward the sky, looking to the moon that glowed in the darkness. A vise tightened around his chest, keeping the relief he should feel from seeping inside.

This wasn't over.

God help them. Any man willing to burn three innocent people alive wouldn't stop coming after Samantha until she was dead.

31

It took two hours for the volunteer firefighters manning the pump wagon and the neighbors with buckets and wet blankets to fully extinguish the fire. Samantha had tried to help, but Asher insisted she stay with her aunt and uncle, and even then, she'd felt his watchful gaze on her, as if he worried someone might emerge from the crowd and steal her away.

Or maybe her own fears were coloring her perceptions. Every time she closed her eyes, she saw her bed engulfed in flames. What had she done to make someone hate her so?

Thank God Aunt Regina and Uncle Obadiah were all right. Someone had fetched Dr. Abbott, and he had examined the three of them. After encouraging them to move farther away from the smoke, he'd listened to their lungs and hearts and prescribed a great deal of rest, clean air, and a pile of lemon drops to soothe their scalded throats. He ordered Uncle Obadiah not to preach for two weeks, but Uncle only promised him one, teasing the doctor about trying to shorten Sunday services with an overzealous prescription.

Once the immediate danger passed, her aunt and uncle's cheerful demeanors gradually resurfaced. It truly was remarkable. The way they smiled and thanked their neighbors for helping, all while everything they owned turned to rubble and ash.

People began making their way back to their homes. Volunteer firefighters shut down the steam pump, packed up their gear, and drove the fire wagon back toward the heart of town. The jangle of harnesses and clopping of hooves faded as the team turned down a side road and disappeared from view. As the commotion diminished, a somber emptiness expanded in Samantha's chest.

Such devastation. Because of her. Oh, she knew it wasn't really her fault. The man who'd started the blaze was to blame. Yet she couldn't escape the knowledge that her aunt's house would still be standing if she hadn't been sheltering beneath its roof. A roof that had fallen in, collapsing the second story and making the residence completely unlivable.

Aunt Regina, still dressed in her nightgown and wrapper, hair hanging down around her ears, soot smearing her face and clothes, came up beside Samantha and wrapped an arm around her niece's waist.

Samantha laid her head against her aunt's shoulder. "Your poor house."

Her stomach churned as she surveyed the blackened remains of what had been a home full of keepsakes, handmade treasures, and family photographs. A home containing books, sermon notes, and original treatises on biblical topics spawned from decades of research and scholarly study. A home whose door had always been open to anyone in need, whose cozy parlor offered an inviting place for comfort and conversation. So many things lost. So much that couldn't be replaced. Cherished memories turned to dust.

Why had God allowed such a tragedy to befall two such faithful servants?

A ragged inhale lifted her aunt's shoulder beneath Samantha's head for a moment before a heavy sigh dropped it back down. "Jesus admonished his followers not to lay up treasures in this world, material things that can be destroyed by moth and rust—and fire." Her voice, roughened by smoke, hitched on that last word. "Our treasures are to be stored in heaven instead." She turned to face Samantha, her arm slipping from around her waist as she instead clasped her niece's hand. "What happened tonight has given me an entirely new perspective on that teaching. When you woke me, all I cared about was getting you out. Getting Obadiah out. Making sure you both were safe. I didn't spare a thought for anything else." Her attention turned back to the crumpled heap that used to be her home. "Now that the danger has passed, I admit to being a little heartsore over what the fire took from us, but dwelling on sorrow only begets more sorrow. So I'll do my best to steer my thoughts away from what has been lost and focus instead on what we have gained."

"Gained?" Samantha stared at her aunt in disbelief. "What could you have possibly gained from all of this?"

A smile broke across her aunt's face, and a light seemed to glow from within her. "We're about to have a front-row seat to a glorious performance. God at his finest. Working for the good of those who love him."

Samantha shook her head, humbled by her aunt's faith. "You're amazing."

"No, sweetheart. I've just lived longer than you, that's all. Experienced more hardships and witnessed God's provision in the aftermath." Her thumb rubbed the back of Samantha's hand. "No one enjoys adversity, but nothing can draw a child of God closer to the Father. It is easier to rely on his strength when we've been weakened. Easier to trust his guidance when we know we are lost. Easier to seek his presence when pain makes us crave his comfort.

"God has promised to provide all we need, and his people are already heeding his call. Your uncle and I have been offered several places to stay over the next few days, and I have no doubt that we will have food to eat and clothes to wear." She looked back toward the house. "And who knows what treasures might be found when we sort through the rubble? The Lord is so good about providing unexpected joys. Maybe we'll uncover an undamaged photograph or an unbroken teapot."

Samantha's lips twitched as good humor began to restore itself in her spirit. "If anything is stubborn enough to survive a fire, it would be that ticking torture device you keep on the mantel."

"My mother's clock?" A laugh bubbled out of her aunt that brought an answering smile to Samantha's heart. "I had no idea you disliked it so much."

"Neither did I, until we were forced to keep company for so long."

Samantha chuckled, and her aunt joined in, releasing the heartache and inviting optimism.

"That's a sound I love to hear."

Samantha turned toward her uncle's voice and picked out the forms of three men heading their way. Asher led the group, his arm outstretched with a lantern to light their path. Her pulse fluttered at the sight of him. His gaze sought hers, and while a smile played at the corners of his mouth, the grave look in his eyes warned that the unpleasantness of the night was not yet over.

The men formed a circle of sorts—her uncle coming alongside her aunt, Asher positioning himself close to Samantha, and the sheriff closing the loop.

Asher set the lantern on the ground in the center of their gathering. When he straightened, he placed his hand at the small of her back, the touch soothing the nervousness that had sprung to life when Sheriff Jeter's gaze latched on to her.

"Monty has a few questions for you, Samantha." Uncle Obadiah tipped his head toward the lawman. "But he promised to keep the interview brief."

Aunt Regina folded her arms over her chest. "Can't this wait? She's been through enough tonight."

"With all due respect, ma'am," the sheriff interrupted, "I've found it best to interview folks while things are fresh on their minds. The more time that passes, the fewer details tend to emerge."

"But she's exhausted. We all are."

"It's all right." Samantha placed a hand on her aunt's arm. "I don't mind."

She knew her aunt was just looking out for her, but in truth, she'd rather get the entire incident behind her now than have to dredge it all back up again in a few hours.

Asher's hand settled at her waist. Warm. Steady. Supportive. "You sure?"

Samantha peered into his face and courage seeped into her bones, as if having him at her side was all she needed to be brave. "I'm sure." She turned to the sheriff. "What questions do you have?"

"I understand you were the one who discovered the fire. Can you tell me where it started?"

Visions of flames leaping up from the center of her bed sent a shiver through her. Asher must have noticed, for he wrapped an arm around her shoulders and tugged her close to his side. His nearness banished the vulnerability the memory stirred and helped her find her voice.

"In my room. I had fallen asleep downstairs after doing some reading. I remember a crash of some sort that woke me. I thought my aunt or uncle had gotten up and dropped

KAREN WITEMEYER

something as they fumbled around in the dark. I listened for a minute but didn't hear anything else, so I laid down and drifted back to sleep. When I woke a short time later, I smelled smoke. I ran upstairs and found my bed on fire."

Sheriff Jeter raised a brow. "Your bed? Not the curtains or the floor where a candle might have fallen?"

"No, sir, it was the bed. My window had been broken, and a bottle of some kind lay in the middle of the coverlet. I think . . ." Her forehead scrunched as she concentrated on the memory. "I think I smelled kerosene, though I'm not certain. All I know is that the bed coverings were completely engulfed in flames, and the fire had started climbing up the wall behind the headboard. The wallpaper was shriveled and curled into blackened bits."

Her aunt made a strangled sound. "If you had put the journal away and gone to bed as I'd encouraged . . ."

"Praise God for his mercy," Uncle Obadiah murmured as he wrapped an arm around his wife.

Asher's hold on Samantha tightened, and she thought she felt a tremor pass through him. But maybe that had been her own shiver. Either way, she leaned into him, hoping to dispel the chill the memory induced.

"Well, that confirms that you were the target, not the Hopewells."

The sheriff's matter-of-fact comment did nothing to soothe her nerves, but his conclusion did not surprise her. She'd reached the same verdict hours ago.

"Mr. Ellis told me about the doors and shutters being fastened shut from the outside. The arsonist must have done that piece of work well after dark to avoid being seen. I'll question the neighbors later today to see if anyone noticed a lantern bobbing around during the night. My guess is that everyone was in bed by the time he worked his mischief, but we might get lucky and find a witness."

279

Sheriff Jeter ran a hand through brown hair that was starting to gray and blew out a heavy breath. "I hate to admit it, but this whole situation has me stumped. Thompson was our only viable suspect, and after we cleared him, I haven't had much to go on. I've questioned your father's business associates to see if anyone's holding a grudge big enough to want to hurt him through you, but I gotta say, this don't feel like it's aimed at your old man. Whoever is targeting you must have something to gain by it. If we can narrow down his motive, we'll have a better chance of catchin' him."

He shifted his stance and pinned her with a penetrating look. "In my experience, there are three motives strong enough to push someone into purposely taking a life—revenge, jealousy, and money. Now, I been askin' around about you, Miss Dearing, and far as I can tell, no one in town's got a big enough ax to grind to want you dead. So unless you provoked someone back in Boston bad enough for him to follow you all the way to Texas . . ." He let the implied question hang in the air.

Samantha shook her head. "No. Nothing like that happened in Boston."

"All right. Then we can eliminate revenge." He turned that unsettling stare of his on Asher. "What about jealousy? Any obsessive women in your circle? One who might feel threatened by Miss Dearing and want to get her out of the picture?" He looked Asher up and down. "Can't say as you're any particular prize, but women get odd notions about things like that."

An embarrassed chuckle rumbled from Asher's chest. "Until a few weeks ago, I lived on a ranch with a bunch of cowpokes. The only woman in my life other than Miss Dearing is my mother, and she adores Samantha. I think it's safe to rule out jealous women."

The sheriff grunted. "Didn't think that option held much water, but I needed to ask. That leaves money." He turned those needle-sharp eyes back on Samantha. "You're a wealthy young woman. You stand to inherit half of your daddy's ranchin' empire. Think carefully now. Is there anyone who would benefit from you being gone? Someone in line to inherit your share of the Three Cedars, perhaps?"

Samantha shook her head. "No. There's no one. If I were to die, everything would go to my bro—"

Clarity struck like a lightning bolt. Her hand dropped to her pocket. Felt for her mother's journal.

"What is it?" Her aunt's confused expression begged for answers, but there wasn't time.

Samantha turned to Asher. "We have to go back to the ranch. Now. Before the hands get up and start their work."

Asher nodded, not asking any of the questions flashing in his eyes. Sheriff Jeter, on the other hand, continued to prod.

"Who is it, girl? Who stands to gain?"

How could she make him understand without dragging her mother's name through the mud?

"I don't know. Not yet. But I think there's a way to figure it out. I just need to get back to the ranch."

The sheriff glanced at the hint of light trimming the horizon and scowled. "Guess we better get goin', then."

32

Asher shortened the stirrups on his saddle to the length he knew Samantha preferred, then patted Bruno's neck in apology for making him work so early in the morning. The paint simply tossed his head and searched Asher's hand for another carrot.

"It's a good thing you're so easy to bribe." Asher reached into his pocket and pulled out a second carrot, happy to reward the horse for his faithfulness. "I expect you to take good care of our lady today. No actin' squirrelly just 'cause it's dark, all right?" Bruno lowered his head as if in understanding. Asher rubbed his forelock. "I knew I could count on you."

Which was why he'd offered to ride one of the sheriff's spare mounts instead of keeping Bruno for himself. Samantha was still new to riding, and he didn't trust her on a horse he didn't know.

The sound of his mother's back door closing drew his attention. Samantha stepped off the porch and walked toward the lean-to.

Asher moved away from Bruno and met her halfway. "Hey," he said as he reached for her hand. "How're you holding up?"

She'd washed the soot from her face and hands and borrowed one of his mother's dresses, but she still looked as tuckered out as a cowhand after a week's worth of night duty. If it wasn't for the spark of determination in her eyes, he'd steer her right back to the house and insist she get some sleep. But he knew better than to try. The set of her chin warned that she'd walk to the Three Cedars if she had to.

Samantha laced her fingers through his and tugged him close to her side as they walked back to where Bruno waited. Once there, she pivoted to face him. "I have to tell you something before Sheriff Jeter gets here. In confidence." Her eyes searched his. "My father and brother can't know, not unless it becomes absolutely necessary."

He'd never seen her this tense. Squeezing her hand, he dipped his chin in agreement. "You have my word, Samantha. I won't tell a soul."

Some of the weight seemed to lift from her shoulders, and Asher was glad to receive it onto his. Whatever she needed, he'd do.

"The reason I wasn't in my room when the fire started was because I was reading my mother's journal. Aunt Regina gave it to me yesterday. She never read it herself, so not even she knows what I'm about to tell you."

"All right."

Samantha looked slightly ill, so Asher grabbed the milking stool standing a few feet behind him in the lean-to. "Here. Sit down." He helped her onto the stool, then crouched beside her and nodded for her to continue.

She placed her hands in her lap and crushed the folds of her skirt in her fisted palms. "My parents had a hard time having children," she said in a small voice. "It took them five years to have me, and when five more years passed without a child, my mother . . . she . . . turned to another man."

Asher did his best to mask his shock, hoping the flickering

shadows of the lantern light would disguise his thoughts. But something must have shown on his face. Either that or she guessed his reaction, for she hurried to explain.

"It wasn't a love affair. It was more of a . . . breeding opportunity." Samantha hung her head, hiding her eyes from him for a moment before lifting her chin again. "She loved my father, but she was obsessed with giving him a son. Almost as if she believed her life would have no meaning if she failed to produce a viable heir."

He heard the hurt in her voice, the recognition that she hadn't been enough. It must have shredded her heart to read of her mother's dissatisfaction. Her disloyalty. How could that woman not comprehend that she already had one of the most amazing humans on the face of the planet as a daughter and heir? Clasping Samantha's hand, he brought it to his lips, praying she would understand that for him, she'd always be enough.

"Mother took up with one of the men at the ranch, but she never named him in her journal. It's possible he's moved on and doesn't work for the Three Cedars any longer, but when the sheriff asked who stood to gain, things suddenly started making sense." Samantha shifted on the stool and squeezed his hand tightly. "Whoever fathered Clint would have a claim to the ranch through his son. A claim that would be twice as large if Clint didn't have a sibling around to inherit her share."

Asher's mind took a dark turn. "In order to inherit, though, he'd have to do away with your father, too."

Moisture glistened in Samantha's eyes. She pressed her lips together and nodded. When she spoke, her voice quivered slightly. "I'm guessing he's been biding his time, waiting for Clint to reach his legal majority. When I came home from Boston, and Daddy started trying to find me a cattleman husband, this man must've worried that Daddy would deed over part of the Three Cedars to whoever I married, and he decided he couldn't let that happen."

It was a better theory than anything else they had.

"So how do we flush him out?"

The sound of distant hoofbeats drew Samantha's attention to the road. Sheriff Jeter would be there soon. She turned back to him, an urgency in her manner.

"Clint has a crescent-shaped birthmark on his chest, right below his collarbone. Mama's journal said the man who fathered him has the same marking. You and the sheriff need to make the ranch hands take off their shirts. See who has that mark. It wouldn't be proper for me to be there, so I'll be in the house, running interference with Clint and my father. I'll try to keep them away from the bunkhouse. I realize that my father will probably have to be told eventually, but I want to spare Clint. He's so young. There's no telling what kind of impact the truth will have on him."

To find out that the man you always believed to be your father wasn't, and the man who *was* had tried to kill your sister on multiple occasions? Yeah. That could mess with a kid's head.

Asher had no idea how he was going to convince a bunch of cowpokes to shed their shirts, but maybe if they got there early enough, they could catch the men before they dressed for the day. Hired hands used to bunking together weren't particularly shy, but they could be pigheaded if they thought they were being accused of something.

"I'll find a way to search the men," he said as he pushed to his feet. He held out a hand to Samantha. "Let's get you mounted. The sheriff will be here any moment."

She rose and moved to Bruno's left side, her hand reaching for the saddle horn. Before Asher could bend over to give her a leg up, she abandoned the saddle and wrapped both arms around his waist.

"Thank you, Asher. I don't know what I would do if I didn't have you to lean on."

He closed his arms around her slender form and rubbed her back. "Lean away, darlin'. I'm not going anywhere." He relaxed his hold, knowing they didn't have much time, but when her face tilted back and her eyes found his, the words he'd been holding back, for reasons he couldn't recall at the moment, came tumbling forth. "I love you, Samantha. And I promise to do whatever it takes to keep you and Clint safe."

She didn't say the words back, but she did grab his neck and plant a kiss on his mouth that sent his pulse galloping out of the corral. She pulled away and reached for Bruno before he recovered from the surprise enough to fully engage in the experience, but it left him grinning nonetheless. It wasn't exactly a pledge of undying devotion, but it was close enough to qualify as reciprocation. At least for now.

"You ready, Ellis?" The sheriff's voice echoed across the quiet yard.

"Yes, sir." Asher locked his fingers together and offered them as a stepstool.

Samantha gave him her foot, and he boosted her into the saddle. He handed her the reins, then gathered the lantern from the hook on the lean-to's support post.

Coming alongside her, he secured her foot in the stirrup, more as an excuse to touch her than to check her position. "You feel all right up there?"

She nodded. "I can do this, Ash."

He clapped a hand over her shoe and smiled at her. "I know you can." He clicked his tongue to get Bruno's attention, then started walking toward the street, trusting his horse to follow. "Come on, then. Let's go for a ride."

After Asher mounted, the threesome picked their way through the sleeping town before the road carried them out into the countryside. Asher let the sheriff take the lead, preferring to hang back and stay close to Samantha. They kept their horses to a steady walk until the predawn sky began to lighten. When Jeter urged his mount into a trot, Asher watched to make sure Samantha made the transition. She hung on to the saddle horn when Bruno picked up the pace, but other than that, she handled the change well. He prayed everything else they were about to experience would go as smoothly.

When the house and outbuildings of the Three Cedars came into view, the sheriff reined in his mount and waited for Asher and Samantha to pull abreast of him.

"All right, Miss Dearing, what am I supposed to be lookin' for?"

"I gave Mr. Ellis instructions on how to search the men in the bunkhouse. He can assist you while I notify my family about the fire."

Jeter scowled. "I don't much cotton to being kept in the dark, young lady. If you want my help, you best be tellin' me what we're huntin' for."

"Easy, Sheriff." Asher nudged his mount forward a step to place himself squarely between Samantha and the lawman. "No need to badger. I'll tell you everything you need to know once Miss Dearing is safely in the house."

The two men glared at each other for a moment before Jeter grunted in reluctant assent.

"Best tell your daddy I'm here making inquiries." The sheriff leaned sideways in the saddle to meet Samantha's gaze around the barrier of Asher's head and shoulders. "He needs to know that I'm conducting an investigation on his property and amongst his men."

Samantha nodded. "I'll tell him." She nudged Bruno forward,

moving to the right toward the house while Asher stayed left with Sheriff Jeter and headed to the bunkhouse.

Asher kept his eyes on Samantha until she dismounted and disappeared into the house, then he turned his attention to the lawman at his side.

"You finally gonna tell me what we're lookin' for?"

"A crescent-shaped birthmark," Asher said. "On a man's chest. Beneath his collarbone."

"A birthmark?" The sheriff spat out the word as if it were a wad of tasteless, well-chawed tobacco. "What does that have to do with anything?"

Asher reined in his horse outside the bunkhouse and dismounted. This wasn't a conversation to be had in anything but the closest of quarters. He waited for Jeter to climb off his horse, then walked up beside him.

"It's a delicate matter," Asher murmured in a hushed tone. "I've given my word not to reveal any details, and I aim to honor that promise. All you need to know, Sheriff, is that there is a man who believes he stands to inherit a portion of the Three Cedars—a portion that would be a good sight bigger without Samantha around. We don't know who he is, but Samantha recently learned that he can be identified by that birthmark I told you about. I know you can't arrest a man for having a mark on his chest, but I figure culling him from the herd is the first step. Once we know which cowhand to target, we can start gatherin' evidence and get him to confess."

Jeter frowned. "If this mark is the only evidence we got, we best keep that bit of information close to the vest. Don't want to let the fella know we're onto him until we have enough evidence to arrest him. I'll come up with some other excuse to get them to take off their shirts. Follow my lead."

"Yes, sir."

The sheriff strode toward the bunkhouse. "When we get

inside," he said, "position yourself by the back door. That way no one can slip out with us knowin'."

"Will do."

Glad to let a man with actual authority do the talking, Asher stayed in Jeter's shadow as they entered the bunkhouse. Once inside, he scouted the second door on the back side of the building and planted himself in front of it. A couple of men sat on their bunks, working up the gumption to get out of bed, but most were still sawing wood.

"All right, boys. Time to get up!" The sheriff banged his fist against the front door a few times, and feet began to hit the floor.

"Sheriff Jeter? That you?" Martin rubbed his eyes as if he didn't trust what he was seeing, then slowly rose from his cot. "Whatcha doin' in our bunkhouse?" The drunkenness of sleep fell away from him in an instant as clarity dawned. "Did something happen to Miss Dearing?"

The grumbles and scuffling from the rest of the men fell silent as they all listened for the answer.

"As a matter of fact, someone set fire to the house where she was staying in town. Trapped her and the Hopewells inside."

"God have mercy." Martin braced an arm against the nearby wall. "Is she . . . ?"

Asher's throat tightened as old panic resurfaced inside him momentarily. The smell of the fire, his desperation to get in the house, the fear that he might be too late.

"She's alive, thank the Lord. As are the preacher and his missus."

A collective sigh echoed through the bunkhouse. Asher watched each man's face, looking for signs of disappointment or frustration. Nothing stood out, unfortunately. The men's concern seemed genuine. 'Course some fellas were awful good poker players and knew how to run a convincing bluff.

"We got evidence that the fire was deliberate," the sheriff continued. "Arson. Attempted murder, in fact. Whoever set the blaze sealed off the exits, making it nearly impossible for those inside to escape."

"Who would do such a thing?" one of the men muttered beneath his breath.

Sheriff Jeter widened his stance. "That's what we're here to figure out. We got reason to believe that the man who set the fire sustained an injury to his torso while committing the act. We also have reason to suspect the man hails from the Three Cedars. So I'm gonna need each one of you to strip down to your drawers and submit to inspection."

A roomful of eyeballs blinked at him as if he'd lost his mind.

The sheriff kicked the cot closest to him, causing a loud clatter. "I didn't ride all the way out here before the crack of dawn for my health, boys. Strip. Now!"

Men stood, all in various states of undress. Some tugged on trousers before pulling off nightshirts. Others yanked shirts over heads. One poor fellow had to unbutton himself out of the top half of a union suit.

Sheriff Jeter grabbed a lantern hanging from a nail on the wall by the door, lit it, and turned the wick up high. Then he walked the line, inspecting each man's torso. Asher joined him, scrutinizing every collarbone.

"There has to be some mistake," Martin said after the sheriff moved past him. "The Dearings are like family to us. No one here would ever hurt them. The Hopewells either."

They neared the end of the row, having found nothing resembling a crescent. A few scars and one cowboy with enough hair to rival a buffalo, but no birthmarks.

"I'm gonna need a list of any man on the payroll who ain't here," the sheriff said as he frowned at the final unmarked chest.

"Sanders and Hansen are out with the herd," Martin reported. "I'll send Green and Foster to relieve them first thing. They can be back here in less than an hour."

"That everyone?"

"Everyone but the foreman," Martin said. "Kendrick's got his own cabin behind the main house. Usually has breakfast with the family."

Duke Kendrick had access to the house. Which meant he had access to Samantha. If he was the man with the birthmark . . .

Asher pushed past the sheriff to get to the door. The instant Asher's boots hit dirt, he ran for the main house.

33

Samantha let herself into the house and made her way to the kitchen. Her father usually had the stove stoked and coffee brewing before Mrs. Stewart woke. He wasn't one to let a drop of daylight slip by without putting it to use.

Sure enough, when she pushed open the kitchen door, she found him cranking the wheel on the coffee grinder. He turned at the sound of the door, his eyes widening when his gaze landed on her.

"Samantha?" His hand fell away from the grinder. "What are you doing here?" He took a step toward her, and that was all the invitation she needed.

She ran to him and wrapped her arms around his middle. He hugged her tightly, his cheek pressing against the top of her head. Then all at once he stiffened.

"Why does your hair smell like smoke?" He held her away from him and scanned her from head to toe, no doubt taking in the borrowed dress that didn't quite fit, the circles under her eyes, and the signs of exhaustion and heartache that no amount of soap and water could wash away.

"There was a fire, Daddy." Her voice rasped slightly, her throat still raw from the smoke and her cries for help. Tears rushed to her eyes, but she ruthlessly batted them away. She wasn't a child seeking a father's comfort. She was a woman on a mission to catch a villain and protect those she loved. "We got out—Aunt Regina and Uncle Obadiah, too—but only because Asher found us." She swallowed, hating the residual fear that made her knees tremble as she recalled the horror of being surrounded by fire with no escape. "Whoever set the fire locked us inside. Sabotaged the shutters and bolted the doors. If Asher hadn't smelled the smoke and investigated . . . Well, I just thank God he came when he did."

It seemed her knees weren't the only ones struck with the wobbles. Her father grabbed the back of a kitchen chair with both hands and braced himself.

"I thought you'd be safe there." Sorrow bowed his back as his head hung low. "I don't . . . I don't know what to do."

His voice broke, and his vulnerability tugged at her heart. She came up behind him, wrapped her arms around his chest, and laid her face against his back.

"It's all right, Daddy. I know what to do."

He slowly straightened and turned to face her. "Go back to Boston?"

She shook her head. "No. I'm going to identify the man who tried to kill me."

"How? Did you see him set the fire?" When she shook her head again, he blew out a breath. "Sheriff Jeter and I have questioned everyone we can think of who might have a motive to hurt you, and we've come up empty."

Samantha chose her words with care. "I came across some new evidence that points to someone here at the Three Cedars. The sheriff and Asher are at the bunkhouse now, questioning the men."

Her father stiffened. "Without me present?" He broke away from her and strode toward the back door.

Samantha grabbed his arm. "Please, Daddy, let them handle it. It's better for you to stay here. With me."

His expression darkened. "What aren't you telling me, Samantha?"

She couldn't let him put her on the defensive. He'd pry all her secrets from her in a heartbeat.

"I'm asking you to trust me." She released his arm but moved to place herself between him and the back door. "Just stay in this kitchen with me. Drink some coffee. Sheriff Jeter will check in with you in a few minutes. I promise."

He glared at her, and Samantha swore she could see his internal debate play out in the clenching and unclenching of his jaw.

A movement caught her eye from the hall. Clint. Her priorities shifted as rapidly as sand in an upturned hourglass. Sidestepping her father, she moved to intercept her brother.

"Sam? I thought I heard your voice. What are you doing here?" He rubbed a hand over his bed-mussed hair as he neared the kitchen, his bare feet padding soundlessly on the wood floors.

"Clint. You shouldn't be up this early." She took him by the shoulders and tried to steer him back the way he'd come. He couldn't be here when the sheriff gave his report. Sheriff Jeter wasn't a man to mince words. There was no telling what he might say. She hoped to spare her father from deducing the truth, but he was a grown man. Clint, on the other hand, was still a child. A rather tall and obstinate child, who refused to budge no matter how much force she applied.

He brushed her hands away. "Quit pushing me." He crossed his arms and glared. "I'm not going anywhere until you tell me what's going on. Why are you here?"

Daddy relaxed his stance a little and took a step toward them. "There was a fire at your aunt and uncle's, son."

Clint's breathing instantly grew ragged. "Are they . . . dead?"

Samantha recognized his panic. After losing their mother, both of them tended to assume the worst.

She wrapped an arm around him. "No, they're fine. The house is a wreck," she added with a wry chuckle, "but we all got out."

Casting a glance over her shoulder, she silently pleaded with her father not to tell him about them being trapped inside. It was better for Clint to focus on the good instead of worrying about what could have happened.

"Thank God you're all right, sis." Clint hugged her tightly.

Samantha held on to her brother for a long minute, relishing the connection and praying that nothing would ever change it.

Smoothing his hair down with her hand, she smiled at him as she leaned away from his embrace. "Now that we have all of that out of the way, why don't we both go upstairs and get properly ready for the day? You can't wrangle cows with bare feet."

It was the best idea she could come up with in the spur of the moment to get him away from the kitchen and the conversation that would ensue before long, but Clint wasn't the suggestible young boy he'd been before she left for Boston. He was too set on being treated like a man to let his sister dictate his actions.

Pushing past her, he strode over to the pie safe and scrounged around inside until he found a day-old biscuit to chew on. "I got plenty of time to get dressed," he said around a mouthful of biscuit. "I want to hear more about what happened." He swallowed and gave her a look. "I'm not a kid to be patted on the head and sent off to my room, Sam. I'm old enough to understand the danger you're in and help you fight it. This is Dearing family business, and I'm a Dearing."

The irony of that assertion tore at her heart, but she ignored the ache. He *was* a Dearing. Maybe not by blood, but in every other way that mattered. He was her brother, and no past scandal would change that fact. Not in her mind.

As she scrambled to come up with some other excuse to get him out of the kitchen, the back door opened.

"Hey, Eli, there's a pair of horses outside the bunkhouse. You know anything about—" Duke Kendrick's gaze collided with hers. Shock and something else flickered in his eyes. "Miss Dearing? What are *you* doin' here?"

Clint answered for her. "There was a fire. Everyone got out, though."

Duke's mouth tightened. "A fire?"

Samantha couldn't pull her gaze away from Duke. Dark brown hair, just like Clint. Brown eyes too. How had she never noticed that Clint didn't share the blond hair and blue eyes that her parents had passed down to her? Aunt Regina's hair was a darker blond, almost brown, but her eyes were still blue.

Duke darted a glance to her, then back to Clint.

"Yep," her brother said. "We really gotta catch this snake that's tryin' to hurt her. She coulda died."

Duke clasped Clint's shoulder. "I don't think you gotta worry none. Your sister's resilient. She's still here, ain't she?"

He smiled, but something about the expression didn't sit right. And the way he comforted Clint. He'd always been affectionate with him. Almost . . . fatherly. When he'd learned that Eli hadn't taught Clint to swim, he'd been upset. No. Angry. He'd taken over the duty himself. And the morning she'd witnessed the lesson in the pond, Duke had been wearing a shirt. Clint hadn't. Did men usually swim in their shirts? She recalled the way he'd grabbed at his neckline when Clint had accidentally stretched the shirt and caused it to gape. The bit of exposed skin she'd seen had been pale, as if it never saw the sun. She'd thought Duke had been concerned with modesty when

he'd quickly adjusted the fabric, but what if he'd been conceal-
ing something? Something like a crescent-shaped birthmark?

"Come have a seat," Clint invited. "Samantha was about to
tell us more about what happened." Her brother shot her a
stubborn look. "Isn't that right, Sam?"

She barely heard him over the truth clanging like cymbals
in her brain. "It's you."

A fierceness flashed in Duke's eyes. He covered it quickly
with the cocky, dismissive demeanor she'd come to associate
with him, but that flash had confirmed her suspicions.

"You're the one trying to kill me."

"Samantha?" Her father's voice. Concerned. Confused. She
heard him, but she didn't take her eyes off Duke.

The man laughed. "Girl, you must've barbecued your brain
with all that smoke you inhaled. I been one of the guard dogs
protectin' you."

Things clicked into place. He knew her routine, would've
had access to her horse cart, had been inside her aunt and
uncle's home. "You asked where I'd be the morning of the
shooting at the old Ellis place."

"Your pa asked me to keep tabs on you. Asked it of all of us."

She shook her head, her anger and certainty growing. "Did
you hire someone to throw that rattlesnake into my wagon? Or
maybe it was you all along. All you would have needed to do
was borrow a black hat and ride a rented horse so I wouldn't
recognize you. With that neckerchief pulled up over your face,
your identity was hidden."

Duke held a hand out in front of him as if she were a skittish
horse he was trying to calm. "You've been through a terrible
ordeal, Miss Dearing. You're overtired. I ain't gonna take of-
fense, but I ain't gonna hang around here and let ya malign
me, neither." He turned to her father. "I'll meet up with you
later, Eli."

Duke turned his back and headed for the door. Clint looked between him and Samantha, grooves digging deep ruts into his brow.

"Hold up a minute, Duke." Her father took a step toward his departing foreman. "I think we should talk—"

Duke spun around, his hand flying to his holster and drawing his weapon in a single well-rehearsed move. "I'm *done* talkin'. Done takin' orders from you, too."

"Whoa, now." Her father raised his hands, helpless to defend himself since he wasn't yet wearing his gun belt.

"Duke?" Clint's voice sounded small, high, like the boy he used to be. "What are you doing?"

Not liking that the table stood between her and her brother, Samantha started to inch around the obstacle. "Clint, come over here by me."

Her brother hesitated, and that delay proved costly.

"He ain't goin' nowhere." Duke lunged and coiled an arm around his neck, dragging Clint against him.

When her father darted forward, Duke pointed the gun at Clint's head. "Back up!"

Her father obeyed, hands back in the air. "Easy, Duke. No need to bring the boy into this."

"He's already in this. Has been from the beginning."

"Don't hurt him!" Samantha reached her arms out toward her brother as if she could pull him to safety with an invisible cord.

She reminded herself that Duke needed Clint if he wanted to claim the Three Cedars. He wouldn't hurt him. It was a bluff. But the desperation in the foreman's eyes made it clear he couldn't be counted on to act rationally.

"You!" Duke unfolded his gun arm to point his revolver at Samantha. "You were supposed to stay in Boston and marry some highfalutin Easterner. You never shoulda come back here. You made a mess of everything."

He cocked the revolver.

"No!" Her father yelled and jumped in front of her.

The gun exploded.

Her father fell.

Clint screamed. "Daddy!"

"He ain't your daddy, boy," Duke sneered as he hauled Clint out the back door. "I am."

299

34

A gunshot cracked, and terror ripped through Asher's chest.

Please, God. No.

Visions of Samantha, crumpled and bleeding, rose to torture him as he sprinted toward the back of the main house.

A man emerged from inside. Kendrick. He had a stranglehold on Clint Dearing. A gun in his other hand.

Asher slowed enough to draw his revolver. "Stop!" he yelled. "Let the boy go!"

Kendrick swiveled toward Asher, shifting Clint in front of him like a shield as his gun arm came around.

"Get down!" Sheriff Jeter shouted from behind.

Kendrick fired.

Asher hit the dirt and rolled toward the side of the house. With no cover, movement was his only protection. Another shot pierced the air. Asher flinched but kept rolling. No pain erupted, so he continued sweeping the dirt until his bootheel kicked against a wall. Twisting onto his belly, he brought his gun up in front of him, rocking slightly to his right so he could lean his cheek against his arm and sight down the barrel. His finger hovered over the trigger, but he resisted the instinct to defend himself. He couldn't risk a shot. Not with Samantha's brother in the line of fire.

Kendrick dragged the boy backward to the small cabin that must be his private quarters. Asher spotted a swishing horse's tail peeking from behind the edge of the building. Seemed the man had an exit strategy.

"Follow me, and the boy's dead!" Kendrick brought the gun up to point at Clint's head as he backed toward the cabin. "You hear me, Jeter? I spot anyone on my trail, and I'll kill him."

Asher prayed it was a bluff. Surely the man wouldn't kill his own son. Then again, what father would use his child as a human shield or point a loaded gun at his head? No telling what he would do if he felt cornered.

"You won't get away with this, Kendrick," Jeter yelled from his position hunkering behind the corral's water trough.

Duke made no reply, just disappeared behind the cabin. A knife twisted in Asher's heart. That could be Jack or Fergus. Overpowered by a ruthless man. Helpless to escape. He scrambled to his feet, gun still drawn. He took two steps toward the cabin, desperate to charge after them. But rushing to the rescue might get Clint killed.

Asher diverted to the house instead.

"Check on the folks inside," Sheriff Jeter called. "I'll gather the men and set out after him."

"What about—?"

"We'll stay back far enough to keep out of sight, but I aim to track him. He had to have stashed money and supplies somewhere. Can't make a run without 'em. When he stops, we can close the gap. If one of the men has an idea about where he might be headed, we might even manage to circle around and take him by surprise."

"Be careful out there, Sheriff. Cornered animals are the most dangerous."

The sounds of horse hooves drew the gazes of both men toward the back of Kendrick's cabin. A horse and rider sped away—a rider with a now limp youngster draped over his lap.

The sheriff muttered under his breath. "Animal's right. God help that boy."

Asher repeated the prayer as he turned away from the sight and hurried into the house. An invisible tourniquet tightened around his chest as he stepped into the kitchen. Dread sat heavy in his gut as he braced himself for what he might find.

"Samantha?"

He didn't see her at first. A plump grandmotherly woman fluttered around by the cabinets closest to the door, grabbing tea towels. The tail of her long silver braid nearly flicked him in the face as she spun around with a gasp at his entrance. In a blink, she had a wicked-looking carving knife in her hand.

"Who are you?"

"Asher Ellis, ma'am. I'm here to help. Is—" He choked a bit. "Is Samantha injured?"

The woman deflated and dropped the knife on the counter with a clatter. "No, thank the Lord, but Mr. Dearing's in a bad way."

She stepped aside, and Asher strode past, his gaze scanning the room as he moved. There. Behind the table.

He lurched forward, pushing a chair out of his way as he went. Eli Dearing lay on the floor, blood seeping from a wound beneath his left shoulder. Samantha knelt at his side, leaning over him as she tried to staunch the flow with her petticoat. Her hands were stained with blood, and when she turned her face at Asher's approach, his heart throbbed at the tears streaming down her face.

"I have to save him." Her voice sounded so lost, so small. "Help me save him."

"I will." God willing.

302

Tea towels suddenly materialized above him. "Here. Use these."

Asher nodded to the woman he assumed to be Mrs. Stewart, the cook Samantha had told him stories about. He took the clean white towels and folded them into dressings.

"Is it safe to go outside?" Mrs. Stewart asked. "I need to send Martin to fetch the doctor."

"Yes. You'll need to catch him quickly, though," Asher said, darting a glance the cook's way before refocusing on his folding. "Sheriff Jeter is rounding up the men to form a posse to go after Kendrick."

"I still can't believe it. Mr. Dearing has always treated Duke like a member of the family. Why on earth would he turn on us like this? And Clint? If he hurts that boy—" A small sob cut her words off.

"Get Martin," Asher reminded her. Now wasn't the time for fretting, especially not in front of Samantha. She had enough heartache on her plate.

After Mrs. Stewart left, Asher gently touched Samantha's arm. She sniffed, then twisted her face toward him.

"I'm going to open his shirt so we can get a proper dressing on his wound, all right?" He waited for her nod. "Once that's done, you can peel back your petticoat, and I'll add the towels."

Asher tugged Eli's shirttails from his trousers and was about to reach for his knife when a pair of shears dropped into his line of vision. He looked up to find Ida Mae standing at Eli's feet, her face pale. She held a pair of scissors in one hand and clutched her son tightly to her chest with the other.

"I've set bandages on the table."

He glanced backward. Sure enough, four rolls of bandages lay waiting at the edge of the table, ready to be used.

"Thank you."

Asher cut Eli's shirt up the center, then set aside the scissors and started peeling away the blood-soaked cloth.

He nodded to Samantha. "All right, sweetheart, sit back."

As she retreated, Asher pulled aside the rest of Eli's shirt. Blood oozed from a deep hole two inches below his collarbone. Asher quickly covered it with the dressing and applied firm pressure. He must've pushed harder than Samantha had been because Eli groaned, and his eyes opened.

"Daddy? Daddy, can you hear me?" Samantha huddled by her father's head. She rubbed her hands on her skirt to remove the worst of the blood, then stroked her father's hair.

His gaze scanned her, and his brow furrowed. He reached for her. "You're hurt."

"No, Daddy. You saved me. You're the one who's hurt." She clasped his hand and brought it to her lips for a kiss. "Lie still now. Asher's dressing your wound, and Martin is going to fetch the doctor. You'll be good as new in no time. You'll see."

"Clint . . ."

Samantha turned to Asher, her heart in her eyes.

Asher cleared his throat and drew the older man's gaze. Eli Dearing seemed the sort to appreciate straight shooting, so Asher didn't mince words. "Kendrick's got him. Sheriff Jeter is gathering the Three Cedars men to ride after him. Do you know where he might be heading? The sheriff seems to think he might've set aside money and supplies somewhere in case he ever needed to make a run for it."

Eli's eyes squeezed closed. "Shack . . . saw some gear . . . when . . . confronted . . . Leroy."

His voice was growing weaker, and Asher didn't like the pallor of his skin. He'd lost a lot of blood.

"I'm going to help him sit up," Asher explained to Samantha in a low voice. "Pull off the rest of his shirt. If there's an exit wound, we'll need to dress that as well, then wrap the bandages." He swiveled to address Ida Mae. "Grab as many pillows as you can find. We'll prop him up to keep the wound elevated."

Ida Mae nodded and dashed down the hall.

Asher turned back to Samantha. "Ready?"

She set her jaw. "Ready."

They worked together to dress and wrap the wound. Eli moaned and hissed as they jostled him, but Asher found it encouraging that he remained conscious.

Mrs. Stewart returned in the midst of their ministrations and took charge of Jimmy so Ida Mae could arrange the cushions. "The men have headed out," she reported as she snuggled the toddler against her breast. "I caught Martin before they left. He's on his way to town to fetch the doctor."

Asher nodded to let her know he'd heard, but he couldn't stop a frown from tightening his mouth. He turned to Eli. "Can you tell me where this shack is? The sheriff can't risk following too close, so there's a chance he might lose the trail. If I could get to the shack from another route, I might be able to take Kendrick by surprise."

Eli's eyelids drooped as he fought to hold on to consciousness. "Dry Creek Gulch . . . She . . . can show you." He tipped his head, not toward his daughter but toward Ida Mae.

She backed up a step, her eyes widening in dismay.

"Please," Eli rasped. "For . . . my son."

Asher slowly pushed to his feet, making sure not to crowd Ida Mae. He didn't want to frighten her or make her feel like she was being coerced. "You wouldn't need to take me all the way there. Just point me in the right direction. Once I have the place in sight, you can return to the house. You have my word."

"There's an old game trail," she murmured, lifting her chin slightly. "It leads up to the line shack from the direction of town. We'll have to backtrack along the main road for me to be able to spot it, but that trail will take you to the rear of the cabin. It backs up to a pair of cedar trees. No windows on that side. If you approach on foot, he might not know you're there."

Ida Mae's attention dropped to the man on the floor, then shifted to Samantha.

Samantha's blue eyes glimmered with moisture. "Thank you."

Ida Mae fisted her hands in her skirt. "Your father gave me work and a place to stay when I had nowhere to go. Besides, if someone stole Jimmy from me, I'd move heaven and earth to get him back." She released her crumpled skirt and straightened her posture. "I'll go."

"You can ride my paint," Asher said, the beginning of a plan running through his brain. "His saddle is already adjusted for a shorter rider. I'll bring my rented mount around and meet you by the front of the house."

"I'll get my boots." Ida Mae crossed the kitchen to the small chamber that served as her bedroom.

"And I'll watch over your boy," Mrs. Stewart promised.

Ida Mae stopped briefly to catch her son's waving fist and bring it to her mouth for a kiss. Then she slipped into her room to prepare for their ride.

"Asher?"

He turned to Samantha, his heart squeezing at the devastation etched into her beautiful face.

"Yes?"

He stood ready to vow whatever it took to give her a grip on hope. If she wanted him to swear to bring Clint home alive, he would. If she needed him to promise to make Kendrick pay for his crimes against her family, he would. Shoot, if she wanted him to guarantee that her father would pull through, he'd find a way to give her that, too. Whatever she needed.

"Be careful." She peered up at him, her eyes pleading. "I can't lose you."

Asher's heart twisted as the truth radiating from her gaze penetrated his chest. What she needed was *him*.

His throat tightened, and his voice rasped slightly when he answered her. "I'll come home to you, sweetheart. I swear it. And Lord willing, I'll bring Clint with me."

Please be willing, he prayed, *for I can't bear the thought of breaking her heart by coming home without him.*

35

The kitchen felt colder after Asher and Ida Mae left. Samantha sat on the floor, holding her father's hand, her mind too numb to pray. All she could manage was to watch her daddy's chest rise and fall.

He'd passed out again. Once Asher and Ida Mae departed, his iron will had succumbed to his body's weakness. He'd done all he could to ensure his son's safe return. All either of them could do now was wait. And hope.

She tried to be glad that he slept. Oblivion dulled pain. Aided healing. Yet she craved the reassurance of seeing his eyes. Of hearing his voice. The quiet rasp of his breathing heightened her apprehension and left her feeling alone and adrift. What if he never awoke?

"Here, sweet girl." Mrs. Stewart unfolded a blanket and extended a corner toward Samantha. "Help me cover him."

As if emerging from a fog, Samantha slowly released her father's hand and pushed to her feet. A tingling ache radiated through her knees and back, making her movements awkward as she rose. How long had she been kneeling on the hard floor? Apparently long enough that Mrs. Stewart had dressed for the day and put up her hair.

Clasping the blanket edge, she helped stretch the covering over her father. She bent to arrange the top edge around the bandages on her father's chest, then started to sink back down into her position at his side. Mrs. Stewart caught her by the elbow, however, and halted her descent.

"I'll grab a low stool and sit with him for a bit." The kind woman's gaze felt like a hug as her lips curved into a sympathetic smile. "Why don't you go upstairs and get cleaned up?"

Samantha glanced down her front. Dark red stains marred the dress she'd borrowed from Asher's mother. Her petticoat would be worse. And her hands. She lifted them. Turned them over. Dried blood caked her skin in a thin layer. Seeing it brought on an itch she couldn't dispel.

"Go on, sweetheart. Just think how much hope you'll give your daddy if he opens his eyes to find your pretty face smiling over him."

Samantha wrapped her arms around her middle, knowing Mrs. Stewart was right but finding it nearly impossible to move her feet. "What about Jimmy?"

Mrs. Stewart gently tugged Samantha away from her father and steered her toward the hall. "He's in his high chair. The teething biscuits I gave him will keep him occupied for a while." As if she sensed Samantha's thoughts, Mrs. Stewart gentled her grip and stroked her arm in a comforting caress. "Your father is the toughest man I've ever known. He's not going to fade away in the few minutes it takes you to wash up and put on a fresh dress."

"But—"

"If his condition changes, I'll call for you. I promise."

Out of excuses, Samantha nodded and headed to the stairs. Feet as heavy as her heart dragged her to her room. She wanted to collapse on top of her bed and weep into her pillow, but she refused to surrender to despair. She was a Dearing. The only

Dearing available to tend to the Three Cedars and its people. She'd not abandon them. It was her job to instill hope, to give direction, to be stalwart and steady.

Samantha crossed to the washstand, lifted the ewer, and poured water into the basin. Taking a cake of soap, she scrubbed the blood from her hands and scraped it out from under her nails. Queasy at the sight of the pink water, she dumped the basin's contents into her chamber pot, then poured new water and washed her face. With mechanical movements, she stripped out of her dress and underclothes, ran a wet cloth over her limbs, midsection, and neck, then dressed in a simple blue skirt and striped shirtwaist. Sitting at her dressing table, she brushed out her hair and twisted it into a sensible bun at her nape. She brushed away her emotions as well, rolling them into a tight knot to examine later.

Determined to fulfill her duty as mistress of the Three Cedars, Samantha rose and headed to the door. But as she reached for the knob, a flash of insight glued her feet to the floorboards. She was imitating her mother. Closing off her emotions. Hiding her anxiety behind a veneer of confidence and poise. Relying solely on herself.

Samantha covered her face with her hands and pressed her forehead against the door.

Forgive me, Lord. This isn't for me to carry alone. You've promised I can do all things if you strengthen me. I can face all things if you strengthen me. Lend me your strength, Lord. Help me to be brave for Daddy. For Clint. For everyone at the Three Cedars. Help me to lean on you and not my own understanding. Give me courage to face whatever must be faced. But please . . . if there is any room in your will to spare Daddy's life, I beg you to do so. And Clint. Protect my brother. Please let no harm come to him. Or to Asher and Ida Mae. Bring them all home safe.

She let the solidity of the door support her weight for a

long moment before straightening. Once upright, she tipped her head back, closed her eyes, and imagined a heavenly ewer pouring strength over her like a stream of warm water.

"'Thou anointest my head with oil,'" she murmured softly as she visualized endurance and fortitude soaking through her skin and into her spirit. "'My cup runneth over.'" Bowing her head, she folded her arms and rubbed them as if to ensure not a single drop would be wasted. "'Yea, though I walk through the valley of the shadow of death, I will fear no evil: for thou art with me.'"

God was with her. She believed his promise. Felt his presence. She was not alone.

Opening her eyes, Samantha set her shoulders and strode out of the room. Her father had not worried about what he might lose when he leapt in front of the bullet meant for her. He'd simply let love drive his actions. Time to stop fearing what she might lose and focus instead on how best to love and support the people around her.

"There you are." Mrs. Stewart smiled as Samantha entered the kitchen. The family cook rose awkwardly from the cushioned footstool she had pilfered from the parlor and pressed a hand to her lower back. "Goodness. It's not as easy to get up and down as it used to be. Best I leave the stool sittin' to you young'uns."

"I'm happy to take over." Samantha gripped the older woman's elbow to steady her as she found her balance.

Mrs. Stewart patted Samantha's arm, then edged away. "I'll get breakfast going. Not sure how many we'll be feedin', but I'll make sure we got plenty of food on hand to fill the men's bellies whenever they make it back to the ranch." She grabbed a towel and wiped Jimmy's slobbery face as she passed the high chair, then laid another teething biscuit on the tray. "When Martin returns, we should ask him to help us move

Mr. Dearing into a proper bed. Ain't right for him to be layin' on the floor like that."

"Good idea." Samantha tucked her skirt beneath her and lowered herself onto the footstool.

She brushed her fingertips across her father's brow, tidying the way his hair lay over his forehead. His eyelids twitched, then cracked open.

"Sam?"

Strange how the name she'd turned her back on now soothed her heart with sweet nostalgia.

"I'm here, Daddy." She collected his hand and placed it in her lap, circling her fingers around his.

His head turned toward her. "How did . . . you know about . . . Duke?"

Her heart broke at his question. How she'd wanted to spare him this pain. "I didn't. Not until this morning. Things just . . . clicked into place when I saw him."

His brows lifted in silent entreaty. He wanted more details. Details that would only increase his suffering. Yet withholding the truth might torture him even more.

She stared at his work-roughened fingers cupped inside her hands, unable to look him in the eyes. "Mother kept a journal. Aunt Regina found it among her things and held on to it for me, wanting to pass it along once I was older. She gave it to me yesterday, thinking it might help me pass the time during my confinement."

Samantha fell quiet for a moment, searching for words that might soften the harsh edges of the truth. "Mother wanted to give you a son so badly. An heir to the Three Cedars. I think her obsession twisted something inside her, enabling her to justify whatever means were necessary to achieve that goal. She never stopped loving you, though, Daddy. I know it sounds absurd, but she likened it to pairing a heifer with a bull. No emotional attachment. Strictly a breeding exercise."

He groaned and turned his face away from her. She tightened her grip on his hand and curled her body downward, as if she could shield him from the betrayal. But such a thing was impossible.

"What Mother did was wrong. Deep down, she knew that. Her journal is filled with guilt and regret."

He stared at a spot on the ceiling, his jaw tight. "I had my suspicions. The more time passed without a baby, the more distant she became. And short-tempered. Complained all the time. I found excuses to stay away from the house. Then something changed. She started going out of her way to please me. Had this forced cheerfulness about her that felt . . . artificial. I didn't question it. I was just glad she wasn't pickin' me apart anymore. When we learned she was finally carrying another babe, we were both so happy, our troubles no longer mattered. Then Clint was born, and I about burst with pride. Didn't matter that he didn't look like me. He was my son, and I loved him with my whole heart." He turned his face toward Samantha. "Just as I loved you." His attention returned to the ceiling as he exhaled. "I didn't want to believe he was anything other than mine, so I didn't. Told myself he'd inherited my uncle's darker coloring."

His words had started to drift a bit, and Samantha worried that he was wearing himself out. Then his right hand balled into a fist and banged against the wall next to his shoulder.

"I trusted him. With everything. The ranch. The cattle. My family. He's been my best friend for nearly thirty years. How could he do this?"

Samantha shook her head. "I don't know." Nothing could justify such a betrayal.

Her father grasped her arm with a grip that belied his weakened state. "No matter what happens to me, you gotta get Clint back. Tell him he's *my* son. Always will be. In my heart and in the eyes of the law. Nothin's ever gonna change that. He's a Dearing." A cough broke up his words, but he continued despite his quickly flagging energy. His eyelids drooped, and his grip loosened. "Heir to the Three . . . Cedars. *My* boy."

"I'll tell him, Daddy." Samantha blinked away a tear and pressed a kiss to his knuckles. "You rest now." She didn't like him talking as if he might not make it. He had to pull through. "Clint's going to want to see you when Asher brings him home."

"Asher . . . good man." His eyes blinked slowly, almost not opening again. "Good . . . for you."

"I think so, too. I love him, Daddy."

"Thought . . . you might."

Was she imagining it, or had his lips curved a tiny bit at the corners? The hint of a smile disappeared, replaced by tension and the etching of pain. His eyes closed, and she thought he had slipped into sleep, but after a long minute, he forced them back open and melded his gaze with hers.

"Love . . . you . . . Sam. Proud . . . of you. Always . . . have been. Glad . . . you came . . . home."

"Me too, Daddy." A tremor vibrated through her chest, quivering out through her voice. The affirmation she'd craved her entire life showered over her like a gentle rain, yet it felt too much like final words to bring her any comfort. Her pulse pounding, she bent her face close to his. "I love you, Daddy. And I need you so much." She choked back a rising sob. "Please don't leave us."

He reached for her face, his calloused fingers rough and infinitely precious against her cheek. "In . . . God's . . . hands."

As he spoke, his hand fell away, as if the physical were relinquishing its handhold so the spiritual could take its place.

He *was* in God's hands. As were Clint and Asher. She prayed those hands would protect and heal and knit her family back together before everything unraveled.

36

Ida Mae drew Bruno to a halt and pointed west. "That's it."
Asher reined in his mount and scanned the landscape
until he spotted a roofline peeking out from behind a large
tree in the distance. The terrain didn't offer much cover between here and there. Might be best to stash his horse in the
brush somewhere. Wouldn't want to tip off Kendrick that he
had company.

Twisting in the saddle, he faced Ida Mae and offered her a
confident smile that was about as genuine as a wooden nickel.
"I've got it from here, Miss Forrester. You can head on back
to the ranch."

"Are you sure?" She'd obviously not been fooled by his bravado. "Maybe I should keep watch. What if you or Clint end
up injured? You'll need someone to fetch help."

Not a chance he'd let a single mother stay anywhere close
to harm's way. Even letting her lead him out here jabbed his
conscience.

"Sheriff Jeter and the rest of the men are in the area. If they
hear gunshots, they'll come running." No guarantee they'd find

them based on sound alone, but he wasn't about to admit that to Ida Mae. "You should be with your son."

She nibbled her bottom lip, clearly dealing with a few conscience jabs herself.

"You know what would help me the most?" Asher shifted in his saddle, the leather creaking loudly in the still air. "Send Martin out here. He's likely on his way back to the ranch by now after fetching the doctor. You might even meet him on the road." Chances were slim, but having reinforcements in the vicinity would sure be nice. Might require a bit of divine timing, but with God, all things were possible, right?

"Yes. Martin." Ida Mae tugged on the reins and turned Bruno around to face the direction of the road. "I'll send Martin. The moment I find him."

"Good."

If nothing else, the idea had successfully diverted Ida Mae's attention and assured she would be a safe distance from any danger that arose. If that was all his impromptu plan accomplished, it would be enough.

Bruno must have sensed the mission for he grew restive. Ida Mae kept him reined in, though, as she glanced back at Asher. "Samantha's never been one to have her head turned by men. She cares about you. Deeply. Getting home to her is more important than proving yourself a hero. Remember that, all right?"

"I will."

She nodded to him, then touched her heels to Bruno's sides and gave him his head. Asher watched her for a moment before returning his attention to his target.

I don't need to be her hero, Lord, but if I can restore her brother to her, I don't mind paying whatever price is required.

Spying a small stand of cedars to his left, Asher nudged his mount into a walk down the hill that led to the line shack.

He'd tether his horse among the trees and approach the cabin on foot.

Any confidence he'd built up from his years of scrapping his way through life dissolved the moment he dismounted and started creeping toward the rear of the line shack.

What did he know about chasing criminals or rescuing kidnapped boys? Nothing. That's what. Asher crouched as he darted from one scraggly bush to another, trying to keep his head low while scanning the area for any sign of his quarry.

Duke Kendrick outranked him when it came to life experience, familiarity with the surroundings, and straight-up ruthlessness. Asher was nothing more than a two-bit cowboy with passable intelligence and an inability to stand down when people he cared about were threatened. Rocks versus feathers. If he had any hope of coming out on top, the Almighty was gonna have to do some serious scale-tipping.

Asher made it to the oak tree at the rear of the cabin and pressed his back to the trunk as he closed his eyes and caught his breath.

David had had five stones and a sling when he faced Goliath. Asher had six bullets and a gun. If God joined the fight, he wouldn't need anything more. But if God chose to let men settle their own squabbles today, things could deteriorate in a hurry.

A little help would be mighty appreciated. If you're willing.

Asher concentrated on slowing his breathing and his heart rate as he listened for hoofbeats or voices or anything to signal that company was fixin' to pay a call. Hearing nothing but the wind rustling the leaves above his head, he drew his revolver and slid away from the tree to plant his back against the windowless wall beside him.

Scraping his shoulder blades along the weathered siding, he stalked to the edge of the small shack and stole a quick glance around the corner. Clear. He continued along the north side of the building, keeping his body angled backward and his gun hand up and ready. When he reached the corner, he led with his revolver as he edged around to the front of the shack. Spying neither horse nor man, he lowered his weapon and peered in the single window. His gaze swept the dim interior. Bed on the back wall. Small stove in the northeast corner. Skinny table and a pair of chairs beneath the window. Some shelves on the south wall above a square cabinet. Something was piled in the corner behind the cabinet, but the shadows made it impossible to identify. Could be the supplies Eli Dearing had mentioned. If so, that would mean that Kendrick hadn't made it here yet, and Asher had a chance to stop him before the scoundrel disappeared with Clint.

Holstering his gun, Asher hurried to the door and let himself inside. If he could find Kendrick's stash of funds, he could delay the man's escape. Maybe even enough for Jeter to catch up.

Asher closed the door behind him and started his search. The west-facing window did little to light the room, but Asher couldn't afford to leave the door open. The shack needed to look empty should Kendrick approach.

The cabinet housed a skillet, camp-sized pans, and a dented coffeepot. The shelves above stocked tinned meat, beans, jerky, coffee, and enough ammunition for a small army. The shadowy pile behind the cabinet proved to be a pair of saddle-bags, but when Asher opened the flaps, all he found were clothes, a flask of whiskey, and a leather document case with a copy of Eli Dearing's will. No money.

He checked behind the stove, under the bed, and in the rafters. The floor was dirt, so nothing was hidden there. Where was the money? Could Kendrick have buried it outside somewhere? Asher hadn't noticed any disturbed ground, so he doubted it. Besides, that would take too long to retrieve. Kendrick would want to snatch and run.

Thinking of Fergus and the places he tended to hide his notebooks, Asher lifted the mattress, moved the cabinet, and even checked the undersides of the table and chair seats. Nothing.

Where could it be? Moving away from the window, Asher scanned the room again, this time making a mental list of the things Kendrick would likely grab. Food. Saddlebags. Cooking gear. Ammunition. What else?

Bedrolls.

There were two under the bed. He'd moved them when he'd searched for a packet or lockbox, but he hadn't taken the time to unroll them and look inside.

Dropping to the ground, Asher snatched the pair of bedrolls and dragged them out from beneath the bed. He unfastened the straps on the first and unfurled it with a flick and his wrists. Nothing flew out of the folds, and Asher tamped down a barrage of disappointment. For good measure, he yanked the blanket out from within the canvas covering and shook it out. No packet. He grabbed the second roll, undid the straps and flung it open. A thick leather pouch bounced against the bed frame.

The money. It had to be.

Asher lunged for the pouch, unbuckled the flap, and opened it to find a stack of greenbacks. His breath stuck in his chest as he fanned the bills with his thumb. Had to be at least three hundred dollars. He'd never seen so much money in one place. Enough to take care of Mama Bess and the boys for a good long while. Not that he would steal it. Asher closed the flap and fastened it in place. Best not stare at temptation too long.

He tucked the packet into his waistband at the small of his back, then kicked the unrolled bedding against the wall. He needed Kendrick to know the money was missing. It would slow him down, and maybe give Asher some bargaining power. After shooting Eli in front of witnesses, Duke had to know he was a wanted man. There'd be no returning to the Three Cedars. His only hope was to outrun the law, and to do that he needed funds. Funds Asher would gladly trade for Clint.

A dull, rhythmic thudding filtered through the crevices in the shack wall. Hooves. Asher lurched away from the window and positioned himself in the southwest corner. When Kendrick entered, the door would hide Asher from view. Not for long, but hopefully long enough to give him the advantage of surprise.

Asher eased the revolver out of his holster and focused on the sounds coming from outside.

The hoofbeats grew louder, then stopped.

"We ain't got much time, but the horse needs to rest a while before we ride again. There's a pump on the side of the shack and a bucket hangin' from a nail on the wall. Fetch some water."

"With my hands tied?" Clint spat the words with a heavy dose of disdain.

"You're a clever boy. Figure it out."

Boots tapped against earth. Asher tensed. Readied his gun.

"Where're you goin'?" Kendrick's call was muffled, as if he'd turned away from the door.

"Home."

"You plannin' on walkin' all that way in bare feet?"

"If that's what it takes to get away from you," Clint shot back.

Running footfalls took Kendrick away from the cabin. "Listen here, boy. I ain't got time for this nonsense. If I have to sock you in the jaw again and sling you over my shoulder like a sack of taters, I will."

"Is that your plan, Duke?" Clint's voice rose, as if he'd turned to face his captor. "Keep me on a leash for the rest of my life?

'Cause that's what it'll take. I ain't stayin' with you willingly. First chance I get, I'm runnin', and when I do, I'm goin' straight to the nearest lawman and tellin' him exactly where to find you."

A smack followed by a whimper had Asher reaching for the door handle.

"Why are you doing this?"

Clint's angry shout halted Asher's motion. He dropped his hand from the door and settled back into the shadows.

"I loved you!" Tears roughened the boy's voice. "Trusted you."

"Eli stole my life," Kendrick snarled. "Made me a measly employee instead of a partner. Took the woman I fancied. The position in the community that should've been mine. The wealth. All of it! He pawned me off with scraps as if I were a faithful hound. Wages and a puny cabin, while he lived high on the hog in that fancy house, hobnobbin' with the likes of Charles Goodnight and the other cattle barons. I've worked the Three Cedars just as hard as he has. I've poured the same sweat and blood into the land. It should belong to me!"

"It'll never be yours!" Clint shouted. "You're a murderer. Wanted by the law. You'll never touch the Three Cedars."

"Maybe not. But *you* will. A Kendrick will sit on the cattle king's throne. I'd hoped to be there with you, work side-by-side with my son, shape you into the cattle baron you were born to be, but now I guess I'll have to enjoy my victory from a distance. *After* you and I make up for lost time. Put the pretendin' behind us, and start actin' like the father and son I've always wanted us to be."

"You are *not* my father."

"The mark on my chest says otherwise. Recognize it?" Kendrick asked after a moment. "Looks just like yours, don't it? You're my son, Clinton. Your loyalty belongs to me. The sooner you accept that truth, the better."

"I'll *never* be loyal to you. You tried to murder my sister and shot my . . . shot Eli."

Asher's heart broke at Clint's use of his father's name. Kendrick had gotten into the boy's head. Had him questioning things a child should never have to question.

"I'm done arguin' with you, boy." Kendrick grunted, and the sounds of a scuffle ensued.

"Let me go!"

"That leash idea of yours has merit. Think I'll tie ya down in the cabin while I fetch our supplies."

Asher tensed. If Kendrick was lugging Clint around, he'd likely use the boy as a shield again. With no shield of his own, Asher would likely end up with Kendrick's bullet between his eyes. Flipping the gun around in his hand, Asher prepared to use it as a club. If he could knock out Kendrick from behind . . .

The door swung inward so hard, Asher had to block his face with his left arm to protect what little line of sight he had.

Kendrick stomped into the cabin, his boots pounding against the dirt floor as he wrested an uncooperative Clint into the room.

Not daring to so much as breathe, Asher raised the butt end of his revolver. *Come on, Kendrick. Just a few more steps.*

The footsteps stopped, and a quiet curse fell from Kendrick's lips. He must have spotted the bedrolls.

Out of options, Asher slid out from behind the door and swung his pistol butt at the back of Kendrick's head.

Alerted to the intruder, Kendrick dodged sideways. Asher's blow glanced off the side of his head. Kendrick roared and spun, fist raised. Asher blocked the punch with his arm, but the force of the collision knocked the gun from his hand. Desperate to immobilize Kendrick any way he could, Asher lunged and wrapped him in a bear hug.

"Run, Clint!"

As Kendrick's skull rammed into Asher's forehead with the force of a mountain goat, Asher held on to a single thought, one he prayed Clint could hear. *Take the horse and ride for the Three Cedars.*

Stranding Kendrick out here without a mount provided the best hope of stopping him if Asher failed.

37

Speckles of light danced in Asher's vision from the blow Kendrick had just delivered, but he held on to the bucking foreman as if he were a wild bronc. A flash of movement registered in Asher's periphery. Clint darting outside.

The instant the boy exited the cabin, Asher swiped Kendrick's leg with his foot. When the foreman stumbled, Asher pressed forward with all his weight, hoping to topple his opponent. Kendrick twisted as he fell, though, bringing them down sideways on Asher's arm. The force jarred his elbow and broke his hold.

Kendrick scrambled to his feet. Asher latched on to the man's boot and yanked. Kendrick crashed into the table by the window. He grabbed one of the chairs and swung it at Asher's head. Asher ducked and twisted. The chair missed his head but smashed against his right shoulder blade, splintering the wood and nearly splintering his shoulder in the process. Pain shot down his arm, making it hard to form a fist. Kendrick had no such trouble. Granitelike knuckles ricocheted off the side of Asher's head.

The room teetered in Asher's vision. He groped for something solid to steady him, found the edge of the bed, and leveraged himself upward. He reached for the knife at his belt, but the click of a gun being cocked froze him in place.

"Where's my money?" Kendrick's growl carried the volatility of a cornered animal.

Asher blinked as the two gun-toting villains swimming in his vision merged back into one. "What money?"

"The money you took out of them bedrolls!"

He couldn't tell him, of course. Soon as he did, he'd be sporting a new hole in his chest. But Kendrick didn't seem the patient type. If Asher delayed too long, the fella would shoot him out of spite and search the place on his own.

A quick glance out the window told him Clint had made off with the horse. Confirming the boy was safe lifted a weight from Asher's shoulders and brought a level of calm to his soul.

"You hid it outside, didn't ya?" Kendrick must have noticed his eyes dart to the window.

Asher's mind whirled. His coat should hide the packet he'd stashed in his waistband. And a treasure hunt might buy him enough time to figure out a way to turn the tables. It would mean leaving his gun behind where it had fallen, but the weapon wasn't doing him any good at the moment anyway.

"I'll show you," Asher said.

"Get on with it, then." Kendrick waved his gun toward the door. "Keep them hands up," he warned as Asher slid past him.

Having a gun pointed at one's back proved rather unnerving. Asher much preferred having danger out in front of him, where he could keep an eye on it.

"You play this smart, Ellis, and I just might let you live. Return my money and point me to where you got your horse stashed, and I'll put my bullet in yer leg instead of yer head. Give you a fightin' chance."

"Charitable of you." Asher turned right, leading Kendrick in the opposite direction from where he'd secured his mount.

"Where's my money?" Kendrick demanded.

Good question. Asher scoured the landscape for anything that might pass as a hiding place.

"See that rock?" Asher pointed to a stone roughly the size of man's head sitting a couple of yards away. The thing looked to be half buried, but it was the best option he could find. "Fetch it."

The man was getting nervous. Asher could hear it in his voice. Probably disliked being out in the open. Maybe Asher could use that to his advantage.

Keeping his steps slow and deliberate, Asher glanced over his shoulder. "You know, using your son as a shield to aid your escape probably wasn't the best way to foster loyalty with the boy."

"Shut up. Ain't none of your concern."

Asher returned his gaze forward, but he'd barely taken two steps before Kendrick started justifying his actions.

"Clint woulda forgiven me in time. A single misstep can't undo a dozen years of good memories. Besides, the kid was never in any real danger. Not from me, at least. And I figured no one else would risk shooting the beloved heir of the Three Cedars. The bluff paid off. When the kid's older, he'll understand why it was necessary."

Asher slowed as he approached the rock. If he managed to distract Kendrick enough, he might be able to pivot and charge. Take him by surprise. Get control of the gun. But he needed his opponent to come closer. "Doubt he'll understand you tryin' to kill the people he loves."

"He was never supposed to know!" Kendrick's shout echoed off the cabin wall. "That stupid sister of his was supposed to stay in Boston and marry some fancy gent who'd keep her away from the ranch. When that didn't work, I intended to grieve with the rest of 'em when she died in an unfortunate accident. But the little she-cat has nine lives. She ruined everything! I only had six years left. Once Clint turned eighteen, I could start lacing Eli's coffee with arsenic, just like I'd done with Victoria's medicine. With the rest of the family gone, Clint would turn to me to help run the ranch, and I'd finally have everything I deserve. The Three Cedars and my son!"

Asher fought to tamp down his outrage over the ugly truths Kendrick spouted, as if the people on his mental chessboard held no more value than ordinary wooden pieces.

He reached the rock and began to circle it, glancing at Kendrick to judge if he stood close enough to make a move. His opponent hung back too far, though. Instead of causing him to close the gap on Asher, Kendrick's distraction had brought his feet to a standstill a good three yards away.

Before Asher could decide if a charge was worth the risk, Kendrick snapped to attention. "Twelve years of plannin' gone in a single morning, thanks to Dearing's brat." He stalked forward, his gun arm rock steady, his demeanor alert. "And don't think I'm unaware of *your* role in all this, Ellis. We wouldn't be here today if you'd just let that runaway wagon do its job in the first place."

Thank God he hadn't. He never wanted to return to a life void of Samantha's vibrancy.

"Now quit stallin' and fetch me my money." Kendrick's dark eyes carried all the warmth of frozen obsidian.

Asher hunkered down beside the rock, keeping his right hip angled away from Kendrick. As he squatted, he inched his hand toward the knife at his belt.

"None of that!" Kendrick took a menacing step forward. "Touch that knife, and it'll be the last thing you do."

Asher brought both hands up and stretched back to a standing position. "Easy. I'll keep my hands where you can see 'em, all right? I'll kick the rock free with my boot." If he couldn't retrieve his knife, he didn't want to fold himself into a crouch and limit his mobility. Quickness was the only weapon he had left.

Lord, I'd really love not to die today. Asher kicked at the rock he knew hid nothing more than dirt and bugs. *But if I do . . .* He kicked the rock again, dislodging one side. *Watch over Mama Bess and the boys for me. Samantha too.* Using extra force, he slammed his toe beneath the loosened edge and flipped the rock, praying Kendrick's greed would divert his attention. As the rock flipped, Asher reached behind him for the missing money.

"Liar!"

Before Kendrick could pull the trigger, Asher flung the packet at the foreman's head. "Here's your money!"

Kendrick made a grab for the packet, and Asher charged. A gunshot fired into the sky as Asher drove his shoulder into Kendrick's ribs and tackled him to the ground. He grabbed for the gun. Kendrick grabbed for dirt. A thick spray of sandy soil pelted Asher's face and burned his eyes. Unable to see, Asher missed Kendrick's fist until it collided with his temple.

The blow disoriented him. As concentration slipped, Kendrick took advantage. He wrestled free and kicked Asher beneath the chin. Asher's head snapped back. He fumbled for his knife as he rolled onto his side and tried to rise. He swiped his left sleeve over his watery eyes, desperate to see more than a blur. He blinked in time to find Kendrick gaining his feet and bringing his gun around.

A shot exploded. Asher dove to the side, but the expected pain didn't rip through his chest.

Instead, Kendrick fell to his knees, then pitched forward, his face hitting the dirt inches from Asher.

A movement at the edge of the cabin drew Asher's attention. Martin, smoking rifle still tucked against his shoulder, stood beside a lathered horse.

"You all right, Ash?"

Asher struggled to his feet, kicked Kendrick's gun away from the man's motionless fingers, then managed a nod. "I am now."

Seemed the Lord wasn't ready to welcome him through those pearly gates just yet. A fact that suited Asher just fine. He had a mite more livin' he wanted to do here first. Starting with wrapping his arms around a certain blue-eyed woman and assuring her she was safe. Kendrick wouldn't be hurting anyone ever again.

———

"Miss Samantha, come quick. It's Clint!"

Mrs. Stewart's call from the doorway popped Samantha's eyes open from the prayer she'd been offering and galvanized her into action. Jumping up from the padded chair at the rear of her father's bedroom, she hurried to meet Mrs. Stewart at the door.

Her heart thudding with hope, she clasped the cook's hand. "He's home?"

Mrs. Stewart's dewy-eyed nod inflated Samantha's soul with an air so light, her feet seemed to lift from the ground.

"He's riding in now with a couple of the hands. Hurry!"

Samantha paused for only a moment, glancing back at her father's form in his bed. Dr. Abbott bent over him, sutures in hand.

"Go ahead, miss." The doctor tipped his head toward the door. "You're father's out of danger for now. We'll need to monitor him for infection, but there's a good chance he'll come out of this with nothing more troubling than a stiff arm and a new scar."

"Thank you, Doctor."

And thank you, Lord!

Samantha hurried from the room, her thoughts shifting to her brother and Asher. She ran through the kitchen and out the back door, reaching the yard at the same time a trio of riders reined in their mounts. She didn't see Asher among them. Sheriff Jeter must've caught up to Duke before he made it to the cabin and rescued her brother.

"Clint!" Samantha ran to him, tears of relief clouding her eyes.

"Sam!" Clint dismounted before his horse fully halted and ran to his sister.

Samantha opened her arms and embraced him, her heart swelling to twice its normal size. *Thank you, God. Thank you.* She held him out from her and examined him from head to bare toes, ruffling his hair, rubbing his arms, and running a tender finger along his jaw where a bruise was beginning to form.

"It's nothing." Clint ducked, then tracked down her hands and clasped them in his. Wide, tortured eyes peered into her face. "How's Da—Eli? Is he . . . ?"

"Daddy's alive. Dr. Abbott's in with him now." She started tugging him toward the house. "Come. I'll take you to him."

He shook his head and pulled his hand free of hers. "No. He'll not want to see me."

Samantha's chest ached at the lostness in his voice. She snatched his hand back and squeezed it tightly. "You're wrong, Clint. Our father loves you. Always has, always will. He told me himself that what Duke said made no difference to him. You're *his* son. In his heart as well as in the eyes of the law. He's never giving you up. And neither am I."

Moisture glistened in Clint's eyes, as he struggled to come to terms with a new identity and pick up the pieces of the life Duke's revelation had shattered.

She tugged again, and this time he followed. His body dragged heavily with reluctance, but it moved.

"He woke up when we moved him to his room and made a special request of Dr. Abbott." She paused at the base of the back porch, her gaze locking with Clint's.

"What'd he ask?"

"He wanted the doctor to stitch his wound in such a way that the sutures would form the shape of a crescent. Even if it meant sewing more than was strictly necessary. When Dr. Abbott asked him why, Daddy said he wanted to match his son."

Clint rubbed the spot near his collarbone where his crescent-shaped birthmark lay beneath his shirt. Something shifted in his stance. He stood a little taller. His chin lifted, and some of the light returned to his eyes. "I want to see him."

Not trusting her voice, Samantha nodded and led him into the house. The moment they stepped into the kitchen, Mrs. Stewart swooped in and engulfed Clint in a hug.

"Oh, my boy. I'm so glad you're home." She sniffed as she released him, then grabbed the corner of her apron and wiped her eyes. "You must be starved. I've got biscuits ready and will scramble up a big batch of sausage and eggs now that you're back. Here." She reached into a towel-covered basket, pulled out a biscuit, and pressed it into his hand. "Now go on and see your daddy. I'll call you when the rest is ready."

"Thanks." Clint met Samantha's gaze, a light in his eyes that reminded her of a smile.

She touched his arm. "Do you want company, or would you rather see him alone? He'll probably sleep a while longer. Dr. Abbott dosed him with ether before starting the sutures."

Clint gave her his best I'm-a-man-not-a-boy look and stepped away from her to move toward the hall. "I'll be fine on my own."

"Just remember, you're not alone, Clint. In this or in anything. You have family and friends who love you and a God who is willing to carry your burdens."

He glanced over his shoulder, his eyes softening as he met her gaze. "Thanks, sis."

She watched him go, a prayer on her heart that God would heal the wounds Duke had inflicted.

"Here." Mrs. Stewart handed her a pair of biscuits wrapped in a napkin. "Take these out to the fellas who brought our boy back. Tell them there'll be a feast ready for them in twenty minutes."

"I will."

Samantha smiled. It was just like Mrs. Stewart to try to erase sour circumstances with good food. Her biscuits were up to the task, fluffy enough to lighten anyone's mood. Samantha had partaken of one herself while they'd been waiting for the doctor to arrive.

Her gaze traveled to the road, searching for Ida Mae. She should've been back by now. As should Martin. Dr. Abbott mentioned that Martin hadn't waited for him. He'd headed right back out to the ranch after informing the doctor of Eli's condition. Had Martin decided to search on his own? Maybe he ran into Ida Mae, and she'd taken it upon herself to show him the way to the cabin. They couldn't have known that Clint had been found.

Samantha turned her gaze back to the barn, determined to curb her worries. The sheriff had matters in hand. Clint was safe. The others must be, too. Yet unanswered questions poked holes in her peace.

Firmly setting those questions from her mind, she pasted a smile on her face, then strode into the barn, where she found the hands rubbing down their horses.

"Biscuits from Mrs. Stewart," she called in lieu of a greeting.

The men turned and tipped their hats to her.

"Thank you kindly, ma'am." Red Watson, who got his name from the flame-colored beard he wore, stepped forward and helped himself to one of the snacks she offered.

"It's you who deserve the thanks, Red, for bringing my brother home safe." She turned to Zeke Jones to include him in her appreciation. "Both of you. I can't thank you enough."

"How's the boss man doin'?" Zeke asked as he reached for the second biscuit. "Clint told us 'bout the shootin'."

"Dr. Abbott expects him to pull through."

"That's good to hear." Zeke chomped off half the biscuit with one bite.

"It will be a good while before he's back in the saddle, though." Samantha shook out the crumbs from the napkin, then stepped deeper into the barn. A third horse waited for attention, his head bent to the water trough.

"Is that Duke's horse?" She'd been so focused on her brother, she hadn't noticed what horse he'd ridden.

"Yes'm." Red drew alongside her. "Clint took him when he made his escape. Said that Ellis fella was lyin' in wait at the line shack. Got the jump on Duke and gave Clint the chance to get away."

Asher was the one who'd confronted Duke? Not the sheriff?

"Me and Zeke got escort duty while Sheriff Jeter and the others headed in the direction of the shots to lend a hand."

"Shots?" Samantha reached for a nearby stall to steady her wobbly knees. If Asher had been alone with Duke, there were only two possible options for where those shots had been aimed.

"Now you done it," Zeke muttered under his breath as he shoved Red into the sawhorse that held his horse's saddle. "I'm sure your fella's fine, miss. He seems the scrappy sort."

Oh, Lord, please let him be all right.

"You hear that?" Red turned toward the barn door. "Riders comin' in."

Samantha sprinted past the men and out into the sunshine. She held up a hand to shade her eyes as she scanned the riders for the one she sought. One wore a skirt. Ida Mae. But the men all looked the same from this distance.

Then one horse broke away from the rest, his rider's form lovingly familiar.

"Asher!" Samantha hitched up her skirt and ran to meet him, her heart so full her chest throbbed.

When he reached the yard, he reined in his mount, leapt from the saddle, then swept her completely off her feet. His arms circled her back and pressed her flush against him. Samantha laid her palms atop his shoulders, laughing and crying at the same time.

Thank God Almighty. Asher was alive. Strong. Healthy. Covered in dust and bruises, but beautifully, wonderfully, alive.

His grip loosened slightly, and she slid down Asher's chest until her feet found purchase on the ground. The moment they did, a new light-headedness assailed her, for Asher's lips had found hers. His hands stroked her back, his touch the tiniest bit desperate and entirely thrilling. She rose up to meet him, giving in to her own desperation as she clung to him, and kissed him with all the love flooding her heart.

As his kiss gentled and slowed, her hands moved from his shoulders to cup his bruised face with tender delicacy. She leaned back just enough to meet his gaze as her thumbs feathered over his stubbled cheeks.

"I love you, Asher."

His mouth curved in a saucy half grin. "It's about time you admitted it."

She laughed, the release glorious.

He kissed her again, a tender meeting of lips that made her belly ache from the sweetness of it. It ended far too soon, but perhaps that was for the best, seeing as how they weren't alone.

"Duke Kendrick is gone, Samantha." Asher's serious words penetrated the passion-induced fog swirling around her with razor-sharp precision. "He'll never hurt you or your family again."

She pressed her cheek to his chest. It seemed odd to mourn a man who had tried to kill her, but Duke had been part of her life from the day she was born. It wasn't so much losing him that hurt as losing the idea of who she'd once believed him to be. How much worse would it be for Clint?

"Martin's fetching fresh horses. He'll ride back to the line shack with a spare mount so the sheriff can take the body to the undertaker." Asher's fingers ran up and down her back, soothing away the ugly image as soon as it rose in her mind. He fell silent for a long minute, but his hands kept rubbing, comforting, easing her distress, and hopefully easing some of his own in the process. "How's your father?"

She leaned back in his arms and peered up into a face filled with empathy. He'd lost his own father, after all.

"Dr. Abbott expects him to recover, as long as infection doesn't set in."

Asher squeezed her against his side. "That's good."

"Maybe we should have Dr. Abbott take a look at you, too, while he's here. You look pretty banged up."

"I'm all right. Just a few scrapes and bruises. Martin stopped the damage from being any worse."

Samantha heard what he wasn't saying. About how close he'd come to serious injury or perhaps death. She hugged his waist and thanked the Almighty for keeping him safe. "God bless Martin."

"I pray he does."

The clanging of a dinner bell echoed across the yard. "Breakfast is ready," Mrs. Stewart called. "Come and get it!"

Asher looked down at Samantha, and her stomach fluttered at the love in his gaze. "I've got all I'll ever need right here."

She pressed a hand to his chest, a thrill coursing through her at the powerful thump of his heartbeat beneath her fingers. "Me too."

38

TWO WEEKS LATER

Asher drew the team to a halt in front of the two-story ranch house at the Three Cedars. Perspiration slickened his hands where they gripped the reins. *Get ahold of yourself, man. It's not like you haven't been here a half-dozen times before.* Yet tonight was different. There were no villains to thwart, no protective details to man, no highfalutin balls to sneak into in search of evidence of supposed wrongdoing. He'd not be hiding tonight. Asher swallowed, his Adam's apple bumping against his too-tight collar.

"Relax, sweetheart. Everything is going to be fine." Mama Bess touched his arm, her smile slowing the stampede of panic bounding through his chest. "The Lord brought you and Samantha together. Trust him to work out the details." She gave his arm a pat, then turned to collect the rectangular basket she'd brought, a basket heaped with potatoes.

Why she thought she needed to bring a bunch of raw potatoes to a family dinner, he'd never understand. She'd insisted it would be rude to show up empty-handed, though, and he'd

338

been too consumed by imagining all the various ways this evening could go horribly wrong to argue with her.

Mama Bess twisted to call to the boys in the back of the wagon. "Jonathan, be a gentleman and help me down, son."

"Yes, Mama." Jack hopped down from the tailgate and hurried around to offer a hand.

Fergus moved a little slower, taking an extra minute to tuck his tablet and pencil into the pocket of his Sunday coat.

They'd all taken care to dress their best for tonight's dinner. Asher most of all. For tonight was the night he planned to ask for Mr. Dearing's permission to court his daughter. Samantha assured him it was a mere formality, that her father would never keep her from the man she loved, but Asher found it hard to share her optimism. When he compared himself to the wealthy cattlemen who'd been at her ball, men Dearing had handpicked for his daughter, Asher fell far short. No money to speak of, no land, no impressive accomplishments or beneficial connections. All he had to offer was his heart, his honor, and a strong work ethic. He prayed it would be enough.

As he climbed down from the driver's seat, the front door opened, and Samantha stepped through the opening. The blue of her gown brought out the blue in her eyes, but it was the sparkle of delight shining within them that made his pulse leap. She rushed down the front steps as if she hadn't seen him in days instead of mere hours. He opened his arms, and she came into his embrace without hesitation. For propriety's sake, he didn't hold her long, just enough to remind himself how good she felt against him and to drop a kiss onto her cheek.

"Don't you look handsome." She patted the lapel of his coat before stepping back and turning her attention and compliments to the other Ellis males flocking around her.

"What about me?" Fergus tugged on her hand, his little chest thrusting forward.

Samantha clasped his hands and held them wide as she examined him from head to toe. "You look fine, indeed, Sir Fergus." Her gaze shifted to Jack and widened with comic extreme. "This distinguished gentleman couldn't possibly be the rascal Jack Ellis, could he?"

Fergus snickered and Jack blushed, but he stood tall and proud with their mother on his arm.

Samantha leaned close to Jack and smiled. "Better not let the girls see you all shined up, or they'll never leave you alone."

Jack quirked a grin that had *rascal* written all over it.

"Bess." Samantha greeted his mother with an embrace, and the two women shared a secret smile. "Is that the—?"

"The potatoes. Yes." Mama Bess shot an odd glance at Asher before she waved Fergus over and handed him the basket. "I thought Mrs. Stewart might enjoy having something that you helped harvest."

"How thoughtful." Samantha linked arms with Mama Bess and led her toward the house. A few steps later, she glanced over her shoulder. "You can leave the basket on the table in the front hall, Fergus. Best not to interrupt Mrs. Stewart's dinner preparations."

"Yes, Miss Dearing." Fergus's eyes twinkled with mischief.

What was that about? Asher took a step toward his little brother. He needed Eli Dearing in the best mood possible tonight. Boyish pranks would not help his cause.

"Asher?" Samantha's voice beckoned. "Are you coming?"

Settling for shooting Fergus a quick warning glare, Asher lengthened his stride to catch up to Samantha and Mama Bess so he could hold the door open for them while they entered the house.

Dinner was a warm, cheerful affair filled with laughter, stories, and food so delicious Asher would likely dream about it the next time he drew night duty with nothing but tinned beans and jerky in his pack.

Eli Dearing presided at the head of the table, his smile ready and his manners impeccable. Only the sling over his arm offered any reminder of the brush he'd had with death. Mama Bess sat at his right as the guest of honor while Parson and Mrs. Hopewell sat to his left. Asher had been glad to see Obadiah Hopewell looking much recovered after the scare they'd had the night of the fire. His voice still carried a hint of a rasp, but that didn't keep him from bragging on the generosity of his congregation. It seemed they'd taken up a special collection to help Obadiah and Regina rebuild.

Clint and Jack sat at the end of the table with heads together, jabbering as if they'd known each other for ages while Fergus and Mrs. Hopewell discussed church mice and whether or not there were secret rodent worship meetings happening under the floorboards on Sunday mornings.

Seated at the center of the table, Samantha served as an elegant hostess, contributing to the various conversations around her with charm and grace. Yet it was the way her gaze consistently returned to him that swelled his heart with pride and restored a bit of his confidence. This amazing woman loved him. Saw something worthy in him. Surely her father would too.

The confidence he'd collected throughout the meal vanished the moment Samantha rose from the table and suggested they all retire to the parlor. She nodded to him as he hurried to help her with her chair, her eyes brimming with encouragement. He wished he hadn't told her of his plans to talk to her father tonight. What if things went badly? Then he'd have her disappointment to carry along with his own.

Happy chatter flitted about Asher's head like a swarm of mosquitos, irritating in its relentless buzz. His gut tied in knots, he dipped his chin to Samantha and slowly made his way around the people milling into the hall to find Eli standing at the head of the table talking to Mama Bess as he waited for his guests to precede him.

His mother excused herself the moment she spotted Asher, giving his forearm a squeeze as she passed him to join the others.

"Mr. Dearing, sir?"

The smile Eli had been aiming at Mama Bess flattened into a straight line as he turned his attention to Asher. He raised a single brow in silent question.

"I, uh, wondered if we might have a word. In private." He shoved his hands into his pockets, hoping Dearing hadn't noticed them shaking.

The man smiled and pounded Asher on the back with his good arm. "Let's go up to my study, shall we?" His eyes narrowed slightly. "I believe you know the way."

Asher bit back a groan. Could there possibly be a *worse* place for this conversation?

Keeping pace with Eli, Asher climbed the stairs, silently castigating himself for not anticipating this scenario. He and Samantha's father might have come to terms regarding his little foray into illegal activity, but that didn't mean his slate had been wiped clean.

At the door to the office, Eli stepped aside and gestured for Asher to enter ahead of him. He smiled and dipped his chin in thanks, but it was all for show. The last thing he felt was gratitude as he stepped into that study. Immediately, his gaze locked on the sofa he'd hidden behind. Then the desk he'd rummaged through and the shelves he'd scoured. Even the window taunted him, tempting him to make another rapid escape.

Not this time. Asher squared his shoulders and turned away from the window to face the man he hoped would be his future father-in-law. He'd already owned up to his mistakes. All he could do now was plead his case and pray Eli Dearing saw more potential than pitfalls in his proposal.

Inhaling a fortifying breath, Asher braced himself and drove straight to the heart of the matter. "Mr. Dearing, I'd like to ask permission to court your daughter, and, if she agrees, to marry her. I realize I don't have wealth or prestige to offer, nor do I have land of my own, but I know what it means to be responsible for a family, to put their needs ahead of my own. I promise to do the same for Samantha. I will work hard to provide a good life for her. It might not be as lavish a life as she would have back in Boston or here at the Three Cedars, but it will be rich with the things that matter most—love, mutual respect, joy, and faith."

Eli sat on the corner of his desk and leveled a steely stare at Asher. "Love and joy are all well and good, son, but a man needs to have a way to put food on the table and a roof over his family's head. How're you plannin' to do that without wages from the Bar 7?"

Asher lifted his chin. He'd been anticipating this question. "I signed on with the Double J this mornin'. I start on Monday. It might take a couple years to save up enough to buy a small spread of my own, but I'll not propose to Samantha until I know I can provide for her."

"The Double J's a good outfit. Alvin Johnson and I have driven a few herds to market together over the years. He'll work you hard, but he pays solid wages. You coulda done a lot worse."

"My foreman at the Bar 7, Walt Ricker, recommended the Johnsons. Put in a good word for me with the hirin' boss, too." Asher had been thanking God for Walt's kindness from the moment he'd received his letter two days ago telling him about the position.

"You could hire on here." Eli pulled a pen from its fancy

brass holder and rolled it between his fingers and thumb. "I'm still short a couple hands. I promoted Martin to foreman, but his old position is vacant." He stopped fiddling with the pen and lifted his gaze. "Seems the least I can do after all you've done for my family."

Asher's gut tightened like it did when he'd been a boy in school, called upon but completely unsure of the rightness of his answer. "As much as I appreciate the offer, sir, I've made a commitment to the Double J. I'll be ridin' for them."

Eli placed the pen back in the holder, then stood and clasped Asher's shoulder. "I respect a man who honors his word. And I can appreciate you wantin' to build something with your own two hands. But the man who marries my daughter stands to inherit half of the Three Cedars. You willin' to take on that kind of responsibility?"

Asher nodded. "When the time comes."

"Good." Eli released his hold on Asher's shoulder. "I hope to be around for a few more decades, but if the last month has taught me anything, it's that life doesn't always go according to plan. I need to know that Sam will be taken care of. Clint too. That boy's been through a mess of hurt. He puts on a good show, but it's gonna take time for him to figure out who he is. Clint looks up to you, Asher. Shoot, you've saved his life twice now. I'm hoping you can help ground him. You're in a unique position to show him that family is defined by love, not blood."

Asher locked eyes with Eli, feeling the weight of his plea and accepting the charge with a sacred vow. "I give you my word, sir. Clint and Samantha are family, and I don't turn my back on family. Ever."

"No, I don't believe you do." A grin creased Eli's face as he slapped Asher on the back. "You've got my approval, but you oughta know, Samantha's the one who'll be making the final decision. She's made it clear I ain't to be pickin' beaus for her."

The knots in Asher's gut began to unwind. "I'll do my best to prove myself worthy of her love."

"You can't earn a gift that's been freely given, son." Eli's expression sobered as he reached for the family photograph at the edge of his desk. "All you can do is cherish it and give your own gift in return." The pad of his thumb caressed the glass, then he set the frame aside. "My girl's got a big heart and a zest for life that can energize everyone around her, but she ain't perfect. She's stubborn, opinionated, and has a tongue sharp enough to shave whiskers off a man's chin. There'll be days when your will clashes with hers, when feelings are hurt, and anger is roused. Those are the days that need more love, not less. Remember that."

"I will."

"Good!" Eli clapped Asher's shoulder once more for good measure. "Now let's get back downstairs. I imagine my daughter's eager for your company."

As he was for hers.

When they reached the parlor, Asher scanned the room for Samantha. She was sitting in front of the hearth chatting with Mama Bess and Mrs. Hopewell. As if she felt the touch of his gaze, she glanced up. A wide smile bloomed across her lovely face.

"I have an announcement to make." Eli Dearing's voice boomed near Asher's ear as the man barreled into the room behind him. "Mr. Ellis, here, has just gained my permission to pay court to my beautiful Samantha." He bowed in the direction of his daughter, who pinkened at his compliment.

Asher doubted the dusty rose painting her cheeks could compare to the tomato red that had to be climbing up his neck, judging by the unwelcome heat around his collar and the way Jack was pointing and snickering with Clint by the window.

Parson and Mrs. Hopewell gave a good-natured cheer, and

Mama Bess turned in her seat to smile at him, her face alight with pleasure.

"I told the boy that gaining my permission was only half the battle, though. My daughter must also approve, and her criteria are much more stringent."

Asher looked to Samantha, thinking to share a smile with her, but her expression had gone quite severe. She rose from her chair, clutching something behind her back.

Her father gave him a not-so-gentle push deeper into the room. Samantha met him halfway across the rug, her arms still behind her back, her expression regal.

"My father has granted me the honor of choosing the man to whom I will one day be betrothed." Her blue eyes danced, and knots tightened in his stomach. "Asher Ellis, you have proven to be a man of honor and steadfastness."

Her eyes darkened slightly, the way they did right before he kissed her. His pulse jumped straight from a walk to a canter.

"You have exhibited tenderness and humor in good times and remarkable courage and sacrifice in times of tribulation. You have not only passed but exceeded every test I could have asked of you. But one remains."

Asher blinked. One what? Test? His hands immediately started sweating again. Until he found her eyes once more and discovered a delightful mix of love and laughter glimmering there. His breathing eased as trust calmed his racing heart. Samantha loved him. She'd not concoct a test for him that he couldn't pass.

"You see, I found something the night a mysterious stranger saved my brother from drowning. Something that stirred my heart with imagination and the hope that I might meet a man such as he. A man who would put the needs of others before himself. A man willing to set aside his own agenda to do what was right.

"I dreamed of this stranger, building him into the man I wanted him to be. A man of kindness and godly character. A man slow to anger and quick to lend a hand. A man who would see me for the woman I am and not the inheritance I represent." Her mouth quirked into a saucy half grin. "A man of rugged good looks who could ride like the wind and teach me to do the same."

Asher's heart warmed at her description, and his arms ached with the need to hold her close and tell her of all the dreams she had fulfilled for him as well.

"The ideal suitor I'd created in my mind left behind some mighty big boots to fill. But I don't want to settle for anything less. Therefore, the man I marry must fit the boot I found the night of my ball."

Samantha withdrew the item she'd been hiding from behind her back—a man's dress boot, black leather upper, brown leather lower, fancy stitching along the edge.

A laugh rumbled through Asher's chest.

He stepped close to her and placed his hand on the boot, his fingers close enough to brush against hers. "I'm sure I'll fail to live up to that ideal man of yours more than once, but if wearing his boot will convince you to let me love you for the rest of my days, then hand it over."

Chuckles and smiles filled the room as Jack rushed over with an ottoman in hand. Asher sat down and yanked his left boot off, then shoved his foot into the boot that would walk him into his future.

"Wait, Ash. You gotta finish the story properly." Fergus scurried forward, Asher's other boot gripped in his hands. "You need this one, too. It's too big to fit in your pocket like the slipper did, so we hid it under the potatoes."

"Under the . . ." Asher stole a glance at Mama Bess, who didn't look the slightest bit guilty about her tuberous Trojan horse.

"Come on, Ash," Fergus urged. "Put it on."

Questions about how many people had actually known about this fanciful shoe test vanished in the face of Fergus's earnest expression.

"All right." Asher ruffled his brother's hair, then took the boot.

Fergus grinned. "If the boot fits, you get to marry the princess."

Asher smiled up at Samantha. "Yes, I do."

Only, when he tried to push his foot in, the boot was too small. Frowning, Asher pulled it off, gave it a shake, then tipped it downward until a potato spilled out.

Laughter filled the room again, especially from Jack's vicinity. Asher shot him a mock glare, then turned back to Fergus. "Let's try this again, shall we?"

This time his foot slid into the leather like a knife into a custom sheath. He stood and reached for Samantha's hands. "What do you say, Princess? Do I pass the test?"

Her smile heated his blood. "With flying colors."

"Well, now that *that's* settled," Eli said from his place across the room, "I have one more announcement to make."

Tugging Samantha against his side, Asher wrapped his arm around her as they turned to give her father their attention.

"Since Samantha has accepted Asher's suit, and the Ellis clan is soon to become kin, I've decided to rent out my daughter's dower property at the family rate of six dollars a month should Mrs. Ellis and her two young boys wish to take occupancy of their old home. I understand there's an extensive garden there in need of a regular caretaker."

Asher's heart thumped an erratic rhythm as he struggled to process what he was hearing.

Mama Bess rose from the couch, her eyes glistening in the lamplight as she looked from Asher to Fergus and back to Eli. "Six dollars? But that's a fraction of what it's worth."

Eli waved away her concern. "It won't make me any money sitting vacant waiting for these two lovebirds to tie the knot. Beware, though, once they wed, you'll be getting a new landlord, and I don't know if he'll be as generous."

Samantha patted Asher's chest as she smiled at Mama Bess. "I'll be sure to put a good word in for you."

His family all together in one place? Asher hadn't thought this night could get any better, but it had. Not only could Mama Bess return to the house and garden she loved, but with the ridiculously low rent fees, he'd be able to save most of his earnings, which meant he could marry the love of his life in one year instead of two.

"I guess we *all* get to live happily ever after," Fergus murmured, a touch of wonder coloring his voice.

"I guess we do." Asher turned to Samantha and drank in the amazing woman who'd just promised to be his.

Her eyes radiated a love so deep, he knew he'd never tire of seeing it. Bending his face to hers, he pressed a gentle kiss to her lips. A feathery touch that carried the pledge of a lifetime of kisses to come.

"Any more tests, my love?" he whispered close to her ear.

Her lashes lifted, and those lips he'd just kissed stretched into the sweetest of smiles. "I'm sure there'll be many, but we'll handle them all together."

He squeezed her waist as his smile stretched to match hers. "That we will."

Life with this woman would be an adventure, and he'd cherish every page of the story they'd write together.

READ ON
FOR A *SNEAK PEEK* AT
THE FINAL BOOK IN

THE TEXAS EVER AFTER

SERIES

AVAILABLE DECEMBER 2024

The Pinkertons trained their detectives to use any and all available resources when it came to procuring information pertinent to their cases, but Phillip Carmichael still felt a twinge of guilt about using his fellow agents. Somehow he doubted Wendell and Harper would appreciate his cunning once they realized he'd duped them.

"I never thought you'd be one to chase the great white whale, Carmichael."

Phillip grinned as he propped a hip on the corner of Gregor Wendell's desk. "I doubt Miss Radcliffe would appreciate your choice of metaphor."

Wendell chuckled as he leaned back in his chair. "Prob'ly not, but since no one can find the slippery woman, her opinion's not terribly relevant."

Stanley Harper stood at the window overlooking Prairie Avenue, idly stroking his thick dark mustache as he watched passersby go in and out of the Lone Star Hotel across the street. The agency didn't have official offices in Houston, but Robert and William Pinkerton had arranged for a small space to be available for agents working cases in the area. Wasn't much to it. Just a narrow second-floor room with two desks and a small filing cabinet in the corner. Bare floors. Bare walls. Nothing to induce a man to linger. Yet it provided a discreet meeting place to discuss Pinkerton business without worrying who might overhear.

"I didn't think Radcliffe was hiring Pinks this time around." Harper turned from the window and pinned Phillip with a suspicious look. "Something 'bout being fed up with us not getting the job done the last four times. As if he expected us to pull the girl outta thin air with nothing but a name and an outdated description to go on."

"I'm not fool enough to think I can do any better than what you and Wendell did." Phillip raised his hands in a conciliatory gesture, hoping to mollify Harper's bruised ego. "The two of you are local legends for what you accomplished three years ago. Tracking down the woman who found that photograph of the missing heiress in her luggage and questioning her about her travels? That move gave us our first break in the case. Thanks to you, we know the girl is somewhere between here and Little Rock, Arkansas. Or at least she was, as of three years ago."

Harper blew out a disgusted breath. "I traveled that rail line and stopped in every stinkin' town along the way. Questioned every porter I could get my hands on. Took me over two weeks, and I still came up empty. Radcliffe was so upset, he refused to reimburse my train fare. Said I could waste my own money on a fruitless endeavor, but he'd not have me wastin' his. Cheap louse."

Now they were getting somewhere.

"A man that wealthy cheating his employees out of their due?" Phillip wagged his head. "Seems bad for business."

Wendell scratched at the beard that was starting to gray a bit at his chin. "I ain't sure the man is as wealthy as he lets on. He's got all the trappings—fancy house, expensive suits, memberships at all the right clubs—but I've heard rumors that it's his brother's side of the company that's keeping Radcliffe Shipping afloat."

Phillip had heard the same rumors. From what he'd been able to gather, Drake and Lowell Radcliffe had started Radcliffe Shipping together some thirty years ago. The two had capitalized on the cotton trade at first, investing in riverboats to travel the Brazos, Colorado, and Trinity Rivers to bring the product to market before shipping it back east out of Galveston. The War between the States brought hard times, but the Radcliffe brothers found a way to continue turning a profit. They were some of the first to invest in local Houston railroads, and by the mid-1870s, Radcliffe Shipping had become one of the richest companies in Texas.

At the height of their success, however, the two brothers had a falling out and decided to go their separate ways. They divided their individual holdings and investments while each retained half ownership of the parent company. Until Lowell died in 1880. Lowell's daughter inherited his shares, but since she was a minor, her shares were placed in a trust with her uncle as trustee, giving Drake sole control of Radcliffe Shipping.

Lowell's wife inherited control of her husband's subsidiary businesses. Fifty percent of those profits fed into Radcliffe Shipping's coffers, and those funds were keeping Drake Radcliffe from declaring bankruptcy after a string of failed personal investments had pauperized the man.

Phillip leaned forward slightly. "Do you think Drake's search for his niece has more to do with money than familial obligation?"

Wendell shrugged. "Radcliffe professes to be devastated by the loss of his niece. Talks about how he owes it to his dead brother to keep searching until she is found. Hires a new round of detectives every few years. But I've been in the man's house. Never spotted a single photograph of the girl. None of his brother, either. Has a big portrait of himself over the mantel in the parlor, though."

Harper strode away from the window, his dark gaze peering at Phillip as if he were trying to mine his motives. Phillip forced himself to maintain his casual position—hip propped against the desk corner, hands relaxed, breathing even. It was natural for a detective to be suspicious. One wouldn't be very good at solving cases if he took everything he encountered at face value.

Still, a little deflection might aid the cause. So before Harper started throwing questions at him, Phillip threw one of his own.

"What do *you* think motivates Radcliffe, Harper?"

"Money." Harper drew to a halt a few steps away from Phillip. "He's gotta have something to gain by her return. My guess is it's something pretty substantial. It would have to be to offset the thousand-dollar reward he suddenly decided to offer for her return." Harper tilted his head. "Is that why you decided to take this case, Carmichael? For the reward?"

Phillip grinned even as his gut tightened. "I don't know about you fellas, but I don't plan to be a Pinkerton forever. A thousand dollars would buy a real pretty piece of land somewhere. Maybe I could finally settle down. Start a family."

Ever since he'd been hired by the Pinkertons, he'd done his best not to break the ninth commandment. A man of faith shouldn't follow the path of the Father of Lies, after all. Yet a man didn't have to lie in order to deceive. Phillip had gotten quite adept at weaving vague truths into a camouflage designed to mislead and, therefore, hide his actual intent. He used to take pride in his semantic subterfuge, but he'd grown weary of the constant word-watching and the bruises it left on his conscience.

"I wouldn't go property shopping just yet," Harper warned with a scowl. "Radcliffe will likely find an excuse not to pay out, even if you do manage to track the girl down."

"Appreciate the tip." And the insight into a man with murky motives.

Wendell slapped his palms on his thighs, then pushed up from his chair, Phillip's cue that the meeting had reached its conclusion. He rose from the corner of the desk.

"I appreciate you taking the time to bring me up to speed. Reading case notes isn't the same as talking to the agents who worked the assignment." Phillip extended a hand to Harper first, then to Wendell.

Wendell grinned as he shook Phillip's hand. "Don't suppose you're looking for a partner, are you? I might be convinced to give finding the Radcliffe heiress another go. Especially if it means splittin' that reward."

"The lone wolf take a partner?" Harper scoffed, then shot Phillip a sardonic glare. "I'll believe it when I see it."

Phillip chuckled good-naturedly as he extricated his hand from Wendell's grip. "You know how it is, boys. Old habits and all that."

He'd established a reputation at the agency for discretion. He always worked alone and was willing to take on the less sensational cases. Glory, power, recognition. He didn't care about those things. A fact that made him attractive to a certain clientele. One desperate to keep their secrets out of the press. He didn't particularly enjoy spying on cheating husbands or digging up dirt on potential investment partners, but the work was steady enough to keep him occupied so he didn't have to hire out for the more questionable duties associated with the labor unions. That work was rife with corruption, and Phillip wanted no part of it.

"I'd wish you luck," Wendell said as he led the way to the door, "but it's gonna take a lot more than luck to find Scarlett Radcliffe. That trail is as cold as they get."

"Kinda makes me wonder why he's wastin' his time." Harper raised a brow. "You uncover some new information, Carmichael? Or are you workin' an angle?"

"No angle, I swear. I just want to bring Miss Radcliffe home."
But not to her uncle.

Phillip bid his two colleagues good-bye and collected his
horse from the hitching post outside the building. In case his
departure was being monitored, he guided his gray north on
Main, then east on Congress, as if heading in the direction
of the grand houses of Quality Hill. He wound through the
area that housed Houston's elite before turning south. Large
oaks shaded the thoroughfares. Sculpted hedges and flow-
ers formed decorative gardens, and women dressed in high
fashion gowns strolled along the walkways or drove about in
open carriages, impressing their fellow socialites with their
style and knowledge of the latest gossip.

A shudder twitched along Phillip's spine. He couldn't imagine living a life where a person's worth was judged by one's
finances, social connections, and fashion sense. Could anything be more superficial? These people had no substance, no
purpose beyond themselves to give their lives meaning. One
lady clad in vivid green with a hat the size of a wagon wheel
studied him as he neared her carriage. Her eyes roved over
his chest as if he were a side of beef hanging from a butcher's
hook. Phillip dipped his chin and touched the brim of his hat
as politeness necessitated, but he voiced no greeting. He'd
been a Pinkerton long enough to recognize trouble, and her
version came with a capital *T*.

He rode Steele a full block before enough tension drained
from his shoulders for him to relax back into his saddle. Rich
people made him itch. Ironic since they also made up the bulk
of his clientele. Maybe the itch had developed because he'd
worked for so many, giving him the opportunity to witness
their greed and selfishness up close.

Not all wealthy people possessed low moral standards and
inflated egos, though. He'd met godly men and women of

means who sponsored philanthropic endeavors like building hospitals and schools, funding mission work, and establishing orphanages. But they seemed to be in the minority. Drake Radcliffe and his ilk were far more prevalent.

Which was why Phillip wasn't working for *that* Radcliffe.

Phillip drew his mount to a halt outside a modest home on Jefferson Avenue. A handful of kids played in a yard down the street. A woman swept her porch next door, not giving him more than a cursory glance. An old man sat in a rocking chair smoking a pipe across the way. He raised a hand in greeting. Phillip waved in return as he casually glanced down the road the way he'd come. No evidence that he'd been followed. The neighborhood seemed normal. Nothing out of place. Still, he walked his horse around to the back, finding a chicken coop and a shed that offered a bucket he could fill at the pump. Once Steele was situated and out of sight from curious onlookers, Phillip strolled back to the front of the house and knocked on the door.

A stately man, likely in his sixties, opened the door. "Yes?"

"Phillip Carmichael from the Pinkerton agency. I believe I'm expected."

A smile creased the formality of the man's bearing, and a hint of what Phillip could only call excitement lit his eyes. "Come in. Mrs. Radcliffe awaits you in the sitting room."

Phillip stepped inside and pulled his hat from his head. He rubbed a hand over his short blond hair as he handed the hat to the butler. "I hope she hasn't been waiting long."

The man's gaze drifted past Phillip to an open doorway a few feet past the entryway. "About fifteen years, sir."

Winner of the Christy Award, ACFW Carol Award, HOLT Medallion, and Inspirational Reader's Choice Award, bestselling author **Karen Witemeyer** writes historical romances because she believes the world needs more happily-ever-afters. She is an avid cross-stitcher, tea drinker, and gospel hymn singer who makes her home in Abilene, Texas, with her heroic husband who vanquishes laundry dragons and dirty dish villains whenever she's on deadline. To learn more about Karen and her books and to sign up for her free newsletter featuring special giveaways and behind-the-scenes information, please visit KarenWitemeyer.com.

Sign Up for Karen's Newsletter

Keep up to date with Karen's latest news
on book releases and events by signing up
for her email list at the link below.

KarenWitemeyer.com

FOLLOW KAREN ON SOCIAL MEDIA

 Karen Witemeyer's Author Page

More from Karen Witemeyer

Beauty has been nothing but a curse to Penelope Snow, and when her beauty is discovered, her mistress arranges her disappearance. Texas Ranger Titus Kingsley is assigned a robbery case tied to Penelope—and all evidence points to her—but he might be convinced that the fairest woman of all has a heart as pure as her last name . . . if only he can prove it.

Fairest of Heart
TEXAS EVER AFTER

Step into the rugged terrain of Texas with bestselling author Karen Witemeyer in this gripping series that follows a gallant band of mercenaries dedicated to safeguarding the defenseless in a lawless land. Saddle up for a riveting journey of courage, sacrifice, and love, amid the untamed backdrop of the Wild West.

HANGER'S HORESMEN:
At Love's Command, The Heart's Charge, In Honor's Defense

⬥BETHANYHOUSE